CW01498169

A WORLD
AIDS DAY
CHARITY
ANTHOLOGY

Benefitting
The Names
Project

SAY THEIR NAMES

Featuring short stories by:
A.M. Arthur, Ana Ashley, Lee Blair, L.C. Chase, Courtney W. Dixon,
Aries France, J.L. Gribble, AE Lister, Evie McGlynn,
Shane K. Morton, Breanna Rae, Marie Sinclair, and Essie Sloane

Say Their Names

Published by Sinbooks Ink

www.sinbinbooks.com

Inquiries contact: marie.sinbooks@gmail.com

Copyright of each story is held by the individual authors.

Cover design by LC Chase

Formatting by Leslie Copeland

Digital eBook ISBN: 978-1-958257-22-7

Print ISBN: 978-1-958257-23-4

Content Warning: Though these stories focus on living and loving with HIV/AIDS, many of them contain references to death, loss of loved ones, and mental health issues. Please see the authors' notes at the end of the book for any content and trigger warnings specific to an individual story.

CONTENTS

ABOUT SAY THEIR NAMES

The first time I saw the AIDS Quilt was in the early 90s on the University of California, San Diego, campus. To say that it was a moving and transformative experience is an understatement. I don't remember how many panels were on display, but I do remember the moment it truly hit me that each of these panels—each measuring 3' x 6' (the size of a grave)—represented someone who was now dead because of AIDS.

At the time, I first saw the quilt, we were still in the midst of the AIDS crisis. The legendary "No Obits" headline in San Francisco's Bay Area Reporter wouldn't happen until 1998 to signal that, for the first time in seventeen years, they had no obituaries to report. According to reports, men and women cheered, cried, and hugged each other in the streets. Years later, that headline still resonates as a turning point in the epidemic.

This collection of stories grew out of my memories of seeing the quilt, of growing up aware of the toll AIDS was taking on the gay community, of seeing the discrimination and prejudice experienced by people with the disease, of knowing people who lost family members and lovers and friends, of recognizing that every gay man over the age of fifty is a survivor even if they are not HIV-positive, and of recognizing how powerful a memorial the quilt is.

The quilt was first displayed on the National Mall in Washington DC on October 11, 1987. At the time, it covered more area than a football field and contained 1,920 panels. More than half a million people visited the quilt, leading to a four-month, 20-city national tour that raised money for AIDS service organizations and also collected additional panels. By the time the tour was over, the quilt would contain more than 6,000 panels.

The last time the entire quilt was displayed was in October of 1996, again on the National Mall. At that point, the quilt was too large to be displayed in any single location. With years to go before effective antiretroviral treatments would become available, the quilt continued to grow. Today, the AIDS Memorial Quilt weighs 54-tons and includes nearly 50,000 panels representing more than 110,000 people who lost their lives to AIDS. It is the largest work of folk art in the world, and is considered to be the largest community arts project in history.

In 2023, I was reminded of that power when I saw a few sections displayed in New York City during Pride Month. What Cleve Jones and his friends created in San Francisco in 1986 was an intensely personal memorial for people lost to AIDS as each panel displays the person's name and, in many cases, memorializes their lives through poetry and artwork. But when the panels were displayed together, they became something more. They became an overwhelming statement of the totality of this loss, of the way governments had failed to protect these people by refusing to see AIDS as the devastating disease it was and put adequate funding into finding a cure. The quilt is at once a personal expression of pain and grief and a political statement of outrage. Even viewing a small selection of those panels brought that home for me, and I decided to put together an anthology to raise money so more people can experience the power and beauty of this incredible work of art.

The National AIDS Memorial relies on donations to continue to maintain, preserve, and display the quilt, which is why I and all the authors who contributed to this anthology say thank you to you, the reader, for reading our work. And why I, as the coordinator, say thank you to each of the authors who gave their time, energy, and creativity to this project.

I always say that love is the most powerful force on this planet. With love, we can change the world.

-Marie Sinclair

P.S. I also want to offer a very special thank you to Leslie Copeland for providing her invaluable assistance, experience, and enthusiasm for this project!

SOLVING THE PUZZLE

A.M. ARTHUR

CHAPTER 1

"Damn, Atty, you weren't kidding when you said it was crammed to the door, and you needed Todd's van," Jessie said, after I'd rolled up the door on my latest storage unit clean-out. The ten-by-twenty unit was, indeed, crammed right to the edge with neatly stacked rows of plastic totes, boxes, and other mismatched containers.

All taped or sealed so their contents would be a complete and utter surprise.

That was part of the fun of buying storage units.

Jessie hated surprises, but her husband owned a small fleet of rental limos and vans, and Todd was great about letting me use their biggest box truck for clean-outs. Discounted rate, of course. I paid Jessie for her labor in food, gas, and first pick of any vintage clothing or purses I uncovered for her consignment boutique.

She wagged her finger in the air as she began counting the first row of visible containers, much like I'd done yesterday during the auction, guess-stimating exactly how much we'd need to move. "Dude, you've got to have a hundred boxes of crap in here," Jessie said. "Maybe more. It's going to take at least two trips for us to empty this sucker out."

"Maybe less if only the first wall has stuff in it," I teased with an exaggerated eyebrow wiggle. After I'd won the locker, I had poked around a little, and the first row was pretty solid. I wasn't tall enough to see behind it, though, but whispers from the other bidders gave me the impression it was full all the way to the rear.

Sometimes it sucked being only five-foot-six, but I made up for my lack of height with muscles. Muscles built not only from working out at the gym after my divorce three years ago, but also from hauling my merchandise around.

Jessie pulled a scrunchie out of her pocket, tied her thick brown hair up with it, then rolled up the sleeves of her hoodie and said, "Well, let's get started. I want to look through something today and not just move shit around."

I laughed. "Yes, let's."

With the help of a lift gate and two dolleys, we managed the first load faster than I expected, locked up, and headed to my house.

Home was in a suburb of Wilmington, Delaware, a place I'd lived my entire life. I'd even gone to college locally, so I could stay near my parents, who had already been aging when I turned eighteen. Told their entire lives they couldn't have kids, I'd oopsied into their lives when Mom was forty-six, and despite doctor's warnings, she'd had me.

Sure, I was grateful for that choice, but it had taken its toll on her health, and she'd had multiple medical issues my entire life. Dad, too, thanks to smoking four-packs-day until right before I was born. But despite their limitations, I'd loved growing up on the little piece of land they'd owned, in the single-story ranch-style home that I'd inherited after their sudden deaths last year.

Sometimes thirty-nine felt way too young to be an orphan. And sometimes all the space was too big, all the empty rooms too damned lonely. Especially after once having a wife and stepson in my life.

After emptying load number one into the detached garage, I treated Jessie to hoagies from Wawa, before we went back for round two. By the end of the day, we were sweaty, exhausted, smelled like wet cardboard, and all I wanted was to face-plant in my bed. The back of Jessie's SUV was loaded with garbage bags of clothes for her to sort. I didn't like dealing with clothes, but she knew to bring back any vintage band tees she found.

I had a good customer who always bought those from me at fair prices.

Once Jessie left with her haul, I nuked a frozen burrito, and then took it outside to admire my wall of boxes, neatly stacked in the two-car garage. The cleanout had been exhausting, but participants agreed to complete it within a specific time frame when registering for the auction. I wanted to get it done so I could dive into the fun part: digging for treasure.

I really should go inside, take a shower, play a video game, and leave all the work of sorting for tomorrow. But my curiosity wouldn't let me. After scarfing down the scalding burrito, I unfolded a work table, put on a pair of gloves, and grabbed a black rubber tote with a yellow lid. It rattled and rumbled, hinting at small things inside, possibly games or toys.

Shaking it too much ruined the surprise. Even as a kid on Christmas morning, I wouldn't shake the package. I didn't want hints before the big reveal.

I used a pair of shop shears to snip the zip ties on two ends, and then pulled off the lid. And cringed.

Games. Mostly kiddie games and not even cool vintage ones. They were maybe ten or twenty years old, the kind that sold for a buck max at a yard sale. Which I did hold occasionally at the house to get rid of excess inventory that wasn't worth donating to a thrift store. My best donations went to my favorite family-run store called All Saints Thrift Shop. Games were okay thrift items if complete, but that was a lot of work I wasn't into. And I'd only opened one tote.

No way was the entire storage unit full of someone's game collection.

Right?

That night, I dreamed I was running across a massive game board, an amalgamation of Candyland and Backgammon, and I was being chased by Monopoly pieces, the top hat and shoe, in particular. Games were on my brain after going through eight totes and boxes of them. A few had been vintage, including a Monopoly set from 1961, but most were not. I'd gone to bed exhausted and discouraged.

After returning the box truck and retrieving my own car from Todd's car lot, I resumed sorting. The first things I'd opened were the last things we'd retrieved from the unit, which meant they were the first things stored by the previous owner. Hopefully, the good stuff was somewhere in the middle.

Bored with games and eager for something new, I shoved some stacks aside to pull out a random gray tote. It was smaller than the others, maybe thirty gallons, and it was heavy. And full of paperwork. Letters, envelopes, postcards, most with postmarks from the 80s and 90s, so older stamps but not necessarily collectible. Bummer again.

With rock music blasting from my vintage Pioneer radio, I steeled myself for this unit to be a break-even buy at best, and kept going.

Between managing my online storefronts, shipping orders, rummaging around at a church-run yard sale on Saturday, and other odd jobs that kept me out of the garage, it took about two weeks to go through everything from the storage unit. And by "go through," I mean open the tote or box, give it a cursory sort, pull out anything that seemed immediately valuable, and then move to the next. I'd mostly shifted the massive pile into four large ones, one of which was for further research, plus one jumbo tote of "immediately valuable."

There was money to be made, for sure, especially in the research pile, which included six totes of vintage Halloween costumes in their original boxes, metal wind-up toys whose age I could only guess, a huge collection of PEZ dispensers, and other miscellaneous bits and bobs from dozens of franchises. I was right that the best stuff had been somewhere in the middle.

The most perplexing pile was the massive stack of apple boxes holding at least three hundred (probably more) jigsaw puzzles. Everything from fifty pieces to five thousand pieces, animals and scenery and paintings, and brand-named things like Barbie, Thomas Kincade, and 90s TV shows. Most of them were opened, which greatly diminished the resale value of any puzzle. It would take weeks, if not months, to check if all the pieces were there, and other than some of the vintage ones, I honestly didn't care enough.

Could you recycle puzzles?

Jessie texted that she'd be by at noon with lunch and a clothing swap. A dozen single-stitch music tees for me, in exchange for a few more bins of purses and clothes for her. I was in the garage shoving the boxes of puzzles closer to the front when I heard her car engine outside.

She breezed in through the open bay door with a tray of drinks and food in her hands and a brand-new purse on her arm. Well, new-to-me, because I'd never seen it before, with its colorful stripes and brown leather handle. She put the food on the worktable with a flourish. "Hey, dude, the rest of it's in the car, but mama couldn't wait to eat. I've been going since seven a.m. on a protein bar and grande iced coffee."

I laughed and reached for the Styrofoam drink cup with the cola tab pressed in. Jessie was on a clear-sodas only kick, even though she drank her coffees black. I learned a long time ago to let Jessie do her weird food phases and not argue.

Jessie nattered on about some of the clothing she'd added to her boutique yesterday. She loved what she did, just like me, and we'd bonded twenty years ago over two important things: our love of junk-ing/thrifting, and us both being bisexual and (at the time) in straight-facing relationships. And while we'd both married our college sweet-hearts, Jessie and Todd were still going strong, while Elizabeth and I had been separated for nearly two years before our very bitter divorce was finalized.

You could say I'm relationship shy now. Thankfully, Jessie never hounds me to try dating her friends, or teases me when I go out to local bars to scratch the occasional itch. I might prefer single, but I wasn't going to commit to celibacy.

Once we'd cleaned up from lunch, Jessie strolled around the garage and poked at my piles of boxes and totes. "I can't believe how much stuff we pulled out of that unit," she said as she lifted the lid of a green tote. "Dude, is that a Hungry Hippos from the eighties? I think we had one of those at my grandma's house."

"Yeah, I think it is. The most recent dates I can find on a lot of this stuff in from the late nineties, so either the owner stopped collecting toys at that time, or that's how long all this has been in storage."

"Wow. It kind of sucks that you never get to learn the history of the person who owned this stuff."

I eyeballed the small black tote I'd shoved under my work table. "Well, I did find some personal papers and shit, but I haven't looked at it. Doesn't feel right to invade their privacy, you know?"

"I'll invade it for you. I mean, whoever this toy collector was, they also had decent taste in women's clothing and shoes. I'm talking vintage Balenciaga mixed with some pretty ugly plaid muumuus."

"I'll pay you tend bucks to take a picture on a muumuu and post it online."

"Forget it." She made her way to the puzzle pile. "Damn. Someone had a lot of time on their hands. Are all these used?"

"I haven't put my hands on every single one, but so far, they are. I don't want to dump a bunch of puzzles on a thrift store, but I'm also not sure I want to bother piecing them out, you know?"

She picked up the top box and studied the image of a colorful rainforest. "Don't artists upcycle puzzles sometimes? Or make jewelry out of them?"

"I'm sure theydo, but there isn't exactly a shortage of puzzles for them to choose from, not between thrift stores and Dollar Tree."

"Good point. Can you recycle them?"

I chuckled. "Uncertain, but that's where my mind was going, too."

"Then let's find out." Jessie whipped out her phone and began typing. Scrolling. Her dark eyes reflected the light of the screen while she read. "Oh look, a whole article on what to do with old puzzles. Yes, you can recycle them, but you should take them directly to a recycling center. Don't mix them in with other stuff."

"Okay, noted."

"Oooh, this is different. It says take them to a puzzle swap."

"What's a puzzle swap?"

"Hold, please." She scrolled more. "It's literally like how it sounds.

A place where people gather and swap puzzles they've completed, in exchange for a new one. That's actually super-cool. And...." She looked up, beaming. "There's a local group meeting on Thursday night at the Edgewood Community Center, seven o'clock."

I stared at her, not computing. "You think I should haul all these to a puzzle swap in the city?"

"Not all of them at once, dummy. Take a few and test the waters. I bet most of the people who go are retired Boomers who do puzzles while watching *The Price is Right* in their lift chairs."

"That's kind of rude, Jess."

"I'm sorry, but do you ever see people our age or younger doing jigsaw puzzles?"

"Not really." Heck, I probably hadn't put one together since I was twelve, and I was nearly forty.

"Well, there are plenty of places you can probably donate puzzles," Jessie said. "What about senior centers and nursing homes? Children's hospitals?"

"Hospitals probably prefer new stuff."

She huffed and threw up the hand not holding her phone. "I'm trying to give you suggestions here, okay? I think you should do the puzzle swap. I'll even go with you so you aren't entering new territory alone."

Thank gods for friends like Jessie, who understood how going to new places still aggravated my anxiety, which had been a lifelong battle. Despite attending auctions and watching my dad haggle at yard sales for most of my life, I still got a rush of acid in my gut when I had to do it. Sometimes my hands still shook, too, but it's gotten better.

"You really want to go to a puzzle swap on a random weeknight?" I asked.

"Sure?" She flipped her hair over one shoulder. "I might drum up some leads on old ladies looking to downsize their clothing and purse collections."

"Thought so." Couldn't blame her for always thinking about business, though, since I did the same. And a neighborhood puzzle swap that was likely to be attended by a lot of elderly folks? Definitely a good place for leads. "Fine. Puzzle swap. Thursday."

Jessie squealed. "It's a date."

&

I spent way too much time overthinking the puzzles I was taking to the swap, and by the time Jessie picked me up Thursday evening, I'd decided to hell with being strategic, and I'd randomly tossed a dozen puzzles into an empty box.

Edgewood Community Center was in a small neighborhood not far from the areas of Wilmington I preferred to haunt, which included the city's best gay bar, Pot O Gold. I hadn't visited in weeks, but I'd also been busy. As Jessie and I passed within blocks of its street, I gave serious consideration to checking it out on Saturday.

I'd been damned lonely recently, on top of being busy with work. Maybe I could find someone to keep me company for a few hours.

The community center was a squat building with a fenced-off parking lot, which was surprisingly more than half-full of cars when we arrived at six-fifty-five. I got the box out of the back and followed Jessie up a cement ramp to the front door, which had a yellowed, handwritten sign in the window announcing the swap date and start time. A small table was set up in the middle of the foyer, manned by a pair of middle-aged women, and they greeted up with cheerful smiles.

"You two must be new," the blonder of the two women said. "You have the wide-eyed look of newbies."

"It is our first time," Jessie replied with a familiar, disarming smile. "My friend Atticus here has recently come into a big collection of puzzles, and we hope they'll find some good use here at your puzzle swap."

"Oh my, that's a big box." The woman rose, as if she could see through the box's lid by standing up. "Typically, we run a one-to-one swap with puzzles. You bring one to trade, and you take one home. Are you looking to take this many home?"

"Fu—uh, heck no," I said. "I just want to give these away. The community center seemed like a better place than, um, the dump."

"Oh, no, please don't throw them away," the second woman said, also standing, her voice as raspy as sandpaper. "Even if they don't all get swapped tonight, we can find them good homes."

"Oh, great, that's what I want." The door opened behind us, letting in a blast of hot air, and I sensed someone coming inside before I turned around, not wanting to block the entrance.

An elderly man leaning on a walker came in first, followed immediately by the cutest guy I'd seen in person since college. Younger, probably twenties, tall and slender, with dark brown hair twisted into dozens of braids, more than I'd ever seen on a guy before. His braids were pulled back and held there by a green scarf, and he eyeballed me with open suspicion before his expression settled.

"Oh, Trace!" Blonde Lady said in a newly-chirpy tone. "Perfect timing. This lovely young couple is new to the swap, and they have a whole box of puzzles to give away. Can you and Gerald show them where the table is?"

Trace blinked several times, probably thrown by being volunteered on the spot, and then smiled. "Of course, Dottie. Always nice to see new faces." Something in his eyes suggested otherwise, and despite his hotness, this Trace guy wasn't impressing me with his attitude.

He gave us a wide berth as he circled the table and headed for another propped-open door. I let Jessie go first, while Gerald brought up the rear. Through the door was a large auditorium with a scuffed wooden floor, a stage directly ahead, and rolled up mats against a wall, as well as stacks of chairs and folding tables. Someone had set up a small coffee station, complete with two white boxes of pastries, About a dozen rectangular tables and chairs littered the front half of the space, many of them occupied by wrinkled faces and gray hair.

Trace went to the only round table in the center of the others, where a small pile of puzzles already waited for more to join them. "You can add your puzzles here," he said. "If you want to take a puzzle, that isn't until seven-thirty, so help yourself to refreshments."

"We're just here to donate," I replied. "I have hundreds of puzzles at home, so I don't need more."

"Hoarder?"

"Reseller." I didn't usually introduce myself as a reseller this early in a conversation, because sometimes folks got weird about it. Like I was immediately looking to get something out of them, or to cheat them somehow. But the topic had come up, and I didn't want to lie to a new acquaintance.

"So you're giving away your garbage?"

The soft, almost too-innocent way he spoke sent my hackles right up. "I don't pawn my garbage off on other people, dude. I have way too many to try and resell them all, and Jessie thought this was a good place to bring some. That's it."

The guy—what was his name? Travis?—slow-blinked at me, then cracked a smile. "I believe you. Sorry, guy, I just hate the way some people think the less fortunate or the elderly will take any old garbage that rich folks will toss at them."

I nearly choked on laughter. "I am not rich by any stretch. I don't want to insult anyone, either, just give a gift."

"His name is Atticus, by the way," Jessie said, inserting herself into our conversation. Gerald had already wandered off to sit at a table. "But we all call him Atty. I'm his BFF, Jessie, and we aren't a couple. What was your name again?"

I tried to glare at Jessie, but she only had eyes for the hottie. I knew this maneuver.

"My name's Trace Johnson," he replied. "Nice to meet you both."

"Likewise." Jessie pretended to see something on her phone. "Since the puzzle swap doesn't happen for, like, thirty minutes, why don't you two go sit and talk? I need to check a message." She marched across the auditorium, tapping away at her phone.

Trace shook his head then angled toward me, his body language more open than before. He had at least six inches of height on me, maybe more, and I could have sworn ink peeked out around his shirt sleeves. "Why do I feel like there will be repercussions if we don't do what Jessie said?"

I snorted. "Good call. Um, buy you a cup of coffee?"

"The coffee here is free."

"I know. I, uh, it was a…um." Major fail.

Trace smiled. "I know what you meant. We can get coffee and chat, if you want?"

"Sure! Um, yes, let's get coffee. Do you need to keep an eye on Gerald, though?"

"Gerald? Why?" Trace glanced around until he spotted the man. "He seems fine."

"You aren't here with him?"

"He's a little old for me, Atticus."

The complete dead-pan delivery made me snort again. "I didn't mean as a date." Yeesh, I was really out of practice at this. Going to a bar required alcohol, dancing, and maybe some info swaps later, but not this level of conversation. Especially sober conversation.

"I know, I know, you're too easy," Trace replied. "No, we just happened to arrive at the same time. I held the door for him."

"Oh. Then why are you here?" Boy, that had sounded rude. "Not that you aren't allowed to come to a public puzzle swap, but, I mean, are you into puzzles?"

"Human puzzles."

I blinked, unsure if he was being serious or joking. The guy could be a psych major. I'd met enough pretentious college students who loved showing off the latest thing they'd read for class, even if the person they were talking to didn't want to be psycho-analyzed. But Trace had a different vibe from those guys. Less ready to attack the world with his big brain, and more weary of trying to survive day to day.

Thankfully, Trace saw me struggling with his response and gave me more. "I used to come here every week as part of my community service hours." Firm, almost challenging me to make a big deal out of it. "Now, coming back is a habit I can't break, but it's a good habit. Everyone here has a story, and most will talk to you or anyone else who will listen to them." He gazed around the auditorium. "Sometimes we just need someone to listen."

"Yeah." I wasn't patronizing him, either. I understood that from my own business. People loved to talk, especially about themselves and their own lives and tragedies, and sometimes a good story helped sell an item faster than a cheap price tag.

Trace admitting to doing community service also dinged my curiosity bell hard. He was too old to be earning a Boy Scouts badge, and had the look of someone who'd probably been sentenced to those hours. But I had enough tact not to bring it up. And as if reading my mind, Trace said, "I bet in your line of work, you know all about talkative people."

I chuckled and nodded toward the coffee area. "You have no idea. Thirsty?"

"Coffee, yeah."

We joined the short line for the two large coffee dispensers. The setup was basic with foam cups, a choice of sugar or blue generic sweetener packets, powdered non-dairy creamer, or a carafe of half-and-half. I took mine black, which had been an acquired taste born of necessity. Sometimes I was too busy to bother with sugar or cream.

Trace added sugar and half-and-half to his, turning the cup nearly white, and I'd bet money he was used to grande, double-foam macchiato concoctions. I followed him to a spot by the wall, not too far from the tables of waiting puzzle swappers, but private enough to keep talking.

"So how did you end up with these hundreds of spare puzzles?" Trace asked then blew over the top of his steaming coffee. "You said you're a reseller, but I can't imagine used puzzles are in high demand."

"Some puzzles can be valuable, especially if you find something that's media-related and complete, like *Masters of the Universe* from the eighties. I found one of those once for a buck at a yard sale and resold it for thirty, but I don't typically buy puzzles. Counting them is a pain in the ass, and even if you count three hundred pieces, there's no guarantee they complete that picture unless you put the puzzle together yourself."

Trace nodded along, his lips quirking over the rim of his foam cup. "If they're so much trouble, then why do you have so many to donate to our quaint, neighborhood puzzle swap?"

Oh, yeah, I hadn't answered his question. Babble brain took over sometimes when people asked about my job. I loved what I did and enjoyed sharing random information with people. "I bought a storage unit at auction, and the puzzles were only a fraction of what I found inside."

"You said you had hundreds."

"I do. It was a packed unit. I bought it a few weeks ago, and it takes a while to get through the entire thing. I have to move everything to my storage area, sort it, organize it, decide what I can sell, give stuff to Jessie in exchange for labor. It's a process."

"So Jessie isn't your partner?"

"Nah, best friend." I described her boutique in greater detail than necessary, especially when Jessie herself was likely to reappear at any moment and promote her store herself. "She helps me empty and haul storage units, in exchange for first dibs on any clothes or purses I come across."

"Not a fan?"

"No, I hate dealing with most clothes, and I avoid them as much as I can, and when I can't, I pawn it off on other people."

"Kind of like puzzles?"

"Pretty much. I know a little about a lot, a lot about a little, and everything else I research as I go." It hit me that I'd been talking for the better part of the last ten minutes, with Trace only asking the occasional question. He was learning truckloads about me, and I still knew little about him. "So, Trace, what do you do when you're not attending weeknight puzzle swaps with the elderly?"

His dark eyes seemed to twinkle, and he finally smiled. A real smile that he needed to make more often. "I'm a barista."

Of course, someone so young and pretty was a barista. "Starbucks?"

"Fuck, no, at a little place called Half-Dozen. It's owned by two guys who met at a bar, ended up best friends, and now have a business together. It's a great place, the coffee is amazing because Ezra is a huge coffee snob, and all the muffins are homemade same-day. Plus, the owners are both big on second chances. And they're right next door to a used bookstore, so you've got coffee, books and pastries in one building. The hours are great, and it's full time, but it also leaves my evenings pretty empty, so I have to find other things to keep me busy. Hence still coming to the puzzle swap when I don't have to."

This was the most animated and excited Trace had been so far in our conversation, nattering on the same way I had about my work and Jessie's boutique. Needing to fill in his lonely evening hours was a refrain I'd heard before, usually from people who'd given up a hard-partying lifestyle for something a lot more sober. Combined with the comment about community service, I couldn't help wondering if Trace was in recovery.

"I've heard other people mention Half-Dozen, but I've never been there," I admitted. "Is the coffee worth the trip?"

"Absolutely, especially if you're familiar with that side of town." He mentioned the neighborhood.

"I definitely am. It's not that far from a bar I like." He'd gently dropped the knowledge that Half-Dozen was owned by two guys who met in a bar, and it was well-known bar lore that Ezra Kelley and Alessandro Silva had met at Pot O Gold, and then opened a coffee shop together. Time to put it out there and see if Trace's interest was dinging my gaydar correctly. "Pot O Gold. Have you heard of it?"

Trace's smile tightened a fraction. "I know it. It's been a few years since I've gone inside. I order the food for delivery sometimes, but the bar scene isn't really my thing anymore. A little too much… temptation."

He held eye contact longer than a straight guy would, and my chest warmed with interest. It had been ages since someone as handsome and hip as Trace Johnson had showed the slightest interest in me, and I wasn't going to fumble this chance.

Jessie would never let me hear the end of it if I didn't at least make the play.

"So where do you go to meet people?" I asked, leaning more directly into his personal space. "Besides puzzle swaps?"

"Oh, you know, the usual. Book club meetings, Sunday School, picnic days at the Brandywine Zoo." He laughed, a soft rolling sound that rippled over my skin. "I'm a barista, remember? I meet people all day long."

"So management doesn't frown on you dating the guests?"

The instant Trace's smile flattened, I knew I'd stepped in something, and the easy conversation between us screeched to a painful halt. "I mean, there's no set rule, but dating is complicated for me."

"Because you're an addict?" Shit, fuck and hell, I hadn't meant to let that slip out of my stupid-ass mouth.

Trace frowned and took a single step backward, putting a chasm of distance between us now, when we'd been getting so damned cozy a moment ago. He looked more annoyed than embarrassed, but I'd also known the guy for twenty-odd minutes, and I wasn't an expert on his expressions.

Thankfully, Dottie put me out of my misery by clapping her hands and asking for silence. I spotted her by the puzzle table, along with the other lady from the entrance. Jessie was striding toward me, phone in hand, and when I turned to try and fix what I'd broken with Trace...he was gone.

Well, hell.

I spent the next two weeks working around my puzzle pile, mostly so I didn't remind myself of how spectacularly I'd blown it flirting with Trace, and I had plenty to keep me busy in the meantime. The remnants of that storage locker ended up sorted for online listings, allocated for a future yard sale, or piled into the back of my van for a donation to All Saints Thrift Store, which happened on a Thursday morning. Doris and Raymond Burke were thrilled with everything I brought them—or they were really good at faking it, but who didn't like free merchandise for their mom-and-pop store?—and I was happy to help fill their stock room with inventory. And get my receipt for taxes.

But when I returned to my garage after lunch, the puzzle mountain mocked me from the corner where I'd shoved it, and I couldn't put it off any longer. I also really wanted to talk to Trace again, maybe apologize for being so rude two weeks ago, but tracking him down at his coffee shop felt way too stalkerish. Who did that? Even if it *was* a public business and wouldn't be weird for me to go in and order coffee...nah.

So I grabbed a random box of puzzles, shoved it into my van, and at six-thirty that evening, headed for the community center. Alone this time, because I did not need Jessie pestering me about being hung up on a guy I'd known for half-an-hour. A hot, intriguing barista with a lot of secrets behind his devilish smile.

Dottie greeted me with a hug I didn't expect. "It's so nice to see new people coming back to these events," she said, "and with more puzzles! Last week, the regulars raved about some of yours. Darlene said the one she chose reminded her of a puzzle she used to love doing as a little girl. The picture on it, I mean. It wasn't the same puzzle, because yours aren't that old."

I blinked dumbly. "Wow. Um, I'm glad it made Darlene happy. I'll just, uh, put these on the swap table?"

"Go right ahead, hon."

The auditorium was mostly empty, since I'd gotten there a little too early thanks to light traffic. I glanced around while I stacked the new puzzles on the swap table. Didn't want to be too obvious that I was looking for someone, or appear as though I was casing the place, and I didn't see—

"Hey, Atticus."

Trace's voice directly behind me nearly sent me out of my sneakers. I spun around, heart slamming into my ribcage, and my pulse jumped with happiness at the sight of Trace, smiling at me like he'd been handed a million dollars. "Hey, Trace," I said, all thoughts of apologizing tumbling out of my brain.

"When I didn't see you here last week, I figured you weren't coming back." His tone was a funny mix of excited and annoyed, and I couldn't figure out why. He's the one who'd ghosted me.

"I had more puzzles." Cue more dumb, obvious statements. "How about you?" Idiot! I knew this.

"Habit." Trace tilted his head toward the far wall, away from the coffee table. "Can I talk to you for a sec?"

"Um, yeah." Had I stepped into an alternate reality where our first conversation hadn't ended awkwardly and abruptly two weeks ago? What the heck? Curious and confused, I followed him to a quiet spot by a stack of plastic chairs. "What's up?"

"When I got here last week, Gerald approached me. He said he took one of your puzzles home and found a letter in it. Wanted me to give it back to you in case you'd lost it. But since it was in the box, I figured it wasn't yours, and I read it, and it was fascinating, and I really want to read more, if you have more letters."

"Huh?" As intelligent responses went, that rose to the level of driveway gravel, but I was confused. Trace wanted more letters that Gerald found in one of my donated puzzles? "Wait, is finding a letter a metaphor for something?"

"No, it's very literal. The letter was postmarked January '87, and it was written on lined notebook paper, in cursive, so it took me a while to decipher it, but the contents…" He gnawed briefly on his lower lip. "I'm sure it sounds nuts, but I really want to know more about the people in the letter."

My brain was finally catching up with the conversation. Personal mail and papers were not uncommon finds in storage lockers, and the tote I'd found in this one was waiting to go through my shredder. I rarely took the time to open cards or envelopes, unless they were obviously vintage. Old greeting cards were valuable to the right collectors.

But unless one of those letters had a bunch of hundred dollar bills in it, I wasn't likely to find valuables inside forty-year-old jigsaw puzzles. "Okay," was all I could stumble out.

Trace's eyebrows furrowed. "Did you give the rest of your stash away? Are they all gone?"

"No. I brought another box tonight, but the rest are still in my garage."

"Great. Come with me." He looped his hand around my elbow and guided me back to the puzzle table, where he began to gently shake the stack I'd brought. One by one. I stood there, face hot, imagining every pair of eyeballs in the auditorium was staring at us in confusion, but too embarrassed to look around and check.

One box sounded less full than the others. Trace opened the lid, reached inside, and produced a thick, standard-sized envelope, and tucked it under his armpit. He found two more letters in puzzles, and then he whisked me back to our spot. The auditorium was filling up with puzzle swappers, but when I did nervously glance around, no one was paying us any attention. Maybe Trace always acted a bit erratically and they were used to it?

Trace looked at the front of each envelope and I tried to peer over his shoulder. Both addresses were blacked out but the postmarks all said '87. He slid a fingertip over the illegible addressee's name. "If there's three here, then I bet there's more in the others."

"Probably." Before I could think through the intelligence of it, I said, "Come over to my garage. We can go through the others, look for more letters. I think I have some old paperwork, too, that was in with the other stuff I bought."

"Yeah?" His dark eyes glimmered, and I loved that I'd put that positive emotion there. "When?"

"Um, whenever."

"Tomorrow? I work until four."

My morning was jammed with appointments, but I could swing that. "Yeah, I can meet you at my place around four-thirty?"

"Okay. Sweet. Give me your phone. I'll put in my number so you can text me the address."

I handed over my phone without much thought, reacting to his gently issued orders and texting my address to a near-stranger, so he could come into my private workspace. I almost never invited anyone over, not even potential clients. We generally met in public places. No one needed to see how much merchandise I had on hand. Despite a good alarm system on both the house and garage, I didn't trust people, as a general rule.

But I was inviting Trace over to root through puzzles for old letters he found fascinating. "So what exactly was in the first letter that made you want to read more?" I asked while Trace fiddled with his own phone.

"A piece of a larger puzzle."

"What?"

Trace pocketed his phone and smiled, but something still lurked in his eyes. Something intriguing I needed to know more about. Much like I needed to know more about the people in those letters. "Tell you what," Trace said. "Give me two hours of your time tomorrow to find more letters. If you look at what I've found and aren't equally interested in knowing the whole story, then I'll buy the puzzles off you and haul them away myself. Take them all off your hands."

"You'd do that just to find someone else's old letters?"

"Yes."

Two hours of my time to have someone else sort through that mountain of puzzles, while I watched (maybe participated), and a chance to get to know more about the mysterious Trace Johnson? To understand why these letters had him so invested that he'd promised to buy the whole lot off me if I wasn't impressed by his findings? Win-win.

"Okay, two hours tomorrow, starting at four-thirty," I said. "You aren't going to give me a hint? Let me read one of the letters tonight?"

"You got a hint. 1987."

"What am I supposed to know about '87? I was a year old."

"It gave us the Frog brothers."

"Was that a country band?"

Trace laughed, the musical sound bouncing around the room despite the droning chatter all around us. "You've never seen *The Lost Boys*? It's a classic."

"Wait, that's a vampire movie, right? I'm not really into that kind of thing."

"What kind of movies do you like?"

"Action. Comedies. Mindless stuff. I don't honestly watch a lot of movies. If I'm not working, I'm probably vegging out with video games or true crime podcasts."

"True crime." Trace cocked his hip slightly, angling his body toward mine. I was no pro, but I was pretty sure he was subtly flirting now. "So you like to gather clues and investigate things? I bet it comes in handy with your day job."

"It does, and I see what you did there." I pointed at the letters in his hand. "You've got the clues. I've got the puzzles. Tomorrow, we start our investigation and put things together."

"Yes, we do, Atticus. It's a date."

A date.

No, it wasn't a real date, but I'll be damned if my body didn't know it wasn't. From the moment I woke up Friday morning, my stomach was in knots, and it remained tangled up and boiling with acid all day, while I got through my other business. Then I spent way too much time worrying about the state of my garage, allowing my anxiety to spike so hard I actually swept the damned floor twice.

By the time four-thirty finally rolled around, I had the air conditioner blasting at Arctic temperatures, I'd changed my shirt twice, and I felt like a wreck. But when I investigated the rumble of a car engine outside, the sight of Trace unfolding his long, lean body from the driver's side of his two-door sedan turned that wormy anxiety into nervous anticipation. We'd definitely flirted last night, he was here at my private residence, and I really hoped we both got something great out of tonight's puzzle hunt.

Trace leaned inside his car, and straightened back up with a brown coffee cup in each hand. I couldn't stop staring at them as he strode across the gravel to where I stood in the open side door, conditioned air circling around my ankles while the summer humidity blasted my face and chest.

Hot coffee in this heat? Was he nuts?

"Brought you a black coffee," Trace said once he was close enough to hold it out. "You didn't put anything in yours the other night."

The other night had been two weeks ago. Trace remembered such a small detail from that far back? The kindness was ten kinds of endearing. "Thank you." I accepted the coffee, careful to hold it around the cardboard sleeve. "I appreciate the caffeine jolt. It's been a long day."

"Same here, but I'm pretty used to early mornings and long days. But the owners are great about allowing employees to help themselves to the drip coffee while we're working."

"Just the hot or the iced, too?"

Trace's smile drooped. "Shit, is it hot in your garage? I didn't even think about iced coffee."

"It's fine, I have an air conditioning unit for the garage. I do a lot of work out here, and I'd melt in the summer without it. Come inside, please." I stepped in and gave Trace room to enter.

He gazed around the space, taking in the rows of sturdy metal shelves and assortment of both cardboard banker boxes and heavy-duty plastic totes. Most of the overhead lights were on, giving us plenty of illumination. I had no idea what it looked like to a stranger, because to me it was just…my workspace.

"How long have you been in the reselling business?" Trace asked. "This is a pretty sick space."

"Technically, I've been doing it off and on since I was in college, both for extra cash and the thrill of the hunt. It's been my full-time job for about three years, mostly because of my divorce."

"I'm sorry to hear that. The divorce, I mean."

"Don't be." I'd lost a lot in the divorce, including a relationship with my stepson, but I'd regained so much, too. "I'm free to be me again."

"I hear that." His eyes reflected keen understanding. "You said mostly the divorce. What's the rest of the reason you do this? I can't imagine it's what you majored in."

"My parents." Heat flooded my chest, and an unexpected wave of grief made my eyes sting. I didn't tell business acquaintances about this part of my life, especially not new ones. New, hot ones who wanted to dig into my puzzles for old letters. Trace's inquisitive eyebrow quirk kept my motor mouth going. "They passed away unexpectedly a little over a year ago. They both loved junking and antiques, but my dad especially encouraged it. In a way, I still do this to honor them."

"Wow, that's really cool, Atticus. Not your parents dying, obviously, I'm so sorry about that. But you doing something to keep their memories alive. You all were obviously close."

"We were." Something in Trace's tone suggested he hadn't been close with his own parents, and I managed to bite my tongue and not scare him off again with rude questions. "I was lucky in a lot of things, so I try not to take much for granted. And to help others when I can."

"Such as allowing a curious new friend to rummage around in your puzzle stash?"

"Exactly." I led him over to said stash. "They're all right here. Every box with a big P written on it, and there are a bunch of loose ones, too. Oh." The small tote of random paperwork I'd saved while sorting was on my main work table, and I snatched it up. Handed it over to Trace. "Here's more pieces for your big puzzle. Good luck."

Trace hefted the tote once, testing its weight. "You aren't helping?"

"I was going to, but I had to reschedule a video chat from this morning to five o'clock, so I have to go inside for a little while."

"You're trusting me alone with all your stuff?"

I shrugged. "I have security cameras."

"Yeah? Ever capture anything salacious on them?"

"Caught two stray cats fucking one night."

Trace laughed out loud, and the sound danced around my garage like it had danced around the auditorium last night. I really liked the way he laughed. "Cats were fucking inside your garage?"

"No, outside. I don't have cameras inside." If I was reading his signals right, this shouldn't go over like a lead balloon. "What happens inside the garage stays inside the garage."

His nostrils flared. "Duly noted." We held eye contact long enough for my belly to squirm with excited wiggles.

Then my phone blared out an alert. "Uh, yeah, my phone call."

"Enjoy the call. Hopefully, by the time you're done, I'll have a lot more letters to show you."

"And then you'll let me in on what's got you so invested?"

"Yup."

"Okay then. See you in about an hour." After another moment of intense eye contact, I took my coffee with me to the house, leaving someone new alone in my private workspace for the first time. I had no real reason to trust Trace already—but I did.

By the time I finished my call, my stomach was rumbling for dinner. I could toss a frozen pizza into the oven for us both, if Trace was still working his way through the puzzle stash and wanted to stay. Maybe offer the guy a soda from the garage's mini fridge. But any thought of food vanished when I pushed open the garage door and spotted Trace sitting in on the floor, surrounded by cardboard boxes and stacks of puzzles, tears running down his face.

"Shit, man, are you okay?" I picked my way around the mess to squat in front of him, trying to suss out the situation in case he'd fallen or something, and my insurance was about to get involved. "Are you hurt?"

Trace looked up, his tear-filled eyes breaking my heart a little, and he rasped, "I'm not hurt. These letters, Atticus. Fuck."

"Letters?" I focused on the folded notebook paper clutched in one of his hands. "You're upset about an old letter?"

"It's what's in the letter. Sit down."

I did, unsure why I listened when he told me to do something, folding my legs into a semi-comfortable position. He was surrounded by at least eight more puzzles, each with a letter on top.

Trace wiped his nose on his shirt sleeve, and then he started to read. *"April fourth, nineteen-eighty-seven. Dearest Teddy. I was with Jerry when he died. I'm glad you weren't here, even though you said you'd come. Bearing it alone was almost too much, but I couldn't stand for you to bear witness to the same horrors as I, especially with you so far away. Jerry is finally at peace, no longer suffering so greatly. So atrociously. To see his skin peeling away like wet tissue paper when they tried to move him…it's the stuff of nightmares."*

My own skin crawled as my stomach erupted into a boiling inferno. The date of the letter, the horrific death. I didn't have to ask what Jerry died from.

"Some of the nurses can't stomach it. It's selfish but I'm glad Jerry's suffering is over. Mine, as well, for this friend. But how many dozens more will follow? Faces I've known, danced with, wept with, dreamed with. And the thousands of faces I'll never know?

"I'm sorry for such a depressing letter, but I thought you should know Jerry's gone. He was your friend too, even if only through my letters. Thank you for the new photo. It helps in the dark times when it's difficult to picture your smile. I miss your voice the most but understand why we cannot telephone. I hope this newest package finds you in good health and better spirits than I send it. Yours always, X."

It took a while to find my voice. "X?" I asked. "The letter is signed X?"

"Yeah." Trace cleared his throat hard. "They're all addressed to Dearest Teddy, and signed X. Every one that I've found so far. And except for two from '88, they're all dated 1987."

I swallowed hard, mouth dry, insides shaky. "It was AIDS, right? That Jerry died from?"

"Has to be. I've heard stories of how some people died of it back then, when there was no real treatment, nothing to do but try and mitigate the worst of the pain." Trace wiped at his eyes again and sniffled, and I wished I had a tissue or something for him. "Ignorance and hate killed an entire generation of gay men during this period. Does anyone even remember Jerry anymore?"

"We do." Without thinking, I reached out and squeezed Trace's knee. "Maybe it wasn't how X intended, but he left a legacy for Jerry. And Teddy, who I'm guessing was the owner of the storage locker I bought." For the first time in my life, a weird sensation passed over my entire body. Like Teddy's ghost was lingering nearby, watching me disperse the remnants of his life like ashes in the wind.

"Those papers weren't for a Teddy or a Theodore. It was someone's collection of old letters sent during World War Two, mostly from England to an address in Pennsylvania. I doubt they're connected to our Teddy."

Our Teddy. And as intriguing as letters from that time period were to the reseller in me, this was more important. "Teddy and X were clearly close."

Trace nodded slowly, fingers lightly tracing lines on the notebook paper with one hand, while the other covered mine. Keeping my hand on his knee. The touch was almost electric, and I turned my hand over so we were palm to palm. "I wish I knew more about X," he whispered. "Were they a nurse? An ex-lover? He or she? None of the letters I've read are specific enough. Everything X writes is about Teddy or other people they knew."

"Then let's keep looking."

More than satisfying my own growing curiosity, I needed to find answers for Trace's sake. We held eye contact—and hands—a beat longer, and then Trace reached for an unopened box.

I'd never been so invested in solving a puzzle in all my life.

☧

We ate the pizza, plus most of a bag of tortilla chips with a jar of salsa, and at least two sodas each by the time we both decided to call it a night. Stacks of puzzles stood all over my garage floor, many of them sorted by Trace during our search for letters, putting them in piles by animals, people, recognizable locations, and general artistic expressions, which was a lot more than I would have done with them.

There was also a small stack of media-related puzzles, including a few from 80s franchises that could have monetary value if all the pieces were there—something I'd do another day, when I wasn't seeing imaginary puzzle pieces floating in front of my eyeballs every time I blinked.

The other major staging area was like a map of sorts. Trace had kept all discovered letters with their puzzle, and he'd moved them into chronological order. We'd read bits of some of the letters as we found them, but mostly we had created a story line to follow at a later time. Maybe when we both weren't yawning every twenty seconds.

"I wonder if my sister could help us find X," Trace said absently, as he surveyed our organized chaos.

"Is she a private investigator?"

"No, she's a partner in an urban planning group that does a lot of work with community centers and nonprofits. But the guy she's been seeing has a lot of cop friends. Maybe he knows someone."

I stood there, a bit in awe of his commitment to knowing everything he could about Teddy, X, and the nature of their relationship. There might be more to discover in the unread letters, but so far, X had been very careful to hide identifying details. "This is really important to you, isn't it?"

"Yes. And you're officially intrigued, right? I don't have to buy all these puzzles off you?"

I chuckled. "No, you don't, and yes, I'm hooked. I'm also about to pass out from sheer exhaustion. Can we pick up our investigation tomorrow?"

"Okay. I get off at four again."

I checked my phone calendar because my brain was mush. "I'll be here." When Trace turned a slightly panicked glance to the floor, I added, "Don't worry about the mess. It won't be in my way tomorrow."

"Great, thanks."

Trace walked out first, and I took a minute to turn off the lights and set the alarm code. Locked the garage door. He was waiting by his car, and I joined him there, a lot unsure of myself, like I'd just walked him to his car after our first date. "Thank you for indulging me on this," Trace said. "You didn't have to, but you did."

"It's no trouble. I'm invested now, too, remember?"

He gazed at me with so many things flickering in his expressive eyes, and I swore they briefly dropped to my lips. I swallowed, unsure what to do next, worried I'd scare him off if I was too forward—or he'd think I wasn't interested if I was too chicken-shit to—

He stuck out his hand. "Thank you. See you tomorrow."

Damn it. "Yeah, see you."

I remembered that handshake—the firm grip, the warm skin, how something seemed to ripple from each point of contact all the way to my balls—until the moment my head hit the pillow, and then I dreamed of Trace Johnson's wickedly sweet smile.

On Saturdays, I had a routine of hitting local yard sales, shooting down to a flea market south of the city if the yard sales were few and far between, and then usually stopping by my vendor booths to swap out merchandise. I got caught up chatting with one of the antique mall owners that afternoon, so I was running late getting home to meet Trace. I'd also skipped lunch and was hungry as a spring bear, so I swung by a favorite pizza joint. The strip mall had a liquor store two doors down, so I got a large supreme and a six-pack. I also texted Trace that I'd probably be about ten minutes late, but I had dinner with me.

Trace was sitting under the shade of a tree, instead of in his car with the air conditioning, and he grinned when I climbed out of the car with sustenance. His smile dimmed when I handed him the six-pack to hold so I could unlock the garage and let us in. The problem didn't hit me until we were noshing on slices, and I offered him a beer.

"I don't drink," Trace said flatly. "I'll take a soda, though."

"Shit, sorry, I shouldn't have assumed." Pizza and beer went together, for me, like macaroni and cheese, or milk and cookies. But that wasn't everyone's jam. I got him a cola from the mini fridge.

"It's fine, I'm used to it. Drinking wasn't really my issue, but it's better to abstain anyway." I bit my tongue, because I'd chased him off once with the nosy question, and Trace impressed me by adding, "I was a heroin addict for eight years before I got clean. Been sober for five."

Damn. "Thank you for trusting me with that. Um." The math confused me, though, because he didn't look that old.

"I can see the question marks floating over your head. I started using when I was fourteen to escape the shithole that was my family life. I didn't know I was trading one living hell for another, not until I ended up homeless. Desperate. Sleeping behind dumpsters and eating in soup kitchens."

His story collided with his attachment to letters written during the height of the AIDS era, and my heart lurched. I couldn't make myself ask, though, not something that insanely personal. Not when we were still just friends.

"But I was lucky," Trace continued, his serious expression gentling. "When I hit rock bottom, my sister April was there. After a few months in jail, she helped me get into rehab. Gave me a place to stay while I got my life in order, got the job at Half-Dozen. I owe her my life."

"I'm glad she didn't give up on you. Some people don't have that unconditional support."

"Didn't you?"

"Mostly. My marriage obviously went to shit, and for a lot of reasons I'm not diving into tonight. But my parents were great, loving and generous. I just wish I'd come out and told them I was bisexual before they died, so they knew all of me, not just the façade I presented to the world."

"Will you hate me if I say I'm envious? My parents weren't around, and when they were they were either fighting, drunk, usually both. It was easier to not be home, but I didn't find anything out there but trouble and drugs."

"I'm sorry."

"Don't be. I'm not. Can't change any of it. My bad choices put me on the path to right now, and while my bed feels really empty most nights, I'm…settled. Things could be and have been much worse."

The empty bed comment wasn't lost on me, and the dark intent in Trace's eyes drew me in. At some point, we'd both put our pizza slices down and stood closer together. I could reach out and touch him. Hold him. Kiss him. "You said before that dating is complicated for you. That why your bed's empty?"

"Yes. Casual sex is one thing, but most people bail when they see the kind of baggage I haul around. Which is why I'm upfront about things when I'm interested in someone. Saves hurt feelings later."

Hope and terror collided in my head, and the only words I could manage were a dumb joke. "I thought you were just interested in my puzzles."

"You're the most interesting puzzle in the room, Atticus, and I really want to know more. Not just about Teddy and X, but about you. I've been intrigued by you since Dottie introduced us that first night."

"That first night when you walked away from me?"

"I'm sorry about that."

"No, it's okay, I was really rude." I reached out before I could stop myself, and I clasped his hand. Gave it a gentle squeeze that he returned. "Thanks for giving me another chance. For being honest with me. And if it helps at all, your baggage doesn't scare me. We all have it. It's always there. But it doesn't have to weigh us down."

Trace sucked in a harsh breath, and then I was surrounded. His arms wrapped around my waist at the same time his mouth covered mine. I expected harsh and demanding, but the embrace was as gentle as the kiss. A quiet questing of his lips against mine that stole a breathy moan from my throat that I barely recognized. I'd never had such a sweet, curious first kiss in my life, not even when I was ten-years-old and kissing a classmate for the first time. Not my first boy kiss. Not my first girlfriend kiss. Not my first kiss with my ex.

This discovery with Trace was the first kiss I'd always wanted, and the one I would never, ever forget.

When it finally ended, we were breathless and hard, and our

hands were tangled in each other's clothes. I could have stood like that forever, holding him, anticipation zinging through my bloodstream, facing endless possibilities as to where this might go. I could have gone straight to my knees and sucked Trace off, and he probably would have let me, but that didn't feel right. I got the sense Trace had had enough quick encounters to last him a lifetime. I know I had.

I didn't want quick and dirty, not this time. Not with him.

"Come upstairs with me?" I asked, barely able to speak above a whisper. "Neither one of us has to be alone tonight."

Trace rubbed his nose against mine. "Okay."

I woke in the dark, the gentle ache in my body a pleasant reminder of the sex I'd had with Trace last night. I'd never fallen asleep so fast or sated in my life, content with my partner by my side. But the other half of the bed was startlingly empty, and I sat up, squinting through the gloom for evidence I hadn't dreamed my encounters with Trace.

No, the sheets were still messy, and an empty condom wrapper was on the side table. My phone's light didn't show any extra clothes on the floor, though, and my heart sank. For the hours we'd played, explored each other's body, and kissed like we'd die without it, I never imagined he'd sneak off while I slept.

I climbed out of bed and padded to the window to make sure—no, his car was still in the driveway. Lights were on inside the garage. I hadn't thought to set the alarm before dragging Trace inside the house and into my bedroom, or I'd have woken a lot sooner. Curiosity overtaking my disappointment, I slipped on a pair of boxer shorts and went outside.

Trace was bent over, rifling inside a box, likewise dressed in just his shorts, and I took a moment to admire the taut ass I remembered so well. Gripped so hard while he fucked me, and even gave playful smacks a few times. Plus, all the tattoos previously hidden by his shirt...

He straightened when he noticed me, his inked chest glistening with perspiration. "Hey. Sorry, I woke up and couldn't fall back asleep."

"It's okay." The a/c was on a timer and had shut off for the night, so I strode over and manually turned it back on. "I'm just glad you didn't sneak away."

Trace's arms slipped around my waist from behind, and he kissed the side of my neck. "I would never do that. What we did was special, Atty. I'd never cheapen it by leaving in the dark like a trick who didn't care about you."

"Thank you." I leaned back against his chest, loving the way he held me so protectively, hands clasped loosely over my belly. "Couldn't stay away from the mystery of Teddy and X, huh?"

"Guilty. I know we were at this for hours last night—"

"The investigating or the fucking?"

Trace pinched my belly, and I laughed. "Both. I just don't want to leave this search unfinished, you know? You don't have to stay up with me."

I reached behind me to gently squeeze his hip. "I'll go put some coffee on."

By sunrise Sunday morning, we'd gone through every puzzle in the garage, plus a few boxes of the games from the same unit, just in case an errant letter had slipped into one of those. Trace had everything sorted chronologically, and after snapping photos of each letter matched with its corresponding puzzle, we took the entire stack of envelopes into my house.

I insisted we break for showers and a simple breakfast of frozen waffles to go with all the coffee we'd both guzzled. Afterward, we settled on the living room sofa with those precious letters and Trace began to read them out loud.

"*September eighteenth, nineteen-eighty-six. Dearest Teddy,*" Trace read from the very first one. "*I found the postcard with your address in my suit-case, you clever boy. Thank you for including it, as I have so many fond memo-*

ries of our time spent together over Labor Day weekend. It was my first ever trip to Rehoboth Beach, and I did not expect to make so many new friends in such a short period of time. Or to meet someone as spectacularly handsome and interesting and sensual as yourself. My only regret is that there is an entire country now between us, and I don't know when or if we'll see each other again.

"But we can write each other, since you thought to make sure our weekend fling was not just a fling. Thank you for that, and for respecting my privacy. No one at home knows, and they can't ever know. I'd lose everything and everyone I care about in my hometown. But I am so tired of living like this. I know you understand."

Trace sighed. "That's so sad."

"Yeah. As much as it's possible X is a woman who had an affair, based on other context clues, I'm guessing he's a closeted gay man from the western side of the country who took a brief, rainbow vacation at Rehoboth Beach and let his freak flag fly. Teddy obviously meant a lot to him."

"I think you're right."

We continued to read aloud the two-year, long-distance love story of Teddy and X. X making gay friends in his home state; losing several to horrible, AIDS related deaths; coming to terms with his sexuality; finally leaving his wife to live an authentic, if terrifying, life in San Francisco and volunteering his time with AIDS patients. His first visit to a place called Club Base. It was the only time X ever mentioned an identifiable location, but it still didn't narrow anything down in terms of who X was.

With four letters to go, we took a break. Trace was hoarse, and I was stiff from sitting for so long. We shared sandwiches for lunch, and as I watched him eat, I marveled at how well Trace fit in here. How easily he moved in the kitchen, how natural it felt to have him in my space. It was way too soon to start dreaming of anything beyond dating, but I basked in the immediacy of it all. And in how much it chased away my ever-present loneliness.

"Part of me wants to save the last few letters," Trace said with a touch of melancholy in his voice. "I'm afraid of what the last one's going to say. But I kind of want to rip off the bandage, so to speak."

"I get it. We're invested, right? Hey, did you ask your sister about knowing any private investigators?"

"I did, and she said she'd get back to me in a few days. She's in the middle of a big project launch at work, and doesn't like to divide her attention too much. But April keeps her promises, so she'll follow through."

"I'd like to meet her." As soon as the impulsive thought crossed my lips, my cheeks flamed. "Um, I mean, not right away, and not as, like, your boyfriend or anything, since we've only been doing this for a day. But she sounds really awesome."

Trace smiled at my babbling. "She's great. And I think you guys would like each other. We also don't have to define what we're doing right now, Atty. No labels. Let's just keep doing what feels good."

Nothing in his tone suggested a come-on in that final statement, but the words still warmed my blood. "Feels good, huh?" I slid my hand across the table to squeeze his wrist. "How good do you want things to feel?"

With a gentle bite of his lower lip, Trace twisted his hand to clasp mine, and rose from the table.

We didn't make it upstairs this time, and after we'd sated ourselves, Trace got a wet rag from the kitchen to clean us both up. By some silent agreement, we cuddled up naked on the couch, a crocheted afghan tossed over us for warmth in the air-conditioned room.

"Ready to hear the end of things?" Trace whispered, fingers tracing circles over the front an age-yellowed envelope.

"It might be the end of these letters, but it's also the beginning of something new. For us?"

"Yeah. Definitely for us." He angled his head to kiss my cheek, and then pulled the letter from its envelope. *"January second, nineteen-eighty-eight. Dearest Teddy. For the first time in my life, I celebrated the new year with likeminded folks, and it was spectacular. Even with the threat of illness in the air, we threw the party of a lifetime. I hope you were not alone yesterday, despite your last letter mentioning you felt poorly. Have you taken the blood test? Perhaps, my love, it's time."*

My heart sank for Teddy and everything X's question implied.

"I'd like to come visit this summer, if you agree. It's been far too long since

I've seen you, and I'm still heartsick over losing the photo you sent. I'm sure we've both changed greatly in the last year and a half. I don't think you'd recognize me from the shy man you first met at the Renegade that weekend. I hardly recognize myself most days, and that is a good thing, I think."

X went on to describe a new patient at the nursing home, a young woman who'd contracted the virus from a blood transfusion, but whose family had turned on her for getting "the homosexual cancer." The ignorance and fear from those times was palpable in X's letters, and it left me agitated. At once angry and sad and all things in between for all the suffering people who'd died alone.

"Thank gods for angels like X," I said when Trace folded that letter and slid it back into the envelope. "He needs a hospital wing named after him or something. I just wish we knew his name."

"Me, too." He held up the final two letters. "Penultimate installment."

"If it wasn't the middle of the afternoon, I'd pour us each a glass of wine for this." I flinched when I remembered too late. "Sorry."

"It's fine, and don't let me stop you. I'm a big boy and can handle being around someone who's drinking, especially if the occasion calls for it."

"Thanks, but getting wine means getting up, and I like this too much." I liked Trace relaxed against my chest, naked, our legs wrapped around each other. Warm and cozy, and so natural I didn't want to break the spell. I rested my chin on his shoulder. "Read to me. Please."

Trace did. The second-to-last letter was dated February 1988 and contained more of the same, making vague plans for a summer visit and tales of X working in the nursing home. He asked again if Teddy had been tested, his concern clear in his words, and I half-expected to see dried tear tracks on the weathered notebook paper. There were also mentions of Valentine's Day and a potential phone call between the pair.

I hoped they got their call. I hoped they had gotten a chance to express their affection in spoken words, instead of just in written ones. I hoped Teddy's letters back to X were as filled with longing and adoration and hope for a future together. I hoped.

But hope had a way of leaving you cold and alone and aching.

Not always, but a lot of the time.

Trace held the final letter in his hands for several long moments before sliding the paper out. It was one sheet, but something was tucked into—a Polaroid slipped out and landed on Trace's lap. I itched to pick it up, but Trace left it face-down on the blanket and opened the letter. Familiar penmanship, but only two paragraphs long.

"March fourth, nineteen-eighty-eight. Dearest Teddy. I wish I could tell you that I bore your news bravely when I received your last letter. I wish I could tell you it filled me with determination and a sense of duty, rather than with dread and despair. I will tell you that I love you, and I still plan on coming to see you. Nothing will deter those plans, they will simply have to be sooner than June. And I promise a longer letter will follow, but I had to send this as soon as I could. I had to tell you.

"I love you, and I will be there for you until the end. It may take time to get my affairs in order and prepare to move east. Until that happens, until we see each other again with our own eyes, please hold on to this photo of us. You sent it to me to replace the one I lost, and I plan on collecting it from you in the near future.

Yours always, in love and life and all matters of the heart, Frederick."

"Frederick," I said. The author of these letters, X, finally had a first name, something to give more identity to such a profound human being. "Teddy and Frederick."

Trace coughed hard and sniffled. "Teddy and Freddy. Huh." With trembling fingers, he lifted the Polaroid and turned it over. Two young men smiled back at us, arms around each other's shoulders, clearly happy and enjoying themselves. The background was dark with slashes of color, possibly the club Frederick had mentioned. The Renegade? They looked very similar in height and appearance, both with sandy hair and slender builds, and both shirtless.

"I wonder who is who?" I whispered, the moment too reverent for loud words.

Trace brushed his fingertip over the face of the man on the left. "This is Frederick. His eyes. They're so joyful, because he's experiencing something so profound. He's experiencing life as his true self for the first time."

I raised Trace's hand so I could study the photo up close. Despite its age and faded colors, I could see in Frederick's eyes the same relief I often felt now that I was also living a more authentic life. "Yeah. I can see that. Do you think Frederick is still alive?"

"If so, he'd be what? Probably in his sixties or seventies?"

"Probably. And if Teddy's stuff all ended up in storage for the last thirty-odd years, it's likely Frederick never made the trip east. Or if he did, he didn't get access to anything of Teddy's. I hope he at least got some sort of closure when Teddy died."

The letter hadn't spelled it out, but I could guess that Teddy tested positive for the virus, and Frederick had immediately made plans to move east and care for Teddy. To be by his side until the end, like Frederick had been by the side of countless AIDS patients in San Francisco. But the photo was in our hands, not in Frederick's, and I'd found it in an abandoned, auctioned-off storage locker.

"Their story deserves a better ending than this," Trace said.

"Hey." I shifted us so he was facing me, the blanket now draped over his shoulders, not liking him this visibly upset. "You gave them a better ending by being curious. By taking that first letter, reading it, and needing to know more. And even if no one else is alive who remembers them, we do. Maybe Teddy and Frederick only loved each other for a little while, but they did love each other. Without that love? Without Frederick sending letters and puzzles to Teddy on a regular basis? We never would have met."

Trace's glimmering eyes widened, hope replacing some of his grief. "Yeah?"

"Yeah. I never would have dreamed of walking into a community puzzle swap if I hadn't bought Teddy's puzzle hoard. Gerald never would have found the letter to give to you, so you could hand it back to me. And I'm hardly a blushing romantic in any situation, but I really like you here, Trace. In my life. And I think Frederick and Teddy would be happy about us finding each other."

"Me too. Liking me here and thinking they'd be happy for us. I wasn't looking for a relationship when I first asked you about looking through your puzzles, but I am truly happy with how things have turned out."

"Yeah." I brushed our lips together, a silent promise that we were both intent on seeing where this new relationship took us. Even if it wasn't forever, it could be a pretty amazing for-right-now.

Trace deepened the kiss, but before things got too steamy, his cell began speaking in a mechanical voice, telling us, "Your sister is calling. Answer the phone, your sister is calling," over and over.

I laughed and loosened my hold on Trace just enough for him to reach out and snag his phone off the coffee table. "Hey, April." He winked at me. "No, your timing is perfect. Any leads on a PI I can call about my mail problem?"

His broad, bright smile answered his question for me.

Chapel Hill House was a strange name for a facility in the middle of a city, nowhere near a hill, much less a chapel of any kind, but that's where our information finally took us. I'd bartered for PI services—the guy was restoring a '69 Camaro and in search of new-old stock for parts, for which I had a few connections—in locating Frederick from San Francisco, using the letters, the Polaroid, and every scrap of paper I'd found in that storage unit related to its former owner.

The leads panned out. Theodore "Teddy" Pavlik took his own life on March 17, 1988, rather than suffer a slow death by AIDS, with which he'd been recently diagnosed. His property had passed to a sibling, and when that sibling passed, everything was put into storage —the unit I eventually purchased. Between Trace's work schedule at Half-Dozen, and my other commitments to my own business, we finally managed to visit Chapel Hill in early July. It was hot as balls outside, and the facility's air conditioning wasn't a whole lot better, but a very nice lady at the help desk signed us in, and then directed us to the proper room. I hadn't been in a nursing home before, and the dreary interior made me hope I never ended up in one in my old age. While Trace and I were still dating and very happy with our three-week-old relationship, neither of us was ready for a hard commitment. I wasn't ready to say, "I love you," but the feelings were definitely growing.

One day I'd say the words.

I followed Trace down the wide, echoing corridor to the room number we'd been given. The door stood wide open, and faint voices trickled out, tinny enough that they had to be from a television, rather than other visitors. Trace knocked on the door and stepped into the frame, me close at his back. I was intensely nervous about this, because visiting an elderly man I'd never met was way outside my comfort zone, so I let Trace take the lead.

I trusted him to lead me steadily forward.

"Who's that?" a gruff voice barked. "Come on in, I don't bite. Ain't got my teeth in."

Trace chuckled and moved deeper inside. It was decorated like a basic hospital room, with a bed, built-in dresser and freestanding closet, but personal touches sprinkled everything like confetti. A red bedspread, framed photos on flat surfaces, some clothes haphazardly thrown on the dresser top, and artwork on the walls. I focused on the art piece nearest my shoulder, which was bright, cheerful, and reminded me of Lisa Frank.

It was also, I realized with a surprised grunt, a sealed, completed puzzle.

A thin, long-limbed man with only a few stray hairs on his otherwise bald scalp sat in a wheelchair that faced a boxy television. He had a crocheted lap blanket over his legs, and he stared at us with a funny mix of suspicion and humor in his deep-set eyes. "You boys got the wrong room?" he asked.

"Not if you're Frederick Marsh," Trace replied. "He's who we're looking for."

"Huh. If you're some long-long grand-nephew hoping old Uncle Freddy's got something for you to inherit one day, don't bother. This place takes it all every month, and what I did have got sold at auction two years ago. Nothing like breaking a hip and a femur to lay you up and make people forget about you."

"You aren't forgotten, Mr. Marsh. In fact, we've been looking for you for a few weeks now."

"Why?" He eyeballed me, probably because I was older than Trace and hadn't said a word yet. "I can't owe you money, and I know I ain't knocked up your sister. Is this some sorta charity thing? Adopt-A-Geezer Week at the country club?"

I laughed out loud, charmed by his snark and sass. "We're hardly the country club types," I replied. "My name is Atticus McMasters, and this is my boyfriend, Trace Johnson."

Frederick's sharp gaze softened. "Well, you seem to know who I am, but call me Freddy. What's brought two handsome young men to my doorstep? Such as it is? Because if it is Adopt-A-Geezer Week, consider me yours."

"As tempting as that sounds," Trace replied with a grin, "we're here because we found something that belongs to you. And we want to give it back."

"Oh? My charming good looks? I think I lost those in the early aughts."

"No." Trace reached into the pocket of his cargo shorts and produced the stack of letters, which were tied together with twine, as well as the Polaroid. "I apologize in advance for reading your private correspondence, but we're here to give them back. And to give you this photograph that you were never able to reclaim."

He held out the bundle. Freddy stared at it, lips parted, frozen in place for so long I nearly reached out and shook him. Then a single tear slipped down his right cheek, and that seemed to unstick his gears. He reached out and took the bundle with shaking hands. Let the letters fall to his lap while he held up the photograph. His eyes filled with more tears that trickled out, almost without notice, as a kaleido-scope of emotions played across his face: joy, grief, fear, awe, humor, and so many unnamable things.

"Oh, Teddy," he whispered. "There you are. I'd forgotten your face."

Trace trembled once, and I wrapped my hand in his. Squeezed. My own throat was thick with emotion, and all my anxiety over this task melted beneath a bright beam of relief and pride. We'd done the right thing.

Several minutes passed before Freddy seemed to collect himself. "Where did you get this?" he asked. "When Teddy died...his family shut me out. Wouldn't tell me anything, give me anything. They never accepted Teddy was gay. All I had were the letters he wrote me, and the puzzles we swapped back and forth for those two years."

"He sent you puzzles, too?" I asked.

"He did. We both loved them. But how? How did you find these?"

"That's a bit of a long story, if you'd like to hear it."

"Sonny, I've got all the time in the world to hear a story from two handsome young men. Please, sit and stay a while."

The room didn't have any other chairs, so Trace and I sat next to each other on the side of Freddy's bed, and we began telling our story. A bit about my business, a bit about his life, and how both had intersected the night of the puzzle swap. As we spoke late into the afternoon, I marveled at how different my life was now.

If you'd asked me back in June what was the most valuable thing I'd ever found in a storage locker, I might have said a stash of one-ounce silver bars, or even an 1871 Colt revolver. But as our story of reading Freddy's letters turned into Freddy regaling us with stories of his own life as a young, closeted gay man, I understood that the most valuable things I'd ever found were in this room.

I'd found the stories and first-hand experiences of someone who'd survived a tragic time in our nation's history. The wisdom of a life lived during a time when so many had died. And, as I leaned my shoulder against Trace's and smiled at my boyfriend, I was pretty sure I'd also found love.

And love was the greatest treasure of all.

UNDER MY SKEIN

LEE BLAIR

CHAPTER 1

HEATH

I approached my childhood home and squinted at the Oregon late-summer sunshine glinting off Mom's mosaic bird bath. A mob of bushtits hung from one of numerous bird feeders dotting the front yard of my childhood home. Weathered gnomes cluttered the ground in varied silly poses between rose bushes and hydrangeas. As I approached the front door, I couldn't help but notice the ranch-style house could use a fresh coat of paint. Guilt gnawed at me as I added that to a mental to-do list for next summer.

I knocked on the front door as I let myself in. "Hey, Mom."

Mom bustled into the living room in a vanilla-scented cloud. She'd been wearing the same perfume for as long as I could remember.

"Heath, honey. You made it!" She tugged me down into a hug.

"I had to before you dragged me over here by my ear." She was strong enough to do it, thanks to her Pilates classes.

There wasn't an ounce of remorse on her face. "Renovations start next week, and I need to clean some crap out of here." She patted my cheek. "Not that your stuff is crap, sweetheart."

I chuckled as I followed her into the dining room. We passed walls cluttered with mismatched frames and shelves full of tchotchkes. All familiar, though I couldn't place the origin of most.

Mom gestured to the plastic tubs and boxes stacked high on the dining room table. "Ta-da!"

It'd been over two years since Dad passed, and Mom had been reluctant to change anything since. The house had always been a shrine to our lives, but after he died, it started to feel more like a mausoleum. It was a big step that she was ready to purge.

I didn't blame her for wanting to keep things the same, but I took the upcoming remodel as a sign that she was healing as much as she could with such loss. It was a cruel twist of fate that Dad's life insurance payout was the only way she'd been able to afford the renovations they'd been saving for when he was alive.

"It probably is crap. Otherwise, I would've taken it with me to college years ago." I'd never been one to hold on to things for sentimentality.

Mom opened the first box and removed yearbooks, fantasy novels I'd read countless times, and middle school reports. I sat and prepared to spend the day strolling down memory lane. She laughed when she pulled out a terrible attempt I'd made at drawing a superhero in elementary school. I'd happily put off grading Introduction to Environmental Science midterms if it meant more of her laughter.

Over the next couple of hours, she paraded things before me that I didn't even remember owning and wasn't interested in keeping now.

"Aww, remember Bearbert Einstein?" She pulled out a beige teddy bear wearing a gray sweater and slacks. It had wild white hair and a bushy mustache to match. "When you were little, you wouldn't sleep unless you had Bearbert in your arms." She smiled warmly at the bear as she attempted to smooth its hair.

I groaned. "Bearbert? Really?"

She booped my nose with a bright-pink fingernail. "That was all your creativity. He doesn't match your minimalist decor, but he's cute. Want to take him home?"

"I don't have minimalist décor."

She arched an eyebrow. "What's one level above minimalism?"

"Tidy."

Mom scoffed.

I took the bear from her and waited for a pang of sentimentality to hit. It didn't. The bear was covered in dust and seemed to have mouse nibbles in its clothes and an ear. "He's dirty and too damaged to donate." I tossed it into the nearly full trash bag.

Mom was used to my ruthless attitude by now, but that one made her wince. She kept *everything*. Too many times throughout my childhood, she'd rescued things I didn't want, like the most mundane homework. I took after Dad. He'd always said memories mattered more than souvenirs.

She rummaged in another tub. "After your grandmother threw out my Beatles trading cards when I was a kid, I vowed I'd never do that to you."

I'd heard the story numerous times over the years. Her childhood had made her keep everything, while mine had made me allergic to clutter. Enough that despite the stack of boxes we'd gone through, the amount of stuff I'd decided to keep could fit in one hand. The best find so far was a framed photo of Dad and me hiking in the Columbia Gorge.

I offered a small smile. "I appreciate that. Are there more boxes?"

"A few in the garage."

I followed her to a room that used to be alive with dusty power tools, partially finished woodworking projects, and piles of dirty rags. The projects were shelved, but evidence of Dad's love for organization remained. The storage units he'd built lined one wall, floor to ceiling.

Mom gestured to purple tubs on the top shelf. "I haven't gone through those yet. They might be yours. Can you reach them?"

I pulled the step ladder off the wall hook and climbed to the second step. Fortunately, the tubs were lightweight, and I easily passed them to Mom.

She carried them over to the workbench and opened one. She removed a plastic grocery bag tied at the top. It bulged with something that looked soft.

"Oh wow." The words were full of emotion as Mom carefully untied the plastic.

"What is it?"

"One of your uncle's crochet projects." Tears filled her eyes.

I wrapped my arm around her shoulders and squeezed as I examined the balls of white, red, blue, orange, and purple yarn. Memories flashed of yarn tucked in every nook and cranny of Uncle Rick's small house and unfinished projects piled on his coffee table.

I'd forgotten about his love of crocheting. Frankly, I'd forgotten a lot about Uncle Rick. His face had faded in my mind to vague features of a wide smile and trimmed black beard. I'd been young when he died, but one thing I remembered clearly was how excited I'd been every time I got to visit him. Uncle Rick had been my hero.

It wasn't until I was a teenager struggling with my own coming out that I comprehended his loss in a new way. When I'd learned about HIV and AIDS in high school health class, I'd grieved even more.

Decades later, I still missed the hell out of him.

"Your uncle always had yarn in his hand." She chuckled. "He was great at starting projects but not so much at finishing them."

"Like Dad's woodworking projects." We shared a smile.

I pulled a stack of crocheted squares from the bag. As I traced the top one, I recalled a memory of Uncle Rick telling me he wanted to make me a special blanket. I'd asked for *Teenage Mutant Ninja Turtle* colors and sat beside him on the couch as he showed me how he made the squares. I remembered thinking he was magic with how fast his fingers worked the yarn.

Mom grabbed a square. "This was his last project. I remember him saying he wanted to make something for you before he—"

I wrapped my arm around her shoulders and pulled her close. "Can I keep it?"

She craned her neck and studied me. "Of course you can, honey. You can take whatever you like. Rick would love to know you have it." She frowned. "I always wanted to learn to crochet to finish what he'd started."

"Uncle Rick never would've expected you to finish them. He couldn't, so why would you?"

Mom laughed and rubbed my back. "Thanks, sweetheart."

Later that evening, I sat on my couch in my *not minimalist but sparsely decorated* home and tried to focus on midterm grading. Instead, my attention wandered to the bag containing Uncle Rick's unfinished project. Well, gift. It would probably live in the corner of my closet, but I had an urge to hold on to it. Somehow, I knew I'd regret it if I didn't.

Worst case, I could get rid of the stuff after having more time to think about it. I almost laughed. The same logic Mom used that had resulted in a house full of crap.

After rereading the same paragraph of a student's essay for the fourth time, I set the grading aside. The students deserved my full attention. There was always tomorrow.

I grabbed my phone from the coffee table and launched Google. After a few attempts at describing the crocheted tiles, I learned they were called granny squares. Search iterations led me through a rabbit warren of tangents and ultimately landed on something that left me staring at my phone in surprise. My gut warmed like it had when I'd decided to keep the materials.

I scanned through a website for an organization called Patchwork Projects, which paired unfinished handmade craft projects started by deceased loved ones or people with disabilities with others who could finish them. I would've never guessed such an organization existed.

I hovered over the *Submit a Project* button. The warmth in my stomach continued to spread. The yarn colors and granny square pattern weren't really my style, but I liked the idea of having something of Uncle Rick's in my home. Something he'd intended for me to have, even if it lived in my linen cupboard.

I clicked the button, and as I filled out a form, I couldn't shake the feeling that something big was about to happen.

CHAPTER 2

BEN

I hummed happily to myself as I collected the chemotherapy cocktail and anti-nausea medication for my patient, Laura. I was pleased that she reported no numbness or tingling in her toes. Her side effects remained minimal, which was amazing.

En route back to Laura, I passed the snack station for patients and their loved ones. There was an array of warm drinks, plain crackers, noodle cups, and other goodies. I snagged a peppermint-chocolate protein bar I knew she loved.

I warmly greeted the wife of a man who'd been coming in for months and smiled at an older woman getting her latest round of chemo when she glanced up from the cozy mystery she was reading.

"Got the goods," I said when I returned to the quiet corner Laura had selected. She wore a soft pink beanie over her bald head and tucked one of our warmed blankets around her legs resting on a footrest. Her latest crochet project sat on her lap. She was always prepared to keep herself entertained on her longer treatment days.

Laura batted her lashes when I dropped the protein bar on the table next to her. She'd lost most of her body hair but had managed to keep her eyebrows and lashes. She'd joked about getting to save on waxing appointments. I was always in awe of patients who maintained such good humor during one of life's biggest stresses.

I wheeled an IV pole to her side, hung the chemo bag from the hook, and connected it to the tube from her port.

"What are you working on this week?" I peered over her shoulder. I wanted to sit and gush about our latest crochet projects but needed to get the medication going first.

Laura raised a crocheted circle of pale-orange yarn about the size of her palm. "Cat butt coasters."

It only took a second to fill in where she'd add legs and a tail and how the circle's center resembled a pucker. "Oh my god, I need that pattern. My brother has a cat, and his birthday is next month."

After getting her drip going, I hung out for a few minutes to make sure she didn't have any side effects. We spent the time talking about our crochet projects.

"You're a terrible influence on my Ravelry project wish list," she accused with a smile playing at her dry lips. I made a mental note to snag her a lip balm from our supply when I returned to do my rounds.

I grabbed my phone to show her a photo of the witch's hat I was crocheting for a friend's Halloween costume. When the screen lit up, I caught a glimpse of an email from Patchwork Projects with the subject line, *Congratulations! You've been matched.*

"Ooh, see something good?"

I told her about applying to volunteer with the organization. "I just got word that I've been matched with someone."

Laura's eyes glistened. "There's a charity for that?" Her voice was thick with emotion.

I smiled softly at her. "There is."

She glanced at one of the larger chemo spaces where a group of older women gabbed. "I want to do that." She smiled wryly. "Guess I need to do a better job of leaving patterns with my unfinished projects."

I chuckled. "You and me both, sister."

"Hey, babe. I got you the green tea you like from the coffee shop next door." Laura's boyfriend approached with a gentle smile. Her answering one was like a burst of sunshine on an overcast day.

"I'll come check on you soon." I smiled at him, then left them to their quiet conversation as I prepped for my next patient. I wanted to read the email, but it would have to wait until later.

Miraculously, I managed restraint as my phone burned a hole in my pocket for the rest of my shift. I didn't get a chance to thoroughly read the email until I clocked out and walked to my car. The project summary indicated it was a granny square afghan that someone local wanted finished. I kicked ass at granny squares.

Once I got home and threw together burrito bowl ingredients, I settled on the emerald-green loveseat in my modest apartment and opened the email again. I stared at the name of the person requesting the project. Heath Hynes. Great name.

I tapped out a text to Heath.

Ben: Hi, I'm Ben. I was contacted by Patchwork Projects about the crochet project you'd like finished. I'd be honored to work on it.

I debated saying more but decided to leave it there for now. I kept glancing at my phone as I ate dinner and watched a nineties sitcom, but it didn't light up. I had about a dozen crochet projects in progress and didn't need to start another, but I couldn't help it.

My phone buzzed as I shoved the last spoonful of dinner into my mouth.

[Unknown number]. Hello, Ben. I'm Heath. Nice to meet you. Thanks for reaching out and your willingness to work on this project. I'm not sure where to go from here. How do you usually proceed?

I added Heath as a contact in my phone.

Ben: This is my first time being paired with someone. We could meet so I can collect the project from you. Or I could give you my address if you'd prefer to mail it. The email said you're in the McMinnville area. I work in McMinnville and live in Dahlia Springs.

Heath: I live and work in McMinnville but spend a lot of time in Dahlia Springs. Are you familiar with A Whole Latte Love? I often go there on weekday afternoons to do some work after leaving campus.

Campus? He might have a job at the local college. I pictured a glasses-wearing, distinguished man with messy, wavy hair and elbow patches on his tweed jacket.

Ben: Meeting there sounds great! When works for you? My shifts end in the early afternoon.

A Whole Latte Love was the only sit-down coffee shop in Dahlia Springs and had the best coffee outside of Portland. Probably in Portland too.

Heath: I'll be there by 3:30 tomorrow afternoon and will stay for a couple of hours. Does that work?

Ben: Perfect! I'll see you then.

I navigated over to Google and searched Heath's name. I told myself it was so I'd know who to look for in the coffee shop, but I was curious. Was he an older guy with a project from his mom who passed? Or someone with a partner who'd loved to crochet?

As I scanned the results, I spotted a faculty page for an attractive man who appeared to be somewhere around his mid-thirties. Short, dark hair, tan skin, no glasses, and a warm smile. Flutters rushed through my stomach. That kind of hot professor would've had me daydreaming through all my college classes.

I stopped myself from reading more about him, but it was hard to fend off the curiosity. If I didn't learn more about him when we met, I'd indulge in digital snooping on the handsome man later.

CHAPTER 3

BEN

I pulled into a parking spot along Dahlia Springs's Main Street. With fall right around the corner, pumpkins dominated the cute small-town storefront displays.

My walk to A Whole Latte Love probably resembled skipping more than a casual stroll. I couldn't help being excited to get my hands on this project, and if I were being honest, Heath intrigued me too. My brother Travis's recent engagement to his boyfriend shined a spotlight on my chronic singledom. I'd always had a thing for intelligent men, so spending a few minutes with a gorgeous professor wasn't a hardship.

Garlands of autumn leaves hung from A Whole Latte Love's windows and a painted anthropomorphized coffee cup hailed the start of pumpkin spice latte season. I loved this place. When I'd rented an apartment in Dahlia Springs, I hadn't known much about the town. I'd picked it for the cheaper rent and easy commute to work in McMinnville, but years later, I couldn't imagine living anywhere else.

I entered the coffee shop and was greeted by the delicious aroma of freshly ground coffee. My favorite scent. I immediately scanned the

room for Heath and spotted him at a table in a far corner. Unfortunately, no tweed jacket, but he wore a snug pale-blue button-up with
sleeves rolled to his forearms that was definitely working for him. His
hair was longer than in his photo and wavy as it curled around his
ears.

He made eye contact and gave an *are you who I'm looking for* face. I
returned a *yeah, I think so* look and wound my way through the tables
to greet him before getting a coffee.

Lordy, Heath was incredibly handsome up close. His hair had more
curl to it than I'd expected. His bright-blue eyes snagged my attention
away from his trimmed beard and mustache.

"Heath?"

"Yes. Hello." He stood and shook my hand. He was a few inches
taller than me, thicker, and had soft hands. "Thanks for coming. It's
great to meet you."

"You too." I jerked my thumb toward the counter. "I'm going to
grab a coffee. Can I get you something?" I needed to escape before the
urge to hug him overwhelmed my rational thought. It wasn't my fault
he had the perfect body type for hugs and cuddles.

Chronically. Single.

He gestured to his mug on the table. "I'm still nursing a drink.
Thanks."

I smiled at him, and he held my eye contact for a few beats longer
than necessary. One side of his mouth inched up, revealing a slight gap
between his front teeth. Too cute.

After flashing what I hoped was a dazzling smile, I turned toward
the counter. "Be right back." Who could blame me for adding some
sway to my hips?

When I reached the counter and stood behind someone ordering, I
looked back at Heath and caught him glancing away. *Why, yes, my butt
does look great in scrubs, thank you very much.*

Several minutes later, I returned to the table with my coffee and
hazelnut scone. My attention snagged on a reusable grocery bag on the
ground next to him. I also clocked papers and a laptop in tidy order on
the table. It was the opposite of my own messy computer desk at
home.

I sat and gestured to his mug of clear-ish green-hued liquid. "What are you drinking?"

Heath wrapped his long fingers around the white mug. "A jasmine green tea. You?"

"A sugary, caffeinated, delicious treat. Caramel macchiato. Do you only drink tea?" I figured easing into things with some mild small talk couldn't hurt. Now that I was in his presence, I wasn't in a hurry to leave.

He shook his head. "I drink coffee in the mornings with a splash of milk and a pinch of sugar, but then it's tea the rest of the day. Otherwise, the higher caffeine will keep me up all night."

"I need coffee to stay awake all day until a reasonable bedtime."

His thick lips curved into a teasing smile. "I find that an apple in the afternoon helps."

I narrowed my eyes at him. "You sound like an after-school special paid for by a medical association."

He leaned forward and tugged his smile to one side of his mouth, revealing a dimple. "I'm afraid I signed an NDA and can't disclose details of my sponsors."

He's funny too? I'm in so much trouble.

I broke a piece off the scone. "Want some?"

Heath shook his head and lifted his hands in a placating gesture. "Don't worry, I don't hate processed sugar or anything."

"Sure," I said, drawing out the word, then winked. "When you do deign to enjoy processed sugar, what's your poison of choice?"

He stared off into the distance and smiled as though remembering something pleasant. "My grandma always made a special treat for Grandpa's birthday. She cooked a plain cake—vanilla, I guess?—in a short and wide round tin pan. It had scalloped edges too. Then she'd top it with gooey, canned cherries. I could've eaten the whole thing if my parents would've let me."

I'd never had that before, but I immediately wanted to make it. "Yum." My mouth watered.

Conversation flowed easily from sharing favorite childhood treats to where we grew up to important things like our favorite *Teenage Mutant Ninja Turtles* as kids. He'd admitted having a crush on

Michelangelo because he liked how fun he was, and I was a Donatello guy because he was the smart one.

Despite having different preferences for many things, we found common ground, and I wanted to know more. So much more. And as we continued talking, I couldn't help but notice our conversation was more of the first-date variety than a brief meeting to pass along an unfinished craft project.

After debating our favorite board games, there was a brief lull in our conversation. My coffee was long gone, and Heath lifted his mug only to find it empty. My attention wandered to the bag. I supposed we should talk about the reason we'd met up.

"So, the project."

Heath tilted his head as though trying to understand what I meant. Then his attention snapped to the bag. "Right! The project." He passed the bag to me.

I gently pulled several granny squares out. Each had a white border, but the bulk of the squares were either solid blue, purple, green, or orange. "These are lovely, Heath." I looked at him. "I'm excited to work on this project."

He let out an audible breath. "Thank you."

"This is absolutely *not* required, but I'd love to know who made these. I can think of them while working on the project."

Heath's eyes softened. "You'd do that?"

"Of course. It feels like the right thing to do."

Heath wrapped his fingers around the mug again, and I waited patiently.

"My Uncle Rick made them. He died when I was young. AIDS." His voice cracked on the last word.

That one word conveyed so much. I reached out and covered his hand with mine as my heart broke for him. For everyone who'd lost someone to AIDS.

"I'm so sorry." It didn't matter how much time had passed after a loved one died. Loss was always hard. Ever since Travis was diagnosed with HIV six years ago, AIDS-related deaths always hit me harder. I was thrilled that my brother had treatment to keep him healthy and undetectable, but it broke my heart that they hadn't been available when Heath's uncle needed them. It was a different world then.

He smiled warmly.

"Thank you. He and my mom were really close. This was a blanket Uncle Rick planned to make for me in honor of my love for the *Teenage Mutant Ninja Turtles*."

I smiled at the orange-and-white square on top of the stack. "Well, the gift is coming a couple decades late, but I'll make sure you get it."

Heath's eyes glistened. "Thank you."

"Did he do other kinds of crafts?"

He chuckled. "I have snippets of memories that feature closets full of colorful craft supplies and bags of yarn in all colors of the rainbow."

I grinned. "I bet you loved to play with all those goodies."

"It wasn't my thing. I preferred mechanical pencils and graph paper over glue sticks and construction paper."

"Mechanical pencils and graph paper?" I mimed clutching pearls. "Give me those bulky pens with a half-dozen colors and neon paper, and I was a happy boy."

Heath's laughter was warm, and his inquisitive gaze ensnared me. I glanced at his tidy pile on the table. "I don't see any graph paper, but it looks like a lot of work. You mentioned when we texted that you come here to work after work?"

Heath straightened the already straight papers. "Such is the life of a college faculty member. Teaching and grading are already a full-time job, let alone the meetings, committee work, and the research we need to advance. I come here to work on my research."

"Does the change of scenery help?"

He nodded. "In my office, I get distracted by the million other things I need to do, but if I want to get tenure this year, I need to get my research written." He glanced at my scrubs. "Do you work in healthcare?"

I wanted to ask more questions about his work, but I could be patient. I wrapped both hands around my mug. "I do. I'm an oncology nurse, though, sometimes I think about moving to an HIV/AIDS specialty." Heath's eyebrows rose. "I have a close family member living with HIV, and I've had quite a few patients with it. It's hard to imagine leaving oncology though." Even on the hardest days, I still loved it.

Heath's smile was sad. "It's important work too." He absently ran his fingernail over a tiny chip on the coffee mug. "My dad passed from cancer."

I winced. "I'm sure if we keep talking, we'll discover something else we have in common that reminds you of your trauma."

Heath let out a startled laugh and then graced me with a grateful smile. "I used to get nightmares as a kid from playing *Bloody Mary*. As long as she's not your distant ancestor, I think we're good."

I mimed wiping sweat from my forehead. "Phew. No mirror ghosts in my family tree."

We lapsed into a comfortable silence for a moment. Despite stumbling into what could've been conversational landmines, we got along well. At least, I thought so, and I wanted to get to know him better. I could always use more friends, and his handsome face didn't hurt.

An idea struck. "You can obviously say no."

His eyebrows rose expectantly.

"But I was thinking I could sit with you—quietly, of course—while you work. If I worked on your uncle's project with you here, you could be a part of it in some way."

"Yeah? That's a great idea."

I perked up. "Cool. Awesome. Great." *Quit it with the adjectives.* "When should I come back?"

"Thursday?"

Two days to figure out the pattern. I could do that. "Perfect."

"I'm curious—how do you get started? There are no written directions in the bag."

"Good question." I smiled at the way Heath sat straighter. I'd bet he'd been a teacher's pet with straight *A*s in school. Hand shooting up with an answer every time the teacher asked a question.

I pointed to the edge of a granny square. "I can count how many stitches are in each row. Each type of crochet stitch looks different, so I can figure out some important pieces of information by studying it. There's a good chance I can reverse engineer the pattern, but if not, there are crochet groups online where I can post a picture and someone else will know."

Heath's mouth formed an *O*. "Wow. That's amazing."

"Beyond figuring out the pattern for each individual square is trying to recreate the colorwork he intended. I'm not sure if he wanted all of one color to be lumped together or to alternate. That's where we'll have to take some creative license."

The furrow in Heath's brow at his concentration was adorable. "This is more complicated than I realized."

I preened. I'd dated plenty of dickheads who'd judged my hobby. I didn't have time for patriarchal bullshit. Heath seemed to respect the craft, which made me like him even more.

"That's part of the fun." Another thought occurred to me. "One thing you should know is that once I go through this stash, I'll need to find different yarn. There's a good chance the hues will be slightly different all these years later."

Heath frowned. "I'll ask my mom if she happened to come across any more yarn, but from what we found in the plastic tubs, he seemed to buy a little at a time."

After finding out how big he wanted the blanket so I could make some yarn calculations later, I decided to make an exit while the vibes were strong. I had a habit of overstaying my welcome, but I should leave Heath wanting more.

"Well, I'd better let you get back to work. I don't want to distract you from getting tenure." I made a mental note to ask him more about his work on Thursday as I stood and gripped the handles on the project bag.

"Ben, thank you so much for doing this. It means a lot." Gratitude shone in his eyes.

I squeezed his shoulder. "It's my pleasure. See you Thursday." I couldn't wait.

CHAPTER 4

HEATH

I stared at my laptop screen, but the letters swam together like alphabet soup. I glanced up as the chime over A Whole Latte Love's door dinged with a new arrival. Again.

You need to focus. I should've picked another spot to meet. It wouldn't help me get my research analyzed if I constantly rubber-necked the door at every sound. Without writing up my research and submitting it to peer-reviewed publications, I wouldn't have a chance at tenure next year.

When my department chair suggested my tenure application would be significantly stronger with one more publication credit, I knew to listen.

What I didn't need was a distraction. Even a cute, charming one that had me thinking about more than work for the first time in a long time. I knew I could've declined Ben's offer to crochet while I worked, but something about him, the way we'd met, the gut feeling that had me leaning into it, told me it was time to figure out a way to date and focus on work.

I huffed a frustrated breath and told myself to relax. Sure, we'd clicked at our first meeting the other day—at least I thought we had—but two queer guys getting along didn't automatically equal romance, despite what my X-rated dreams last night might indicate.

Focus, Heath. This is important. I was writing notes about running some analysis when the door chimed again. Ben entered with a halo of sunlight shining behind him. He wore the same sage-green scrubs as two days ago. They snugly fit his lean frame.

The scrubs barely triggered a negative response, which was certainly new. Ever since Dad had gotten sick, I'd associated scrubs with bad news. Even when I went to the doctor or dentist for routine check-ups, I had to remind myself I was okay. The scrubs weren't a harbinger of death. Getting to know Ben a bit the other day had given me something positive to associate with the uniform, and I was grateful.

Ben scanned the room and waved when he spotted me. I returned it and felt a stretch in my cheeks from my wide smile.

He chatted with the barista while I made a note of where to pick back up. His presence brightened the space as he approached with his coffee and pastry.

"Hey. Good to see you."

He set his coffee and a reusable grocery bag from the local market on the table and then pulled the chair back. "You too. Don't worry, I promise to be quiet and let you work, but I *am* curious how you're doing."

Something about the genuine curiosity in his tone had me sitting taller. "My week's better now." I suppose my mouth and brain had colluded to make room for romance alongside work. Pink colored Ben's pale cheeks. "The research is going slow, but sometimes that happens. How have the past couple of days been for you?" I leaned back in my chair. Maybe if we talked for a few minutes, I'd be able to focus better after.

Ben chatted a mile a minute while he unpacked his supplies. He talked about a patient who got good news and how that had made his entire week. Seeing how he lit up while talking about his oncology patients healed another fissure in my heart.

"I made these last night with the yarn you had." He handed me three granny squares. White and purple, white and blue, and white and red. "This is one your uncle made." He gave me a white-and-orange one.

It was impossible to tell them apart. They were the same size and the gaps in the symmetrical pattern were identical.

"You've been busy. They look amazing."

Ben beamed at me. "I figured out the pattern pretty quickly, but determining the hook size took some troubleshooting."

I asked how he figured that out, and he explained how hook size affected the finished dimensions of the piece. I grew more fascinated by this craft the more he shared.

"Also, I think I found a solid substitute yarn to finish the project. A shipment of the skeins I need should arrive in a few days."

It took me a moment to find my voice. He was taking this so seriously.

"Let me know how much it is. I want to pay."

Ben frowned but nodded. "I had planned to pay for it, but since you brought it up, I had to sign paperwork as a volunteer agreeing to tell you the costs. Damn me for being a rule follower, but I ordered from a place that offers discounts for Patchwork Projects volunteers."

"I'm not worried about the cost. I wish the organization would let me pay for your time." I wanted to invite him to dinner to thank him for all the time he'd be investing, but that felt presumptuous.

Ben smiled graciously as he wound the yarn around the fingers of his left hand and held the hook in his right.

"I'm curious how many squares it will take to finish the blanket. The process fascinates me."

Ben hummed. "Given the size you told me you wanted, I'd say roughly a hundred and twenty."

My eyebrows shot up. "That's a lot. How long does it take you to do a square?"

Ben tilted his head to the side as he stared at the ceiling, and his lips moved silently like he was doing mental math. "Depending on how distracted I am by the TV, probably thirty to sixty minutes." He smiled sheepishly. "If the show has subtitles, even longer."

I wanted to know about his favorite shows to watch, but if I asked that, we'd spend the rest of the evening talking at the expense of my work. Restraint. I could practice that and allow myself to enjoy Ben in small doses while making progress on my research. Balance was key.

I did some mental math as I roughly calculated how much time it would take to finish the blanket. My eyes widened when I arrived at the number. "That's a ton of time. I'm honored you would give so much of yourself."

Ben's smile was warm, but there was something more there. A sparkle in his eyes that had my stomach twisting with joy. Could he be interested in me too?

"It's a lot of coffee shop visits if you're up for it."

The look we shared was more than casual friendliness between two new acquaintances. My pulse quickened.

"It's a good thing I have a lot of research to do."

Ben set the hook down, then raised his coffee. "Cheers to that. Well, I've interrupted you enough. I'll let you get back to work so you don't think I'm a bad influence. I don't want our coffee shop time to end before it has even begun."

The energy shifted away from butterfly flutters to something deeper, more eager. It'd been a long time since I dated anyone. Work had come first for so long, but now that I was on the cusp of earning tenure—finally—I realized I was ready for more in my life. A partner. I couldn't help but wonder if there was potential for Ben to be that person.

As Ben pulled earbuds from his bag, I asked what he was listening to.

Ben eagerly leaned forward. "It's a podcast where the host interviews an expert on a different topic in each episode. I like getting to dip my toes in and learn about a wide range of things, from the lifecycles of cicadas to theories around black holes in space. Last week's episode was fascinating. It was about wildfires, land stewardship, and the importance of indigenous knowledge in fire management."

I had to run through his words in my mind to make sure I'd heard him correctly. "Seriously? That's my area of research. I'm a fire ecologist, and all this"—I gestured to my notes and laptop—"is about predictive modeling of the effects of wildfires in the Pacific Northwest.

I'm working with several local tribes—" I actively stopped myself from going super nerd with too much detail.

Ben slammed his palm on the table. "Tell. Me. Everything." He tucked his other hand under his chin and stared at me expectantly.

So I did. Ben asked thoughtful questions that helped my brain puzzle through some of the places I'd been blocked. After we talked for a while, he put his earbuds in and began crocheting while I typed like my hands were on fire. Instead of being a distraction, Ben might be exactly what I needed to complete this work.

CHAPTER 5

HEATH

"I've never understood why you and your dad like that stinky cheese so much." Mom scrunched her nose as the wind whipped her gray curls around her face. Mist from the crashing ocean waves kept the cool air damp.

Mom pointedly ignored the blue cheese on the to-go cheeseboard I'd ordered for our day trip and selected a slice of mild cheddar and a cracker.

"Blue cheese is the best. You don't know what you're missing." I cut a corner off the hunk of blue and spread it on a graham cracker like Dad used to do. That combination would always please my tastebuds like a warm hug.

We fell quiet as we stared at the expansive Pacific Ocean as waves crashed against the rocks below our perch on the short wall separating Highway 99 and downtown Depoe Bay.

Depoe Bay was Dad's favorite spot on the Oregon Coast and where we'd celebrated his birthday since I was a kid. Dad loved whales, and there was no better spot to try and catch a glimpse. Some years, we got lucky. Others, we didn't. But we always ended the day with clam chowder and fudge for dessert. Mom and I hadn't seen any whales since he'd passed.

"Still nothing?"

I shook my head. "The binoculars are in your bag. Maybe you'll see a spout."

Mom rifled through her backpack and then put them against her eyes after finding them. "I think they're broken."

Shaking my head, I flipped them over in her hand. It happened every year.

"Shut it," she said as she adjusted the dial.

I mimed zipping my mouth closed, then smiled.

It was hard to believe it had been over two years since Dad had died. I still missed him terribly, but the pain wasn't as sharp today compared to last year's birthday. I hoped that meant as time passed, the happy memories would be easier to reach for.

"I can't believe it's been two birthdays."

It was comforting to know our thoughts went to the same place. "In some ways, it feels like months, but in others, it's hit me like a decade of wear and tear."

"I sure feel a decade older," Mom said disdainfully.

I reached over and rubbed her back. "You don't look it."

Mom smiled wryly. "I raised you well."

Neither of us mentioned the new wrinkles and gray hairs we both now sported.

"Do you remember when we got him the whale-watching boat tour for his birthday?" I'd been in elementary school.

Mom groaned. "You mean the time we learned firsthand that your dad gets terribly seasick? The poor man wouldn't have seen a whale unless it swam right under the boat since he spent the entire time with his face hanging over the edge."

I laughed and startled a seagull who'd been inching toward our picnic. It made a low piercing caw before flying into the overcast sky. The clouds threatened an afternoon drizzle.

"Dad was so bummed he missed all the sightings."

We swapped memories of our times on the coast and finished off the cheeseboard as the sun moved out from behind a bank of clouds. I pretended not to see Mom sneak a piece of the blue cheese before smiling at the sky and then wrinkling her nose as she chewed.

"I regret not doing something to thank the oncology office," she said after several minutes of comfortable silence.

I turned toward Mom in surprise as I tried to follow her line of thinking. Tracking thoughts spurred by grief was like trying to predict a pinball's movements. "Where Dad got treatments?"

"Yes. Those nurses were amazing. I feel terrible I didn't think to do something for them at the time."

"You were buried under a mountain of grief. We both were. They don't expect anything from us."

"I know, but I want to do something. Do you think it's too late?" The sadness in her eyes triggered a lump in my throat.

"Not at all. I'm sure they'd love anything you decided to do. Are you thinking flowers?"

She angled her head and stared at the sea. "Maybe a catered lunch?"

"Who doesn't like food?" I squeezed her hand, then let go.

"I wonder if our favorite nurse still works there."

"They might." I had no idea what kind of turnover oncology offices had.

It made me think about Ben, and how much he clearly cared about his patients. Nurses were special people. My thoughts danced to Ben in his scrubs. *Not the time or place.*

"That's a smile I haven't seen in a long time. Who's causing it?" Mom gave me the same eager grin she had in high school when I'd asked to borrow the car to take my date to the prom.

Instead of admitting to my mom that I—a grown-ass man—had a crush on someone, I told her about Uncle Rick's blanket. I'd been meaning to anyway.

"You know that blanket project I kept of Uncle Rick's?"

Mom fished around the remnants of our cheese board, dragged a piece of salami through quince paste, and dropped it on a cracker. "Yeah?"

I explained the Patchwork Projects organization.

Tears welled in Mom's eyes. "Did they pair you with someone?"

I nodded. "They did. A guy who lives in Dahlia Springs."

She shot me a calculating grin. "How old is this guy? Is he single? Is he queer?"

"Cool it with the twenty questions. He's generously donating his time to finish the blanket. That's it." She didn't need to know that what it *was* and what I *wanted* were two different things. It was hard not to talk to her about it because she'd love Ben's profession and adore him too—from what I knew of him, who wouldn't?—but I knew better than to hint at my feelings because she'd go all in. I didn't want to deal with her disappointment on top of mine if it didn't go anywhere.

Mom's smile softened. "I'd love to meet him and thank him. It's a generous way to spend one's free time."

"We'll see. I don't want to put too much pressure on the guy."

She winked at me. Clearly not buying any of my bullshit.

"Your dad would love that too."

As we lapsed into silence, a stream of water shot up from the ocean only a few hundred feet from us. Mom grabbed my hand and nearly knocked the cheeseboard over.

"Did you see it? There's a whale!"

The spout rose again before a fin breached the ocean's surface. My throat burned. *Miss you too, Dad.*

CHAPTER 6

BEN

The days we learned we lost patients were always the most difficult. It was a part of the job I never got used to. The only thing that had gotten me through the day was knowing I'd see Heath at the end.

My shoulders relaxed as I entered A Whole Latte Love. I enjoyed the routine Heath and I had developed of spending a couple of afternoons each week chatting before his research and my crocheting. It was quickly becoming a highlight.

Heath's eager smile triggered my own. I was starting to get sad with each granny square I finished because that was one square closer to losing my excuse to spend time with him.

If I wanted it to continue, I'd need to ask him out. If we'd met on an app, I wouldn't have had an issue because we would've known we were both in the market for something, but meeting someone in the wild and putting yourself out there? That was complicated as hell.

I waved at Heath before approaching the counter. "Hey. How's it going?"

The androgynous barista with the fuchsia hair and hollow plugs in their ears smiled easily. "Good, thanks. You?"

"Hanging in there." I didn't need to trauma dump on them.

"Your usual? The blueberry scones are fresh."

I perked up. "Yes, please." I reached into my bag to grab my wallet.

"He already got it." The barista jerked their chin toward Heath.

I glanced over my shoulder and saw Heath look away and focus *a bit too hard* on his laptop. I bit the inside of my cheek. "That's nice of him."

"*Very* nice of him." They winked. "I'll have your coffee right up."

Minutes later, with my coffee and pastry in hand and my project bag over my shoulder, I made my way to the table. I couldn't have stopped my grin if I wanted to. Being around Heath made me happy.

"Hey. Thanks again for treating me. You didn't need to do that."

Heath tucked a curl behind his ear. "I know, but I wanted to." His smile softened. "Your text earlier said you'd be running late and had a hard day, so I wanted to do a little something."

My eyes stung at his simple act of kindness. "I appreciate that." *I appreciate you.*

Heath closed his laptop and pushed it to the side. "What happened today? Do you want to talk about it?"

I ripped off a corner of the warm scone and told him about the patient we'd lost. After I'd been rambling, I froze as a realization hit me.

"Oh god. I'm so sorry. You're the last person I should be complaining to about this." It was insensitive as hell of me to vent to Heath, of all people. My grief was nothing compared to the pain families experienced.

Heath placed his hand over mine and kept it there after a squeeze. His lips curved into a small smile. "Don't apologize. It actually makes me feel better knowing the people who cared for my dad probably grieved his loss too."

"I'm sure they did," I said earnestly. "We hurt every time it happens, and we celebrate every time someone gets better like it's our win too." I brushed my thumb over his. "I have a feeling all the nurses probably loved your dad."

"Oh yeah?"

"Only a great man could have raised someone like you."

Heath's smile bloomed as something warm spread across my chest. "He had a favorite."

I laughed. "They usually do."

After catching my gaze with his, he glanced at the project bag. "How's the blanket going?"

"I've made a lot of progress." Embarrassingly, I hadn't been working on it at home this week because I wanted to draw it out. I didn't dare admit it to Heath though.

Heath's brow furrowed. "What's that look for?"

I blew out a breath and pulled back my hand. I was so comfortable with his touch that I'd forgotten he was still holding it. "Honestly? I'll be sad when it's finished. I like our meetings."

He licked his lips. "I've been thinking the same thing."

An idea I'd been toying with tumbled out of my mouth. "How about you making one of the squares?"

He immediately shook his head. "My uncle tried to teach me once, and I was terrible at it."

"Weren't you a kid?"

"Well, yes, but I'm not artistic or crafty. I wouldn't know where to begin."

That protest didn't faze me one bit. "I've taught a lot of people how to do it, including men with zero experience working with yarn. People often get antsy when sitting for treatment. When they're not readers, crocheting can help. I've got a good track record with teaching, and I'm confident I could show you." I leaned forward. "Wouldn't it be awesome to have a granny square you made among the ones your uncle created?"

"And the ones you made."

My heart melted at his earnestness.

Heath studied his tea mug for a moment. "Okay. I'll give it a try, but if I mess it up, I'll need you to fix it."

"Of course," I agreed quickly.

"If you're going to teach me how to crochet, I want to cook dinner for you. It's only fair."

That was even easier to agree to. "I'd love that. How about this weekend?" *I'm not eager or anything.*

"I'm free on Saturday."

"It's a date." Feeling a trillion times better than I had ten minutes ago, I pulled a half-finished granny square from the bag. When I glanced up, I caught Heath smiling at his laptop. If I played my cards right, I might finally get that hug I'd dreamed about since first laying eyes on him. Or maybe even more.

CHAPTER 7

HEATH

Olive oil sizzled on the toasted baguette slices as I pulled them from the oven. After letting them cool slightly, I spooned the bruschetta mix I'd made this morning onto the bread, then took a hearty scoop for myself as a chef tax. After adjusting several pieces into a tidy circle on the plate, I stood back to examine the appetizer spread. Bruschetta, spinach and artichoke dip with pita and cut vegetables, and brie with crackers.

Okay, so maybe I'd gone a *little* overboard with the appetizers since I also had a main course planned. The food prep helped keep my nerves at bay. He'd called it a date, but I wasn't sure if he'd meant *date*-date or a friendly hangout. I hoped for the former and had cleaned my apartment *and* body thoroughly, just in case.

After I moved the appetizers to the living room coffee table, there was a knock at the door. I hustled over and opened it to reveal Ben dressed nicely in a short-sleeved, maroon button-up and form-fitting black jeans. This outfit made his tight scrubs baggy in comparison, showing off his strong thighs and arms. It took some serious effort not to give him a *third* once-over.

He clutched the straps of two bags in one hand. One was the familiar crochet project bag, and the other was a reusable grocery bag with two wine bottle necks sticking out above the rim.

Ben glanced at the bag and laughed self-consciously. "You said you had food under control, so I brought drinks. A red, a white, and some Tap That Brewery beer. Probably overkill, but…" He trailed off.

I immediately relaxed and gestured for him to enter. "You're making me feel better about my appetizer spread."

As soon as I closed the door, I turned toward him. He went in for a hug and wrapped his free arm around my shoulders as I hooked mine around his waist. I could've sworn I heard a soft sigh from his lips as our bodies made contact. It was dangerous how much I liked the feel of him in my arms.

When we started to pull apart, I turned my head to offer to take his bag as he turned toward me. My lips brushed the corner of his mouth. Instead of freezing or pulling back, he kissed the corner of my mouth in return. We parted and smiled at each other. There was no shyness in his heated gaze. Tension broken. *Oh yeah, this is definitely a date.*

"Thanks for the drinks. What would you like?" I took the drink bag off him.

Ben looked at the appetizers and laughed. "I'll start with a beer, but maybe we can arrange a drink and appetizer pairing menu." His wink sent flutters racing through my stomach.

"You got it."

He followed me into the kitchen. "That's a lot of food. Are you testing a party menu out on me?"

I chuckled as I put the white in the fridge and pulled pint glasses from my cupboard for the beer. "I cook when I'm nervous."

Ben took a step closer to me. "Are you nervous?"

"A little." My nerves were more about being overly invested in where things went with Ben.

Half of Ben's mouth curved into a devastating smile. "Me too, but the good kind."

After I poured our drinks, we moved to the couch. Ben set his beer on a coaster—*swoon*—and leaned forward, resting his elbows on his knees. The position pulled his shirt taut around his shoulders.

"This all looks delicious. I'm starving. What's the dip?"

After talking him through the offerings, we fell into an easy conversation while filling our bellies. Time passed in a blur of laughter, drinks, getting to know each other better, and the kind of teasing you could only do with someone you genuinely clicked with. My sides hurt from laughter and my cheeks ached from all the smiling.

Thankfully, I'd chosen a light pasta dish for dinner because I was nearly stuffed from the appetizers. After dinner at my two-seat bistro table, we settled back on the couch with the remaining white wine. We sat close together in the middle.

Ben picked the project bag off the floor. "Are you ready for this?" Ben studied me from under his long lashes as he pulled supplies from the bag.

"As I'll ever be." My nerves activated again for an entirely different reason. When Mom found Uncle Rick's project, I never imagined I could be a part of it, but as soon as Ben mentioned the possibility, I couldn't let the idea go. Now, I worried I wouldn't be able to actually do it.

After telling me we'd do some practice rows to get the idea of things before moving into the granny square pattern, he showed me how to hold the crochet hook and yarn. It felt awkward and foreign wrapped around my fingers.

"The tendency is to hold everything really tight, but try to avoid that." He directed me through something called chain stitches.

I pulled my attention away from the lopsided column of loops dangling from my hook to glance at Ben. "Why?"

Ben's fingers sped through a bunch of chains in the time it took me to do one. "Once you start working on the next row like this, it can be difficult to get your hook in when the first row of chains is tight."

I tugged on my yarn to start over, not for the first time. "Does it affect anything if I make them too big?"

"Not really. The tension will sort itself out as you keep crocheting."

I had to trust the process. I did trust Ben, but I wasn't sure I'd be able to progress from simply making a row of chain loops.

About twenty minutes later, Ben proved me wrong. After several more false starts with the chain stitches being either too tight or too uneven, which bothered me far more than it bothered Ben, I moved on to the first actual row of stitches. Our bodies touched from shoulders to hips. Ben kept his hands next to mine so I could mimic his movements as he taught me something called single crochet. His encouragement never waned as I finished the first row.

"Look at that! You're doing great." Ben beamed at me.

I warmed under his praise, which kept growing as he taught me how to identify the different stitches so I could move on to making a granny square. Once I'd successfully identified the parts of a stitch, he wrapped yarn around his fingers in a way that reminded me of a hand-string game from elementary school.

"This is a magic ring. I'm going to start yours because it's not a beginner technique, and I don't want you to get frustrated." His grin softened his words, and I appreciated that he was doing everything he could to help me be successful. He would've been a great educator, but I was sure that attitude made all the difference in his line of work.

Once he'd finished two, he passed one to me, held the other, and showed me how to spot the stitches in a circle instead of the line I'd been doing. Now I understood why he'd hammered home the stitch identification.

"You're right. You are good at this."

Ben's eyes sparkled. "Thank you. That means a lot." He worked his hook in and out of the stitches with ease. "You know, crochet is more logical than people give it credit for. You're following a pattern. Instructions. You can be as artistic as you want by deviating from the pattern and selecting colors, but you can also make it as straightforward as you need."

I considered his words. "I think I get what you mean. Even though all my artistic talent lives in my pinky, this feels doable to me. With more practice."

Ben knocked his shoulder into mine. He didn't have far to travel, given how close we still sat.

I'd always admired people who could take plain materials and make something beautiful. People who had the talent to see things I couldn't. Who could blend colors, shapes, and patterns in ways that mesmerized me. Ben was that kind of person, and I really liked that about him. It turned out I liked a lot about Ben.

My frustration grew with the size of my granny square. It looked sloppy and uneven next to his. Logically, I knew I was a beginner, but usually, I had an aptitude for things when I tried them. The stuff I stuck with, anyway. For better or worse.

"This looks like crap." I held it next to his.

Ben wrapped his hand around mine and lowered it. "Think of it this way. You'll always know which square is yours when I assemble the blanket."

I dropped my head back against the couch and faced him. "You always have a positive response for everything, don't you?"

He shrugged. "It's the truth though. I like that you'll be able to identify it."

One side of my mouth hitched up. "I do too." I tapped his knee with mine.

With renewed determination, I kept going. Eventually, I moved steadier, but I would've abandoned it rows, and nearly two hours ago, if it wasn't for Ben's coaxing and encouraging comments. Before I knew it, I finished my square. White with orange for Michelangelo. Ben had distracted me with stories of his crochet fails until I reached the end.

I stared at the uneven but square-shaped crocheted piece in my hands. "I did it. I finished." I couldn't hide the astonishment from my voice. I would be a part of Uncle Rick's blanket. It was such a silly thing, but it meant the world to me.

"You did." Pride shone through Ben's words.

I gazed into his handsome face, which blurred as my eyes filled with tears. Ben was doing something kind for my uncle and making me a part of it. I expected to be overcome with grief, but a lightness filled my chest. Ben had given me something I would never be able to thank him enough for.

"Oh, Heath. C'mere." The tears flowed more easily as Ben pulled me into his arms. He rubbed my back and murmured soothing words.

I waited for the shame to hit. I was crying in a gorgeous man's arms on our first date, for fuck's sake, but it didn't hit. I supposed I'd gotten to know him well enough over the past several weeks to believe he wouldn't judge me one bit.

I melted into his strong arms. Though my uncle had died decades ago, the pain had never fully gone away. It was worse each holiday he was absent, every Pride month, any time I saw a commercial for HIV treatments that gave people long, healthy lives and wished it'd been available for him.

The soothing circles Ben rubbed into my back brought me back to the present, to him. Warmth and joy filled every space in my body as I buried my face in his neck and squeezed him. I gave in to an impulse and pressed my lips against the skin under his ear. A thank-you kiss against his pulse. An acknowledgment. A wish. An invitation.

Ben's fingers teased into my hair as he held me closer, squeezing tighter. I kissed his neck again, and Ben let out a soft, happy sigh as I forged a path with kisses. I wanted to get as close as I could get. I'd needed the emotional release, but now I craved something else.

Ben.

CHAPTER 8

BEN

My eyes fell closed as he continued kissing the column of my neck. He'd been crying only minutes ago. Was this too soon? Was I taking advantage if I let this go further?

I dismissed the worries. Heath knew himself, and if this was what he wanted, why wouldn't I agree? Because I sure as hell knew I wanted him right back.

I tugged on the silky strands of his hair, eliciting a moan. When his lips reached my jaw, I gently pulled so I could search his eyes for any sign of hesitation, but all I found was desire. Need.

One beat passed. Two, three.

I surged forward and was surprised to find his lips closer than expected. We clashed together. He cupped my face in his hands as I gripped his thigh. His hungry kiss made me dizzy with my own need.

As the kiss continued, we shifted toward each other. I was minutes away from climbing onto Heath's lap or pulling him onto mine.

Heath let out a soft moan as I tugged on his earlobe with my teeth. The sound settled in my heart like the last piece of a puzzle sliding snuggly into place.

Fuck it. I wanted more contact, so I swung my leg over his lap and settled on his thighs, cupping the back of his neck with my hand. It wasn't easy in my snug pants.

"Yes," Heath said with a sigh as he wrapped his arms around my waist.

I tilted my head back as Heath sucked a kiss on my Adam's apple. Each point of contact sent flames skittering across my skin.

Leading to tonight, a part of me had feared our easy friendship and flirting wouldn't have legs outside of the parameters we'd constructed in the coffee shop. I should've known not to worry. Whatever was between us had real potential, and I'd be foolish to ignore the intense spark.

Our slow, languid kisses set a thousand fires racing through my veins. My hips began a slow rotation, and the increased friction made me moan. If I didn't stop, we'd hit a point of no return, with one or both of us coming in our jeans.

I pulled back. "How far do you want to go?" Given the emotional beginning, I wanted him to lead the pace tonight.

Heath slid his hands down into the back of my pants to cup my bare ass. "Is it too fast if I say as far as you'll let me?"

A man who knew what he wanted. I liked that. I draped my arm around his shoulders and leaned close to nibble along his earlobe. He squeezed and massaged my ass. I pressed into his touch, but his fingertips weren't close enough to where I wanted them.

"Do you have condoms?" I whispered in his ear.

Heath had starred in a couple of dreams lately that had left me hard and aching when I'd woken up. The dreams and the way he kissed and held me left me with a need to feel him deep inside. If this were merely a fling, I wouldn't have messed around with bottoming, but I craved it with Heath. I was down to top too. Hell, I was down to do whatever if we were both naked.

"Yeah." He pulled me against him, grinding against my pelvis with more force.

"Good. My last test was a month ago after a hookup. No one since and nothing on my results to report," I offered.

He flicked his tongue against my earlobe. "Nothing positive on mine either. I haven't been with anyone since my physical a few months ago."

Heath urged me to my feet. As soon as we stood, we clumsily removed our shirts while trying to kiss each patch of revealed skin on each other's bodies. By the time we reached his bedroom, I regretted the snug pants. I hadn't expected us to do anything tonight, so I'd opted for a fit that showed off my assets. There was nothing sexy about peeling the fabric off my legs.

I half noticed maple furniture, a fluffy, white comforter, and the absence of clutter like the rest of his apartment, but most of my attention was focused on the three trees tattooed over his pec. A thin trail of dark hair led along his round belly. I couldn't wait to kiss his skin there.

"You look good in those pants." Heath hooked a finger in a belt loop.

I let out a sharp laugh. "Hold on to that image because I'm about to run a deficit on hotness points when you see me try to strip out of them."

"I'll race you. Then we'll both look goofy."

My lips widened into a broad smile. "You're on."

I nearly fell over multiple times in the process, and by the time I kicked the pants off my toes, tears of laughter filled my eyes.

Heath stepped into my space and looped his arm around my waist, pulling me flush against him. "Your hotness points skyrocketed. I like it when you laugh."

"And nearly give myself a concussion by almost careening into your dresser?"

"That too."

I kissed his crooked grin, then moved out of his grasp and flopped onto the bed. As I settled myself against his pillows, he dropped onto the bed on his knees and crawled up my body, dragging his fingernails along my legs. I melted into his touch as he lowered his weight onto me and kissed me deeply. Before I could get my arms around him, he retraced the path of his fingernails with his lips. Each kiss he placed on my chest, stomach, and hips left tingles behind.

My toes curled when his warm breath ghosted over the sensitive skin of my hard dick. "Are you stalling?"

"I prefer to call it building anticipation."

"It's working," I said in a strained voice as my head dropped against his pillow.

My thighs quaked as Heath tongued the crown of my cock and licked the precum before engulfing me in the wet heat of his mouth. All I could do was surrender to his enthusiastic worship of my cock and balls.

Heath pulled off and blinked at me. His lips were red and wet. "Lube? In the drawer." He gestured in the area of the nightstand before sucking me back down his throat.

Without looking, I felt around until my fingers brushed something bottle-shaped. I handed it to him, then bit my fist to hold back a loud groan when he teased slick fingers around my hole. His apartment shared a wall, and I didn't want to piss off his neighbors.

I lifted my head and sucked in a breath at the sight of Heath. His legs were bent at the knee as he sat back on his haunches. His lubed fist stroked my cock while his other hand thrust a finger in and out. As I let my legs fall open, I begged him for more. Soon, he had two fingers, then three, stretching me to take him.

Heath's confident command of my pleasure had my eyes rolling back in my head. If it was this good our first time, how would it be once we learned each other's bodies? I wasn't sure I'd survive that much passion.

When he leaned down to tease my nipple with his tongue, I reached back into the drawer until I touched a plastic packet. I dropped the condom on my chest, next to his face.

With a rough chuckle, he straightened and gently pulled his fingers from me. "I can take a hint."

"Not sure that was subtle enough to be a hint."

Heath's laughter turned into a moan as he stroked himself several times before sliding on the condom and lubing up. He dropped onto his forearms on each side of my head and covered my body with his. I wrapped my legs around his waist. With his slick fingers, Heath reached between us and gave my cock slow strokes. The sensation balanced the pressure as he pushed inside me. I straddled the fine line between pleasure and pain.

As Heath slid home—the front of his thighs brushing the back of mine—I tipped my head back and groaned. *Sorry, neighbors.* He stilled as I adjusted to the feeling of his cock inside me. He wasn't particularly long but thicker than I was used to.

I wished there was a mirror behind Heath so I could watch the slow rock of his ass as he pumped in and out.

First times with guys were *never* this satisfying. It was usually good enough but often bumbling and a little disappointing. My toes never curled to the point where I worried about a foot cramp.

Heath found a steady rhythm, thrusting in and out and absolutely wrecking my world in the best way.

How the hell had signing up to take on a crochet project led to this? To Heath? To maybe us as a couple if things went as I hoped. I wanted more with him. I wanted to stay over and make breakfast together in the morning. I wanted to lounge around and plan our next date between kisses.

I wanted so much more, and Heath's eyes made promises as I stared into them.

He rocked his hips and nailed my prostate, sending a jolt of pleasure racing through my body.

"Feel good?"

"You can't tell?" My eyes rolled back in my head.

Through a rough chuckle, he licked beads of sweat from my neck.

My balls drew close to my body and a familiar tingle in my gut warned me this would end soon. I pushed at Heath's hips and rolled us over because I wanted to drive. Heath watched me with wide sex-drunk eyes as I found a rhythm while jerking myself off. His fingernails dug into my hips with enough force that I wouldn't be surprised to find a patch of crescent moons in the morning.

"Ben, you're so…ngh—" He licked his lips and thrust into me. I'd never felt sexier than with Heath's full attention on me while I brought us both gratification.

The roughness of his grip tipped me over the edge. My strokes stuttered as I shot over Heath's chest. Pleasure crashed through me as I tensed my thighs, pushing Heath as deep as I could get him. I dropped my head between my shoulders as stars sparked in my vision.

Heath pumped into me as he murmured praise about how sexy I was and how good I made him feel. I curled over his body, dancing along the edge of oversensitive and loving every damn second of it. He wrapped his arms around my shoulders and pulled me close until his lips pressed a wet kiss at the crook of my neck while pumping long, forceful thrusts into me. I moaned in his ear, and his body went rigid. He grunted as he filled the condom.

I collapsed against him and kissed the underside of his jaw. "Holy shit."

Heath's laughter was a warm rumble in my ear. "Couldn't have said it better myself."

I angled my face toward his and studied his soft smile in the moonlight. "I wouldn't mind another round if you feed me first."

His smile grew as he teased his fingertips along my spine. "How about breakfast?"

"You read my mind."

CHAPTER 9

HEATH

For quite possibly the first time in my life, I literally woke up smiling. How could I not with Ben snuggled against me? Having him in my arms felt right. I was getting way ahead of myself, but I wanted to hold on to the joy and never let it go. I'd been around long enough to know that when you experienced something like this, you didn't let it slip through your fingers.

When Ben stirred, I kissed his forehead.

His smile was soft and sleepy. "Morning." A face-splitting yawn interrupted the word. He was so cute.

"Good morning. How'd you sleep?"

Ben snuggled closer. "Amazing."

"Me too. Coffee?"

"God, yes."

I chuckled and kissed his forehead again before getting out of bed to take care of business and brush my teeth. When I left my en suite bathroom, I found Ben stretching and yawning with the comforter around his waist. He looked so at home in my bed. I wanted to wake up to that sight again and again.

"I left you a toothbrush on the counter. I'll go start coffee."

Ben hummed. "Thanks."

I pulled on a T-shirt and pajama pants then set out some for Ben before leaving my bedroom. When I got to the kitchen, I started a pot of coffee. I was in the middle of perusing my fridge for breakfast fixings when Ben shuffled in. Seeing him in my clothes tugged at my heart and the Ben-shaped hole that needed to be filled.

He wrapped his arms around my waist and kissed me gently like we'd had a hundred similar lazy Sunday mornings.

"This is nice." His words echoed my thoughts as he rested his head against my shoulder while we watched the coffee pot slowly fill.

"It really is. Hungry?"

"Starved. Got more appetizers hiding in there?"

I pinched his ass, then talked through the options. We settled on buttered English muffins, scrambled eggs, and finishing off the pint of blueberries I'd grabbed at the farmers' market last weekend.

"What are your plans for the day?" Ben asked as he dropped an English muffin into the toaster while I whipped the eggs.

"I don't have anything planned other than grocery shopping. You?"

Ben hummed. "That's all I had planned to do today too. Possibly the farmers' market." He glanced over at me with a tentative smile. "We could go together. Or is that weird? Too much, too fast?"

I dropped the whisk and pulled him close. "Who cares what time-line we move on? No one is scoring us. If it feels right, then that's all that matters, and right now, I want to go grocery shopping with you and learn what kind of bread you buy."

"Whole-grain wheat with as many seeds as possible."

"Dave's Killer Bread has the best seeded bread," I said. We grinned at each other.

The eager smiles and quick kisses continued as we finished break-fast. It was hard not to let my imagination run wild with this easy domesticity. I pictured staying at each other's homes, meeting each other's friends, bringing Ben to work functions, and having dinner with Mom joining us. I wished Dad was still around to meet Ben. Dad would've absolutely loved him.

We started discussing plans to meet at A Whole Latte Love tomorrow as Ben rose from the table to refill our coffees.

"Want to come to my place after? I can cook us dinner," he said over his shoulder as he replaced the pot on the coffee machine.

I was curious about Ben's space. He'd warned me he had a lot more clutter than I did. "Sounds great." I couldn't wait.

A knock at my front door startled me. Who in the world would be knocking on a Sunday morning? As I realized, cold dread filled me.

"What's wrong?" Ben studied my face.

"I think that's my mom. She sometimes drops by on Sunday mornings with pastries from the farmers' market."

Ben glanced in the direction of the bedroom. "I can hide in your room."

I walked over to where he stood at the counter. I wasn't worried about what Ben assumed. If she knew I had a guy here, she'd start a Pinterest board for our wedding. I squeezed his arm. The hesitation in his eyes made my stomach roll.

"I'm not worried about her meeting you. I'm concerned she'll scare you away with her enthusiasm."

Ben's eyes brightened. "You can't get rid of me that easily. And anyway, parents love me."

"I don't doubt it. Well, brace yourself."

There was a more persistent knock, then a muffled "I'm going to use my key" came through the door.

"I'm coming," I called in return. When I opened the door, Mom bustled past me.

"What took you so long? Were you still sleeping? Are you ill? You never sleep this late. I got those cardamom buns you love." She talked a mile a minute as she headed toward the kitchen with a grocery bag hanging off her arm.

I squeezed my eyes closed like it could prevent the train wreck about to happen. "Wait, there's someone I want—" Before I could finish getting the words out, Mom gasped.

As I entered the kitchen hot on her heels, I saw her run into Ben's arms and pull him into a tight hug. Her knuckles whitened with the force of her grip on his shirt.

"Cynthia? Oh, honey. It's so good to see you again. Your complexion is much rosier away from those fluorescents."

Mom's laugh sounded wet as she pulled back and cupped Ben's cheeks. After staring into his eyes for a long moment, she pulled him into another hug. He gripped her just as tightly. I watched them as the gears in my brain tried to figure out how they knew each other. Fluorescents?

He opened his eyes and stared at me over Mom's shoulder. "You're George's son."

How could he know my dad? Oh. *Oh my god.*

Mom let go and turned toward me. Tears formed an inky path down her cheeks, but her smile glowed. She stared at me like I'd won the lottery, achieved tenure, married a nice man, and found a cure for cancer.

"I told you that you'd adore your father's favorite oncology nurse. God, I love being right."

My attention darted to Ben for confirmation as my pulse pounded in my ears. Ben was the man who'd brought my parents joy during their darkest days? The man who'd held my mom's hand as Dad struggled more with his chemo treatments? The man who made them laugh and leave appointments upbeat, as impossible as it had seemed at the time. He was the man they'd spoken about as if he were an angel walking Earth.

Of course it was Ben. He was the most amazing man I knew. That was obvious after only knowing him for a few weeks.

It only took three long steps for me to reach him. I pulled Ben into a breath-stealing hug and added my own tears to the mix on his shirt, then stepped back enough to hook my arm around Mom's shoulders too.

I wasn't sure what I believed about spirituality, the afterlife, or whatever might be out there, but... *Thanks, Dad. I owe you one.*

EPILOGUE
ONE YEAR LATER

BEN

Heath and I walked hand-in-hand from the parking garage in downtown Portland to Waterfront Park, where we blended into a crowd of thousands waiting for the AIDS Walk Northwest to begin. We walked under a balloon arch, and I noticed rainbows everywhere, drag queens all dolled up, kids getting their faces painted, and a deejay filling the air with upbeat music. The Willamette River sparkled under the sun's rays.

Heath read something on his phone. "Mom texted. She found Travis and Beckett, and they're waiting for us behind the HIV-testing booth."

I chuckled. Heath's mom adored them. Ever since we'd introduced our whole families to each other over the holidays last year, his mom liked my brother and his new husband even more than she liked me and Heath. They'd hit it off so well that she'd gotten an invite to their wedding last month.

Cynthia ran over and pulled us into a hug when she spotted us. She sported a red T-shirt for the event with nail polish to match. My eyes widened when I saw another man talking with Travis and Beckett. I caught Heath's eyes after he noticed too.

"Can you boys be any more obvious? Don't make a big deal out of it. He's just a friend."

Heath and I snorted in unison. The "friend" who kept asking her on coffee dates and had helped fix things around the house several times. The "friend" who co-planned a surprise birthday lunch for her earlier this summer with all her loved ones in attendance.

"I'm glad you brought him, Mom." He kissed the top of her head.

Cynthia cupped Heath's cheek. "Thank you, sweetheart." She turned her attention to me. "Don't forget our plans after this. I've already picked out the yarn stores I want to visit." She patted my cheek before walking back to the group.

"You shouldn't have made that bet with her. She's going to clean you out."

I laughed. "I've been fundraising for my brother's AIDS walk team for years. How was I supposed to know that her first time joining us, she'd raise twice as much as me? I thought it'd be an easy bet."

"You sweet summer child. Mom volunteers with a half-dozen organizations and knows a million people. You never stood a chance. You made a bet fair and square, and now you're stuck taking her yarn shopping."

My smile grew. "I love seeing her crochet. She's getting really good at it."

"If we're not careful, we're going to have an afghan for every piece of furniture in our place."

I squeezed his hand and smiled at "our place." Even though we'd been living together for several months, I still had to pinch myself sometimes that this was our life and not a dream. That I'd been matched with my soulmate through a volunteer project.

We'd had an eventful summer between the move, celebrating his tenure promotion, and taking our first vacation together. My tan from our week at an all-inclusive resort in Mexico still lingered, and Heath had even bought a colorful art print on our trip for our new place. I was surprised by how well Heath took to having more color and clutter in our home. He'd encouraged me to decorate because he said he liked my style, but I asked him to do the bedroom. His minimal, soothing style always made me sleep better.

Uncle Rick's finished afghan had a place of prominence over the back of our couch. We often draped it over our laps in the evenings while snuggling and watching TV.

"I heard her mention the other day that she was thinking of trying knitting. I bet she'll be making sweaters before we know it."

He kissed my cheek. "Instead of human sweaters, it might be easier for her to start with dog sweaters."

I tilted my head. "Is she planning on getting a dog?"

Heath turned toward me and grabbed my other hand. "I was thinking we could."

My heart thundered. We'd been kicking around the idea, but Heath had needed more time to mull it over. I was happy to give him any time he needed. "You mean it? You're ready?"

"I am. I want to take our dog on walks to the coffee shop on weekend mornings and cuddle in as a family to watch our favorite shows at night."

"A family." I threw my arms around his shoulders. "I love you so much."

"I love you too, baby." He kissed my neck.

"What are we celebrating?" Cynthia asked as the group joined us.

"We're getting a dog!"

Travis lit up. He loved them as much as I did. They'd just adopted their first dog last year. "Seriously? Are we going to the shelter after this? Portland has several shelters we can visit."

He turned puppy-dog eyes toward Beckett as I did to Heath.

"Why not? The AIDS walk ends around noon, right?" Heath asked.

My brother nodded. A wide smile split his face. "Puppies!" He sounded like an eager kid. We high-fived.

Beckett suggested we head to registration, but Travis paused, and his expression turned more thoughtful. "Thank you all for walking with me today. Your support means the world."

Beckett wrapped his beefy arm around my brother's shoulders as I looped an arm around his waist.

"Thanks for letting us join your team, Travis. It's a privilege to walk with you." Heath squeezed his mom against his side.

"One big, happy family," Cynthia said as she wiped her eyes. "I want to get my face painted before the program starts." She and her not-boyfriend walked toward registration with Travis and Beckett close behind, chatting about what they wanted on their faces. Travis vetoed his husband's idea of something phallic.

I turned toward Heath. "We're adopting a dog."

He intertwined his fingers with mine and pulled me close. "It feels right."

"It does. You feel right too. I love you so much."

"I love you too, Ben." Ever since that first meeting at A Whole Latte Love, he'd gotten under my skin, and there was no other place I wanted him to be.

MY UNCLE CHARLIE

SHANE K. MORTON

CHAPTER 1

"My arm's asleep," Jackson whispered into my ear. I could feel his hot breath, and I curled up closer against him. "Baby," he chuckled and nuzzled into my bedhead. My hair always looked like a rat's nest when I woke up.

"No," I pouted. "Just a little more cuddle before we start the day."

"Any more cuddling and my arm will fall off. The tingling is killing me." I always enjoyed listening to him whine. It was the start of almost every morning. It made him more human instead of the perfect person he usually was.

"But I'm comfy and don't want to get up. I feel safe using you as a pillow." I snuggled even tighter, burrowing myself into his armpit.

"I love it, babe, but I can't even feel my fingers after eight hours of being your pillow. Roll off me."

"No."

He kissed the top of my head and turned towards me as best he could. I knew what was coming – it happened every morning. He unceremoniously rolled me over, smacked my ass, and pulled his arm free before I could get back on top of his shoulder. I liked his arm around me while I slept.

Before Jackson, I moved a lot when I slept. My sleep was fitful and full of vivid dreams that made me jump awake. Now, every night was peaceful, and it was all because of how he made me feel as I snuggled up against him. Over twenty years of snuggling every night – but we had been together longer than that. We were high school sweethearts.

Safe.

Jackson was safe, and I knew I was loved.

"Asshole."

"Yes, but I'm your asshole." He chuckled and sat up on the edge of the bed. "You have a missed call from Mona."

"God, why does Mom call so early on the weekend? She does this every Saturday."

"Old people don't sleep as much. My gran-gran wakes up at four every morning and goes to bed at midnight. It's just the way the body works, I guess."

"Mom isn't that old. She's like… fifty-eight. God, is that old?"

"She's sixty, and it's not young," he laughed as he stood up and stretched. I watched his tight muscles as he bent over. It was a very nice view. "But it's also not old. I read that sixty is the new forty."

"Then that means thirty is the new ten. You read way too many bullshit articles about health." I groaned as I stretched in the bed.

"I thought you liked me healthy."

"I like the muscles." I gestured to him with my finger.

"Why did I marry such a ho." He came over and kissed me lightly.

"I also like how you smell when you come back from the gym pumped up. It makes me get pumped up, too." My fingers circled the back of his neck.

"Are you trying to get me to come back into the bed?"

"Is it working?"

He laughed and kissed me quickly before standing back up. "Pan-cakes instead of morning nookie? I'm starving."

"I didn't say anything about nookie. You should take me out to dinner first. What kind of boy do you think that I am?"

"The nookie before dinner kind."

"Can I have extra syrup, and will there be bacon? There should always be bacon."

"I'll make some just for you. You should call Mona back. Get your ass up and come downstairs, babe. I'll get your coffee ready."

"I love you." I watched him walk naked over to the drawers and bend over as he opened one. Damn, it was a spectacular sight. Most people aged, but Jackson just seemed to get better with every year.

"I know," he chuckled and pulled on a pair of sweatpants, which he had pulled out of the drawer. "I love you too."

"Alright, I'm coming. I mean, you're going to make me breakfast shirtless. So, I'm totally in."

"Call Mona. I don't want your mom calling you back five times today before you talk to her. Avoidance is not helpful."

"Do I get a prize?"

He turned back to me and grabbed his cock in his hands. "Be a good boy," he chuckled as he disappeared around the doorframe. I could hear the sound of his footsteps on the wooden stairs.

"Alright…" I rolled over and picked up my phone. "Three times? Jesus, someone better be dead."

I crawled off the bed and made my way to the bathroom. "Hello, gorgeous." I posed in the mirror. My hair was in full Heat Meiser mode and stuck straight up. I grabbed my toothbrush and turned the water on.

"Alright, Mom…" I touched her name on my favorites list and turned the speaker on. As it rang, I added a large helping of toothpaste to my brush and started brushing my teeth.

"There you are. I figured you and Jackson were sleeping in." She sounded totally put out. Mom could be a lot and, at times, was much more than a handful. She had worked hard and was a single parent – but sometimes, she could really drive me crazy when she wanted to.

"Nope," I brushed my teeth. "Hold on."

"Honey, I can barely understand you. Are you in the shower? This is nuts." Yep, totally put out.

"Bwushing teeth," I groaned, knowing that I sounded like a child.

"Oh, why do you always call me when you're in the middle of doing something? Just call me back."

"Mom, you called thwee times." I spat and put my hand under the water so I could rinse quickly.

"What? Adam, I swear!"

I rinsed quickly and spat it out into the sink. "Three times, I said. You called three times. I thought something was urgent."

"Oh! Yeah, I thought you'd be awake." Her voice changed coyly. She knew full well that we wouldn't be.

"It's not even nine, Mom. Jackson's making pancakes and bacon."

"Well, I'm on my way over."

I gripped the bathroom door. "Are you kidding?"

She sighed heavily. "No, I'm actually not. I... Will you please do something with me today, honey? I never ask you to... I need you to do something with me today. Is that ok?" This was not the way Mom usually asked for anything. It sounded so needful and sad.

"Mom, is everything alright? You're sounding a little... Have you been taking your meds?"

"Yes, Adam. I may be a little manic-depressive, but I'm not a moron. I know what happens when I stop taking them." There she was. I preferred the mom who snapped at me to the sad one.

"Then what's wrong?"

"Your uncle is in town, and... I mean..."

My eyes bulged out of my head. "Mom, are you alone right now?"

"I know he's dead, Adam. That's not what I... I'm getting in the car and coming over. Do you have plans that you can't get out of? I know this is last minute, but I'm not sure I could... I don't want to do this alone, ok?"

"I have no idea what the hell you're talking about, Mom. But..." I sighed. Drama did run in the family. "Yes. But I want to know what the fuck is going on. I'll tell Jackson to make a few more pancakes."

"I love you," her voice broke.

"I love you too, Mom."

"Thanks, Adam. I love you more. See you in about fifteen." With that, the phone went dead. When Mom was done talking, she always hung up first.

"I guess nude breakfast will not be a thing." I grabbed a pair of shorts and a T-shirt I'd laid out last night. I always prepared my clothes the night before. Mental health was not the strong suit of my family, apparently. My OCD had OCD sometimes, but I was as medicated as Mom, and usually, things were fine, and it didn't rear its ugly head. But having small rituals always helped.

I grabbed the shirt Jackson had worn the day before and carried it in my arms as I made my way downstairs. I had no idea what Mom was on about, but knowing her, it could be anything. "Mom will be here in a few minutes and wants a pancake."

"Is everything ok?" Jackson grinned as he put a tray of bacon in the oven.

"Who knows? She wants us to do something with her today. Will that be ok? I didn't think we had any real plans."

"Sure. I love Mona. She's a hoot. What is it?" He took the shirt from my hands and laid it over the stool on the other side of the counter. "I'll just keep it off until she gets here."

"I like that," I laughed happily. "As to what the fuck she's talking about, I have absolutely no idea."

CHAPTER 2

"How did you find out about this, Mona?" Jackson asked as he poured some extra syrup over my pancakes. He knew me well.

"I donate monthly to them in his name. I received an email saying that his square would be here for the installation. Have you ever seen The Quilt, Jackson? It's… beautiful and horrible all at the same time. At least, that's how it feels for me. It pulls the past right back to the surface." She looked at us, and I could see her eyes mist over. Shit. This day could slide sideways at any moment. Mom could be an emotional mess when she wanted.

"I have, actually. When I was a kid, we went on a school trip when it came through town. I didn't really understand it then – not the way that I should have. But I remember my teacher crying, which was… strange, I guess, at the time to a twelve-year-old. I remember that it was beautiful and weird. Each square was so different from the others, and a few of them made some of the kids laugh. After seeing my teacher crying as she walked through the exhibit, I knew better. There was nothing funny about it at all."

"So, Uncle Charlie has a square. How did I not know that?" I shoved a piece of bacon in my mouth.

"Did you know him, babe?" Jackson picked up his green juice and took a drink. It looked gross and tasted grosser, but Jackson had become a complete health nut when he turned forty. I did get to reap the benefits of his amazing, hard body.

I swallowed. "I... yeah. But I was really young when he died. I just remember that he would put me up on his shoulders and run around the yard with me, and I would laugh. He had a great laugh. That's what I remember the most about him. I was what... seven when he died?"

"That's about right." Mom played with her food. "He knew who you were going to be, you know. We were all outside, and you were maybe five at the time, and you fell in the mud and got your favorite t-shirt dirty. He told me that you were definitely Dorothy's friend. Only a gay would cry at soiling their favorite Thundercat shirt in the mud."

I gasped. "I had a real Lion-O kink. He was a very muscular and handsome catman. I loved that shirt."

"He pointed that out, too. He was usually right about most things, you know. He had a sixth sense for everything except the fucking disease that killed him." She looked away from us.

"I also had a thing for the World Wrestling Federation action figures."

"Yes, you did," she giggled. Crisis averted.

"I guess I've always had a thing for muscles," I laughed and glanced over at the bulging biceps of my very hunky husband.

"Let's just say that I wasn't surprised when I met Jackson. You always did have a type," Mom sighed and patted Jackon on his shoulder. "Your Uncle would be so happy for you. He went through it with men, let me tell you. It was a different time, I guess. You two are lucky. High school sweethearts that have always been together."

"Well, not always. We did break up in college." I liked to lord this over Jackson every now and then because it always got a rise out of him.

"It was for two months, and then you came crawling back." He grinned. He was totally playing the game today.

"I remember you being the one who groveled," I grinned happily back. He was right. I did go crawling back.

"We both knew it was wrong. We were right together and always had been. Did you really eat all that bacon?" He looked at me aghast.

"Why? Do you wanna make me more?"

"I want you to start taking better care of yourself. You could go to the gym with me or start eating better protein."

"These are grounds for divorce, and Mom was here to be a witness." I dropped my fork on the plate in protest.

"How long was he sick?" Jackson asked, completely ignoring me.

"It was… I didn't know at first. He was in the city and didn't visit the suburbs as often as I would have liked. But then he didn't show up for Christmas, and that was weird. He had never missed coming home for the holidays, and I realized I hadn't seen him for almost a year. He had been feeling crappy the last time he visited. I thought he might have a bug of some kind, so we stayed in and watched movies for his whole visit. We had talked since then, but the conversations had been pretty short. I started thinking about it and just got so mad at him that I got in my car and drove up."

"It was a surprise?" Jackson frowned. "That had to be hard, Mona."

She nodded and sniffed loudly. "I knocked, and it took a bit for someone to answer. I was mad at him for not coming home. This was right after Christmas, I think. I left Adam with my parents and packed a bag. I stayed there and banged on the door. I was a little shocked when a woman answered. She was very butch with a military buzz cut."

"Are you talking about Sandra?" I ate the last bite of pancake.

"It's the day we met. She was a volunteer and was taking care of Charlie. She let me in, and I got really scared. I didn't understand what was… I mean, I knew what AIDS was, but when she told me that he was quite sick and I should prepare myself – I knew without her telling me what was wrong with him. Charlie was a riot, and he loved having a good time. But he hadn't been very lucky in the love department, like me. He was a bit of a slut. I knew that. But I thought he was being careful. He said he was, anyway."

"I couldn't stop myself from crying when I saw him. He was just a… skeleton of who he was. He had lost sight in one of his eyes, and his beautiful blonde hair was stringy and falling out. The look on his face when he saw me – the fear – it broke me. He cried. I cried. Sandra cried as she came in to check his vitals every so often and to make him eat anything since he had no appetite. She just forced it into him as best she could. I left Adam with his grandparents, and I stayed there for two months helping him, but Sandra had told me that it had progressed too far, and he wasn't responding to the drugs. He had ignored it. Charlie was an ostrich who buried his head in the sand whenever he had a problem instead of facing it. I so wish he would have faced it sooner. Maybe he would still be here." She looked at us, and it broke my heart. She loved him so much, and I had... I was a horrible son.

"I'm... I had no idea, Mona. You guys never talk about him." Jackson reached over and placed his hand on hers.

"Well, Adam was so young. I knew he could barely remember him. I just... I think I've just kept him to myself to feel closer to him. He was my best friend and an amazing big brother. We used to go to gay bars together and watch drag shows, and we danced all night long. I still miss him so much."

"We need to shower," I said way too abruptly.

"You do. Adam, you really do stink." Mom nodded.

"I get hot and sweat when I sleep. Jackson is a fucking inferno."

"You don't have to lay on top of me." He stood up and put his plate in the sink.

"But you're the best pillow."

"Upstairs – both of you. I'll clean the dishes while you get ready." Mom stood up.

Jackson walked over and kissed Mom on top of the head. "I love you, Mona."

"I love you too, Jackson. Now scoot. We can go grab drinks after. I'm sure I'll need one."

Jackson took my hand, and we walked slowly up the stairs. The gravity of my Uncle Charlie was pulling me like a dark planet—an energy source that you couldn't see but knew was there. It gripped all of us, and I tried to picture his face. All I could see was the picture of him and Mom that she had framed and set beside her recliner. I knew nothing about him – not really. How could that be?

"You, ok?"

"Yeah… I'm just surprised, I guess. It's not what I was expecting to happen for the day."

"What did you expect to happen?"

"Lying naked in your arms watching shit TV?"

"That sounds great, but…"

"Not happening, I know." I pulled off my clothes and threw them in the corner. This was the perfect outfit for staying inside all day, but now those plans had been derailed. I'd have to choose something nicer to go to this. "What do you wear to a… art installation? A memorial? All of the above."

"I think we should think of it as a celebration, babe. We're going to remember your uncle. You sure you're ok?" He pulled his shirt over his head, and I had to stop myself from salivating. I was one lucky man.

"Yeah, I just… I barely remember him, you know? I wish that I would have had him to… Our lives are so different from each other, I guess. If he had been born when I had, he would still be here, wouldn't he?"

"I don't know, babe." He smirked as he pulled his gym pants off. He knew I was dick-crazed for him. But there was not enough time, and my mother was waiting downstairs.

"Mom did great. She didn't blink when I told her that I was gay and just hugged me, and nothing changed. But to have a gay uncle who could have helped me – answer questions and be my gay guru as I grew up would have been something special. I could have told him about you."

"But that's not what happened. I get it. But he *was* here, babe. He lived a vibrant life. Maybe it's time you actually learned something about him. You can still get to know him – know things about him, I mean. Maybe that would help?" He walked towards me, and I ogled for as long as I dared.

"Yeah. Maybe?" I shrugged and turned on the shower. "Get your ass in here. I wanna shower cuddle."

CHAPTER 3

"I didn't know you were going to be here, Sandra!" I ran into her arms, and she squeezed the living shit out of me.

"Wouldn't miss this for the world, kiddo. It's so good to see you." She kissed me quickly on the cheek.

"It's been too long. Once a year at Thanksgiving is not enough for a hug like this. I've missed you. We're so close to each other that we should at least meet for brunch every now and then."

Sadra blushed. "I see Mona quite a bit because we're old and have no other friends," she huffed and grinned at me happily. "But I'll come out of my cave for you. You look good, kiddo."

"Hi, Sandra." Jackson reached around me for one of her extra special hugs. When Sandra hugged you – you knew you were loved.

"Hey, handsome, are you keeping this one in line?" Sandra laughed with a throaty laugh that made you smile whenever you heard it. It was so natural and free that it made me jealous.

"Did Moses actually hold back a river?" Mom kissed Sandra on the cheek. "No one can keep that little shit in line."

"I'm like forty-one years old. I have a job and a husband." Yes, I pouted and even stomped my foot. When it came to Mom and Sandra, I swear, I reverted to a teenager all over again.

"Still a little shit to me," Sandra pinched my cheek. "I remember the first time that I met you so vividly that it could have just been last week. You wouldn't stop moving or talking – so chatty and full of happiness. It was so needed at the time."

"I don't really remember meeting you. You've just always been Aunt Sandra. It's like you've always been there, but Mom told me how you actually met. I can't believe I didn't know that. How did I never know that until today?"

She shrugged. "I started working with positive people in the early eighties when I was nineteen. No one knew what to do. Gay men were terrified, and the lesbians stepped up because no one else would at first. Those poor, sick men just lay there in their beds with people afraid to touch them. It wasn't right, so I volunteered, and I wouldn't trade those moments for anything except for them to have never happened. Your uncle was the fifteenth person I sat with at the end of their life."

"That's… a lot." I was stunned. How had I never known this about her? What was wrong with me? Was I that self-involved? I knew the answer. I had only child syndrome.

Jackson put his arm around me. He understood me better than I did after all these years, yet here he stayed. He was a fucking saint. "It's remarkable. I've read quite a few gay history books about that time because when I was a kid, the crisis was still happening. I mean, I was born in nineteen-eighty-one in New York City. My parents had quite a few friends who passed, but school didn't really teach me what I wanted to know. I don't know if I… I hope I would have been able to be strong for my friends, but the fear they felt back then… That palpable sense of death on the horizon."

"Oh, honey," Sandra patted Jackson's cheek sweetly. "It was horrible in every way, but we hoped, and we fought because that was all that we had. We danced as hard as we could and lived even harder because who knew when it could all be taken away? Gay men are strong, Jackson. Strong enough to live and survive as hard as they could. We fucked, and we fought to survive. But those that didn't… I wouldn't wish that on my worst fucking enemy. Not even Reagan himself."

"Did you know him before he... got sick?" I asked, feeling like a stranger to my own family.

"No, honey. We didn't know each other, even if I did know who he was. I mean, it's possible that we brushed up against each other or danced at the same gay bar. But I didn't meet him until he needed someone to help him. But we became fast friends when he wasn't cursing at me because I was making him do something he didn't want to." Mom came over and put her arm around her. "He hated me making him eat. He hated sponge baths, and more than anything, he hated taking those fucking meds. His body didn't respond well to them. He was really sick when he began them."

"Did he have a lot of friends?" I asked quietly. I felt guilty over knowing nothing about my family. I mean, he was my uncle, and all I really knew about him was that he died. I had so few memories of him. I had been too young.

"He was very popular," Mom giggled. "He hosted drag at the Round Up every Friday and Saturday as his alter ego – Ivanna Mann. People loved him, but you learn who your real friends are when you get as sick as he was."

Sandra looked at me seriously. "He had quite a few people who wanted to see him. But he rarely wanted company. There were a few, though, that he would always see, and when he did... Boy, did Charlie know how to turn it on. He was one of the wittiest and filthiest men I have ever met to this day. He could make you laugh so hard that it hurt."

"He sure could." Mom nodded.

"Uncle Charlie was a drag queen?" How did I not know this? I watched Rupaul with Mom on the phone weekly; she had never told me this information.

"Bitch, he wasn't just a drag queen. Charlie was drag royalty at the time," Mom snapped and grinned happily as if she could picture him. "Charlie himself was outgoing and fun, but Ivanna was a force of nature."

"I had no idea."

Mom looked at me and frowned. "I'm sorry that we... that I don't talk about him very much, babe. It's just that you were so young, and it was a long time ago. You remind me a lot of him in a ton of ways, you know."

"I do?"

"Yeah…" She grinned. "You resembled him when you were young. But… You know you're older now than he ever was, right? It… It still hurts to think about him sometimes, but it hurts more not to. I guess I've just kept him to myself because it was easier that way."

"I never asked." I could feel my entire body slump.

"That too," she said kindly.

"But you are now," Sandra reached out and took Mom's hand in her own. "Would the two of you like to meet your Uncle Charlie? His quilt piece was made by all of us who knew him. Twenty-five of his closest friends helped create it. Your mother and I also added a part of it."

"I think I need to," I smiled, and we walked into the entrance together. I was instantly overwhelmed. "There's… It's absolutely huge."

"There are quilts everywhere. How do we find it?" Jackson looked around in awe.

"I have the layout in my hands," Sandra sighed. "So many names – so many people who were lost. Charlie's square is on row twenty-two and number seven. This way." She nodded and gripped Mom's hand tighter.

We followed quietly behind them. The enormity of seeing this was humbling, and it made me so happy to be here – to be alive – not to have been a victim of a world that let so many people die. I knew what had happened back when I was a child, but to see it so vibrant and colorful was something else. It wasn't just knowing – I could now feel it.

"I think I could spend hours here," Jackson's deep voice smoothed the rawness of my emotions as it always did. He was my anchor in a world I sometimes flitted to rapidly in. "All of the colors are so vibrant and alive. I guess that's the point, huh? A celebration of life in the face of death."

"A way to remember?"

"A way to never forget."

"I... That sounds nice." I bumped into him as we walked. "We're too busy in our lives to stop and think about the past, aren't we?"

"You sound so wise. What did you do with my husband?" Jackson laughed. The sound of happiness felt weird as we walked through the squares of people who had died.

"Smartass. I'm serious. We work and deal with our finances. We clean our houses and do laundry – and then in our free time, which feels like we rarely have, we may go see a play or a movie – watch TV."

Jackson rolled his eyes dramatically. "Scroll on our phones. You lose time whenever you open TikTok," he chuckled. "But I get what you're saying."

"I mean, you read a lot of history and nonfiction books. You're reading what right now?" I asked in perpetual awe of my husband.

"A new book about Stonewall. I like learning things."

"Shit... Do I ever stop and learn about the past?"

"You are today. Don't kick yourself about it."

"He was my uncle, and I would have had a hard time remembering his name. I mean, it's been years since we've ever mentioned him."

"I think Mona thinks about him a lot. Sandra too. You just didn't know him, babe. That's ok, you know. My dad's parents... My grand-parents on his side... they died before I was born. I didn't know them, and I can't tell you the last time I thought about them because of that. It's ok not to know. But now you do."

I let his words wash over me. "It's humbling. Each of these... All of the names... This was their life, wasn't it?"

"A part of it. It's powerful. Even more so now that I'm an adult. I understand mortality now – better than I did when I was a child. Forty-*something* isn't twenty, no matter how much we like to pretend it is."

"True that."

"Row Twenty-two," Mom turned and smiled at us.

We turned right and walked down all the bright fabrics that seemed to hover off the ground on both sides of the path. My emotions were complicated, and that was always hard for me. I didn't deal well with any kind of sadness. But this made me... regretful, and I felt so small in the face of all these men who died. I regretted not knowing my uncle, and small because I never tried to learn more about this time or him. I needed to... No, I wanted to change that. Maybe Jackson could lend me a book?

"Here it is," Sandra stopped and pulled Mom into a one-armed hug. "God, it's just as remembered it. It's so much like him."

We stepped up beside them, and I caught my breath. "These panels are so large that they... They're about the size of a person."

"They're the size of a grave," Sandra answered quietly. "Six feet by three feet."

"That's somber." I shivered.

"That's life, honey." Sandra's voice filled with compassion. She, too, understood me and my faults.

"His name is so beautiful. Whoever did that work loved him very much." I whispered.

"Yes, I did," Mom nodded. "Gold metallic thread. He loved Lamé fabric. That was the one thing his taste was shit about." Her giggle brightened up her face. "He had the gaudiest gold Lamé curtains in his apartment. They made me insane. Most of his gowns were the same kind of fabric. It was the one tacky thing he loved."

"He was the best hostess of New York drag shows. He was so funny and changed the lyrics to all the popular songs of the time. He sang live, you know." Sandra smirked. "God, he had a filthy mouth in drag."

"He had a filthy mouth out of drag, too. Dad said one of his first words was fuck, which served Dad right because it was also his favorite word," Mom giggled again. "God, even after all this time, it looks so new. How do they do that?"

"Well, it's not being used on a bed or washed. And it's being cared for by a team of people who make sure they stay in the best shape possible. This is the remembrance of people's lives," Sandra answered proudly.

"What is that on the square?" Jackson smiled as he stared at the block which belonged to Uncle Charlie. "Is it gems?"

"He always wore red heels. So, the center of the square below his name is a replication of the rhinestone heels he wore. That is Diana Ross in the corner with her microphone as she's holding out her hand. His favorite song in the world was one of her songs. Reach Out and Touch, I think it was called. We all hummed it as he finally faded away." Mom scrunched up her face as if she were denying a powerful emotion. "He used to change the lyrics to something very bawdy about balls."

"He sounds amazing," Jackson looked at me sadly. He always knew when I was having one of my moments of feeling overwhelmed.

"I'm sorry that I can barely remember him. How nice it would have been to have gotten older with him and had someone to tell all of my secrets to," I sighed, and Mom walked the few steps between us and took my face in her hands.

"He might have taken you to your first gay bar. He may have given you advice – bad or good – who knows with Charlie," she grinned. "But he loved you. He was the first person to hold you. Did you know that? Even before they put you in my arms – they put you in his. He was there through the entire thing, and I hoped he wouldn't pass out. It was a little touch and go in the beginning, as I screamed bloody murder. You were a difficult birth."

"Oh, God, I bet," Sandra laughed. "I wish I had really known him when he wasn't sick. I know that I missed out on what would have been a very good friend when I might have needed one the most."

"He loved you," Mom nodded to her. "He knew how lucky he was that you were there. He loved you, Sandra."

"He gave me you, Mona." Sandra wiped at her eyes, and I felt reality crush down on me. The things that I had missed out on because he had died too soon. A life unlived. A life devoid of potential and happiness as we grew older together. The dinner parties he could have come to as he regaled us with the stories of his past would never happen. I didn't realize how much I had missed by not knowing him.

"I want to know more about him. This is... nice, but it's just material, isn't it? It's not him. I want to know more about him. Tell me about Uncle Charlie," I pleaded.

"Please?" Jackson added as he took my hand in his again and interlaced our fingers. "He sounds amazing."

"Well, shall we go back to your place?" Mom asked. "Sandra? Want to come and help me?"

"Can we go to yours? I… You have photos and things, right? I'm sorry that I never took the time to think about him or you, Mom. How much loss you felt while I was too young to understand. You were so alone." I saw my mother in a new light. A person who had always been there had I taken a little time to think about her. I wouldn't take her for granted again. How fucking strong she was.

"I wasn't alone, kid. I had you. I had Sandra and your grandparents. For all their faults, and trust me, they had quite a few – they loved Charlie with all of their hearts, just as they loved you. I wish they could have been here with us today." She reached out and touched me again.

I looked up at the sky. The sun was shining brightly, and there wasn't a cloud in the sky. "They're here. They're always here, and so is Uncle Charlie." I hugged her tightly.

"What was Charlie's favorite cocktail?" Jackson asked suddenly.

"Mimosas. He loved anything bubbly." Mom laughed. "He loved the pop of a champagne bottle."

"Let's stop on the way. I think we need to share a drink with Charlie."

"Jackson, he would love that." Mom looked at him sweetly.

I didn't know what my future held, but I was glad that I had Jackson to share my life with. I wish that Charlie could have met someone like him while he was alive. But fate had other plans for him. The government turned a blind eye to his plight until it was too late for so many gay men of Uncle Charlie's generation. I owed them so much for all they had done for the life I now held so dear.

I wouldn't forget.

"When we get home tonight, Jackson, can you give me a book to read about all of this."

"I thought you'd never ask," his grin lit up his incredibly handsome face, and he took me in his arms. We kissed in the middle of all these pieces of people's lives, and just for a moment, I could feel them all watching and smiling back at me.

I had an uncle, Charlie, who sometimes went by his drag name, Ivanna Mann. In the eighties, he was the hostess with the mostess at a very popular New York gay bar, and he loved me.

I would hold that close to my heart while I finally got to know him.

I wouldn't forget.

BITTERSWEET

ANA ASHLEY

CHAPTER 1

JULIUS

I smell it before I see it.

"Open your own coffee shop," they said. *"It'll be great,"* they said.

They didn't consider the lack of available skilled baristas in Stillwater, or bakers for that matter. Or that my kitchen seems to be extra combustible? I really should look into dating a firefighter.

Like you have time to date.

Why didn't I open in the city?

Because you hate the city, dumbass.

"On the house," I say to my customer with a smile, placing extra marshmallows on the hot chocolate I just finished preparing and setting it on the counter. She stares at me, but I don't have time to explain that if I stop to charge her, I'll lose far more than the cost of the drink.

The fire extinguisher is within arm's reach, so I grab it and rush to the kitchen.

Billowing smoke hits me as I push open the kitchen door. The second thing to hit me is the kid who only started working for me last week.

"I quit. Please don't sue me." He coughs.

I can't see an actual fire, so I take a few short strides to the back door, open it, and let the smoke out. The chill of the Connecticut fall is a welcome relief from the heat in the kitchen.

"What happened?" I ask, trying to show a calm I'm really not feeling, but I know I'm a big dude, and the kid already looks ready to shit his pants.

He shrugs. "I don't know. I set the timer to make sure the toast didn't burn. I was checking my messages on my phone and then there was smoke. Lots of smoke. Like *everywhere*."

I glance at the oven.

I choose calm. I choose calm, I repeat to myself as I open the oven door, releasing even more smoke into the small space.

"Which timer did you set?" I ask when what I really want to know is how long he'd been lost in his phone that he hadn't noticed what was happening.

"That one." He points to the oven timer, which was timing the baking of a batch of brownies for an order. I've had a lot of fires in this kitchen, but burning two things at the same time is a first.

"Did you think of using the timer on the wall next to the toaster?"

The kid purses his lips in an *O*, but no sound comes out.

"Do you agree that maybe this job isn't for you?"

"You can't fire me because I've already quit."

I want to shout that it's just semantics because either way, I'm now without an assistant and down a batch of brownies for an order. The brownies aren't for just any customer. Fletcher is a friend, and he's going to be here in just a few hours. Instead, I say, "I'll mail your last check to you."

The kid runs out like his ass is on fire, which is a thought that should make me laugh, considering the current situation. But it's not funny, especially because I can't shake the feeling that this is somewhat my fault for not getting the toaster fixed when the automatic pop-up button stopped working.

I lean over the island in the middle of the kitchen until my forehead touches the cold marble top.

"I release worry and embrace calm," I repeat to myself half-aloud, hoping it'll make the feeling a reality.

"Does that actually work?"

I lift my head to find a guy leaning against the doorframe. It takes a second for my brain to engage. "I'm sorry. I'll be right out to take your order."

He smiles and points at the still-smoking open oven. "Brownies, right?"

"They were, yeah."

"What kind?"

"Triple chocolate."

He releases a moan that goes straight to my dick, and I notice the way his sharp jawline leads to a long, slim, perfectly biteable neck. I trap my lips between my teeth. The guy is shorter than me—at six foot five, most people are—but he's not short. He's all long legs and arms, guarded blue eyes, and an easy smile.

Down, boy. We're in a crisis situation here and your dry spell is not a priority right now. Especially when directed at perfect strangers who walk into our kitchen uninvited.

"They're my favorite," the guy says.

"I'm sorry, I don't have any to sell right now."

"Not yet," he says, crossing his arms.

"I'm sorry, I can't…"

"You keep apologizing. Why don't you go handle the line of under-caffeinated customers while I deal with your brownie situation?"

I crane my neck to look over him into my coffee shop and, fuck, the line is out the door. How am I going to have time to work on the order without any help?

Wait.

"What did you say?" I ask.

"I can't make a drink to save my life, so you better go deal with the hangry crowd."

"No, the other thing."

He walks farther into my kitchen and picks up the Bittersweet apron hanging by the door. "I'm going to bake you the best brownies you've ever had in your life."

I want to argue, but with the line of people needing my attention, I can't afford to waste more time. As they say, beggars can't be choosers, and at this point, I'm definitely the beggar in the situation.

"Hell, what's the worst that can happen?" I mutter, grabbing two slices of bread and putting them in the toaster, making sure to set the timer correctly. His smile gets to me, and I can't help returning it.

"What's your name?" I ask as I go around the worktable toward the front.

"Constantine."

"I'm Julius."

"Hey," he calls as I walk past him, "there's a kid out there. He looks like me but shorter. Can you give him a glass of water? He needs to take his meds."

"Sure thing. Can you butter that toast and bring it out when it's done? I have some apologizing to do outside."

I walk out, trying to ignore the weird feeling in my gut and the possibility that my kitchen might go up in flames before the end of the day.

The crowd isn't angry, just hungry. This is Stillwater, after all. But the line is long, and I can't afford to lose any business.

I spot the kid straight away, so I grab a bottle of water from the cooler and put it in front of him. He's wearing a Hall of Fame T-shirt under his heavy coat, which he still has on, even though it's a cozy seventy degrees inside my coffee shop.

"Thanks," he says, avoiding eye contact.

He looks to be around fourteen or fifteen and is the spitting image of Constantine. Is this his kid? My quick mental math doesn't seem to add up. Not that it matters. I have a job to do.

New priority. Serve customers and then find out what the hell is happening right now.

CHAPTER 2

CONSTANTINE

Fake it till you make it. Isn't that what they say?

I don't feel the confidence and carefree attitude I'm determined to show Julius, but there is one thing I don't have to fake. This will be the best batch of triple chocolate brownies he has ever tasted.

I know my way around a kitchen, so I throw out the burned brownies and give the oven a quick clean. The oven timer is counting down from four hours, so if I were a betting man, I'd say the kid who ran out of the kitchen like a bat out of hell didn't see it was set for the brownies and set it for the toast currently in the trash, still smoking a little.

On top of mixing up the timers, he set them to hours instead of minutes. No wonder the kitchen looked like it was on fire when I arrived at Bittersweet, hoping for the break I so desperately need.

Five minutes later, Julius has freshly buttered toast for his customer and the area is spotless and ready for my magic. Just one more thing.

Take the stinky trash out so I can breathe again.

When I return to the kitchen, Leo is sitting on the stool by the kitchen island.

"You never said he was hot. Like *Mountain Men* magazine hot," he says, holding a half-empty water bottle.

"That's not a real thing." I look inside the cabinets to find the ingredients I'll need.

"Not the point. He's hot."

"Is he? I didn't notice."

Leo laughs. "Sure you didn't."

Okay, I did. But I'm not going to own up to it. Besides, it's not like I can flirt with the man I'm counting on to give me a job and a place to live, is it?

"Are you going to help or just stand there?"

Leo tenses, his hands gripping the bottle tight until it bends under his fingers. He seems to notice what he's doing and releases the bottle, hiding his hands between his legs. "I can't. What if…?"

This is something he's doing more of. Hiding. Pulling away. I'm still not sure the move to Stillwater is a good one for us, for him, but I have to try.

Buckle up, Constantine.

"Do you have any cuts on your hands?" I ask.

"No."

"Did you take your meds on time?"

"Yes."

"Well then, right now, our biggest worry is me getting this job so we have somewhere to sleep tonight."

He nods. "Right."

"Besides—"

"It can't spread through food preparation. I know."

Sometimes, I'm not sure if he struggles to apply the stuff he knows to real life or if he's being a little shit like teenagers often are.

I open the fridge and grab the butter. There's also a block of cheese, which gives me an idea.

"Have you ever baked scones?"

Leo snorts. "Sure, I like to whip up a batch for stress relief. You know, between classes, doctor appointments, and Mom abandoning me."

"Leo."

"Sorry," he sulks. "This just sucks. You had your life, and now you're stuck with a sick kid. How did you even find out about this place?"

I go around the counter and wrap my arms around him. He inherited the Galanis genes, so he's never going to be tall, but he's still far too small for his age.

"A lot of things suck right now, Leo, but having you in my life is never going to be one of them, okay?"

He nods against my chest and holds me back tight. We've been traveling a long time, so he's as tired as I am.

"Okay, how do I make scones? What are scones, anyway?"

I grab my phone and pull up my recipe from the notes app. "Measure these ingredients for now."

The sound of the coffee maker, the ice blender, and people from the front of the coffee shop becomes our background noise. I put everything into the brownie mix, making it a double, and then I help Leo with the cheese scones.

While everything is in the oven, I fix Leo a sandwich. I hope Julius doesn't mind. I'm too nervous to eat right now, but Leo needs to. Then he tells me he wants to go for a walk to explore, and I know he's responsible enough to not get lost or do anything stupid.

I get lost rearranging the cabinets and making an ingredients list, and I don't notice the noise outside has died down until a small cough gets my attention.

"Oh, hi. All good out there?"

Julius has his arms crossed as he leans against the doorframe in the same position I was in just over an hour ago.

"It smells nice in here," he says.

"Hmm...I'd say heavenly, but I'll take nice."

He raises a brow, and when his lips curl into a small smile, two dimples appear on his cheeks.

He fucking has to have dimples.

Pushing aside the way his dark-brown eyes look like they're trying to figure me out, I place a brownie on a plate with one of the cheese scones and hand it to him.

I try to keep still while he breaks off a piece of the brownie and puts it in his mouth.

"Wow. This is…" he says as he chews, making a chef's kiss gesture with his hand. "This is better than my brownies."

Considering what I've heard about his brownies, I suddenly feel a lot more confident. This job is so mine.

He tries the scone, which would go better with some butter, but I used the last of what he had in the fridge. He finishes it off like he hasn't eaten in days.

"I didn't realize how hungry I was. Thank you." He puts the plate on the worktop and looks around. "Where's your kid?"

"He went for a walk to explore the area."

I glance behind Julius and see the coffee shop is empty. When I look back at him, his gaze is intense and laced with curiosity.

"Who are you, Constantine?"

I take a deep breath and hold my hand out. "Connie Galanis. I'm the guy who's been avoiding your calls."

CHAPTER 3

JULIUS

"You're...Connie? I mean, Constantine."

He nods. Well, he's definitely not what I had expected when Fletcher told me he had a friend who was perfect to help me in the coffee shop.

"Sorry, I don't know much about you. Fletcher just gave me your number and said I should call you, so I did."

He laughs. "And you did what he said just like that?"

"What can I say, I'm good at following directions." I cringe when Constantine's smile goes from amused to interested.

"Good to know. Look, I'm sorry. I didn't mean to dodge your calls. Fletcher said you were looking for help and that you'd call, but I've had a lot on my plate this year, and I wasn't ready to move to the East Coast."

I'm not looking for help. I'm desperate for it. The good, non-fire-setting kind, which, judging by these brownies alone, Constantine *is* it.

"And you're ready now?"

"I'm here, aren't I? Do you want to tell me about the job? Again,

Fletcher didn't say much except that I'm the man for the job—as proven by the amazing brownie you just tasted—and that the job comes with accommodation."

Accommodation? Well, this is news to me.

"Accommodation…right." I pretend to look at my watch. "Give me a moment. I'll be right back."

I leave the kitchen, pulling my phone out to call Fletcher.

"Julius, please don't tell me you're calling because your new helper set fire to the kitchen. I need the brownies, dude. George and Megan are having a sleepover with their friends, and if I can't supply the goods, there will be a riot. As it is, Harrison is not happy that I agreed to this sleepover when we were supposed to have the weekend to ourselves."

"Hmm, I know how he feels."

"What do you mean?"

"Did you tell Conn—Constantine—that the job here comes with accommodation?"

"Um…yes? You said you were moving back into your new place and the apartment above Bittersweet would be free. You talked about renting it out. Remember when Sage said you could use it for hookups? Or, more precisely, for *his* hookups."

I sigh. "I remember."

"And that was what, a year ago. Wait—has he…finally taken your call?"

Oh shit, I think I've put my giant foot in my equally giant mouth. "Yeah…kinda."

"Okay, is it going to be a problem? I mean, you're not living in the apartment, are you?"

"No. It's not a problem." As long as Constantine doesn't mind sharing a tiny one-bedroom apartment with his kid and a big dude. I guess I'm moving back home. No point delaying the inevitable. "I was just caught by surprise, that's all."

"Okay. Harrison is picking up the brownies on his way home from work. Can you add two slices of your carrot cake to the order? It's the only way I can make it up to my husband for cockblocking him with a bunch of kids."

"Sure. It'll be ready for pick up." *Thanks to your friend. The friend who clearly hasn't told you he's in town.*

I end the call and turn back to the kitchen. Constantine is bent over the island, looking at something on his phone. He has my notebook open and my pen hovering over something he's already written down.

It should annoy me that he's making himself at home in my kitchen, but it doesn't. Quite the opposite. He looks like the space was made for him. I always feel too big for it and prefer to be behind the counter talking to my customers.

Baking is something I'm good at and enjoy, but it's not my passion. It's just a handy talent.

"So…" I start.

When he looks up, he smiles. His tongue pokes out from the corner of his mouth and my eyes zero in on it as it disappears again.

My eyes meet his, and I know I've been caught staring.

"So…" He tilts his head to the side.

"About the accommodation. I'm kinda living in it."

His face drops.

"You can have it," I add quickly. "It's a small one-bedroom apartment upstairs. I've been staying there because…it doesn't matter. I'll just need to grab a few things, change the sheets, and then it's yours."

"Thank you. I don't want to kick you out of your own place. Fletcher mentioned—"

"You're not kicking me out. I have a house, but most days, it's easier staying here." Not to mention that apart from my bedroom, the whole place is in severe need of a good renovation, which is something I don't have the time or energy for. Maybe with Constantine here, I can finally get the work started.

"Oh, okay. If you're sure. I know we showed up out of the blue, and you didn't know about Leo."

"Your kid?"

He raises a brow. "Eesh, I know I look as tired as I feel, but I don't think I look old enough to be my brother's dad."

"Sorry, I shouldn't have assumed."

He waves me off. "It's fine. He looks younger than he is and weirdly like me, considering we have different dads. I'm not sure I'll ever get used to that."

He mutters the last part to himself. It's a strange thing to say, but I don't want to pry. For some reason, Constantine Galanis decided to come to Stillwater to work for me. The kid is an unexpected addition, but it doesn't bother me. I love kids.

"The couch opens into a bed—"

"Hey, Julius." Harrison calling my name interrupts the conversation.

"I'll be out in a sec," I say, poking my head out of the kitchen door and then turning to Constantine. "That's Harrison, Fletcher's husband."

He tenses, but I hold my hand up. "I spoke to Fletcher. He doesn't know you're here, does he?"

Constantine shakes his head.

"If you're staying, you'll have to tell him because he's a regular and a friend. For now, can you put the brownies in a box? That's what Harrison's here for."

I point to the pile of Bittersweet cake boxes on the shelf and go out to give Harrison a coffee to go. Hopefully, the distraction will work.

Constantine's brother comes back a moment after Harrison leaves.

"Hey. Good walk?" I ask him.

"Yeah."

"Your brother is in the kitchen."

He nods, and with his hands in his pockets and his head held slightly low, like he's trying to make himself invisible, he walks through the space next to the cooler and into the kitchen.

An almost-fire in my kitchen followed by the new kid quitting? I can't say I didn't expect it to happen.

Constantine and his brother Leo? One hundred percent unexpected but not unwelcome.

That feeling I got in my belly seeing Constantine in my kitchen? Well...I probably shouldn't think about it too hard. I have the help I need and that's that.

It's been a long time since someone's knocked me off my feet.

Constantine is capable in the kitchen—something that will never not be sexy for me—and he's also very much my type. Small but not breakable.

I should probably find a hookup before I do something stupid.

CHAPTER 4

CONSTANTINE

Fletcher: I hear you're done playing hard to get.

　　Me: I really don't know what you mean.

　　Fletcher: Don't play dumb. I spoke to Julius. You're moving to Stillwater?

　　Time to rip off the Band-Aid.

　　Me: Already here.

　　Fletcher: Dude, wtf! Why didn't you say?

　　Fletcher: Damn, we have a house full of kids. I want to catch up and do dumb shit.

　　Me: What, like raise your son alone before you get married to the first hot dude immune to your charm?

　　Fletcher: He wasn't the first. You didn't bite either.

　　Me: Which is why we're still friends.

　　Fletcher: Fuck, I missed you. I've still not forgiven you for not coming to the wedding. A Victoria Sponge Cake would go a long way to getting back in my good graces. Just sayin'…

　　Me: We'll see…

　　I put my phone away and let him stew. Predictably, the messages keep coming, but I ignore them. The last time I saw Fletcher, his son, George, was only two. Now, he's married and a stepdad to Harrison's daughter, Megan.

He's not earned just his favorite cake. He's earned a visit.

And since Julius gave me the weekend off to settle in, and Bittersweet is closed, getting familiar with his kitchen is just what my antsy hands need right now.

The kitchen in Julius's apartment is small and functional. Perfect for most people.

Unfortunately, I'm not most people.

Fortunately, Julius said I can use his fully equipped kitchen for my personal needs at any time. I placed a grocery order yesterday, so I have everything I need.

Even though the apartment is above Bittersweet and technically part of the premises, access is through an external staircase outside the back door.

The chill outside hits my face just as Leo comes out of the bedroom. I close the door again to keep the heat inside.

"I'm sorry," Leo says, stopping a few steps away, his blond hair all over the place because he hasn't brushed it.

Damn, I'm acing this parenting gig if he's ready to apologize this quick.

"What are you sorry for? For having a legit concern, or for being a little shit about it?"

He laughs. "Both?"

I set the grocery bag on the floor. "I know you're worried, but you can't hide from the world. You have the right to live your life to the fullest. Have an education, do stupid things, fall in love. Okay, that one, not for a long, looong time," I add quickly.

He looks down, running his hands through the overgrown hair on the back of his head. I need to find out where he can get his hair cut before starting school. "Yeah, like that's ever going to happen."

Fuck, I just want to scoop him up in my arms and make it all better. At just fifteen years old, he was handed the shittiest deal.

"I know it feels that way now, Leo, but you're on the right meds, and your viral load is undetectable. Yes, this is something you're going to live with for the rest of your life, but having HIV is no longer the death sentence it once was."

"You're saying that because you're my brother, but who's going to want to give a job to the guy with HIV? How about when I go on a date and have to disclose my status?"

I take a breath and resist the urge to scoop him up in my arms. Instead, I break the space between us and hold his hands between mine. "I can't promise that everything will always be okay or easy, but I can promise I will always be here for you, okay?"

He sighs. "Do you think it was the right thing moving here?"

"Yeah. I think so."

I may not have taken Julius's calls when Leo's life imploded and I couldn't see past the next doctor's appointment or stop researching everything about living with HIV and treatment, but I knew about Stillwater. When I met Fletcher in Europe years ago, he talked about where he grew up so much that I feel like I already know what it'll be like to live here.

Small-town living was never my thing. I grew up in LA, and the world always seemed too big and full of opportunities to settle in a small town.

That feeling in my gut when I'm creating a new recipe and know how much of something to add? That's the same feeling I get about Stillwater. I know I made the best decision for us. I just hope I'm right about it.

"Okay," Leo says. "I'll go back to school." But then he pauses. "Can I...um...not tell anyone about...?"

"It's your choice to disclose your HIV status," I say with as much finality as I can because I've done my research, and I know he can't be discriminated against because of it. I will fight with all I have to ensure Leo has the best chance at a normal life.

"I'm going to play X-Box," he says, turning back toward the room. I really shouldn't have set up the game with his small TV in the bedroom. I'll never see him again.

"Take your fill because, after this week, I want to see you catch up with schoolwork. Gaming hours will be supervised."

"Ugh. You're worse than a real parent."

I take that as a compliment as I blow him a kiss and pick up the grocery bag again. Having kids was not on my radar. Hell, I can't even hold on to a relationship because who wants to date a pastry chef with irregular hours?

Tasty food on demand? Selling point. Leaving the house before dawn some days and not returning until after dinner? Not so attractive.

I make my way down the stairs, pulling the keys Julius gave me from my pocket.

When I get to the door, it's open.

Shit, have we been robbed?

I go in carefully, trying not to disturb anything that could be evidence. There are three grocery bags on the kitchen island.

Weird.

I hear noise from the front of the building. Maybe the thief is still here and trying to get money from the register. It's unlikely Julius would leave any cash on the premises over the weekend, so when the thief comes out feeling all pissy because there's no money and then sees me, they're going to get extra pissy.

The knife block is nearby, so I reach out for it.

The door opens just as I draw the knife.

"Whoa." Julius holds his hands up.

I drop the knife on the counter and bring my hand up to my chest.

"Sorry. I thought…"

"I was here to rob my own place?" His brow quirks a little, and I try not to fixate on the dimples that make him look like an adorable, huggable giant or the way the coat he's wearing makes him look like a cuddly bear.

"Yeah." I laugh. "Especially when I'm the one who shouldn't be here."

"Nonsense. This is your kitchen now. I'm not used to having someone else around, so I forgot to tell you." He walks over to the grocery bags and takes out all the stuff that needs to go in the fridge.

I put it away for him and then reach over to my own bag.

"You came down to bake?" he asks.

"Yeah, you said it was okay and…I was bored."

Julius leans against the kitchen island, juggling a tin of condensed milk between his hands.

"I have an idea to help you with that while also impressing the shit out of your new boss."

I try not to stare when he removes his coat and reveals a Henley stretched around his big chest and arm muscles. I fail.

When I find my voice again, it's a lot breathier than I'd like. "I'd love to impress my new boss."

CHAPTER 5

JULIUS

"Three éclairs. The chocolate ones, please. And…one of those pretty tarts with the blueberries and two banana muffins."

"Coming right—"

"Okay, make it three banana muffins. One for the journey, right?"

I smile and pack up everything neatly in a box.

"Can I get you anything to drink?"

"No, thank you. I'll just take those yummies."

I ring up the order, and off she goes.

"Who's next?" I ask hopelessly because I've lost count of the people coming in and out of my coffee shop. Breakfast feels like a week ago and lunch is a luxury for those who don't have patisserie geniuses working in their kitchen.

No one answers my question because every single one of my customers is focused on the show they can see through the open kitchen door.

"Hey, Liv, let me take your order."

"Don't rush. I put a sign on the bakery door saying I'll be right back."

I sigh. Not her too.

Not that I can blame her or anyone else. Watching Constantine work is mesmerizing. With his headphones on and humming a tune I don't recognize, he's so focused that I'm not sure he'd know if there was an earthquake in Stillwater.

He glances up and smiles, waving at the line of people waiting to try to take home one…or five of his amazing pastries and cakes.

"What can I get you?"

"Actually," she says, "any chance I could have a word with him? That cake I tried yesterday was out of this world, and I want to know what he put in it. I think it would really work on a bread recipe I'm developing right now."

"Go ahead."

She practically dances over to the kitchen. Constantine removes his headphones and I struggle to pull my gaze away and call the next customer.

"Can I have all of those macarons? I haven't had them since I went to Paris on my honeymoon, and I just bet these are even better."

"Of course. Can I get you a drink to go too?"

"No. Thank you, my dear."

It's the same all afternoon. I hop between serving customers staying and those wanting an order to go.

This certainly beats having the kitchen on fire, broken cups, cakes dropped on the floor, or any of the catastrophes my previous helpers caused.

When there's a short break in the line, I try to check in on Constantine, but the door to my coffee shop opens again, the wind blowing in teenage trouble.

"Hey, Julius. Did you know your muffins are my favorite muffins of all time? Dad says your coffee is the best too."

I laugh and lean against the counter. "Kayleigh Nielssen. What do you want from me? Let me check the calendar." I pull my phone from the drawer under the register and pretend to look. "Yup. I believe someone is still grounded for starting a bonfire in their backyard, and I have specific instructions from someone's dad to not supply any sort of treats."

"It's a good thing I'm not asking for a treat then."

Kay is far too world-smart for a fifteen-year-old, thanks to spending most of her life with her dad, the lead singer of Hall of Fame, and the rest of the band, her honorary uncles. Now that they've settled in Stillwater with her dad's boyfriend, she's become one of my regulars.

"What are you asking for?"

"I need you to supply coffee for a fundraiser."

"You got it. What are you fundraising for?"

She stares like she was hoping to work harder for it, but part of my business plan is to be part of the community and help whenever I can.

I have portable equipment to supply coffee at any location, and the soup kitchen, which also serves as a community center, has my old coffee maker for events stored there.

She hands me a small leaflet. "It's for the Ryan White HIV/AIDS Program. We learned about Ryan at school when Mr. Bradford did a talk about HIV/AIDS education. My group project is to raise awareness in the local community, and I thought it would be a good idea to raise some money to help out too."

"It's a great idea, Kay. Have you spoken to Liv? I'm sure she'd be willing to offer her cookies."

The smile on her face falls. "She can't. Levi and Arlo are going on a honeymoon, so she's closing Lovely Buns to take Ava to visit their aunt in Chicago."

"I'll help."

We both turn to Constantine, who's standing by the kitchen door with his apron in his hand.

"Who are you?" Kay asks. "I know your face."

I bite my lip to stop from laughing. Kay is a force of nature, and the world is not ready for her.

"I'm Connie Galanis," Constantine says, raising his hand. "I've baked everything on that display. Tell me what you need, and I'll do it."

Kay crosses her arms and purses her lips before saying. "I need a sample."

Constantine goes to the kitchen and returns with the end piece of a lemon cake. Kay takes it and tries it immediately. It's like I'm watching a baking competition judge assessing texture and flavor.

Kay hums as she tastes the cake and Constantine brings his finger to his mouth, biting his nail.

"You two are something else," I say. "Kay, stop playing boss dragon when you need shit for free. Constantine, you don't need to be worried. The gig is yours."

"Says who?" Kay straightens her shoulders but hasn't stopped eating the cake.

"Says me." I place a blueberry muffin on the counter and she grabs it, running for the door.

"Love you," she says out the door.

"For the love of rock n' roll, don't tell your dad I gave you a muffin."

"I won't."

"Why do I get the feeling we've both been played?" Constantine asks.

I laugh. "We weren't played. We were Kayed."

"Who is she?"

"Ever heard of Hall of Fame?"

"Yeah, Leo is a super fan."

I walk over to him and put my hand on his shoulder. "You're about to win the Brother of the Century award."

Constantine's eyes widen and the skin beneath them takes on a little color. I didn't know he had freckles. The tiniest, prettiest freckles.

I jump when I hear the door open again and clear my throat. "Yeah...um...Leo will be surprised. You're getting total bro points there."

"Sure." He turns and goes back to the kitchen, leaving me with my embarrassment and the new customer.

What was I thinking touching him? I mean, it was innocent enough, but where was my mind going? If Constantine leaves because of me, I'll never forgive myself. He's by far the best thing that's happened to Bittersweet, and I can't afford to lose him.

CHAPTER 6

CONSTANTINE

I hide in the kitchen the rest of the day. By the time Bittersweet closes, you can't tell anyone's ever baked a single muffin in it because I've scrubbed every surface like I'm competing against Cinderella.

Okay, maybe I'm freaking out a little here. Julius smells nice. Like *really* nice. And he's so tall and big. His arms are like tree trunks and he's…everywhere.

Bittersweet isn't a huge place, and we work well together. Me in the kitchen baking to my heart's content and him in the front making coffee and talking to his customers.

I've seen firsthand how adored he is by everyone in town.

And when he said yes to helping the kid with her fundraiser without even knowing what it was for?

Be still my little heart.

Who can blame me for having a tiny, little, minuscule, barely there crush on my boss?

"Wow, I don't think I've ever seen the kitchen so clean that I could lick the counter," Julius says, taking his apron off.

"Don't." I chuckle.

"You don't have to do everything on your own, you know? I'm happy to clean up. You put in more than enough hours just baking."

I shrug. "It's ingrained in me. Years of military service."

"You were in the military?"

"Michelin-star restaurant kitchen. Same thing."

He smiles and those dimples that make me weak in the knees appear.

"Right, I um...should go up. Leo must be wondering what's for dinner." I hang my apron and turn toward the back door.

"Constantine?"

I turn around. "Yeah?"

"Thank you for volunteering for the fundraiser. You didn't have to do that, but just so you know, I'll help with the cost of the ingredients."

"You don't need to. I'm already planning on using your kitchen. I don't want to abuse your generosity."

"You're not, and I'm glad to work beside you on it."

"Thank you." I feel my cheeks heat again. "It's a cause that...I'm passionate about. I didn't mean to overhear the conversation, but the kitchen door was open."

"Don't worry about that. I'm glad you heard it. It'll be fun doing it together. Kay's dad is the lead singer in Hall of Fame, so I bet the band has been roped in to perform. You said Leo is a fan?"

"He's going to be fucking stoked just to see the band perform."

"I'm sure he'll get to meet them in person too."

He wasn't wrong when he said I'll score all the bro points. I'm going to milk this with Leo for as long as I can.

Don't want to help with the laundry? Who took you to see Hall of Fame?

Room not tidy? Remember meeting Hall of Fame?

"You're making a list, aren't you?" Julius asks, laughing.

"Yup."

"All right, I'll see you in the morning."

"Sure thing, boss."

I climb the stairs to the apartment two steps at a time. Partly running away from the guy who has me all twisted up just by existing and partly to see my little brother. With all the hours I work in the kitchen, we don't hang out as much.

When I get inside, Leo is on the couch staring at the TV with red-rimmed eyes. I close the door and run over to him.

"What happened?"

"What happened is that you told them. You promised, Connie. You promised."

I hold his shaking hands. "What did I tell and to whom?"

"About me. You told the school that I'm HIV positive, and now this holier-than-thou nosy girl is going around the school telling everyone all these facts about HIV/AIDS and organizing some fundraiser thingy."

Ahh, that would do it. I sit next to him.

"Listen to me, Leo. What did I promise you?"

"That you'd always be here for me."

"And that includes not breaking your trust. If I had to inform the school or anyone else, I would tell you first."

His eyes meet mine and he looks so lost it breaks my heart.

"Sweetie, I promise this fundraiser idea has nothing to do with you. It's a coincidence. One of the teachers gave a talk about HIV/AIDS, and it seems to have struck a note with Kay."

He stands all of a sudden. "If you're not involved, how do you know her name?"

"Leo, can you please sit and let me explain?"

"No. Tell me the truth."

Leo starts to calm down as I explain what happened earlier. And then I figure I can cash in the bro credit.

"How would you feel about meeting Hall of Fame?"

His whole body locks in place as he drops onto the couch. "Don't even joke about that."

"You know," I say, dragging it out, "for someone who claims to be a true fan of the band, I'm surprised you didn't recognize Kay."

Leo gasps. "No. Fucking no. I knew her face was familiar."

"I'm sure the AIDS epidemic isn't a new concept for her. As you tell me all the time, the band does a lot of charity work. Maybe you could learn a little from your holier-than-thou friend."

"She's not my friend."

"Maybe she could be?"

He huffs and sits back. "What's for dinner?"

Hmm, interesting. Maybe I'm not the only one with a tiny, little, minuscule, barely there crush on someone.

"How do you feel about pizza?"

CHAPTER 7

JULIUS

I was not ready for Constantine's glued-on jeans and fitted white chef's jacket that highlights his slim frame.

I was not ready for the quality of his cakes and pastries that have caused a continuous line around the block every day for the last month.

I was certainly not ready for the way my belly tightens when I'm around him.

Constantine is a force of nature. He's as passionate about what he does in the kitchen as he is about looking after his brother. More than once, I've seen them bicker about one thing or another until Constantine parents his way to the best solution.

It shouldn't be arousing to hear his don't-mess-with-me or his you'll-do-as-I-say voice, but the moment Constantine took over my kitchen three seconds after we met, I was done for.

"You're thinking a lot over there," my brother-in-law says, holding a couple of beers. I take one as he sits on the chair next to mine.

"No more than usual."

"You sure about that? Kellie called you to throw a ball three times, and when you didn't answer, she went inside to ask Hella if you're sick."

I take a swig of the beer and look up at the sky. It's an uncharacteristically warm day—well, as warm as it can get in the fall in Connecticut—so my sister and brother-in-law invited a few friends over for a barbecue. I close my eyes and take in the warmth of the sun.

"And, naturally, my sister sent you to check on me."

He smiles over the rim of his bottle. "You know what they say, happy wife, happy life."

"I'm not sick, and I'm not overthinking anything."

"Hmm."

"What's that supposed to mean?"

"I didn't suggest you were overthinking anything, simply that you were…thinking hard about something." He leans forward on his chair.

More that what I was thinking about was making me hard.

My sister comes over and sits on her husband's lap with her own beer in hand.

"I think I'm done with this barbecue." I pretend to move to stand up.

Hella laughs, but I see it in her eyes. Her determination and the unrelenting curiosity about my life. "I hear your new helper is causing quite a stir in town."

"He's not my helper. He's a full-fledged pastry chef and too good for this place." I don't know why I voice the worry that's been on my mind since Constantine turned up. Well, the only thing apart from how fucking alluring he is.

"You think he'll move on at some point?" my brother-in-law asks.

"I don't know. His brother goes to the high school, but it's only a matter of time until he gets a better offer. I pay him more than I've ever paid anyone, but it's definitely not what he's worth."

"Sorry, hun. That's a tough situation," Hella says. "He's definitely worshipped in town. I was picking up the bread order for the restaurant from Liv at Lovely Buns and overheard the ladies from Sage's craft group say that Constantine used to be a model. That was a creepy amount of giggling for a group of octogenarians."

I don't know if he's ever modeled, but he certainly has the looks for it. Either way, he's a talented baker, and I don't know what I'll do if he ever decides to move on.

The beer sours in my belly, so I put the bottle down.

"I'll just have to make the most of having him for now. At least the work in my house is finally getting done. Not spending the weekends working on orders or shopping for the week has made a huge difference."

Hella reaches over and squeezes my arm. She doesn't need to speak for me to know what she's not saying. A couple of years ago, our mom was in a bad relationship, and our two younger siblings moved in with me. Running Bittersweet and taking care of two teenagers was hard work. One more reason I really admire Constantine.

After Matty and Jules went to college, Mom moved away with another new boyfriend. Hella still feels guilty that she wasn't able to help out more, but Kellie was still a baby, and I had the space at home.

Hopefully, the cycle of toxic relationships and defining yourself by the person you're with stops with our mother.

"You could always convince him to stay."

I glance at Hella. "What do you mean?"

"Give him a reason to stay."

"I can't pay him more. At least not right now. I'm still paying off the kitchen remodel after the last fire."

"Don't play dumb with me, little brother."

"What you are implying is unethical."

"Only if he's not willing. And the rumors in town…" She trails off, and the hairs on the back of my neck prickle.

"What rumors?"

She looks around to make sure no little ears can hear. "I overheard someone at the grocery store talk about you and Connie like you're together. Like together *together*."

"What? That's insane."

She laughs. "Which part? That you work so well together that people make assumptions or that you don't think you'd be good together?"

I open my mouth, but giving her anything would play into her trap, and I'm too old and wise for it.

Of course I think we'd be good together. Constantine is hard-working, kind, patient, and everything about him does it for me. People talking about us like they know something is up when nothing is up makes me uncomfortable.

"Okay, sis. Good talk, but I need to head back home. I have a sexy date with a paintbrush in my living room."

She grumbles but puts together a box with leftovers and lets me head home without further prying.

I stroll back, enjoying the nice weather. And because I don't have to go to Bittersweet like I usually do, I go through the park.

A dark denim jacket catches my attention. The person wearing it is on a bench, hunched over and staring at the ground in front of him.

My sister's words still play in my head, but it's my gut feeling that makes me change direction because Constantine looks…lost.

"Hey," I say, approaching.

"Oh, hi." He smiles, but it doesn't reach his eyes like when he's pulling something out of the oven or impatiently waiting for me to taste something he made.

"Enjoying the weather?"

He shivers at the same time as he says yeah, and then he chuckles. "It's freakin' cold."

"It wouldn't be if you had a coat on."

"Thanks, Dad. I'll make sure to buy one soon."

The way he says it makes the stone rolling around the pit of my stomach sink a little. Does he think he won't need one because he's not staying in Stillwater?

He never specifically said he was here to stay. Then again, he also didn't say this was a temporary gig for him.

"Hey, do you want to come to my place for a coffee?" The words are out of my mouth before I have time to overthink them. It's only coffee.

"Sure."

I'm not looking to discover his life plans. He'll tell me when he wants to. And I'm definitely not wondering about what could happen if I had the chance to let my touch linger a little longer because that's not what I'm doing.

Hella's voice is in my head calling me a big, fat, Greek liar, but I ignore it.

"Advance warning. My house is practically a building site, but since you're responsible for the advance on the work in my living room, I figure you should see it."

He laughs. "I'm not sure what I've done to deserve the credit, but I'll take it."

My house has been feeling more like a home recently. Maybe because I'm there a lot more than I used to be.

The kitchen is complete. It was what sold me on the house, and apart from new paint on the walls to cover up the old green, it didn't need any updates.

I pull out my French press and fill the kettle with water. The kettle was a gift from my sister when she traveled around Europe before opening her restaurant. To this day, I still don't get why everyone doesn't have one in their kitchen.

While the coffee brews, I show Constantine the house and tell him a little bit about my plans.

"I love your house. It's going to look amazing when it's finished," he says.

I pour the coffee into two mugs and give one to Constantine.

He's still wearing his jacket, so on our way to the living room, I turn up the heat.

"This is delicious coffee, Julius."

"Thanks. It's my own mix. A little stronger than what I have at Bittersweet, but I love it."

We drink the coffee in silence for a bit, and I notice Constantine becoming pensive. His gaze is on a photo I have on the wall where a TV would likely be.

It's Hella somewhere in Europe, smiling with her eyes closed as she tastes some food. The black-and-white photo was taken by her boyfriend at the time, and I love it because, to me, it represents freedom, love, abandon. After her travels, Hella came back and opened the restaurant. She found a home where home always was because she'd been set free when she needed to go.

I stare at Constantine, craving to know more about him. "You said you don't know what you did to deserve credit. You showed up, Constantine. You are here."

He smiles, his eyes still on the photo. "Sometimes I wonder if it was a good idea."

"You regret it?"

"I don't regret moving or working with you. I just...it's complicated."

With my willpower waning to nothing, I reach over and place my hand on the back of his neck, caressing his skin. "You can talk to me."

He turns his head slowly until his eyes are locked on mine.

"Julius." His voice is throaty and...needy?

He takes my empty coffee mug and places both on the coffee table. Before my brain registers what's happening, Constantine straddles my legs and leans his forehead against mine. His breath is warm and smells of my favorite coffee when he says, "What if I don't want to talk?"

CHAPTER 8

CONSTANTINE

Julius releases a throaty sound like he's trying and failing to contain all the energy inside his big body.

I must be on the verge of insanity because I need him to let go. To let it all go on me.

"What are you asking?" he says.

"I need to be Connie for just a bit. And I know this crosses all kinds of lines. I don't want to lose my job, and I don't want to mess with the friendship we're building."

Julius places his big hands on my thighs. "And still, here you are."

"I'm starting to think I didn't have much choice in that either." Because it was a foregone conclusion that I'd end up here one way or another, no matter how much I fought it.

"Are you saying I'm irresistible?" His lips curl up, and I give up resisting his dimples. I lean over and run my tongue over his cheek. My name is a breathy moan from his lips, giving me the encouragement I need to taste more of his skin.

"Irresistible, alluring, magnetic. You are all those things." I run my hands up his arms. "You're so strong. These should be illegal. Every time I see you at—"

"Right now, we're just Constantine and Julius. Nothing more."

The man speaks my language.

I pull away enough to make eye contact, and when I do, I see exactly what I need. I feel it too. Even if Julius seems to be trying to hide it, there's no way the giant bulge under me could go unnoticed.

Will things get that far? I don't know, but—

Julius cuts through my thoughts with a claiming kiss that takes my breath away. When I open my mouth, his tongue is there. Warm, wet, exploring. I lean into the kiss as my brain shuts down and I find the relief I've been craving.

He tastes like coffee and smells like pumpkin spice. I want to rub myself all over him and transfer it to my skin.

"Julius." I don't even recognize my voice. I want to ask for more, but my brain is at war. It wants to fully shut down and enjoy this moment, but it also keeps reminding me why this is a bad idea.

I shouldn't get involved with Julius for all the reasons, and I don't even want to consider what it'll do to my heart. That part of me has been neglected for so long that I can't trust its judgment anymore.

My whole body vibrates with need, and I press my hips against his. We're both so hard. He growls against my mouth and flips us.

My back lands on the couch, and I completely check out when I find myself surrounded by Julius. He's heavy and all-encompassing. I can't move, which should make me want to run, but instead, I open my legs to give him more room.

"You smell so good, Constantine. I want to lick every inch of your skin."

"Yes…"

He takes my hands and pins them above my head. His face is buried in the crook of my neck and his cock rubs against mine. My eyes roll to the back of my head. I'm so close, yet we're still fully dressed and it's not enough. I need skin.

"Julius, please. I need…"

"What do you need, Constantine?"

"I can't think with you doing that. Fuck."

"Should I stop?" He chuckles, dragging my lower lip between his teeth.

"No! Don't stop. I need to come before I lose my mind."

"That ship has sailed, baby."

I moan at the term of endearment. He's just going with the flow. Too far gone to think.

"Touch me, Julius. Take our cocks out and rub them together. I want to feel your soft skin and hard dick against mine. I want... want..."

With one hand still holding mine, the other roams down my body. I groan at the sudden absence of his weight, but when he cups my erection through my jeans, my whole body shakes.

"More."

He struggles with the button on my jeans. "Fuck, Constantine. Why are your jeans so fucking tight?"

"Don't tell me you haven't checked out my ass at work."

He growls.

"That's why." I move my hands, he releases them, and I quickly undo my jeans and push them and my underwear down. At the same time, I go for Julius's.

"I don't know why, but I didn't think you were a black boxer shorts kind of guy," he says, his hand hovering over my stomach and making its way down too slowly.

"I'm not, but there isn't a whole lot of privacy when you live with a teenager."

He claims my mouth again and wraps his hands around both our cocks before letting his weight settle on top of me again.

My brain completely checks out. Between the grip of his hand, the feel of our cocks rubbing together, his rock-hard body on mine, and the way he claims my mouth, I don't even know what my name is anymore.

"Tell me I can see them one day," he rasps, and my brain struggles to remember what he's talking about.

"Make me come, and I'll promise anything you want."

His hand moves between us furiously. The tell-tale sign of an impending orgasm builds from my balls, spreading through my body, leaving me with tingles of pleasure.

This is going to be a good one. I try to stave it off because I'm scared of how good it'll be. What if no other orgasm matches this one? What if this is the only one I'll ever have with Julius?

"I can't be doing a good job if I can't get you to let go, Constantine."

"Say my name."

"Constantine."

"No...Conn—"

"Your name is Constantine. I don't care what other people call you. To me, you're Constantine. Beautiful, strong, capable. Constantine."

"Say it again."

"Constantine. Constantine."

I hold on to his arms, and with my name coming from his lips, I let go. My release coats my stomach and our cocks.

The high lasts longer than it ever has, but I have enough presence of mind to open my eyes and watch as Julius's big body locks up and he comes all over me.

He's so beautiful and gentle. Maybe that's why I like him. He's strong but caring.

We exchange small kisses as we catch our breath, surrounded by the smell of sweat and sex.

I'm terrified of what happens next, but the regret I thought would hit must have escaped through the cracks in my heart because I can't find it.

As I lie on the couch, boneless and sated, while Julius grabs a cloth to clean me up, one thought intrudes my mind.

He did it. He made me feel like myself again.

CHAPTER 9

JULIUS

"Hey, I have a desperate single mom who needs birthday cupcakes for her son to take to school tomorrow."

Constantine looks up from the cake he's decorating with buttercream flowers.

"Sure thing, boss. Might have to stay here late." His lips curl up in a teasing smile. "You know, after hours. All on my own. Unsupervised."

I close the kitchen door and go around the island to stand behind him. A tiny moan leaves his lips when I press my growing erection against his ass.

"I'm not sure you can be trusted on your own," I breathe onto his neck, and he shivers. "My kitchen does have a history of setting itself on fire."

"I guess you better stay with me then. To supervise."

I press a kiss to the back of his neck. "I guess I will."

Yeah, pretending that what happened in my living room was merely between Julius and Constantine and wouldn't affect our work together lasted all of twelve hours.

After seeing his face as he came, the bliss in his eyes, the way he gave himself to me? I'm only fucking human, and Constantine is the first man in a long time that's made me feel like I could lose myself to someone else.

Hella's always said to throw caution to the wind once in a while and let life happen before I wake up one morning and find myself old and alone.

"You should tell your customer we can work on the order before she thinks you're ignoring her. She can pick it up tomorrow when we open," he says with a chuckle, and that's when I realize I haven't moved.

"You smell nice." Like cake batter and citrus.

"So do you, but I can work with a boner. Your anaconda is harder to hide under that thin apron."

"Constantine…" I sigh. I'm so hopelessly in lust with him.

It's been five days since our living room sex, and apart from stolen kisses and a blowjob where he sucked my brains out through my dick a couple of days ago, we haven't done anything.

Bittersweet is busier than ever, and Constantine's focus is on work and Leo. I don't blame him for that. It's what I really like about him.

I just wish…for things I have no business wishing for. Constantine hasn't expressed any desire to discuss what's happening between us, so I won't be the clingy one demanding answers.

I can do casual. Isn't that what I've been doing for years?

Then why does casual feel like a bitter word when it comes to Constantine?

I'm confirming the order with the customer when Fletcher comes in.

"Hey, Julius."

"Hey. Give me a second, and I'll be with you."

"No problem. Okay if I check in with Connie?"

"Sure."

When the customer leaves, I clean the counters and rearrange the baked goods display to keep distracted from wanting to be a fly on the kitchen wall.

Fletcher isn't shy about sticking his nose in everyone's business, and he can sniff out a hookup from a mile away.

When he comes out of the kitchen, he's wearing a suspicious smile.

"Can I get you a coffee?" I ask, straightening the pile of to-go cups.

"That's really generous of you."

"I'm a generous kind of guy."

"So I hear."

Shit.

"As they say, don't believe everything you hear."

His piercing blue eyes and long blond hair make Fletcher one of the most attractive men I know. He knows it too and uses it to his advantage. Shame my eyes and dick are tuned only to his friend's personal frequency. Not to mention, Fletcher is happily married.

"Dammit. You're not budging either. I could swear you and Connie are hooking up. And if you're not, you should be."

I snort. "Glad to have your approval."

"You're welcome. Now, can I please take two bribes with extra sprinkles to go?"

"Peanut butter and chocolate?"

"Yup."

"You got it. What is it this time?" I ask, my curiosity peeked.

"We need to convince George and Megan to stay with my parents for a weekend next month so I can take Harrison away."

I laugh. "How does Harrison feel about your underhanded tactics?"

"It was his idea. We really want to spend a weekend at the lake cabin. No clothes. No treasure hunts. No arguments about bedtime. Just us."

I put a lid on his coffee and hand over the box with the two cupcakes, extra sprinkles for Megan. "I hope it works."

After Fletcher leaves, we have a quiet moment in the coffee shop, so I grab my laptop and reconcile some invoices. Something I used to do at home over the weekend, but since I don't have to spend all my free time in the kitchen, I'm getting better at managing the business.

"I didn't tell him."

I glance at the open kitchen door where Constantine stands with his hands in the pockets of his jeans that I know for a fact don't have enough room to make them usable, but somehow, he still manages.

"I know."

"I figured you wouldn't want people to know."

I cross the space between us until I'm close enough that he can hear me but far away enough that anyone walking inside Bittersweet won't be able to tell we're having this kind of conversation.

"That's not true. I don't want people to know until we've had a chance to talk about it and decide if this"—I point at him and me—"is something we want to tell people about."

He lets out a breath. "I don't know if I can make you promises."

"I wouldn't ask you for them. All I want—"

The door opening stops the conversation and Constantine smiles when he sees Leo coming in from school.

"Hey, Mini Constantine," I tease, and he rolls his eyes. "How's school."

"It's fine."

"Do you want something to eat?"

"Nah. I'll grab something upstairs."

Constantine narrows his eyes, giving Leo an assessing look.

"Gee, stop it with the parental. I'm just stressed because I have a test to study for and I missed a few classes. It'll be okay, but I have to go up and study," Leo says.

Constantine squeezes his elbow. "I'll be up later because we got a last-minute order, so you have extra quiet time. I'll make you pasta for dinner."

"With peas?"

Constantine laughs. "No, dude. That's a sin. I'll make you proper pasta like the Italians eat. You can get the peas on the side."

"Fine." Leo walks past us through the kitchen door to the back.

"You seriously denying a kid his veggies when he specifically asked for them?"

Constantine stares at me with wide eyes. "It's. A. Sin. And I don't want to get my chef credentials revoked because I served my kid pasta with nothing but butter and peas, which is what he'd have if he had his way."

Before I can stop myself, I bring my hand to his face. "You're a really good dad, you know that?"

"I have no idea what I'm doing, Julius. I wasn't there for most of his life, and then our mom practically abandoned him just as he"—he shakes his head—"never mind. I never planned for kids, but he's my baby brother, and I'll do anything for him."

"I know." And because I'm a sucker for punishment, I brush my lips against his, breaking the kiss way too soon for my liking, but with our conversation interrupted, I don't want anyone to catch us. It's bad enough that my sister keeps sending me messages asking about Constantine and if I've made my move yet.

CHAPTER 10

CONSTANTINE

The community center is buzzing with this energy that's making the hairs on my neck stand up. It's electric, all due to the force of nature that is Kay Nielsson.

"Doors are opening in five minutes. You guys ready?" she asks, tapping a pen on the clipboard she's holding.

We both nod, and I'm a little frightened as she inspects the baked goods display on the table.

"When did she start wearing glasses?" Julius asks when she walks away.

"Beats me. You've known her longer, but I swear she didn't have them earlier."

A loud whistle gets our attention. Kay is on the stage looking more confident than I've ever seen a person her age.

"Hi, everyone. Thank you so much for helping me and my class with this project. Ryan White was a kid, just like us, who only wanted to go to school. His courage and perseverance have inspired many people since he was diagnosed with HIV, and even after his death, his program continues to help others. Let's be a little like Ryan today and do some good for those living with HIV. In the words of my dad, let's rock and roll this place down!"

The band comes onto the stage, playing the first chords of a song. The lead singer gives Kay a kiss as she steps down from the stage.

"I swear kids these days are so much more put together than in my time," I say to Julius.

"Hell yeah. I was more concerned with the three pubes I called a mustache than trying to help others."

I smile, trying to picture Julius as a teenager with a baby face, with those cute dimples and barely there facial hair. "I may need to see photos."

"Never."

We don't have a chance to chat much longer because as people enter the hall, kids go to the front to dance and parents hang back, grabbing a free cup of coffee and a baked good in exchange for a donation to the Ryan White Program.

I'm serving someone a slice of my almond and apple cake when Leo walks into the hall.

"Look who's here," Julius says, leaning closer so I can hear.

I nod without taking my eyes off Leo. Julius takes over and hands out the cake and a coffee to the lady waiting. Leo walks toward the crowd and talks to another kid. My heart tightens when I see him smiling and dancing with the other kids.

He's wearing his Hall of Fame T-shirt, and my next thought is that he walked here from the apartment without a coat on, even as my brain sees the rest.

He could get sick.

He made friends.

He could get sick.

He's having fun.

"I'm sorry, Julius. I need a moment. I'll be right back."

I practically run toward the closest door. It leads to a hallway that runs along the side of the building, where there are a couple of offices and meeting rooms.

One of the rooms has the door open so I go inside, not bothering to turn the light on. My hands are shaking as I struggle to pull air into my lungs, and I feel stupid for running out on Julius.

"Constantine?"

"I'm here." I should have known he'd come for me. How do I explain it to him?

He comes into the room, and before I overthink it, I run into his arms. "I'm sorry. I didn't mean to leave you hanging out there. I just need a minute."

"What happened? Is it about Leo?"

He runs his hands over my back, soothing me. It fucking works, and I'm not sure if I hate or love him for it.

Love?

My panic shifts from Leo to Julius.

"Hey. Hey. What's going on?"

I look up at him, and even in the relative darkness of the room, I can see his face. We've spent so much time together that I could draw it without trying that hard, and I'm shit at drawing. But I know all his expressions, the worry lines, the depth of his dimples, depending on what's making him smile or laugh.

"I need to tell you something, but…"

"Constantine, I need you to know that—"

"What's your problem?" Kay's voice sounds right outside the room.

"My problem is you."

Leo?

I move to go outside, but Julius holds me tight. "Shh. Let them talk it out."

He's right. I know he is, but my overwhelming feeling is to help and protect Leo.

"What have I done?" Kay asks.

"You think you know everything," Leo snaps. "But you don't know anything. You don't know what it's like."

"I did my research, thank you very much. I grew up with men who lost friends to HIV. I heard the stories. Wait—what do you mean I don't know what it's like?"

Leo doesn't reply, and the silence breaks my heart.

"I'm…the reason I'm so angry at you is…is…"

I try to move again, but Julius's grip on me is strong. Tears start running down my face. "Baby."

"I can't let him do this alone, Julius," I whisper back.

"Do what?"

When Leo's voice returns it's so small it's barely audible.

"I'm HIV positive."

I expect to hear two gasps, but there's only one, and it's not from the man holding me like I'm the most precious thing.

"I'm really sorry, Leo."

I hear a thud. "What are you doing?" Leo squeaks.

"Hugging you, dumbass. What did you think? I would push you away or be mean? I've organized a whole freakin' fundraiser to help people like you. I don't know what it's like, Leo, but I'd like to know. I'd like to be your friend."

"You're not scared?"

"I'm scared of many things, but not of you."

"I'm undetectable," Leo says.

"That's great, and for your health, that makes me really happy. But for me, it doesn't matter."

"I'm sorry I was mean and rude to you."

"Why?" Kay asks.

I can almost imagine Leo's usual shrug as he finds his words.

"Because I thought I would get found out. That people wouldn't stop talking about it, and eventually, they'd figure out I have it. I've never told anyone."

"And you never have to unless you really want to. Want to go dance?"

"Okay."

"Cool. I'll introduce you to the band later."

"Really?"

"Yeah, Dad has this stupid rule that he wants to meet all my friends. He gives them this lecture about not being scared of me or some crap."

Leo's laughter pulls a sob out of me.

"I'm not scared of you," Leo says.

"You should be. I'm freakin' crazy."

"You're also pretty awesome."

The following sound is of the hallway door closing.

"Oh my god." My knees buckle, and I almost fall down, but Julius catches me, pulling out a nearby chair and sitting on it, dragging me onto his lap.

"You wanted to tell me," he says.

"I couldn't. Leo made me promise."

"Your loyalty is one of the things I love the most about you."

I rest my head on Julius's shoulder. "What else do you like about me?"

"It's a long list. Might take me a long time to read it all out."

I hold Julius's head between my hands and pull him in for a kiss.

"Don't start what you can't finish, Galanis. We still have plenty of coffee and cake to give out," Julius says.

I stand and hold out my hand. He takes it, and we leave the room.

As much as I want to check in with Leo, I need to decide whether to tell him I overheard the conversation or wait to see if he tells me.

An hour and a half later, Julius and I pack up the empty trays and clean the coffee maker. I don't know how much money we raised, but the tin where people placed their donations is heavy as we hand it over to one of the organizers working with Kay.

"Hey, Connie?"

I school my expression before turning to Leo.

"Hey. Having fun?"

"Yeah. Um…can I sleep over at a friend's place?"

I bite my tongue. "Sure. Who is it?"

His cheeks go a little pink. "Kay. She's, um…my friend, and I'm going to meet the band."

"I'm not sure… I should meet her dad properly first."

He rolls his eyes. "Kay told me she's lesbian and their place has like a gazillion bedrooms. That good enough for you, *Dad*?"

"Okay. If you promise to call me if you need anything."

"I will."

"And please take my jacket with you. It's on the hook in the hallway. You're hot now, but I don't want you catching a cold when you go outside."

"Yeah, sorry. I was really excited to see the band, I didn't know what to wear, and then I was running late. I ran here and forgot my coat."

I ruffle his hair.

"Connie."

"Love you too, bud. Have fun."

He runs over to where his friends are all together.

I go back to Julius. "Hey, I have a little problem. I was wondering if you could help me out."

"Sure."

"My schedule has cleared out for tonight, so I was wondering if—"

"Fuck yeah."

I laugh at the way he takes a step forward like he wants to touch me but is holding back.

"Glad we're on the same page because I neither have a warm coat to go home with nor the willpower to stay away from you."

"We can come back tomorrow to clean up the rest." Julius drags me by my hand, only stopping by the coat stand to grab his and put it over my shoulders.

I slide my arms through the sleeves, drowning in the coat.

"Fuck, you look really cute like that," he says, pulling me closer.

"Like what?"

"Like you belong to me."

"How possessive of you. I kinda like it."

"Good. Let's go so I can show you how possessive I can be."

CHAPTER 11

JULIUS

Even though I dragged Constantine out of the center ruled by my dick, during the drive to my place, my brain is in overdrive.

It's not a long drive so we don't say much, and it's clear from Constantine's silence as he follows me inside that we need to talk.

"Do you want to take a shower with me?" I ask.

He toes his shoes off by the door and hangs my coat. "I get to see you naked and wet? Yes, please."

His teasing tone doesn't quite hit the right note. I'm not sure if his sudden change of mood is because of the emotions he's going through after witnessing Leo and Kay's conversation, because I overheard it, or if he's afraid it will scare me off.

I may have to wait until we're both naked and he's talking before I can reassure him, but I'm determined to do that. I knew from the moment I met Constantine that he was special, but the stolen kisses, the flirting, the working together?

Falling for him was as inevitable as cinnamon and apple or peaches and cream.

"Come on, let's go upstairs." I take his hand and don't stop until we're through my bedroom and in the attached bathroom.

Constantine removes his shirt and throws it on the floor. His chest is covered in tattoos.

"Fuck, Constantine. You…" I shake my head, my tongue too big in my mouth to generate any words. I trace them slowly, loving as his breathing changes under my touch. The outline of his cock makes my mouth water, so I drop to my knees and help him out of the rest of his clothes.

I look up and see him watching me.

"Like what you see?" he asks.

I stand and get rid of my clothes. My hard cock answers his question for me.

"You're so big."

I laugh. "What can I say? I'm perfectly proportional."

"That you are." He licks his lips and bends over, taking the head of my cock into his mouth.

"Oh fuck, fuck, Constantine. Give a guy a warning."

He sucks my resolve to take things slow and to talk first out through my dick, so I pull him up and turn the water on. It's still warming up when I drag us both into the shower and push him against the tiles.

"Tell me you want me inside you because I need you so fucking much," I growl against his neck, sucking his wet skin. He still smells like his cologne and cake batter, a mix I feel was made only for me because, with just one lick of his skin, I want more. I want every little inch of Constantine.

He gives my cock a good long stroke that makes my eyes roll back. "I've been dreaming of being railed by you since that first time, and I barely even saw it. Now I'm just wondering how long you want to drag this shower out before you can take me to bed."

With great difficulty—because I'm only human and Constantine has skills—I grab his hand and bring it to my lips. "I want to lose myself in your body more than I've ever wanted anything, Constantine. But I want you to be there with me. If we do this, I need to know you're not using me to hide from anything."

He runs his hands over my chest, stopping at the tattoo I have over my heart. A word cloud of the names of everyone in my family.

"I'm sorry I made you feel like that." His eyes meet mine. "I've never felt this way about anyone."

"How do you feel?"

"Like everything is so heavy, but one look at your smile, and it all evaporates."

I swallow dry, tracing his jaw with my thumb.

"My mom was always a little wild. She looked after me, but she didn't care if I went to school or got good grades. She wanted a friend, not a son." He releases a choked laugh. "When I was in elementary school, I was jealous of my friends who got in trouble with their parents and couldn't come out to play. Sometimes, I'd go to my friends' houses, and when their moms said they were grounded, I asked if I could stay anyway."

"You wanted to experience boundaries."

He nods. "That's where I got my love for cooking and baking. My friends' parents would make dinner and tell me all about it. Eventually, I started helping and wanting to know more about it. As soon as I was old enough to go to culinary school on a scholarship, I left. Leo was a baby, and by then, the next-door neighbor was his regular babysitter, so I didn't think he wouldn't be looked after."

Constantine pauses, so I run the water over us to get rid of the soap and turn it off.

"Come on, let's finish this in bed."

"No. I want to do it here because once we're out there, I want to be with you. No ghosts of the past or responsibilities."

"Okay. Let me at least wrap you in a warm towel."

He chuckles. "Thanks. So, while I was gone, I kept in touch. I sent money I saved from working in restaurant kitchens and made sure she was taking care of Leo. My goal was to make a name for myself and then get Leo to come live with me. Out of the blue, my mom disappeared with Leo. No one knew where they were. I was in Europe at the time and came back. Moved all over the country taking temporary cooking jobs while I looked for them. When I found them, they were back in LA. Leo barely remembered me and couldn't tell me where they'd been. I stayed close to them until there was an opportunity to work at a Michelin-star restaurant in London. Mom didn't want Leo to come with me, so he stayed. I returned when Leo called me saying Mom had decided to move to Florida without him."

"Fuck, Constantine. That must have been so hard for you."

"No. I love my brother."

"I know that. But you also loved your job, and it couldn't have been easy giving up your dream because of your flaky mother. Sorry."

He chuckles. "You're right. She's flaky but not a bad person. She probably shouldn't have had kids, that's all."

"I'm glad she had you. And Leo. I've become quite attached to both of you." I wrap the fluffy towel around him like a burrito and hold him tight.

He sighs. "Let me finish this so we can get naked…more naked."

"Okay, go on."

"After Mom left, Leo got sick. The doctors couldn't figure out what was wrong until they did some tests and discovered he was HIV positive. That was a year ago. The doctors don't know how he got it. There's no indication that he was ever exposed to anyone with HIV, but he did have a blood transfusion when they were in a car accident when he was ten."

"Medical negligence?"

He shrugs. "Who knows. I was really angry in the beginning. Angry with my mom, the system, anything. Until I figured the best thing I could do was be there for Leo."

"So when I was pestering you to come save my coffee shop, you were busy saving your brother instead."

"Yeah. Sorry."

I smile and kiss his head. "Nothing to be sorry for. What's his status?"

"Undetectable. His current meds are working. It's everything else that's been really hard. He's a kid, Julius. He struggles with it, and I struggle because I can't take it away from him." He pauses. "When I saw him dancing with his friends tonight…it was the first time I've seen him have fun. I caught a glimpse of the person I want him to be—HIV or no HIV."

"That night downstairs, I caught a glimpse of you, Constantine. I've been addicted to it ever since. I want more of it. I want to help you carry that load and be there for Leo."

"Can we start with a good dicking? Because I'm so ready for that."

I pick him up in a fireman's lift and carry him to my bed.

"Talk time is over."

CHAPTER 12

CONSTANTINE

"Thank fuck."

I'm glad I opened up to Julius. He makes me feel safe and capable, like I'm doing a good job. Most of all, he makes me feel wanted, and being wrapped in a fluffy towel with his big arms around me has my heart doing all kinds of dances. Not to mention my dick. He's more than ready for some fun.

Julius pulls out the drawer in his side table and grabs a bottle of lube and a couple of condoms. I give my cock a couple of long strokes to take the edge off.

"God, you're so beautiful, Constantine."

"I'm skinny and long. You're the gorgeous one. I could lick those arms, and the thought of riding you and painting your abs with my cum…" I bite my lip.

"Keep talking like that and it'll be me painting you with my cum in about three seconds."

"Then I guess you better hurry up and get me ready for you." I pull my knees up and hold them with my hands. With anyone else, I'd feel exposed and vulnerable. With Julius, I want to show off and make it very clear I'm all his.

"Christ, Constantine."

Julius runs his hand over his face, looking exasperated. What? A guy isn't supposed to show what he wants? And from the way his cock is standing at attention, all purple and hard, I'd say it's very much on board with my plan.

"Are you going to fuck me or what?"

Julius's eyes meet mine and those two dimples I love so much appear.

"All in good time, baby." He ignores the lube and the condoms and falls face-first onto my ass.

I squirm as he kisses my hole like it's a competition he has to win. Sweat beads on my forehead. "At this rate, I'm not going to last, and I want to come with you inside me."

He doesn't reply or stop licking me, but the sound of the lube cap gives me a measure of relief.

It's short-lived because, damn, the man can do things with his fingers. He stretches me slowly, teasing my prostate whenever my cock starts to wane, making it rock hard again.

"Julius," I gasp. "I'm ready. So fucking ready."

He crawls up my body and kisses me. "You're ready when I say you're ready."

"Am I ready?"

He chuckles. "You so fucking are. Your beautiful hole was made for my cock, and I'm going to show you."

He pulls back just enough to roll the condom down his length, and then it's there, pressing against me, seeking entrance.

"Fuck. Fuck. Julius."

"It's okay, baby. I'll go slow."

"No, don't. I need this."

His eyes search mine. I don't know what he's looking for, but doubt isn't something he's going to find. I dig my heels into his butt and push him against me.

I hiss as his cock passes through the outer rim.

"Constantine!"

"You were taking too long."

"I don't want to fucking hurt you."

I reach up to his face and touch his cheek. "You won't. Like you said, I was made for you."

He pushes in, and I take a deep breath to adjust.

Inch by inch, Julius bottoms out, and he is right. I was made for him. I feel so full, and there's this tingling under my skin, traveling all over my body.

"I need you to move, Julius."

"Baby, give me a sec."

His breathing is labored and his eyes are closed tight. When he opens them, it's like I'm staring into the man I'm meant to be with for the rest of my life. It takes my breath away and tears build at the backs of my eyes.

I pull him closer because I don't want him to see me cry if those stupid tears come out without permission.

"Constantine, I…"

"I know, baby. Show me."

He pulls back slowly, making me gasp when he pushes back in. I've bottomed plenty of times, but it's never been like this.

My ass burns so good. It's never been this stretched. My cock is rock hard and leaking all over my stomach.

"God, you feel so good, Constantine. So warm. Tight. Perfect. I can't hold out much longer. I'm sorry."

"Don't. I need this. Need you. We have until the morning to do everything else."

He grunts against my neck, and I feel the pull of the skin beneath his lips. I won't be able to hide that one because it's too high up.

"You're playing with fire, Julius."

"I'm not playing, baby. I'm ready to get burned."

"Don't joke, Julius. My heart can't take it." And my brain is too far gone for this conversation when every time his dick brushes against my prostate, I feel like I'm soaring above the clouds.

"Let me take care of you, Constantine."

Words become superfluous as we both moan and grunt our way

toward orgasms, and as if he can read me like a recipe he created himself, Julius wraps his hand around my cock.

I fuck into his hand as he fucks into me until he spills his release into the condom. My orgasm follows, and I cry out his name.

I'm boneless and sated. My brain is switched off and don't ask me what day it is. All I know is that when Julius leaves my body, I feel the absence in my bones. When he returns with a damp cloth to clean me, I realize I would do this again and again with him.

And when he pulls the bed covers over us and curls up around me, I know that I'm in love and the decision to stay in Stillwater permanently is no longer mine. My heart has decided it now belongs to this loyal gentle giant of a man with sexy dimples and a big dick.

Sleep takes me under and I'm dead to the world until light shines through the window. The weight I fell asleep under is still on me. Safe and warm.

I smile as I feel his cock pushing against my leg, which makes my dick react.

"Feels like a good morning for both of us," he mumbles, still half-asleep. "How do you feel?"

"Like I was railed by a monster dick."

He snorts.

"So, no butt stuff this morning. Got it."

"Hey." I punch his shoulder. "No need to get all extreme like that. Some butt stuff is allowed."

He moves so he's on top of me and claims my mouth. My sleepy brain struggles to catch up, but my dick is wide awake and ready to play with his.

"You like some butt stuff, huh?" Julius asks.

"Let's just say that if you ever want me to spread out so you can eat dinner off my ass, just tell me where and when, and I'll be there."

"I'll take you up on that, but for now…"

Julius presses me into the mattress. There's no space between us, and we rut against each other until we both come.

We make out until our drying cum becomes uncomfortable.

"How about breakfast?" he asks.

"Sounds perfect. Mind if I have a shower first?"

"Sure. Let me clean up, and I'll get started on coffee."

I get up and look for my clothes. I'm pretty sure my phone is still in my jeans pocket on the bathroom floor.

Julius gives me an appreciative once-over, so I make a show of it by sticking my ass up while I look for the phone.

There's a message from Leo on the screen, so I unlock it.

Leo: You're not home.

Me: Sorry, bud. I got caught up with something. I'll be home in thirty minutes.

Leo: Hurry up. We need to talk.

"Shit."

"Everything okay?"

"Not sure. I need to get home."

"Okay. I'll make your coffee to go." Julius gives me a lingering kiss, and then I get in the shower, wondering how my dick is already ready to rally. He's going to be disappointed.

A moment later, another ding comes from my phone. I see Julius in the bedroom, so I call him.

"Hey, can you check my phone? Something's up with Leo, and I'm worried."

"Sure."

I can't see him properly because of the steam from the shower, but it takes him a moment to say something. It feels like a lifetime in which all the bad things happen in my head. I clear the glass in time to see him look up.

"It's not Leo."

He turns and leaves the bathroom.

That was weird.

I rush through my shower and check the phone as soon as I'm out. I don't recognize the number.

Hey Constantine, this is Piper from Nobu again. The restaurant manager has just returned from maternity leave and is keen on meeting you. I can set up a meeting for next week. Let me know.

I dry off, get dressed, and go downstairs to the kitchen. Julius looks way too good for someone in sweatpants and a T-shirt. He's holding a travel cup of coffee in his hand.

"Here. I'd make you breakfast, but you probably want to get back to Leo."

"Yeah. I'll call you later?"

"Sure."

The space between us suddenly feels too big. I go over and kiss him. It feels wrong, and I don't like it. But he's right. I need to check in on Leo. I should have been home before him, but I didn't think he'd be back so early.

CHAPTER 13

CONSTANTINE

When I get home, Leo is on the couch. He doesn't look upset, and when I look for signs that he's been crying, I see none.

"Hey. How was your sleepover?"

"How was yours?" He laughs.

"I didn't—"

He holds his hand up. "Don't even try. You're wearing last night's clothes. Did you spend the night with Julius?"

I open my mouth and close it again. I'm not ready for this conversation. We didn't talk this morning because I rushed home for Leo, and now I'm getting the third degree.

"It's not your business."

Leo narrows his eyes. "It kinda is because if you break up, not only will we have to move out, but I like Julius, and I like Stillwater."

"What are you talking about?"

"I want to stay here."

"What makes you think we're moving? We just got here."

His face goes all red, and he shifts his gaze away.

"I deleted a message from your phone."

"You did what?"

He huffs. "I know you applied for that job at the fancy restaurant in LA."

I sit next to him. "I did."

"The other day, when you were in the shower, you got a message from them. I panicked and deleted the message."

"How do you even know my passcode?"

He rolls his eyes. "It wasn't hard to guess. It's my birthday."

Great. And now I feel old.

"Okay. Time to change my passcode. Why did you delete the message?"

"Because I don't want to go. I've made friends here."

"Would one of these friends be Kay, by any chance?"

He shrugs. "She's nice."

I don't press the Kay topic because he'll tell me when he's ready. He always does.

"I told Kay about me."

"Oh yeah? And how did she take it?" I ask, pretending I didn't hear the whole conversation. Somehow, I don't think it would go down well, even though it was unintentional.

"She hugged me."

"Wow, that must have taken you by surprise."

"Yeah. You were right. The people who matter won't care. Kay and my other friends are pretty well educated on HIV, thanks to the charity project. I'm not ready to tell everyone, but I'm really happy I have a friend who knows."

I reach out and squeeze his shoulder.

"I'm really happy for you, bud. And if you need any kind of reassurance, we're not moving anywhere."

"Serious?"

"Of course. I love it here. I like baking for Bittersweet, and Stillwater is a pretty nice place."

"And how about Julius?"

I raise my brow.

"Come on. Don't treat me like I'm a kid. Last week, I know I walked in just after you'd been kissing."

"How do you know?"

"Because your face was all red like you were running a marathon and you wouldn't look at me. Plus, all your answers were one word."

Yeah, I remember that. I'd thought it was a close call, but we were caught anyway.

"Okay, so how would you feel if Julius and I were dating?"

"If you're serious about him, then I don't care. I'm happy for you. You've already given up so much for me. I don't want you to think you have to stay single forever."

I pull him into my arms and squeeze him tight.

"Dude. My hair!"

I laugh, and for the first time since I found out about his diagnosis, I feel he's going to be okay. We're going to be okay. Yeah, our lives will always be different, but we have all the important people around us.

"Shit. The message." I pull out my phone and touch the screen. The message from Piper flashes right in the center, which means Julius saw it.

"What's wrong?"

"I ran out on Julius after you sent your message. When my phone dinged again, I thought it was you and asked him to check it."

"He's going to think you're leaving."

"Yeah."

"You have to fix it, Connie."

"I will."

I unlock the phone and reply to Piper's message, declining her offer. I never really liked LA anyway.

Then I pull up Julius's number.

Me: Are you home? Can I see you?

Julius: I'm visiting my sister today.

No other messages follow, and I'm gutted that he hasn't acknowledged my second question. If he's with his sister, I'm not going to hunt him down, but I will see him today.

Julius is mine, and I'm his, and by the time I'm finished with him, there will be zero doubts of that.

"How do you feel about going to the Academy for brunch? We haven't done anything together in a while," I say.

"Yeah, sounds good."

"Great. Then you can tell me all about your sleepover."

"Not a chance."

"Remember who's paying the food bill."

"Ugh. You're the worst."

"Nah. I just love you too much. And I can be as nosy as you."

"Fine. But I want to know all about Julius."

I laugh. "Fair trade."

CHAPTER 14

JULIUS

"Again!"

I throw the ball, and Kellie tries her best to catch it but fails.

"She's never going to get a spot in the Women's Football Alliance," Hella says, leaning against the door to Kellie's bedroom. "Also, what did I say about throwing balls inside?"

"Mommy, it's cold outside. I get sick."

"She does have a point," I say.

Hella crouches and Kellie goes straight to her. "Huggle."

"Hey, sweetie, how about you make a picture for Uncle Julius to take home?"

"Okay, Mommy. Uncle Julius, what's your favorite color?"

"Pink," I say, and she scrunches her nose. "Yellow?"

She shakes her head.

"I tell you what, why don't you pick what you think should be my favorite color."

"Purple!"

"I love it."

Hella sets Kellie up at the small desk in her bedroom. I know exactly what she's doing, and there's nothing I can do to stop it.

"Out with it," I say when we get to the kitchen and she puts a cup of coffee in front of me.

"I don't know what you mean."

"Don't play coy, Hel."

"Fine. People saw you leave the fundraiser yesterday with Connie. This morning, you show up here like someone kicked your puppy."

"We...there's something between us. Something really good."

"That's great. Why the kicked-puppy face?"

"Can you stop saying kicked puppy?"

"Can you stop making the face?"

I make an exaggerated grin.

"Ew. Stop that."

I chuckle and then tell her what happened this morning.

"So you think he's going to accept this job?"

"He'd be stupid not to. He has responsibilities and is the sole carer for his brother. I can't pay him what a fancy restaurant like Nobu can. And I won't stand between Constantine and his dream job."

"Hmm."

Hmm? "What's that supposed to mean?"

She hits me upside the head. "You're assuming that the most important thing to him is a job. You know, the same person who moved across the country to work for you while looking after his little brother. Yeah, I can see how you'd think he'd jump at the chance to work twenty hours a day in a kitchen rather than a place that is literally a flight of stairs away from home."

She has a point. "I know, but I'm scared."

"Of what? I'm sure you can hire someone else."

I can't even believe I'm willingly walking into her trap. "I really like him, Hel. Fuck, I'm falling for him so hard. I'm scared of him leaving and taking my heart with him."

"Then you have to tell him."

I shake my head. "I can't. I'm not going to make him choose."

"It's not your choice, little brother. It's his, and he needs to know all the facts. He needs to know he has options."

I hate that she's right, so I don't tell her. "I should go. Think I can slip out undetected?"

She laughs. "Good luck."

After posing for my niece for half an hour, I am the proud owner of a purple portrait that captures my essence better than an actual photograph. Purple with some green squiggles and questionable ears.

I walk back home, thinking about what Hella said. It was a dick move not replying to Constantine's request to come over, but I needed to think.

As I approach my house, I see a figure huddled against my door.

"You really need to get a proper winter jacket," I say.

Constantine practically runs down the steps in my direction and wraps his arms around me. "Why do I need one when my boyfriend is more than happy to keep me warm any time I want?"

My heart stops.

"Boyfriend?"

He bites his lip. "Can we talk inside?"

"Yes, of course." He keeps hold of my arm and laces his cold fingers with mine. "You also need to buy gloves. Your hands are freezing."

"Not for long."

He goes straight to the couch when we get inside. I turn the heat up and join him.

"I know you saw the message," he says straight away.

"I'm sorry. I didn't mean to, but you asked me to check. I shouldn't have read it once I saw it wasn't from Leo."

He shakes his head. "It was unavoidable. I just want to make it very clear that I don't intend to take that job or move anywhere." He looks around. "Maybe here one day, when you have the place all fixed up and we're ready to have some giant kids of our own."

My heart is stuck in my throat. "Do you mean it?"

"Did you not hear me when I called you boyfriend earlier?"

"I'm still trying to wrap my head around that."

He tells me about the conversation he had with Leo.

"I'm really happy he's got a friend he can confide in. He's a great kid, and it'll be a privilege to see him grow up and become a funnier, better version of his amazing older brother."

"Ass."

"What's that? You want to eat my ass?" I tease.

Constantine straddles me the same way he did that first time.

"I'm falling for you, Julius. I know you feel the same way."

"I do. I fucking do, baby." I pull his lips against mine and show him exactly how I feel about his decision to stay, be my boyfriend, and even have our own kids in the future.

I'm so fucking in love with this man.

"Hey," he says, pulling his lips away from mine. "I've been given permission to stay with you for the rest of the day. *Apparently,* Leo has a test to study for and doesn't want me pining for you from afar."

"Pining, huh?"

"Don't know where he got that idea from. Point is, I need to go home later. But I'm yours for the next"—he looks at the clock on my wall—"six hours."

I pull his shirt up and pay attention to his nipples one at a time until he's squirming and hard. "I can do a lot with six hours."

"Then let's get to it, boyfriend."

I put my hands under his butt and take him with me as I stand and walk to my room. I've never been anyone's boyfriend, but I'll be anything Constantine wants me to be. Best friend. Boyfriend. Husband.

I've watched so many of my friends find their soulmates, but between kitchen fires and frustrations, I never thought my soulmate would be the one to find me.

I guess I'm just lucky.

SUMMER FLING

ARIES FRANCE

CHAPTER 1

JASPER

Blow jobs always get me in trouble.

At twenty-three, I should know that.

Some part of my brain keeps trying to waive red flags and put up caution tape, to no avail. This blow job should have been easy. Anonymous. Safe.

And while my mind is partially focused on the fact I am standing in the law firm where I will be interning this summer, there is a fair bit of mental real estate being taken up by thoughts of last night. And waiting for the other shoe to drop.

It always drops, and today feels more ominous that most.

A hookup off an app shouldn't occupy this much space in my brain, but...damn. The guy was tall, older, and hot as hell. And the way he liked it was exactly the way I liked to give it. That's rare enough to warrant a little bit of mental replay.

I cough, willing my thoughts to control themselves. This is an important day, not one where I can be distracted by how perfectly some guy sank his hands into my hair or how his thighs shook against my cheeks.

Nope. Not today.

Today is the first day of a summer internship that will set everything I've worked for into motion. It's my last year of law school and as the editor of the law review and top student in my class, I intend to go out having left my mark.

I pause in the long hallway, one of the only places in this law firm that doesn't seem perpetually flooded with natural light. I stare at the portraits. That's right, honest-to-god oil paintings of the firm's three current partners. The paintings are displayed in a way that is imposing and at the same time, somehow effortlessly cool.

This internship is over 1600 miles from my law school. But I'm interning with one of the premiere AIDS and HIV advocacy law lawyers in the country. Shadowing him—Marshall Caffrey—during a huge trial he has this summer will make my Law Review article perfect.

I sigh just a bit, a smile pulling up the corners of my mouth. I am the architect and engineer of the perfect summer.

But no. Too soon.

Blow jobs are going to get in the way of all that, I realize as my eyes go back to one particular painting and my mind goes back to one particular blow job.

And, come on, is it really my fault that I love the intimacy of the act? The ability to feel my partner find release with nothing but my mouth? Okay, and maybe a bit of help from a finger or two?

And yet… Despite my mastery of oral love, it always gets me in a pickle.

My skills should be considered a superpower, or at least acknowledged as both art and skill honed from years of watching what my partners like and dislike. Far too few ever get the same sort of high off the act that I do.

But then, when the pants are zipped and the cum has cooled…

Sometimes guys will start to wonder how I got to be so talented with my mouth. It would be easy to explain if they bothered to ask— which they don't. I am young, unattached, and have chosen to live in towns with lots of available gay men for most of my adult life. I didn't have that kind of freedom growing up.

Back then, kids told me my sexuality before I got to figure it out for myself—not in a nice way—and by the time I did figure it out, I realized my small town had slim pickings for experimentation. Then the later years of high school happened and I found that not all straight-presenting guys are straight once you get behind closed doors. And a hell of a lot of them played football.

Sure, later there were the college dalliances where guys didn't mind being open about their sexuality and guys who loved that I loved blowing them, until they got jealous of how I learned the art. Also, not a reciprocal bunch.

So, thanks to you, my love and talent of blowies. All you have left me with over the years are the jocks who wanted me to be a secret and the never quite reciprocated affections of the other men in their wake.

But I still love you, despite the trouble.

Now, the occasional hookup on an app when the bar scene gets too tedious yields about the same results as those high school and college experiences.

And now there is this.

Maybe the biggest trouble blow jobs ever got me in.

And this trouble matters. Way more than jocks or frat boys.

My feet walk me to Marshall's office. A sleek teak wood door seems to laugh at me, or my reluctance to knock on it. I have to say, million-dollar law firms do not scrimp on aesthetics.

"Did you knock?" a clipped and faintly amused voice asks. The paralegal from the front desk, the very one who had sent me back here, swishes by on red-heeled shoes that look perfect with her pencil skirt and tailored blouse. I could believe she borrowed Meghan Markle's wardrobe from *Suits*.

Instead of waiting for my answer, she raps loudly on the door, and with the briefest of pauses where she's making some sense out of the muffled reply, she opens the door, sweeping toward me with her other hand as if to usher me in.

I swallow and nod at her, straightening my bow tie as I do. I'm not nervous about the internship. I'm editor and top of my class for a reason. I know my shit.

I'm nervous because the trouble here isn't the guy rising to meet me, well it is, but not because he's a big shot. Which he is.

I am here for an internship with Marshall Caffery. *The* Marshall Caffrey.

All six-four, dark hair, light-eyed inch of him.

And he might throw me out before we even shake hands.

Because I recognized him in his painting in the hallway.

Marshall Caffrey is the guy I blew last night.

CHAPTER 2

MARSHALL

My husband always gets me in trouble.

He's been dead five years so you would think he would quit speaking in my brain, but there it is. His voice loud and clear.

Although, sometimes I wonder if it's him or my subconscious trying to tell me what I need to hear.

Maybe it's both.

Maybe it doesn't matter.

Thanks, Keith.

Some days I feel lost without him. I was twenty-four and more or less fresh out of law school when we met. He was older by fifteen years and a hell of a lot of life experience. This past May I turned the same age as he was when we started dating—thirty-nine. It was a birthday I had dreaded coming. I wracked my brain trying to determine what it meant. Was it a full-circle moment somehow?

To celebrate the occasion, my good friend and former law partner, Lincoln Rutherford, had invited me to vacation with him. He knew that birthday would be an odd one for me, so I traveled down to Lin's place on The Wyn, a resort island off the Gulf Coast of Florida.

Lin had been the voice of reason on that birthday and had been damn right about me not spending it alone. Instead, I had spent it with Lin and his husband, Ryke. They had an age gap similar to the one Keith and I had shared. Same for their best friends who lived down there too, but somehow I never was the odd one out even with the two couples.

There was sun and beaches and attractive boys in tight shorts who set out my chair and umbrella each morning. There were drinks and five-star dining experiences and friendship with old pals. Not just pals, but former law partners. We had been through some things together.

Still, it was Keith, or his voice at least, who noticed that I was watching the young men more intently than the older ones.

We weren't perfect, but I had loved Keith. Most people never have that much, so I never looked for anything but one night of companionship in the years after he was gone. Not even a night, really. Always with older men—what I knew. What I had been attracted to since I was eighteen and first acknowledged that it was only men, and not women, that got my engine running. Only men and the older the better.

But, that birthday trip had turned everything on its head.

I struggled in the months since my birthday with the fact I am now the older guy, and instead of being attracted to other older men as I had assumed would always be my preference, I'm now attracted to younger men.

All I got from Keith was a smug little "uh huh" in the back of my brain, like he wanted to welcome me to some club.

Until this last month, when that smug little voice started having commentary.

Yeah, definitely cute, he said of the guy stocking the produce in Trader Joe's.

Were you checking out his ass, Marsh? I did, he said of the college kid jogging by me in the park.

So here I am, the older guy, checking out guys a decade younger with my dead husband's voice as a guide. Perfectly normal.

And then there is last night.

Holy shit last night.

There sure was. Keith's voice kicks in like he's lounging in bed with a cigarette in some post-sex scene from a black and white movie.

I had used an app and found the hottest young guy I had seen in a while. He was tall but muscular, with curly light brown hair and hazel eyes.

There was a light in those eyes, a spark of something, that ensnared me from the moment he opened the door to his extended-stay hotel room. It was playful but intelligent. I wanted to ask him where he was from or what he did for a living, but those were not the kinds of questions one asked on a hookup.

He had kissed me like a desperate man, and something clicked. A need to slow it down and show him that one could be eager and still savor the moment.

After that, I was fucked because it was clear he was used to the quick and easy of hookup culture. The idea of showing the earnest young man the world of pleasure? To lead him to it? It got me off like nothing ever had before.

And we had savored everything—right through the most epic blow job of my life.

I shake my head in the present day, trying to clear it of last night's escapades and focus on the case in front of me. That's never a problem—I can always focus on a case. Always get the job done.

Except today, I want to remember last night.

"Yes?" I answer to the sharp rap at my door, not looking up, but moving my computer tabs back to the arrangement that suit me to work on this case.

I click out of the tab I had open for the private investigator the firm sometimes uses. Not that I would engage firm resources to track down a hookup, of course. That would be…crazy.

"Your intern is here," Penny calls, and I can tell she dropped that bit of information for my benefit, as I had indeed forgotten he was arriving today.

Lin sent me one of his eager 3L, or last-year law students, who was working on a law review article and could both get experience from my work that specialized in his topic of AIDS and HIV advocacy as well as help me out on a big case this summer.

"Come in," I call, straightening my typical button-down and khakis I wore for a day in the office as I stand to meet him.

Only, the guy standing awkwardly in my doorway isn't some intern Lin had sent me, but my guy from last night.

Keith, at least, was blissfully silent.

Not even a chuckle.

CHAPTER 3

JASPER

This is awkward, but I owe it to Professor Rutherford to at least try and salvage this internship and my 3L year. He told me he and Marshall are friends and former law partners too, so the stakes here are enough that I have to swallow my embarrassment and try to move forward.

"Hi," I manage, sticking my hand out to be as professional as I can be. "I mean, hello. I'm Jasper Dawson."

Marshall looks at my outstretched hand for a beat, and then shakes it, and I swear I see his full lips curl into a smirk.

Lord help me, that's sexy.

"A bit beyond handshakes, aren't we?"

I swear I see his eyes darken as he asks the rhetorical question and he doesn't act as if his skin prickles and sparks. Mine does.

My brain falters a bit, wanting to go back to the night before when I had opened my hotel room door to greet this snack of a man waiting on the other side. He had worn dress pants and a button-down shirt, signaling he was some sort of professional. Of course, I had no way to know it was a profession that actually mattered. He smelled fantastic when I got close to his skin. Like sandalwood and soap. Maybe leather too, but a fainter scent than the rest.

The smirk on his face in the here and now rises to show a flash of white teeth that looks sexy as hell with the contrast of his dark stubble, and it jars me back to the present and the fact I'm standing in his office.

I look anywhere but him. The expanse of windows, the dark wood bookcases, the couch.

Fuck, not the couch.

"This is awkward," I finally acknowledge, going with the advice to always say the quiet parts out loud. I can tell my straightforwardness surprises him. I am much younger, so maybe he thinks me less mature than someone who would be so up-front.

Marshall raises an eyebrow and then rests his ass on the front of the desk, so his height difference isn't quite so pronounced, or at least, I no longer feel like he's looming over me.

Not that I minded that last night when I was on my knees for him, and he was…

I clear my throat.

"This is awkward, but it is also—" I falter, reaching for the right word, trying to get my bearings.

"Did you know who I was? Last night?" Marshall interrupts me. It's startling for a moment, because he seems much more like the kind of guy to wait out talking and awkward silences. The kind of guy who will let someone else fill those silences so he can read into their words.

I clutch the leather strap of my messenger bag across my chest. "I did not," I answer truthfully. "It was the painting in the hallway that tipped me off." I try a smile that doesn't work. "Thirty seconds before Penny knocked on your door."

He just nods.

I lick my lips, wondering if I should stay as silent as he is, some sort of refusal to talk stand-off. Then I remember why I am here.

I ignore the rush of heat that I get from watching him watch me lick my bottom lip nervously.

"I can…compartmentalize…how we might otherwise know each other, Mr. Caffrey. I am sure these things happen more often than I could guess."

Marshall would know, of course, he seemed smooth as hell last night. No stranger to hookups. And he is the lawyer between the two of us. Well, make that The AIDS/HIV law expert. Capital "T" on "the." He is famous in certain circles. Circles I have a chance to touch right out of law school if I correctly leverage this internship and the chance professor Rutherford handed me.

And I intend to do just that.

Marshall raises an eyebrow, looking at me for a long minute.

"Well," he gestures with his large hands, palms up. Given my body's reaction to just seeing those hands, this is going to be harder than I thought. "The truth is, Mr. Dawson, I owe Lincoln Rutherford far more than taking on a competent law student for a summer internship. You aren't my employee. You wrote and applied for the grant that's funding your time here. But, what I signed on for was to have an intern help me on this rather large case this summer and I still need that warm body." He gives me a look I can't read. "Yours is just as fine as anyone else's."

I nod slowly, feeling the heat of something that is part anger and part blush heat my cheeks. This guy is an asshole, that's for sure, trying to make it sound like he is doing me a favor by letting me stay in the internship. The internship I worked for that benefits him. He's getting a free paralegal for this case, but I don't say that.

Warm body, I cringe internally at his choice of words, feeling them tumble over my brain and bristling at his insinuation about last night. He didn't have to go there. For a moment, a feeling I thought I was long past threatens to come up. Not quite shame, but something close enough to make me feel cheap.

I bet he used to be a jock. I clock the muscles under his dress shirt and the square cut of his jaw. Probably a former frat boy, too. Figures.

The first item on my to-do list after work will be to move up my flight home. Originally, I had given myself a few days of cushion after the trial, but now I can't imagine staying longer than necessary.

Even then, it's going to be a long summer.

CHAPTER 4

MARSHALL

Keeping Jasper here is a mistake, but I owe it to Lincoln Rutherford to see it through.

I had warned Lin that I wasn't easy to deal with during big cases, and the one this summer is big. He had laughed, said he knew that, and that he had just the student to send me. Someone who could "handle me"—his words.

From what I knew, Jasper was intelligent and driven. Lin said Jasper was hoping to turn his experience with me over the summer to not only satisfying his internship grant requirements but much more. Jasper is associate editor of the Law Review and is preparing a special edition on AIDS and HIV Law. My specialty. He also has, in conjunction with the special edition, been on the planning committee for a symposium on the same topic at the law school.

I know because I signed up both to submit an article for the special edition and to give a lecture at the symposium in the fall. That was equal parts favor to Lin, wanting to be back on The Wyn, and just good professional practice.

And now, well, last night, I managed complicate all of it.

Last night had been a dream. I remember how the casual pants he was wearing draped just right on his lean hips, his t-shirt suggesting definition as much as it begged to be stripped off.

And I had. The awkwardness I knew I would feel with an app hookup was gone when I looked at him. I wanted him and apparently that was enough to cut through any situational awkwardness.

Well, not the present kind of situational awkwardness. This unprecedented moment of being turned on in my own office, because last night I received an epic blow job from the man I would be working with side-by-side all summer.

There is no fault here. After years in this business, I am adept at telling when someone is lying to me, and Jasper hadn't been when he said he didn't know who I was last night.

And I hadn't been either when I said I wasn't his boss. For a moment, I wish I were because it would make the ethics of keeping my hands off him so much clearer. But, still, he is my intern and that is clear enough.

If he wants to learn what it is to fight a system that has no intentions of changing, then he's in the right place.

But, there will be no repeat of last night.

No return to him on his knees, wrapping that talented mouth around my cock. The look on his face, too, was a remarkable sight. The way his eyelashes fluttered, eyes tearing at the effort. The way he sounded when…

Holy shit, I need to get it together.

Problem, Marsh? Keith unhelpfully chimes in.

My teeth grind together. Of course, Keith now wants to give advice.

He can compartmentalize, Keith continues, and I can feel the smirk in his words. *Can you?*

I sigh and try not to look anywhere but Jasper's face. Not at the adorable bow tie and khakis and how they wrap his…nope, not there.

I throw words at him, harsher than I should be, and I see the hurt cross his eyes, quickly hidden. There is resignation, too.

He's used to nasty words from men, I realize, feeling shock that such a pretty and sexy young man would have such a reaction even for a moment.

Reading people well has its drawbacks. People always show things they don't realize. Jasper's reaction takes the wind out of my sails a bit.

I sigh, sorry for being so harsh. But the words have their intended effect.

It puts distance between me and the all too tempting summer intern.

CHAPTER 5

JASPER

"Are we ever going to talk about the case?" I ask, ready blurt out anything so as not to be overwhelmed by the presence of Marshall in the conference room where we are working.

It's my third day on the job—the rest of the first one and the entirety of the second I spent with Penny, who caught me up to speed on the back-office side of things. I learned how to get into the file on this case and how to access the firm's calendar and research platforms. That was on top of getting an office ID, email, and all the rest.

This is the first time Marshall and I have spent time together—even been in the same room—since the awkward morning of finding that my sexy hookup was now the person I would be working with all summer.

He quirks a brow at me and slides a take-away cup of coffee across the table.

"Let's caffeinate first?" he suggests. "I don't know your order, yet, but let Penny know and she will coordinate someone for the coffee runs."

"I assumed I would be doing coffee runs."

"You are much more helpful to me on this case than on a coffee run. We are heading to trial in a few weeks. You need to familiarize yourself with the file."

I nod, pulling it up from the firm's file management system and my notes that I have made so far on my laptop.

"Get up to speed today. Start with the Complaint and the Summary Judgement Motion and Order we just won."

I nod again, fingers flying as he continues, and I make notes of what he's saying, a little proud of myself that I would have started in the same place he suggested and that I can keep up with his bullet-point tempo.

"The depositions are also in the file—read those. In fact, your whole life this summer needs to be *Ashby v. The City of Trenton*."

I look at him to gauge if he's joking. He isn't.

"I'm going to lay the facts of the case out for you," he says, gesturing to Penny to join us as she enters the conference room. "I want both of you to write down questions. What you don't understand, what has holes—especially you, Jasper, as you haven't heard this before and can give us a sense of how the jury will understand the facts. Most of this will be in my opening statement, so I need to know what lands."

Penny nods right along with me, and I can see why Marsh, I mean Marshall, and Professor Rutherford are friends. They have similar energy when it comes to discussing a case.

"After that, we need to go through the evidence. Piece by piece. I want an index card for everything we might offer into evidence. I want to be clear on what point we are proving with every piece we offer. What objections can be made and what is our response? Every piece. Then, the same for them. What the evidence is, what it can prove, and our arguments. If there is a case one way or another, I want it cited. Got it?"

Penny and I again nod in tandem. I know a few things about being prepared for trial. I've taken the trial class the law school offers and even sat in on a few trials. What Marsh wants is a level of dedication beyond what anyone has mentioned to me before.

Every piece of evidence? The man is thorough.

What would it be like to have that kind of thoroughness applied to other things, I wonder. Sexy things.

I'm transfixed as Marsh starts laying out the facts. He doesn't have the background of a courtroom, just the windows of the sleek conference room. It's less grand in a way, but his presence is still filling the space.

Hell, he isn't even in a suit. It's just him in business casual, reciting the facts of the case.

Doesn't matter though; he's mesmerizing. He's the kind of handsome that draws you in, makes you want to listen.

I can see why he's good in the courtroom.

I want to believe him and every word he says.

CHAPTER 6

MARSHALL

"Let me tell you about this case," I say, willing to say anything so that I'm not overwhelmed by Jasper's dark gaze on me.

He's still undeniably gorgeous, despite me doing my best to keep my distance in the few days since he started.

Show him what you got, Keith urges in the back of my head.

I shake off those thoughts. This case is too important for grand-standing due to my crush on the young intern and his beautiful, talented mouth.

So, I go through the facts, slowing to be careful to enunciate. If Jasper can't grasp the reality of what these cases are about, the tragic facts, then he is of limited usefulness this summer.

AIDS/HIV law takes a certain amount of empathy, just as any advocacy. If Jasper wants to pursue this niche as a career path, he needs to be the kind of person who can use the injustice of the world to fuel his work.

Something about Jasper tells me he has that ability. Maybe it was that flash of hurt in his eyes from my too-harsh words on his first day. I don't know, but something tells me Jasper would be willing to fight for the underdog.

I clear my throat and start telling them about our client, the estate of Fred Ashby. The estate, as it were, is Fred's surviving sister, Pearl.

Fred was forty-two, in the prime of his life, working as a radiographer at the local clinic in the small town of Trenton. He had moved into administration, something he often told his friends at their weekly meet-up at the local bar was more money and more headaches. But, he saw it as something he could do into the future, even when the usual demands of the job might be too much as he got older.

He coached his niece's swim team. He was known in the small town for being a good coach and a good friend. Someone you could call if your car broke down. Someone who would say hello and call you by name if he ran into you at the grocery store.

He was also gay. That was well known, too. It was Colorado, known for a certain independent spirit and openness, but it was also a small town, and the tolerance everyone assumed was there was largely untested.

I can feel Jasper listening to the story. Not taking notes, just listening to understand the very real person he will never get to meet, but to whom we owe our best work.

Fred was driving home after taking the late shift on Halloween. He had worked a double shift, and as he had no children himself, he was known to volunteer on kid-friendly holidays so his co-workers who were parents could enjoy the time with their children.

He was in an accident, caused completely by a drunk driver. Of that there is no question, no concern. No one, even the driver himself, contends that Fred had anything to do with the accident other than being at the same four-way stop.

This case is not an automobile case. It is not an accident case or personal injury. It's a discrimination case, and that part of the story comes next.

The driver of the car, Oliver Trent, was impaired, yes, but he had the presence of mind to call 911 and to go to Fred's car to give help when he broadsided Fred at the four-way stop. Fred's car was in a deep ditch off the side of the road because of Oliver's driving. While Fred was proceeding through the stop at an under-the-limit rate of forty-five miles per hour, Oliver did not see the stop sign and was going well over seventy-five.

Oliver had basic first aid and CPR training. He could see that Fred was struggling to breathe and was able to attempt to perform CPR.

As soon as he started CPR, he was pulled off Fred before he could fully perform the series of compressions and breathing exercises.

He was pulled off by an on-duty officer, Stanley Holmes. Holmes not only stopped the compressions and CPR series, he told Oliver that Fred had HIV. Oliver still attempted to render assistance, but Officer Holmes did not allow him to continue, citing Oliver's safety due to Fred's HIV/AIDS status.

Officer Holmes then stood between Oliver, other bystanders, and the vehicle with Fred until EMTs arrived. All of this is something Oliver will tell you himself. He was impaired but his story of what happened at the intersection that night has never changed. It is also the same story documented in Holmes's own police report.

When they arrived, the EMTs immediately began CPR and demanded to know why CPR had not been done yet at that point.

All officers are trained in CPR. They are required to up their training yearly. Officer Holmes was fully trained in CPR. The EMTs knew that and were shocked that it had not been performed.

Despite the efforts of the EMTs on site and the efforts of those at Valley County General, where Fred was taken, Fred succumbed to his injuries.

A doctor who was there, an EMT who was there, and doctors who reviewed his file can all testify that if he had received the CPR that Oliver offered, then he likely would have survived.

They will also tell you that the chances of contracting HIV from CPR is almost nonexistent.

But, it would not have mattered in this case.

Fred did not have HIV or AIDS. Not at all. But, he was gay, and Officer Holmes knew that.

And being gay was enough.

CHAPTER 7

JASPER

Oh hell, I really want to do well this summer, and not let my stupidly large attraction to Marsh mess that up.

Hearing the facts of the case we are working on was enough to inspire anyone. Even my organized, detailed work has been kicked up a notch. My mind just keeps telling me how I can't lust after Marsh and do this job well. And then I realize that's a quick ticket to burnout.

One of the things Marsh already warned me about in pursuing this kind of work is how hard it is to let go, even just to go home and live your life. Like when I didn't want to take lunch the afternoon after his talk. There is always work to be done and always a client and a case that deserves it.

Drawing those boundaries sounds easy, but I can see now they aren't.

So, by the end of the first week, I quit caring so much if my eyes linger on his ass, or if I noticed the kind way he let a potential client know that her case had no merit to pursue. If anything, those little glimpses of him as a man, as well as my steamy memories of our night, make the work worth it.

He's asked me to call him "Marsh" rather than Mr. Caffrey, and I guess that's good for our working relationship, but it's hell on my libido that loves the feel of his name in my mouth.

Just like I enjoyed the feel of *him* in my mouth.

I sigh, pushing the stack of evidence index cards I've been working on to the side.

Marsh looked adorable yesterday when he explained the system, and he sort of blushed when he explained how he knew modern technology allowed other ways for this kind of trial prep, even more efficient ways. But this was his way, and so I dutifully set to the task as he asked.

"That looks good," he says, taking the stack in his ridiculously large hands. He plants that plump left ass cheek on my desk...again. It's a thing. His ass on my desk.

His eyebrows rise as he looks at me, a smirk forming on his mouth. Yep, definitely former frat boy.

I'm sure he's reading my face as easily as he reads a case.

Instead of planting his ass, giving me directions, and then leaving, as has been his *modus operandi* all week, Marsh folds his hands together. The gesture is sexy, showing off his rolled-up shirt-sleeves, making my eyes draw to those large hands.

One can perfectly wrap the back of my head and hold me in place, as I well remember. And he also draws my attention to his forearms, the muscle there marking the landscape of his skin in long lines.

"We have a bit of an office tradition on Fridays," he says.

"Oh?" My interest is immediate. I've met Penny, but that's about it in the week I've been here.

"We go over to a local bar—The Black Diamond—for drinks at about three. Close the office early. I wanted to make sure you were invited."

I nod. "Black Diamond. I'm guessing that's next to the slopes." I actually haven't been to that part of Bear Valley. I'm staying in the more commercial area of town and haven't ventured into the beautiful slope-side of town I've only admired in pictures.

"It is," Marsh confirms. "Next to the lifts. You can grab a ride with me, if you like."

I would like, very much, so I nod. If he's offering to treat me just like everyone else, then fine, that is what we agreed to. I shouldn't be surprised that it's easy for him to do. Of course it is. It's always easy to set me aside. There's no reason for Marshall to have a different take than every other man I've ever been with.

I swing my bag over my shoulder and clean up my area as quickly as possible to follow him to his vehicle.

It's a large, dark SUV, and it suits him. Marshall seems to be the kind of guy that molds the world around him to fit his tastes, and his vehicle is no different.

He opens the door for me, which gives me pause, and I feel my face blush too hard to look him in the eye. He is far too likely to be able to read how flushed such a simple gesture makes me.

All I catch is a cool raised eyebrow—one of his quirks—out of the corner of my eye as he closes my door and walks to his own.

The drive is short, thankfully so for the way my cock wants to respond to the enclosed space and scent of Marsh all around me. Marsh is such the host, pointing out distinct parts of town that might be interesting to me as a visitor, and before I know it, we are walking down the cutest pedestrian walkway toward the ski mountain that looms ahead. The walkway is wide, lined with shops, bakeries, restaurants, and entrances to condos that are on the floors above the commercial spaces below.

We get to the end of the street, almost to the lifts, when Marsh gestures toward a beautiful building, all industrial modern with lots of glass and natural light. It reminds me of his office space.

This time he holds the door open for me, and I feel myself flush as I pass him, his arm outstretched above me. That's all it takes. Just get me close to him and I'm basically a puddle.

There is another set of doors ahead of us, and a large party comes out, pressing me into Marsh's body to make room for the group to pass. He smells amazing, and I long to press my face into the curve of his neck.

I look up before I can tell myself not to, and the scorching heat of his gaze over me makes me wish I had kept my messenger bag so I could pull it discreetly in front of my khakis. The air in the small vestibule is gone with the group as they pass through.

We just stare at each other until I hear Marsh's sharp intake of breath.

"We should meet the others," he says, and I can do nothing but nod.

CHAPTER 8

MARSHALL

Oh hell, I really don't want my ridiculously large crush on Jasper to mess up this case or Jasper's summer.

I've never had someone get under my skin like this, though. Never felt electric just being next to someone in a bar entrance.

My intention as I enter the bar is to sit a bit away from Jasper, but of course, the only seat is right next to him.

Quinn Mann, the owner of the bar, is here this afternoon, and gives me a hand raise in acknowledgement as he talks to someone else across the room.

Before the drinks arrive, Quinn himself walks over with a large tray of shots. He sits the tray on the table and I stand so he can engulf me in a big hug, which I return. Quinn and his family are cornerstones of Bear Valley.

Penny passes out the shots while Quinn and I quickly catch up. Once distributed, Quinn grabs his as I do mine and we all look at Keith's picture on the wall over by the stage. The framed photograph is one of my favorites. It's from the stage here in Black Diamond, the very stage the picture hangs near, and it shows Keith playing guitar during a set with Quinn's brother, Baylor, who is a successful songwriter and plays Black Diamond from time to time.

This toast is always for Keith. A little tradition that started even when Lin was still at the firm. Keith was from Bear Valley and knew the Manns well. Quinn is a good man to always remember my husband.

The best, Keith agrees.

"To Keith!" We all say, before tipping back his favorite bourbon— Pappy Van Winkle, of course, so it costs me a pretty penny each week, but at least it isn't as pretentious as Macallan.

Quinn grabs up the empty shot glasses with a grin, expertly placing them on the tray.

"Good to see you, man," he says as he gives me another hug, arms squeezing quickly.

"Um," Jasper's voice asks, his face adorably flushed by the shot, "Who is Keith?"

"Marshall's husband, of course," Quinn says scooping up his tray and heading back to the bar, where I can see Quinn's own husband waiting. Quinn was always a good man, but I've never seen falling in love look so good on someone as it does him.

Jasper makes a sound, a cough or something like it, before quickly grabbing the water the server set on the table when we arrived and taking a long drink. He looks mortified and I quickly realize why that is.

Maybe I was an ass that first day, and sure, I've been trying to put distance between us, but that's because I'm worried about my ability to resist him.

Now he thinks he helped me cheat on my husband.

You better clean that up, Keith advises.

Get it together, Marsh. That's my own voice, thankfully, not Keith's.

The point is, Jasper's used to a certain amount of disappointment where men are concerned, that much is obvious just from my casual observation this past week and the look on his face when I was an out-of-line asshole.

The desire not to be one more thing that disappoints him surges strong.

Right on time, the server shows up with our orders and passes them around, providing me a moment to lean into Jasper. It's a mistake, because I can smell him, feel the body heat rolling off him. Just like in my SUV that always seemed large until he was in the space.

So close.

So much I want.

Still, I swallow down how my mouth waters this close to him. I'd kissed him when we hooked up, but those had been more heat and teeth. What would it be like to really taste him, soft and sweet. Would he fall apart? Whimper under my kiss like he did around my dick?

GET. A. GRIP. That's Keith. Loud and clear.

"So, Keith," I gesture to the picture we saluted earlier, "that was my late husband." I pause, making sure that the words land as they need to.

I have Jasper's attention and realize it's not something I want to give up too quickly.

"Keith was a doctor at Bear Valley General. He grew up here." I gesture over at Quinn, who is back behind the bar. "Quinn Mann and his three brothers—their family that is—sort of own most of Bear Valley. Most of the properties and many of the businesses around here, including this bar. Keith was older than the brothers, they are closer to my age, so they didn't go to school together or anything, but they got close once he moved back."

"So that's how you ended up here."

I see-saw my hand back and forth.

"Kind of? I knew Bear Valley would be a great place to live and work because I went to undergrad at Rollins University, just down the road in Mirror Lake. So when Lincoln," I correct myself, "well, Professor Rutherford to you, I suppose. But, anyway, we decided to create our own firm instead of staying on at Smith-Parsons in Denver, and this seemed like the perfect place to land. The other partners thought so too. I was already dating Keith, and it all sort of fell together."

Jasper looks around as the noise continues on around us. I can tell he has a million questions he won't ask right now.

"So you and Rutherford go way back. I applied to Smith-Parsons, and he said it was a great place to work." It's a comment, not a question.

"It's a world-class firm," I tell him. "I met Lin there and the rest is history," I smile, making the small talk while my mind catalogs the fact that Jasper may only be an hour away after he graduates.

CHAPTER 9

JASPER

If Marshall doesn't quit being so damn hot, I'm going to lose it.

It's not just his face or his body, which sure, I am definitely down with both of those things.

No, it's how he interacts with the rest of the firm, buying everyone a round, which is apparently what he normally does. Every week. Of the expensive stuff, too.

The salute to his late husband, keeping his memory alive is not just regular guy sort of stuff.

It's not just that, though, but how he greets and speaks with the other people here, too. There is a real sense of community in Bear Valley and Marshall is part of it. He must stand up a million times to shake a hand or step away from the table for a quick chat with someone.

I've met my share of the locals, too. Everyone is welcoming, and every time some guy shakes my hand, I feel Marsh's eyes hot and heavy on me. I like it, the feel of his gaze. I want to do whatever I can to keep those eyes on me.

Bear Valley makes me want a career like Marsh's. So far, the three-year slog of law school has me focused on which law to practice and what to avoid, more than the life I would build around that practice.

Watching Marsh makes the idea of a small-town life quite appealing. Not that anything about Taylor Law Partners is small. They have a large reach, but due to the kind of work they do, they can choose a small ski resort in Colorado as their headquarters.

Of course, if I can pull off this summer internship, and the symposium and special edition of the law review next year as the editor, then I can put myself in a position to make choices like this for myself. I can create this kind of life.

"You ok?" Marsh's voice is low and I can feel his breath across my neck as he takes his seat from yet another quick word with a local.

Suppressing the twin needs to shiver and lean into him, I just nod.

"It's about five, and that's when we usually wrap up. Or," he smiles, and it's so relaxed, my brain instantly remembers the smile he gave me leaning against the doorway of my extended-stay room. "Actually, I make sure to leave about five, so no one feels obligated to stay later," he confesses, still leaning into my space. "Would you like a ride back to your place?"

I watch a bit of blush creep across his cheekbone and wonder if that's because he's remembering how he knows where I'm staying.

I nod and in no time he's paid his tab and we are back in his car.

"I apologize," he says, his forearms catching my attention even as he shifts the car into gear, "I didn't think about how you might take our ritual with Keith." His eyes are warm and intense when he looks over to me while we are stopped at a stop sign. "But, rest assured I'm not cheating on anyone—" Marsh blows out a breath. "Wasn't, I mean."

"That's your business." My words come out sort of primly, but this conversation is taking off for dangerous waters.

"What about you? Someone back home?"

I catch my breath—that's not the question I was expecting next.

"N-no. I don't think I could ever cheat on a partner," I say. "Plus, I'm focused on school, really. Top of the class isn't easy."

He smiles a slow sexy smile that matches a look in his eye I can't really describe.

"I remember."

He then switches to asking about law school, thankfully, as he navigates the short distance to my hotel.

"Let me walk you up," he says, already out of the car so that my "that's not necessary" reply is swallowed by his closed door and the quiet of his vehicle.

I hastily exit, and he frowns as he rounds the car, looking at the door as if he is offended that I opened it. Was he going to open my car door? Who even does that?

It's a short walk to my room, just through a mostly empty lobby and up the elevator. I should say something, make small talk, but I can't think of anything to say because my mind is so overwhelmed with the idea that he might want to come in.

I settle on "thanks," as I reach into my pocket for the key, awkwardly standing in the hall by the door.

When I look up, he's close, dark eyes heated and on me.

"Just wanted to see you safe," he says. "You never know who is staying at these places."

I shake my head before I can stop the movement. Maybe he's right, but something is off about his statement.

"That's not it."

A slow smile takes over Marsh's face, and I swear the heat in this hallway cranks up and the oxygen evaporates. That smile is lethal.

"I wanted to tell you that you are sexy as hell, Jasper."

I blink—not what I expected him to say at all.

"You—"

I'm cut off by his hand cupping my cheek, fingers trailing across my skin. I shut my mouth tight against the needy whimper that wants to escape.

He's so close, so warm, and smelling divine. What I wouldn't give to press my nose right into that soft spot under his neck, the one that made him give the needy sounds the night I blew him. But, I'm rooted to the spot.

I'm not going to spend all summer playing his hot and cold games. Maybe he's struggling with how to handle an intern who he hooked up with, and I get that. But, he's had a week to get his shit straight.

I let out a breath, not moving as his eyes roam across my face, chasing answers to unanswered questions. Swallowing hard I resolve that he's had his time to process and I'm not going to beg to hear whatever conclusions he's come to. If he wants more, he can damn well ask.

"I should go," he says, and I try not to let my eyes flutter under his touch, but it's hard. "I don't want to—so I should."

I nod, the resolve of seconds ago still in place.

I press the key card to the door, and as soon as it's closed behind me, I slump against the door with a smile.

At least Marsh is the kind of guy who isn't afraid to show he's interested, or at least turned on. That he finds me sexy. I definitely like him showing that he's struggling with our attraction to each other.

Our mutual attraction.

Damn, it's nice he validated that.

Still. He's had a week to figure it out. If he keeps up this game, I'm going to call him on it.

CHAPTER 10

MARSHALL

If Jasper doesn't stop being so sexy, I'm going to lose it.

Not that he is doing anything overtly sexy. He doesn't have to.

All he has to do to get my attention is exist, apparently.

He's being a competent intern—one of the best I've ever had, and we have employed several law students over the years. He clearly earned the fellowship grant that got him here and has the drive to make something of his plans for next year.

When I've needed case law this past week, he's found it. Same with arguments to get evidence introduced when we are in trial. My index cards are ready to go.

He's as engaged in this case as I am, and while I have reasons for my practice almost exclusively representing AIDS/HIV discrimination cases, I don't know what drives Jasper.

I want to ask.

I want a whole lot of other things too. The amount of times I've found myself staring at his lips or thinking about that hot night...*his mouth on me. Hazel eyes full of heat and want looking up at me as his sinful mouth wrapped around my cock. Damn, the way he looked. The way he was totally into the experience. His hand working himself as his eyes fluttered back. The sinful sounds that could be the soundtrack of any porn I'd ever seen, punctuated by the low, guttural noise he made despite his mouth being full of me.*

I stand up from my desk, as if it will help my swelling dick. I pace behind my couch, using it as a buffer from any prying eyes into my office until I can get my body under control.

Outside my office, I can see everyone working as normal. Penny, my perpetually unimpressed paralegal, smiling at Jasper as he hands her something. I do a double take, and yep, she's actually smiling at him.

She looks up at me, and I force myself not to flinch. Pen's asked what is wrong with me at least fifteen times the past two weeks.

Now she just walks in my office, closes the door, and watches Jasper's retreating back, headed to the library, where his office is.

"Just ask the kid out, Marsh."

I do give a start at that comment.

Keith laughs in the back of my brain.

"What are you talking about?"

Pen comes off the door and walks closer, analyzing me like I'm under a microscope.

"You obsess before trial. We all know that, but we aren't close enough to go-time for you to be there just yet. And you look at him like he's the answer to all of your prayers."

She's mostly right. If I ever had prayers for blow jobs, Jasper far surpassed them.

"Oh," her eyes flare wide. "You've already gone there." I freeze at her perceptiveness. "Good for you."

"W-what?"

Pen crosses over to my hidden liquor cabinet and pours us each a few fingers of whatever is in the crystal decanter.

"Come on," she smiles, handing a glass off to me. "It's after five. How's a bit of liquid courage to go after what you want."

"He's an employee," I argue, taking a sip.

"He isn't," she quickly retorts. "We both know you know that. What else do you have?"

"Lin—"

"The Lincoln Rutherford I know would tell you to go for it. And so would Keith. What's wrong with some summer fun?"

I stare at the liquid as I swirl it in my glass.

What indeed.

It's an hour later before I am sure the office is empty except for me and Jasper. I find him in the library carefully packing away his things into his messenger bag.

"Hey," he says with an easy smile when he sees me enter.

"I thought you would like a ride home. It's raining pretty hard." I notice he walks home unless he leaves with Penny.

"Oh," Jasper looks out the window to see the rain pelting down. He gives me a nod and follows me out. "You don't have to do that, but I won't turn it down."

I hold an umbrella for him, and open his door, enjoying the flush on his skin in the low light of the summer storm as he sits in my car.

"I lied," I tell him as I navigate out of the parking lot. Before he can argue, I continue. "Not a lie," I correct, "but I did lure you into my car on false pretenses."

"Not to take me home?" Jasper asks, his lips quirking in a smile that threatens to take over.

I feel my shoulders unbind at how he completely trusts me.

"How about my house?" I ask, but not until I have stopped at a traffic light, just so I can watch his reaction and see his eyes heat.

They do, and I can't help but smirk as I drive on.

CHAPTER 11

JASPER

Going home with Marsh may be a bad idea, but I'm not sure I care anymore.

Sexual frustration will do that to you.

Marshall's home is a lot like him. It's in the Wilson Park neighborhood of Bear Valley. Older homes with beautiful and varied architecture are set off from the street but all face the park the space is named for. His home is cedar shingles and white trim with river stone making up part of the columns at the porch.

I love it immediately, before I am even inside. And then, to make it even better, Marshall pauses at the door leading into his house from his tidy garage.

"Hope you don't mind dogs," he says, right before the most beautiful border collie sticks a curious nose out the door as Marshall opens it.

I can feel the smile across my face and hear Marsh laugh. "Guess that answers that," he says, as the dog comes to me and I at once get on her level for all the dog love she wants to give.

It doesn't take long before she is rolling over, making me laugh as she clearly tries for more affection. I can feel Marsh's hot gaze on me.

"Katz loves people," he says with a smile, and at his voice saying her name, Katz contorts herself off the garage floor and over to him, butting his hand for more attention. He gives it to her until she heads inside, looking back at us as if she is waiting for us to join.

"'Katz' as in K-A-T-Z for the famous wiretap case or for the cat pun?" I ask.

Marsh stops for a moment, hand frozen on the door. "No one ever gets that, Jasper. Thank you for validating my sense of humor." He visibly relaxes as his hand comes off the door. "And for the wiretap case, of course. When we were first married, Keith and I had a terribly ugly fish we named Roy Cohn and the punny pet names sort of stuck after that."

I follow them in as Marsh lets Katz out to his backyard. There is a wide covered porch, so she doesn't even have to brave the rain.

"We can take her for a walk after dinner if the rain slacks off. She usually comes to work with me, but the neighbors have a daughter looking to make some money pet-sitting."

I nod, unsure of what to say. My plans for the evening had been some leftovers in my hotel—the extended stay that is wearing thin. Just being in Marsh's home makes things way better than the day I had planned.

It's just so sudden, like we took a turn somewhere.

This is the anonymous stranger from our hookup, not the guy I've been working with for the past few weeks.

And it looks good on him.

As good as the rolled-up sleeves of his shirt and the dress pants that stretch across his ass.

"Do you like red or white wine?"

"I like both, depending."

Marsh smiles, and grabs a bottle, his arms working as he places two glasses on his butcher block island. I know the stemware must be expensive given its simple elegance.

I notice myself caught in his smile, staring at his full Henry-Cavil lips. He catches me, his gaze heating.

"Salut." He offers, clinking his glass against mine and I respond in kind, taking a drink of the wine.

The flavors burst across my tongue, a swirl of rich grapes with a spicy finish.

I give an appreciative sound as I try to remember everything I learned from a tasting class I took with a friend back in undergrad. Focus on the flavors. Swirl the first sip…something else, but it's hard when Marsh is staring at me like he is.

"Why am I here, Marsh?" I ask, setting the glass down. I want him to want me, more than I have ever wanted to be desired by someone. I remember what it was like to be on the receiving end of his sexual energy, the focus of it. The kind of feeling that could get addictive very quickly.

Yeah, I watch his eyes track the movements of my mouth as I savor the last of the wine. I want him to want me, but the thing is, I have tremendous respect for Marsh and what he does. These are challenging cases. Soul-breaking in a way. His life's work is to fight for people who have been harmed by prejudice and ignorance.

I respect him.

And I really hope he's not about to shatter all that by acting like I owe him a hookup. Or saying something like he did that first day that makes me feel cheap.

That move doesn't seem like the Marshall I've gotten to know, but after my past experiences, I guess it's what I expect.

CHAPTER 12

MARSHALL

Maybe bringing Jasper home with me was a bad idea, but I don't care.

Sexual frustration can be like that, I guess. Not just general sexual frustration, but a very targeted, pinpointed frustration for this exact man.

I watch the emotions play over Jasper's face. He's not easy to read, but I'm learning.

He's definitely wary.

"Jasper," my voice comes out low, rough, and that's due to nothing other than how attracted to him I am and how close we are.

Alone. In the stillness of my house.

"I want to be honest," I start, keeping the island and the wine between us, "you are incredibly distracting."

I can see the words play over his face and rush to explain.

"I am very attracted to you and—"

"You want me to go. Leave the internship."

He says the words evenly, but there is still a finality there, too.

I round the corner of the island to stand next to him.

"What? No. That's not what I want. You are good at this work,

Jasper. You deserve what you earned this summer. This isn't about that. At all."

"What is it about?"

"I want to ask you out," I tell him. "Dinner, tonight, with me. You don't have to agree to date me to have dinner, but...I was hoping you wanted that, too."

"Wait," Jasper looks like he just landed on a strange planet and is trying to survey alien terrain. "You want..."

His gaze lands on mine, hot and hungry, and I swear if he doesn't say yes, I might not make it past his rejection.

"I'm not your boss," I remind him, closing the distance to cup his cheek like I had in the hallway of his hotel. The feel of his skin under mine makes the hair on my skin rise and I hear him inhale a sharp breath. "But this is just between us, after hours. Nothing to do with work. I can't be distracted from the clients."

"A summer fling," he offers.

I grin, loving that he understands me so completely. I can only hope that is because he wants the same things.

My thumb caresses his jaw. "I can't be around you and not want you, Jasper. It's like breathing oxygen." He holds back a choked sound and that makes me braver to be honest, "So I figure, maybe you wouldn't mind if we did something about that. Maybe you want me, too."

My words are rewarded with Jasper in my arms, and my first instinct is to pull him tight against me as our mouths collide. I want my arms locked against his smaller frame. Protective. Closing him off from everything but me.

The kiss has heat and promise but I slow it down, taking the time to savor his taste, his feel.

Jasper kisses like no guy I have ever known, and I am enraptured before we even come up for air. The press of his mouth, the slide of his tongue against mine is perfection. The answering pounding of blood in my cock has me at full attention.

"Dinner," I whisper across his lips. "Dinner before anything—"

An almost whine bubbles up from him, and I laugh before pecking his lips.

"You fried my brain with that talented mouth of yours the first time, Jasper. Tonight is my turn."

I cup his ass, pulling him up, and he gets the idea of what I want, jumping enough to wrap his legs around me as I slide my hand under his cheeks to support him.

I can't help the short thrust of my hips. He's too perfect.

He grinds against me, his hard cock and mine trying to get acquainted through the fabric.

Our lips meet, and Jasper takes it slow and sensual.

Damn that mouth.

"Dinner can wait," he whispers between kisses, and I agree, too eager for him to wait like I had planned. I could easily become a man obsessed.

I walk us through to the open living room. My bedroom is upstairs and far too far away, but my ottoman is a huge fabric-covered monstrosity that takes up plenty of space on the rug that covers the hardwood.

Gently, I lower Jasper, splaying him out on the ottoman as I start taking off his clothes. The slide of his shirt over his head, his belt through its loops, the lowering of his zipper—each move that unwraps him is punctuated by hungry kisses and hands that want to devour each other as much as our mouths do.

He's finally in nothing but tight briefs. It's hot as fuck to see that scrap of silken material on his body, so I leave him there on the ottoman splayed with damp spots of precum forming on the lime-green fabric.

Little sounds of protest follow me as I move to my knees, turning to almost a purr of pleasure as I start taking my own clothes off.

A quick shake of my head is all it takes to keep him laid out for me.

"Don't move," I tell him, "I want to look at you just like that as long as I can."

His face flushes and while I've found that to be adorable when we're at work, seeing it now, in the middle of sex, is somehow both incredibly endearing and adorable.

Who is capable of both? Jasper's the only guy I know who is.

I've never gotten naked faster.

CHAPTER 13

JASPER

Holy hell, this is so much more than a summer fling.

I think I knew that a few minutes ago when I threw that term out there, but with the way Marsh is looking at me? I want it to be. It's going to be hard when this ends at the end of summer, but it's a pain I can get over when this fucking amazing chance is over.

Marshall is bare to me. We never got this far on our hookup. It was a hot blow job by me and then his hand jerked me off on him.

His cock is beautiful. Long, hard, cut...but that matters less to me than the expression on his face while looking at me.

Me.

Blood rushes to my own hard cock, leaving nothing but a roar of static in my ears.

Marsh's long fingers reach for the band of my briefs, and I hope he doesn't see how my cock jumps at the anticipation of his touch.

The smirk on his face says he definitely notices.

I'm still sprawled out where he left me, up on my elbows, and he peels the tiny scrap of fabric down my body.

"Are you always wearing something this sexy under your clothes?"

I smile. "Probably."

He groans. "I'm going to be thinking about that." Marsh looks like he wants to say more, but he stops, gaze riveted on my dick.

"Look at that," he growls, a finger running the vibrating length of my shaft, collecting all the precum I'm leaking. I watch, my brain damn near its own orgasm as he takes a slow lick of his finger. "Fucking hot as hell, Jasper."

He kisses me, and it's a rush to taste myself on his tongue. Like I've just been blown by him except I'm not spent. Nope. Absolutely not.

"Didn't plan ahead enough for lube," he says with a frown before another flash of his smirk as he pushes off the ottoman to walk backward to the kitchen and swipe something from the island and makes his way back.

"Marsh, what—"

"Don't you dare move, beautiful."

A metal cap rattles across a glass bottle and the distinctive scent of high-end olive oil wafts. His large hand wraps around my dick, and I can't hold in the audible gasp at how slick and wonderful it feels.

"Can't wait to make you come," Marsh rasps, and my eyes fly open at his dirty talk. I love it so much it makes me squirm.

He bats my hand away from helping.

"Lay there, fucking taking my breath away, Jasper. Lay there and let me bring you pleasure. I want to see you come apart. I want to be the one who does it."

Dead. He's going to kill me dead right here and now.

He strokes slow, watching me squirm, but not giving me enough to take me over the edge. No, he just builds up the mountain I'm going to fly from higher and higher.

A slick finger rubs my entrance and my eyes roll back. The dual sensations are too much, especially when all I can do is clutch the ottoman.

"Let me touch you, suck you, Marsh. Something," I pant.

"No," he growls, giving me a fierce kiss. "Take the pleasure, Jasper. All of it."

I whine as he circles my hole, fingers strong but light. The slow strokes to my dick continue, and soon he's crooking two fingers inside me, lighting me up like never before.

"Marshall!"

"That's right," he grins a feral smile, "call my name, Jasper."

I think my brain short circuits, because I am right on the edge of a major orgasm, but instead, he slips his fingers from me, causing my hips to buck in frustration.

My hips lift as he moves over me, driving my dick against his as he lowers down to catch both of us in his hand.

He strokes with purpose now.

"Gonna come," I manage, my back bowing off the ottoman.

"Yesss," he hisses, a wild look on his face that I can no longer see when the whole world goes very bright, only to flood with black spots a moment later as the tsunami of pleasure he's been building crashes over me.

"Fuck!"

I come hard, my whole body getting in on the action as I spasm against the onslaught of what has to be pure fucking bliss. He's right behind me, head thrown back, Adam's apple bobbing as he inhales and groans loud, dick throbbing against mine.

Our sticky combined release between us, his mouth crashes into mine and he winds his arms around me, somehow taking me from the ottoman to the couch as we pulse against each other with aftershocks and kisses.

I'm on top of him as we lie across the couch, coming down from the orgasms. The kisses slow but Marsh's arms hold me tight, like I might fly away if he were to let go.

CHAPTER 14

MARSHALL

This is so much more than a summer fling.

I can feel a tug toward Jasper and he's just across the living room.

"So, you can cook," Jasper says. He's in nothing but his briefs and a too-big shirt of mine.

For some reason I can't stop looking at his bare feet on my floors. He is looking through the built-in shelves that line the living room, oblivious to my new obsession.

The smell of sex is still in the air, tempered now by the smell of steak and mushroom ravioli I am finishing for dinner.

There is nothing left to do except wait for the steaks to rest for a few minutes, so I walk over to where he stands, enjoying the view of his long, bare legs sticking out from under my shirt.

Jasper swirls a glass of wine and smiles up at me.

"This must be you and Keith." Jasper gestures to a picture sitting on the bookshelf of us on our wedding day on the beach. Keith looks younger in this one than the one at Black Diamond.

I like that picture, Keith says.

He always says that. That's why it's here. It's his favorite.

"It was Keith's favorite," I tell Jasper, only to hear Keith's quiet hum of appreciation at being acknowledged.

This is where most hookups have gotten…squirrelly, for lack of a better word.

He's no hookup. I'm not sure if that's me or Keith I'm hearing.

But Jasper doesn't shy away from the fact I was married before to a man I loved. Just like he hasn't shied away from the intensity of the cases we handle at work.

Out of the corner of my eye I see his lips rise as he watches me look at the picture of me and Keith.

"Tell me about him."

It surprises me for a moment, but it shouldn't. Jasper is a straightforward kind of guy.

Still, it pleases me somewhere deep when he wants to know about Keith.

I move back to the kitchen area so I can finish our dinner. If I'm being honest, I'm giving my hands something to do.

"Keith was a lot older than me. Like I said at lunch the other day, he was from Bear Valley originally. I met him when I worked for a firm in Denver."

"You said he was a doctor here."

"Yeah. And Keith was HIV positive," I tell Jasper in a rush. All he shows is compassion and a look that prods me to tell more.

"He's the reason you do what you do?" he asks, sliding onto a barstool to watch me slice up the steaks at the island counter in front of him.

"I met him when I worked on his case. I was a young lawyer, really green, but I did know a lot about employment law, and I worked at a big firm that wanted me to get experience. He chose the firm due to his friendship with Lin—Professor Rutherford. His employment discrimination case was our meet-cute. A hospital in Denver started discriminating against him because of his HIV status. At the time, he was positioned to be chief of surgery."

Jasper takes a drink of wine, rolling his hand for me to continue.

"Keith was very involved in advocating for HIV/AIDS rights and issues. He never shied away from who he was and what he wanted. Not even in the rough last days."

"Do you want to talk about that?"

I shake my head. "No. We had it better than most. Money wasn't an issue. But, he missed out—just bad timing—on all the experimental stuff. He caught a respiratory infection, something that would have been nothing, and didn't even make it halfway through the time we thought he had."

"That's tough."

"It is, but he also wanted me to live on. With our age gap, that was something we had talked about well before, even before the disease was an issue. Keith always told people about my work on his case, a case I won by the way, and one thing became another."

"It became your career."

I smile. "It did. I'm proud of the work I do," I pause, grating the last bit of cheese over the dish before I finish it with some Italian parsley. "When Keith died, I wondered for a while if part of my drive for this work was because of him. But, I found that it had morphed into my own sort of passion."

"I'm glad."

I slide over a napkin and fork for our dishes as he tops off our wine. "Jasper."

He blinks up at me, as if he's a million miles away thinking.

"This looks amazing, thank you," he says, noticing the food.

I lay a hand on his arm as I slide onto my own stool next to him.

"You should know that I told you that first night, what's on the app, is true. Despite our years together, we were always careful. Keith was a doctor and knew the risks. Knew the limits. I get tested regularly, of course, but if I were to have contracted anything from Keith, I would well know by now. I haven't. But, I know what most guys think about hooking up with someone who had an HIV positive lover." I search his eyes, not wanting it to be a shock.

"And what I said that night was true. I'm on PrEP. We even used a condom that night."

I groan. Despite how well he drained me earlier, my dick wants to rally at the thought of his blow jobs. And yeah, he rocked my world even over the dulled sensitivity of a condom. It was so good; I had even forgotten that fact. I can't imagine what it would be like with his lips on my skin.

I knock my shoulder into his. "Dinner. The least I can do is feed you a decent meal, beautiful. Eat."

CHAPTER 15

JASPER

Holy shit. Best. Summer. Ever.

A great summer job that might lead to something bigger?

Amazing sex with a hot as hell older guy?

Either of those things might be enough to make this summer memorable, but together? Together they make it the best I have ever known.

If this is adulting, sign me up.

Don't get me wrong, it's not all play and no work.

We are working our asses off as this case ramps up the closer we get to the trial date. But, in the weeks since we started our summer fling, I've stayed at Marsh's almost every night.

My daily routine is that Marsh, Penny, and I spend long hours at the office in trial prep. A row of white binders sit on the desk, each with tabs and indexes to help Marsh coordinate the flow of trial.

I have the same thing, digitally, on my tablet in an electronic notebook.

Today, I'm driving to Trenton, the small town where the events of the case took place and where the trial will be held. It's a nice distraction from how much my mind wants to dwell on Marsh. And his hands. And voice. And sex.

The approaching trial date has us all keyed up, and for some reason, sex seems to be the distraction we both want.

He's an amazing man, that's for sure. Keith was a lucky guy.

The road to Trenton is empty. There are few towns in the foothills, where the land looks more like Kansas than Colorado. My mind wanders easily in this open space.

I think about standing in Marsh's living room in nothing but a pair of shorts a few days ago when he came up behind me, pulling me to him. His hands ran up the back of my legs, grabbing by ass.

"Fucking cake," he mumbled in my neck as he manhandled me upstairs to bed, putting me on my hands and knees. He had groped and stroked my ass while removing my clothes until I was begging for something more. Then, naked, he had rimmed me until the begging became sobs. He had brought me off with his fingers and tongue in my ass, and I almost came untouched. Then he pushed me down and came on my hole.

A shiver runs down my spine at the thought. It was filthy, sexy, and amazing.

I'm used to blowing a guy or an occasional rough fuck, but Marsh continues to blow my mind in an entirely new way.

I sing along to a playlist I haven't queued up in ages on the rest of the drive.

But, I'm here to do a job. So, I cheerfully hand over the subpoenas to the clerk of court for her to issue back to me for our witnesses. I try to make a good impression on everyone I see and meet, knowing it will reflect on Marsh.

One of Professor Rutherford's first lessons in our trial practice class was that you can never be too nice or polite to the courthouse staff. It matters.

I also smile through a brain-numbing show of the court evidence presentation equipment. The equipment is so outdated it is the same as what I used for presentations in high school, but at least I know how it works.

By midday I've accomplished all my tasks for the case, but I place the paperwork in my car and walk across the courthouse square to the diner that sits at one corner. I want to get a feel for the town, some local flavor I guess. I keep a pleasant smile affixed to my face, careful of my manners like my grandmother was watching.

This is the kind of small town where visitors are noticed, and absolutely talked about.

The door to the diner doesn't make a sound, but every head in the lunch crowd turns toward me when I walk in. There is no sign guiding whether I should be seated or to wait, and the older servers behind the counter wait in a lengthy silence before finally signaling me toward a seat at that same counter.

The talk finally resumes as I peruse the menu, quickly deciding what to order.

I try for a "what's the special?" Or "what do you recommend?" But I am met with a blank stare as if I am speaking a foreign language.

The server says nothing, doesn't even look me in the eye. The other customers also give off so much ice it feels glacial.

I pick up the sandwich that is set in front of me, determined not to be aloof on my phone, nor to rush through it. I tip generously and still feel the eyes of the patrons on me as I leave.

Walking back to where I parked my car at the town square, I can still feel eyes on me. I pause for a moment, keenly aware the townspeople are watching as I slide in the car.

Turning it on, I see the notification on my control panel that my passenger door is ajar. I take a deep breath. No one has ridden with me today and it was closed—no alerts—the entire drive here. I hadn't opened it when stowed my things before heading to the diner.

I look to the seat next to me, opening the padfolio where I placed the paperwork from the courthouse and sure enough, the subpoenas are gone.

My hands shake a bit as I send out at text to Marsh.

Come straight to the office, he replies. *And be careful.*

CHAPTER 16

MARSHALL

Holy shit. The best summer ever just took a turn I don't like.

By the time Jasper arrives at the office, I am pacing the floor, ready to put eyes on him and see that he's okay. A few stolen subpoenas are an annoyance at best, I can find other ways to serve them.

My worry is for Jasper. He doesn't have experience with the kind of bullshit that can happen in these kinds of cases. Suing the government, especially a small town, is not for the faint of heart.

People don't mind being bigots, you see. What they mind is when someone dares to call them on their bigotry.

Jasper looks fine but when he walks in and his eyes meet mine, I can tell the events of the day gave him more of a shock than he wants to admit.

I go to him, a hand to the back of his neck is all I need to ground myself that he's okay. Penny's eyes are on me, and while Jasper and I have kept our sexual relationship out of the office, I wonder if anyone has puzzled it out. Her look is curious, though, so maybe not.

I realize that I don't care.

"You okay, Jasper?" I ask, trying to read his face past his nod and quiet "I'm fine."

"Seriously," he says, stepping slightly away from me, which I hate. "No one did anything more than stare at me and take the papers. I'm fine. Well and then…"

"And then?" I prompt with a growl.

"I was followed by a local police cruiser until I got on the interstate."

I am cut off from saying anything more or processing how the very idea that someone could have hurt him is crawling all over me. He's mine to protect.

Mine.

"Mr. Caffrey?" Nina, my go-to for situations like this, enters. Jasper was in the firm's car and I don't trust that some missing paperwork is all they did.

"Can you give Nina the keys, Jasper? She will need to check the car to make sure no one put a listening device or tracker in it since we know it was messed with."

Jasper steps closer to me, pulling out the keys with an unsteady hand.

"People do that?"

I give him a smile, resting a hand on his shoulder. "Usually more of a divorce law thing, but it's happened in a few of my cases when the stakes were high. It's really just a precaution."

He hands the keys over and I nod to Nina. "Nina is the best, she is brilliant with this sort of thing."

"I'll take good care of it, promise," she says to me, and Penny follows her out.

As soon as they are out of my office, I pull Jasper tight to me, his hands clutching my shirt as I cup his face to raise it for a kiss. I make it slow and tender, but Jasper shivers, responding with hungry sweeps of his tongue.

I maneuver him to my desk, finally satisfied when I stand between his thighs and his legs wrap around my waist. I grunt an affirmation. He's exactly where he should be.

Pulling back, I knock my forehead gently against his, watching the rapid rise and fall of his chest.

"What do you need right now, beautiful?"

His eyes flutter, and I realize it's one of the rare times he's being completely vulnerable with me.

"You."

I chuckle, ghosting my lips across his. "You got that. What else do you need?"

"I was scared, Marsh," he admits, shaking his head. "I know I could have filed a police report, but what good would that do? You know it had to be someone in the system who took the subpoenas. And subpoenas—it's not like they are essential or anything. It's just more paperwork. More like a scare tactic," he continues rambling, breath racing across my lips, "and why try to scare me? Or us? Do they just want us to know they are watching?" He takes a deep breath. "I could have gone to the local copy store, reprinted them and had them reissued, but I didn't think of that until I was halfway back here. But I have the file on my tablet. It would have been easy."

I step back just enough to be able to search his eyes. "You did the right thing, Jasper. It was a scare tactic, for sure. Just someone wanting to know they don't appreciate us coming into their town and saying they did anything wrong. They want to throw us off our game before we even get there. You also have to factor in that we are suing the city itself, too. People don't take that lightly."

He nods, but his eyes still hold this sort of wariness I haven't seen from him in weeks.

I kiss his nose and he makes a light laugh that has me feeling better.

"Do you feel like being around people right now?" I ask.

"Bear Valley people?" he asks in response, and I nod. "Then yes. You, then double yes."

I peck his lips this time, just lingering long enough to let him know there will be more of that later, if he's up to it.

"What about Black Diamond? I want to speak with Quinn's husband, if he's around, and he usually is on a Friday afternoon."

I step back and straighten my clothes, and Jasper follows, straightening his own and reaching to fix my tie.

We've done this move a few times now. Those occasions where a quick kiss led to more in the library or the copy room.

"Isn't Quinn's husband an English professor? Is this about a case?"

"It's about this case. He was an FBI agent before he became an English professor and I want to talk to him. I planned for us to stay in Trenton during the trial, and if we go through with those plans, I need to know everyone is safe."

I need to know that Jasper is safe, but I don't say that.

CHAPTER 17

JASPER

Marsh cuts a dashing figure in the front of the courtroom. He has on a navy suit, what he's told me one should always wear for a small town trial.

"The people on this jury will mostly have jobs and lives that don't require a suit. It may even be something they would have to go out and buy for a funeral or other occasion, and if they are buying one, the default would be navy," he told me that morning as I watched him from his bed, drawing out getting up until the last possible moment. Watching Marshall Caffrey trying to be Everyman was adorable. Watching him roam his eyes over me, even through the mirror, was heady. A hell of a way to start the day.

We are arguing motions and selecting the jury today. Marsh wants to make a certain kind of impression, and my brain once more wants to orgasm over the attention to detail. Is competence a kink? Do other people find that sexy?

Because watching him in front of the 1950s-style courtroom arguing our motion for three additional witnesses to be able to testify—witnesses that the Defense is dead-set against—is sexy. It's also important to this case. Important to the justice that the family deserves. Lack of access to emergency care is a big deal. This may be a small town, but national media are already here to cover the case.

Marsh starts arguing again, citing cases that are familiar to me because I helped research them. He even uses the arguments that I found, too, making me feel less like an observer and more like part of the team.

"Well," the judge casts her eyes back to the last rows of the gallery, where some media already has presence before the trial starts tomorrow, "I'm going to let you make your case, Mr. Caffrey. So, my ruling for now is that these witnesses can testify." The defense attorney, a stern woman with sharp, angular features, begins to protest, but the judge hushes her with a look. "All I am ruling right now is that the witnesses can be called and sworn. The questioning will have to meet the rules of evidence just like any other witnesses. But, I can't see anything that would prevent them from being called at all. We will deal with any issues of relevance the City has at trial. I will clear my calendar for the week, if that's what it takes. However, I expect you can make your case in that time, Mr. Caffrey."

Having made her ruling, she nods with finality when Marsh says, "Of course, your honor."

Marsh turns from the bench, catching my eye as he moves to collect his things at counsel table. Marsh, who showed no emotion when handed a big pre-trial win a few seconds ago, flashes me a brief smile, his eyes warm.

When opposing counsel catches his arm he lifts a finger to me, silently asking me to wait before I head back to his car. Penny stands with the family of the deceased, our clients, and Marsh says something quick to them as well.

The exchange is swift, and Marsh's hand guides me from the courtroom, down the stairs and into a small bathroom on the first floor.

He locks the door behind us, despite the bathroom having several stalls for multiple people.

Eyes dark and hungry, he pushes me against the door and kisses me hard.

"That was you, Jasper," he buries his hands in my hair, kissing me until I whimper. "Beautiful work, beautiful."

"Thanks?"

He chuckles, moving his mouth toward mine, only to take it away, like we are in one of those "don't kiss" challenge videos on TikTok. His eyes darken at every pass where my mouth wants to follow his.

"You will be a brilliant lawyer," Marsh says. "I want you to know that. Those cases, your research, was exactly what I needed."

"This is your area of expertise. I was excited to help."

"You did. Damn, you did." He presses his hips against mine, the feel of him hard against me is heady.

"You want me to do something about that in the courtroom bathroom?"

He smiles. "Want? Yes." He draws away. "But not a good idea." He looks sheepish as he looks at me through his lashes. "There is a bit of a high that comes with courtroom work, seeing you there turned it into…" His eyes drag down my body, "Something else."

I cup him on the outside of his pants and he groans, eyes rolling back.

"Too tempting," he says with a kiss, pulling away to run a hand over his face and step back a few feet. "Here's the plan. We will get ourselves presentable, then we will take the client to lunch as agreed upon and make sure they are ready for tomorrow. Then, we will look over our case, and make sure we are ready for tomorrow."

I wiggle my eyebrows. "And then?"

A wicked smile crosses his face. "And then whatever you want."

Later that night, I'm more than ready to make good on his promise. I've intentionally not looked at when my flight leaves. I honestly can't remember, but with the case starting, I know it is soon. Something niggles in the back of my mind about it, but with Marsh making his way across the bed, walking on his knees over to me, I really can't think about much else.

I meet him in the middle of the tangle of sheets, our mouths and hands devouring each other. My heart skips a beat no matter how many times we have done this.

Marsh pulls away, hands running down my ass and to my knees and he flips me down on my back with a grin.

"Sorry about pulling you in the bathroom at the courthouse," he says, placing kisses along the inside of my thigh as he stretches out my legs. "It was a rush. Like after a fight or a football game. I needed your lips on mine."

My blood rushes south and my head starts to spin with how wonderful he is.

"Glad I could oblige," I manage, closing my eyes before he reads too much there.

At least you had this, I remind myself. At least now I know what it's like to have something like how we are together. Not only that, but the couples I've met in Bear Valley? It gives me a lot to consider as I think about where my future lies.

"Beautiful," Marsh mumbles, his kisses at my neck now.

"Hmm?"

"Sex," he smiles, "I want to top you. I know you said you like to bottom, but do you like that for tonight? We haven't—"

I cut him off with a fierce kiss. Yes, I want that. I want everything with Marshall, so I better take what I can get before this summer fling is over.

CHAPTER 18

MARSHALL

The way Jasper looks in my bed is absolute sin. I can't get enough, either.

Having the green light to top him has my desire skyrocketing and puts this case somewhere to the far corner of my mind for the first time in days.

Jasper squirms, lean legs looking like art as they stretch across my white sheets and the shadows of the low light play across them.

I think I'm in love with him. I should *know*; I loved Keith. I think I was expecting that if I ever found love again, it would feel the same. It doesn't. This love is different than what I felt with my husband. My first husband. Because damn, I can see Jasper as my second.

It's good between us, even if it is this whole other thing than what I had with Keith. It feels different. It's my love for Jasper and love is a unique sort of thing.

But still just as good, just as valid, Keith's voice says.

I blink back into the moment, not wanting to miss a second of this. Jasper, on his back, panting.

"Baby," he says, causing a flood of emotions through me at the endearment. Keith and I didn't really use them. Not the usual ones like "baby." It hits like a punch in the gut.

Keith will always be a voice in my head, of that I'm sure, even if I'm in love with someone else, too. But my focus right now is on Jasper and only him. He might as well be the only thing to exist in the entire universe.

Looking into his eyes, I can see the love there, and I can't help but wonder if he can give me the same love with his heart as well. Falling for him complicates things I don't want to complicate.

He has his whole life ahead of him, and I can't hold him back because I fell in love with him. I can't ask him to ditch what is ahead of him for a small town in the Colorado mountains. He has to go at the end of the summer and I have to let him.

I have to not think about our conversation a few days ago that involved a job offer in Denver that would be one the best offers on the table. One he wants.

He wants. Not my call. So I tried not to tip my hand during that conversation and managed—somehow—not to beg him to take the job closest to me.

"Marsh," Jasper growls, impatient for me to quit watching him and start touching. I feel my face stretch into a smile. No problems there.

"Stay close," I tell Jasper. Closing arguments are over and the jury has the case. That means a whole lot of waiting as we are asked to remain in the courthouse, as is typical.

Jasper has seemed preoccupied since closing arguments. I can see the side-eye Jasper gets—has gotten the entire week of this trial. He's been a great assistant, handing me case law, notes, exhibits. He's even good with the witnesses—not everyone is early on.

But there is one bailiff in particular who raises my hackles when he stares too long at Jasper. In a small town it isn't strange for a bailiff to also be a patrolman, and I wonder if he's the one that followed Jasper. I wonder if that is what has Jasper looking panicked every now and then.

Only a few more hours until this jury does what the Constitution intended it to do, and we put this one in the closed case file.

I feel confident. Everything went as well as it could. There is always a hiccup or two in litigation. I never make predictions or try to feel a certain way, but in my gut, I always know the outcome, and I've never been wrong.

My gut tells me to call ahead and reserve some tables at Black Diamond tonight, but I don't. Lawyers are as superstitious as athletes, and I never count a win before the jury foreman reads it.

But, still, when the jury comes in, I know. And sure enough, the Ashby family gets the justice they were long denied.

After we finish the formalities and clear out, I catch Jasper's arm and he startles, like I've caught him unaware.

"I'll meet you at Black Diamond," I tell him, "if you want to ride back with Penny. I just need a few more minutes with the Ashbys and to give a statement to the press."

CHAPTER 19

JASPER

Walking out of the courthouse after the big win, I feel like I am in a daze. Maybe it was the closing arguments. Or cross examination. Or... just seeing Marsh do his thing so well to bring justice to his clients. But somewhere during that trial, it became less about my internship and my ambitions for the last year of law school and more about watching Marsh.

One minute I was sitting on the hard bench of the gallery of the old courthouse and the next...well, I looked down and my heart was gone.

My hands are still shaking from that realization.

I say the right things, enjoy the win I helped craft and the team I helped craft it with, but by the time I slide into the back of Penny's car, I'm in a panic.

I cannot fall in love with Marshall. That has to be the golden rule of summer flings. Do. Not. Fall. In. Love.

I stare dumbly out the window as the landscape flashes by, taken out of my circling thoughts only when my phone vibrates.

Looking down, I see the airline confirming my check-in. I blink a

few times, trying to figure out why I would be getting on a flight back
to Florida.

Oh shit. When I first arrived, I had moved my flight up because
Marshall was being an ass, and then I got caught up in the case and
him and I never changed it.

Tomorrow morning, it reminds me.

I can check in now.

I stare at the screen, swallowing hard.

Six weeks later, I am riding high on the pace of the third year of law
school. The work is hard—would have been crushing in my first year
—but by now it's shockingly manageable. It allows me to focus on the
Law Review, the symposium, and the way my heart aches in my chest.

I stare out at nothing sometimes. There are days it feels part of me
is still in Bear Valley. I don't go out much. But, otherwise...I'm fine.
Perfectly fine. Even as I sit here at the Law Review offices at school
doing nothing except avoiding the quiet solitude of my apartment.

Professor Rutherford passes by in the hall but then backtracks.

He pauses like he might just linger in the doorway, but then plops
down in the unused chair of the other desk in the office.

"You want to talk about it?" Professor Rutherford asks.

"The symposium is going fine, Professor. I just checked in on the
reception tonight—"

He holds up a hand.

"That's not what I meant, Mr. Dawson."

I blink at him, feeling my cheeks heat as his look gets more knowing. He is my professor and I did spend the summer doing very
naughty things with his best friend and former law partner. I feel my
face ignite in a blush.

"I know Marshall Caffrey pretty well, as I have gotten to know you.
And I am just wondering what I will be walking into when you are
both at this reception tonight."

I start. "He's coming to that?"

"I didn't pick him up from the airport for a weekend of fun. He's the keynote at the symposium and you and I both know the fact he wrote one of the articles for the journal is, standing alone, a fact that will draw national attention."

I swallow hard. I hadn't thought he would be here until at least the symposium itself, which is a few months away. I thought I had more time to get over him. Him being here just reinforces what I knew—it was just a summer fling for him. He hasn't called or tried to reach out since I left after the win, and I've been telling myself that's a good thing.

"So I'm right," Professor Rutherford continues. "Something went down this summer."

I almost snort a laugh. Yeah, something went down. Me. And all I got was a broken heart.

I wet my lips, sliding my now-damp palms down my thighs. "He won his case—"

"I know, I read your article for the review, Jasper. I do turn on the news every now and again as well."

"Then what?"

Rutherford huffs. "I know heartbreak when I see it. And it's all over both of you. My suggestion is that you go talk to him before tonight." He reaches into his pocket and hands me a piece of paper. "He's staying out on The Wyn," he says, referencing the resort island just a bridge away from where the law school is located. Rutherford lives there with his husband. "I know the owner of the resort, and that's Marsh's room number. Do with it what you want, but you didn't get it from me."

The paper burns in my pocket during the short trip out to the island. I'm not thinking about what I will say when I get there, I just get there and in front of his door as soon as I can. I want to pause, but I don't. I knock before I can talk myself out of it.

My heart hammers in my chest, threatening to crawl up my throat.

I'm just here to clear the air, I remind myself.

The door opens with a jerk, "Damn you, Lin, I told you I—" Marshall halts mid-sentence, his eyes roaming over me like he's cataloguing every change from the last time I saw him.

I do the same, tracking the dark stubble, the sunken eyes. He looks just as sexy as I remember him, but if I'm honest, he also sort of looks like shit.

"Want to come in?" he asks, opening the door wider.

I nod and enter, with him so close behind me I can feel his body heat.

Strong arms wrap around my waist, and I melt into him, burying my nose against his neck and feeling just for a moment that all is right with the world. I shiver in his arms as his nose runs down my neck.

"Jasper," he breathes, catching my lips as I try to get as close as possible, and he doesn't hold back from clutching my ass and pulling me to him and pushing me against the wall.

"This isn't what I expected," I manage between kisses.

He nips my lip. "You left." Another nip. "Didn't say a fucking word to me, Jasper."

I moan when he kisses me even more aggressively, making me forget why I left in the first place.

"Never work," I tell him, while still kissing the hell out of him and rubbing my body all over his with no shame. "I was getting too involved, Marsh," I whisper, and his hand tangles into my hair, making me look at him.

His eyes are full of heat and questions, bouncing from one of mine to the other.

"Did you think I wasn't in it?"

I blink up at him.

"We were a summer fling."

Marsh's grip relaxes, his hand cups my jaw. "That's not all we are. I know love, Jasper. And it showed me what I fool I was when I didn't chase you down and keep you from getting on that plane. I love you."

CHAPTER 20

MARSHALL

Jasper is going to be an amazing lawyer. I can tell just by watching him help Lincoln host this dinner full of all the people who do the same kind of law that I do. To a person, they can be a tough sell—especially for some baby lawyer who hasn't even passed the bar yet.

He's good with a crowd. Charismatic. And that's not just the post-sex haze from the love making—and promise making—of just a few hours ago talking.

I catch his eye across the room and give a slight tilt of my head to encourage him over. We are at the desert and wine and mingling part of the evening, and there are people here I want him to meet.

But more than that is the promise still ringing in my ear for us to see where this goes.

It goes forever. Keith's voice is loud and clear in my ear.

Maybe, I toss back, but I know down to the very core of me that he's right.

While my eyes trail Jasper around the room, I hear Keith's rich laugh in my head.

So much for a summer fling.

A FRIENDLY PRESCRIPTION

AE LISTER

Featuring characters from the Paging Dr. Griffin series by AE Lister.

PART 1

GEROME

Gerome: *Hi, Scott. This is Gerome. Do you remember me? I was your server, but you decided you wanted dessert back at your place? And I was dessert?*

I stared at the text on my phone as memories assaulted me. Memories of a beautiful and sweet young man who'd been our server at a cute little restaurant when we'd been on holiday in Wakefield, Ontario, and had accompanied us back to the cottage we were borrowing from friends. But that had been a long time ago. We'd said we'd keep in touch, but we hadn't.

Me: *Good, good. How are you?*

Gerome: *I've been better. Would love to meet up to talk to someone.*

I smiled at my phone, glad to have heard from the young man of whom we had such fond memories from our stay at Duke's cottage two summers ago.

I texted back right away.

Me: *Of course! I'm free right now.*

Gerome: *Can we…meet somewhere in person? Is that possible?*

Me: *Are you still in Wakefield?*

Gerome: *Living in Ottawa now.*

Me: *Oh! Where would you like to meet? It's a nice day. In the mood for a walk?*

Gerome: *Yeah, that would be great. How about Hog's Back Park? I'm living in an apartment near there and I don't have a car.*

Me: *See you at two?*

It was one o'clock right now, and that would give me time to change into better clothes and get there.

Gerome: *Great! I'll be near the concession stand.*

I knew where that was. I doubted it would be open. Actually, I had no idea if the city still stocked and ran it. They had when I was a kid. We used to bike there and stop for a snack.

In Ottawa, you could live close to downtown but still be in a wide-open green space in about ten minutes. I'd briefly tried to live in downtown Toronto, and while the vibe and hustle-bustle had been cool and invigorating for about three months, I'd soon tired of the high rises and concrete. People called a block of grass between two streets in Toronto a 'park', but it didn't feel like one. When I got back to Ottawa, it seemed even more beautiful than I'd remembered.

Hog's Back Park—not the most auspicious name for such a pretty spot—was between Prince of Wales and Riverside Drive, near Mooney's Bay Beach and across the Rideau River from Carleton University. The entire area along the canal and through the university campus was a naturalist's dream.

There was lots of parking in the dedicated lot. It was a weekday afternoon in the middle of the summer. A yellow school bus sat by the curb, and a group of kids played some game in the field near what became ideal toboggan hills in the winter. But the concession stand was in the other direction, right beside the viewing area. The sound of rushing water filled my ears as I noticed a young man in grey bermuda shorts, flip-flops, and a wine-coloured t-shirt. It had been a while since I'd seen Gerome, so I approached slowly, hoping the person would turn around.

I realized it was him as he turned and lifted a hand to wave.

"Scott!"

"Hey! So nice to see you!" I said.

We greeted each other with a quick but affectionate hug, and then Gerome looked me over.

"Still sexy. Goddamn."

I blushed. "Well, you too."

He nodded and looked away, as if unsure of what to say next.

"Let's go look at the falls," I suggested.

"Okay."

We walked along the path and down some steps to a paved look-out area with a black metal fence to keep people off the rocks.

"I'm always impressed with the beauty of this place," I said, leaning on the fence and watching the whitewater fall to the left of us and cascade over the rapids below.

"Yeah. It's something special," Gerome said.

"Want to tell me what's going on?" I asked.

Gerome gripped the metal rail and looked down at the rocks. He took a shaky breath and started talking. "So...I got a call yesterday from this guy that I hooked up with a few weeks ago. And he told me he just..." Gerome struggled to speak. "Oh God, I can't even believe I'm saying this. It's making it even more real and terrifying."

"It's okay. Tell me."

"He said he tested positive."

My blood went cold.

"For HIV?" I said, my voice hushed like it was the horrible, unspeakable thing it used to be in the eighties and early nineties.

"Yeah." He took a steadying breath. "Scott, I'm so fucking scared right now."

He stared at the roaring water that coursed over the rocks below, as if it reflected the turbulence of his mind.

I was from a generation that had barely missed the whole AIDS epidemic and the echoes of that era still hit hard. I moved closer.

"Can I put my arm around you?"

The gratitude in his eyes and the look he gave me as he nodded reassured me. I embraced him and squeezed his shoulder.

"I'm glad you called me."

He shook his head.

"I don't know what to do..."

"I hate to be so practical, but you need to get tested."

"Yeah, I did. I went this morning. But now I have to wait and I don't know how to manage between now and then. It's literally all I can think about."

I sighed. "I'm so sorry you have to go through this."

"I feel so bad for him, too. He sounded so sad and scared on the phone."

"Is he a friend? Or just a casual fling?"

"Not even a fling. We met at a club and went back to his place. I wasn't planning to see him again." He shrugged.

I took my arm away but stayed close, leaning on the rail beside him. The spray from the falls made a cooling mist around us.

"Can I ask you—"

"We fucked. He used a condom for that."

"Oh, thank God. I mean, I don't really believe in God, but...yeah."

"I never let anyone top me without a condom."

"Good," I said with a nod.

"But Scott. I sucked and swallowed."

Ah. That's where the fear came from.

Gerome continued. "I knew it was a risk but, for some reason, it didn't register. I can't even remember if I did that with you guys."

"I don't think so. We were conscious of your safety and ours, at the time."

"I feel like an idiot. But I mean...blowies are low risk, right?"

"Sweetheart, they're *lower* risk. But there's still *some* risk."

"Fuck, fuck, fuck. I was hoping to get on PrEP. I've discussed it with my doctor. I don't know what I was waiting for."

I saw movement out of the corner of my eye and instinctively moved a step away from Gerome. A couple of teenagers were coming to look at the falls.

"You want to come over to our place? We can talk some more and get pizza when the others get home in a couple of hours."

"I'd love to. I don't want to be by myself right now."

I texted our address to Gerome, then texted Pascal and Jericho to fill them in.

Pascal: *Flame emoji. Hot dog. That night in Wakefield still features pretty big on my wank-off list.*

Me: *He's not coming for sex and we're going to be gentlemen. I'm afraid he's had an STD scare, and he's freaking out a bit.*

Pascal: *HIV?*

Me: *Yes. Someone he hooked up after us tested positive.*

Pascal: *Shit. Poor kid.*

Jericho made the same assumption, that Gerome was heading over for a sexcapade, but I explained what was going on.

Jericho: *Oh damn. So, pizza, beer and a movie?*

Me: *Yep. He just needs to chill and talk about it.*

"Let's go, then," I said, and Gerome followed me to my car.

As I drove back to the townhouse I shared with Pascal and Jericho, I told Gerome about a health scare I'd had a few years ago.

"I know a bit about waiting for test results."

"Shit, are you okay?"

"I'm fine. I had to get a biopsy, though, and that was terrifying. It turned out to be benign." I waved my hand in the air. "Not to minimize your situation."

"No, no. *Please* minimize it," Gerome said, leaning back in the passenger seat and watching me drive.

I laughed.

Gerome looked appreciatively at the home I shared with my two partners when I pulled into the drive.

"This is such a cute house."

"Yeah. It was Jericho and Pascal's place first. I moved in a few years ago."

He followed me inside.

"Make yourself at home. Jericho and Pascal will be here soon."

He looked around, and his eyes bugged out.

"Wow, this is a fantastic place. Who does the decorating?"

"Pascal mostly."

Gerome sat on the leather sofa, stretching his legs out. "Do you still go up to the cottage?"

The cottage…

"Yes, but it belongs to my friend, Duke. We're usually up there with him and his husband."

Gerome raised his eyebrows, and I laughed. "No, no. They're just friends. It's the three of us and the two of them."

The thought of being sexual with Duke and his husband was hilarious. Not because they weren't attractive, but they were almost family.

"Oh. Not the weekend we met, though."

I grinned, remembering. "No. They let us borrow it for the weekend. Trust me, you were a lovely amuse-bouche after a couple of days of rampant debauchery. Want something to drink?"

"Sure."

"I've got lemonade and soft drinks, beer and wine…"

"A glass of wine might chill me out."

"Wine it is. White or red?"

"Red, please."

I went into the kitchen and poured a glass of red wine for Gerome and one for myself. Then I returned to the living room and handed him the glass.

"Thanks," he said. He took a sip. "Oh yeah. This is what I need." He frowned, then leaned forward with his elbows on his knees. "Scott, do you think…do you think I'm reckless?"

"Gerome, come on. You said you've discussed PrEP with your doctor. I think it might be a good idea…" I gazed at his morose expression. "Do *you* think you're reckless?"

He sighed. "Maybe a little." He took another drink of his wine, then placed the glass on the coffee table.

I sat down beside him and put my glass next to his.

He continued. "I keep thinking back to it, and wondering what I was thinking. Why did I go down on the guy? Why did I have to swallow? I knew it was risky, but in that moment, I didn't care."

"Remind me how old you are," I said in a soft voice, gazing at him with kindness. I knew he was much younger than me, but I couldn't remember his actual age. I was pretty sure he'd been twenty when we'd had him for a spontaneous dessert.

"Old enough to know better. I'm twenty-two."

"Jesus. I was not as responsible at twenty-two as you seem to be. I've taken my share of risks. Luckily, I wised up before it was too late, and I've had numerous negative test results since then."

"Are you guys on PrEP?"

"The two of them were, when we met. But they've stopped taking it, as we're keeping things exclusive between the three of us now, and…" I met Gerome's bashful gaze, "Being safe with anyone new."

He raised his eyebrows.

"We don't fuck other people. We might play around a little, but there are minimal bodily fluids involved and we don't do it often. Honestly, we've only ever done it with you."

"Really?" He seemed astonished.

"Yeah. What did you think? That we picked up a new twink every weekend?"

He blushed and shrugged. "I don't know. Maybe."

"Well, we don't. God, for one thing, we don't have the energy. But that was a fun night. And we played safe."

"You guys took very good care of me, as I remember," Gerome mused, letting his gaze run down my body. "I wish I was here for something other than moral support, except I can't even think about sex right now."

At that moment, a key turned in a lock and the front door pushed open. Jericho and Pascal came in.

"We're here, we're queer, and we're gonna order pizza!" Pascal said boisterously as they came in. "Gerome!"

"Hey! Oh my God, it's great to see you guys."

"Gerome," Jericho said. "Scott told us about your predicament. Well, not the details. If you want to talk about it, we're all ears."

"Thanks," Gerome said. "I don't know any other guys your ages to talk to. Well, except my *actual* Dad, but there's no way that's happening. We don't talk much these days and I'm not telling him about this, or what lead to it."

Pascal started laughing. He elbowed Jericho. "Our ages. Did you hear that? We're fucking Daddies! Whoop whoop."

Gerome smiled. "I only mean that I look up to you."

"Thank you," I said. "We do have a considerable amount of experience between the three of us."

"And FYI, I'm the youngest, if you didn't already know," Jericho said.

"And also the kinkiest. I can't remember, does Gerome know about Dr. Griffin?" Pascal asked.

Gerome's gaze flew between us. "The what now?"

"Ooooh!" Pascal said with great excitement. "He doesn't know what a kinky fucker you are, Jericho."

"I don't think we need to tell Gerome all of our dirty little secrets," I muttered, embarrassed about the way Jericho and Pascal and I played sometimes. There was medical kink and there was *medical kink*, and we were into the serious kind.

Gerome sat up straighter. "Oh yes, you do. Because if you can make me realize I haven't been the biggest slut on the block this year, that would be amazing."

"Trust me, it's him," Pascal said, pointing to me. "No, wait. It's him." He pointed to Jericho. Then he shrugged. "Or it could be me. It's definitely not you."

"Fine, we'll let you in on our little secret," Jericho said, winking. "But only after the pizza's been ordered. I'm starved."

After a discussion with Gerome about what he liked and didn't like on pizza, we ordered two large pies—one with meat, and the other all veggies. Then Pascal and Jericho said all the same things that I had to Gerome, to reassure him about the probable results of his blood test.

He seemed to be calming down.

"Don't forget that a positive HIV test result isn't a death sentence anymore," Jericho murmured. "The treatments have come a long way."

"I don't think many people, at least in North America, actually go on to develop AIDS," Pascal agreed.

"Oh, what about Grant and Christopher?" I said, remembering the couple we'd known for several years.

Jericho nodded. "They're HIV positive and have been married for what, eight years?"

I nodded. "Yes."

"Undetectable. I hardly remember they have it," Pascal said.

"That's encouraging," Gerome said, a hopeful look in his eyes.

"I can give you their contact information if you want to talk to them about it," I said. "I don't think they'd mind."

"Thanks," Gerome said. "Now, about this little secret. I'm dying to know what it is…"

"Oh boy," I said, glancing at Pascal.

He laughed. "Maybe we should just show Gerome the exam room?"

Gerome coughed. "Excuse me?"

Jericho leapt up from the couch. "Come on. I'll take you to my office."

"What is happening?" Gerome asked, glancing to me and Pascal.

Pascale winked. "You're getting a look at how perverted we are. That should distract you."

Gerome, Pascal, and I followed Jericho down the hall to a door on the right of the hallway.

Jericho put his hand on the knob and turned to Gerome. "You ready?"

"Sure."

Pascal and I exchanged a look.

Jericho twisted the handle and pushed the door open, letting it swing wide while he crossed his arms and nodded. "There you go."

An audible breath left Gerome as he got his first look at *Dr. Griffin's* exam room. *Dr. Griffin* was Jericho's alter ego when we were engaged in this kind of play.

"Holy shit," Gerome said, eyes wide as he took everything in. He swallowed, then looked at us. "So which one of you is the doctor?"

Jericho raised his hand while Pascal and I pointed his way.

"Dr. Griffin, at your service," Jericho purred. He glanced at me. "But I'm not taking outside appointments anymore."

I smiled. That was a concession to me, although I didn't think Pascal was all that upset about it. There were three of us now. We were unlikely to get bored.

"Honestly, in a way, I'm relieved to hear it," Gerome said, eyeing me and Pascal, probably imagining both of us submitting to weekly or monthly 'exams'.

I raised my hand. "I'm the patient. Pascal is Dr. Griffin's assistant."

Gerome's eyes went even wider. "You!"

I shrugged, giving him an indulgent smile.

"Yes, well, Scott was quite the surprise," Jericho said, leaning on the doorframe. "We picked him up at a kinky Halloween party and brought him home. Decided to keep him."

"Hardy, har," I said. "It was a little more complicated than that. But, yeah, it worked out in the end."

Jericho grinned. "Oh, it definitely worked out in *the end*."

Pascal hooted.

"How are you the king of dad jokes when you aren't even a dad?" I asked.

"Oh, Scott. You are a naughty, naughty boy for implying that I'm not *at least* your daddy. And probably his," Jericho said, gesturing toward Pascal, who barked.

Gerome's eyes went even wider.

Jericho held up his hand. "Oh, I'm so sorry. Not daddy to you then. Master?"

Pascal barked again.

Gerome was grinning from ear to ear. "Wow, this relationship has layers."

"It certainly does," I said, blushing.

"May I?" Gerome asked, gesturing to the contents of the exam room.

"Of course," Jericho said. "Just don't touch anything. Most of these things are sterile."

"Jesus Christ," Gerome muttered. "Okay, you guys win."

"See?" Pascal said. "You're not the sluttiest."

Gerome walked into the room with some caution, glancing back with various expressions on his sweet face as he took it in—the steel exam table with stirrups; the IV stand with enema bag and tube; the sterilized implements on the tray.

"Jesus. If I'd known about this, I might have been into it back in Wakefield."

"Yeah, I didn't have all my stuff at Duke's cottage," Jericho admitted.

"Some of it, though," I muttered.

"Well, I wouldn't be a good doctor if I wasn't prepared for emergencies," he said, looking me over.

I couldn't help laughing, remembering the milk enema he'd given me that weekend, much to Pascal's delight. And mine, if I was being honest. I loved that Jericho was so damn creative and such a fucking pervert.

Gerome turned to Pascal. "So, you're Dr. Griffin's assistant?"

"Yes."

"And a...pup?"

Pascal nodded and yipped, then grinned.

"Huh. You guys are wild."

"Just kinky and with minimal hangups," Jericho said. "Now, that's enough gawking at my medical equipment, young man. Let's go pick a movie. The pizza will be here soon."

We wanted to watch something light and upbeat, so we chose The Devil Wears Prada. Just as it was starting, Jericho jumped up.

"Hold on."

We exchanged curious looks until Jericho returned, carrying a colorful tin jar that I recognized immediately.

"Ah," I said.

"Yes!" Pascal muttered, holding out his hand.

"Dessert," Jericho said, taking the top off the tin and holding it out to Gerome.

"What the fuck?"

Jericho pulled the tin back to his chest, staring at Gerome in shock.

"You've never seen a tin of Chuppa Chups?"

Gerome looked confused. "Um..."

"These are the best lollipops you can buy," Jericho explained. "They were super popular in the eighties, apparently. Luckily, you can still get them."

"Lollipops?" Gerome asked, grinning.

"Mm hm," Jericho said, pulling one out and checking the wrapper. "How do you feel about blueberry?"

"Good."

Jericho handed the lollipop to Gerome, then held the tin out to me and Pascal. We each took one. I got raspberry.

Jericho had become obsessed with the popular retro lollipops when he'd quit smoking many years ago. He always had a tin of them on hand.

"Maybe sucking on something will soothe you," Jericho said to Gerome, grinning.

Gerome frowned. "That's what got me into this mess in the first place."

"Okay, but a Chuppa Chup is harmless. And they taste so good."

Gerome unwrapped his sucker and popped it into his mouth. "Mmm."

I stared at sweet Gerome wrapping his lips around the blueberry lollipop and tried not to get hard. But it was hopeless. I glanced at Pascal, who seemed to be having the same problem.

I jumped up. "Anyone want popcorn?"

"You want me to hit pause?" Jericho asked, the white stick of his lollipop jutting from between his teeth.

"No, no, I'll just catch up. I've seen it a few times. It's all good."

I went into the kitchen as Pascal stood and followed me.

"Hey, I'll help."

I set up the air popper while Pascal got the jar of kernels. I put a whack of butter into the melting pan and set a bowl underneath the chute, then turned on the machine. Now we could talk without worrying about being overheard.

"Jesus. He's just as cute as he was last summer. I'm trying to ignore it, but it's difficult," Pascal muttered.

"Yeah, me too. He's such a nice kid. I feel bad that he's stressing out over these test results."

"Maybe everyone has to have a close call before they truly wise up and start taking these risks seriously. He's so young," Pascal said.

"Compared to you and me, sure."

"Jericho's not *that* much younger than us," Pascal said.

"But he's closer in age to Gerome," I pointed out.

"Sure, sure. But does it matter?"

"No, I guess not."

Pascal leaned against the counter. "You thinking about Duke's cottage?"

"Yeah. How can I not?"

He shrugged. "So rein it in. Like I'm doing."

I grinned. "Of course. I'll have you know, I'm a gentleman."

We exchanged a look, remembering every debasing thing Jericho had ever done to me, and burst out laughing.

I shrugged. "In some circumstances."

"Right."

"And who knows? If Gerome's test results come back fine, maybe he'd want to give us a go again, and we could have even more fun together."

Pascal shrugged. "You know, if he *is* positive—I hope not, but it could happen—we could still have some safe fun with him, and show him that he's not a pariah. Not right away, obviously, but once he gets on track with his meds. When he's in the right headspace. If he even wants to."

"Sure."

There were two things we had to do. One was to make sure Gerome was supported through the anxious waiting period, and two, through whatever the results turned out to be. If he was neg, we'd encourage him to get onto PrEP, or even get a prescription for Doxy-PEP. If Gerome was going to be sexually active, even if he continued to use condoms for penetrative sex with strangers, taking those further precautions would be wise.

PART 2

RESULTS

As the movie credits rolled, someone tapped my shoulder. I turned my head to see Pascal. He pointed to Gerome, who had fallen asleep on Jericho's shoulder.

"Is that the sweetest fucking thing you've ever seen?" he whispered.

"That's pretty fucking sweet," I agreed, meeting Jericho's gaze.

"He probably hasn't been sleeping well," I whispered.

"No. I'm sure he hasn't," Pascal said.

"I hate to wake him," Jericho murmured. "But I need to piss."

"Should we offer the couch for the night?"

"Yeah, of course," Jericho said, reaching over and jiggling Gerome. "Hey, Sleeping Beauty. Time to wake up."

Gerome moaned lightly and snuggled into Jericho even more.

Pascal put a hand to his heart. "So precious."

Jericho spoke a bit louder as he jiggled Gerome again. "Gerome. Wakey, wakey."

Gerome opened his eyes. He stared at Jericho in surprise.

"Oh shit. Sorry."

He sat up, blinking.

"I need the washroom," Jericho said. "And it's eleven thirty, so I think we're gonna go to bed. You can stay the night, if you want, though. The couch is yours."

Gerome looked at Jericho, then at me and Pascal.

"I'm pretty tired. Are you sure that would be okay?"

"It's Friday. Do you have to be anywhere tomorrow?" I asked him.

"No. I've got an entry-level admin job now. Which means weekends off. Finally."

Pascal opened his arms. "Well, just stay here, then. We'll probably sleep in, but if you want to get up and go, that's fine, too."

"I'll get you a blanket and a pillow," I said.

"I'll say good night," Jericho said. "Scott can show you where the bathroom is on this level, all right?"

"Yeah, thanks. Good night, Jericho."

"Good night, Gerome," Pascal said with a little wave. "Sleep tight."

Gerome smiled. We kept a basket of throw blankets by the sofa, so I pulled one out and tossed it onto the end of the couch for him.

"Bathroom's the last door on the right."

"Thanks, Scott. This is so nice of you all."

"Gerome, it's the least we can do. You need to sleep, and if that's easier here with us, then that's fine."

"Good night, then."

"Good night."

I left him and went upstairs. Pascal and Jericho were getting undressed.

Pascal eyed me.

"You, uh, still having that problem we discussed earlier, Scott?"

"In a general sense, I guess." I had managed to subdue my erection, but at Pascal's words it started to make a reappearance.

"What problem?" Jericho asked, glancing over as he pushed down his pants.

I glanced at the open bedroom door, then walked over and closed it, turning back to Jericho.

"A problem with *not* being a huge horny slut for the gorgeous, but understandably anxious, twink downstairs."

"Ah," Jericho said. "If it makes you feel any better, that was also a problem that I was having."

"Jesus. You guys are such perverts," Pascal scoffed, grabbing his dick and aiming it at me and then Jericho.

Jericho gave Pascal a sober look. "Don't you tell me that you weren't having flashbacks to that oh-so-perfect evening back at Duke's cottage."

Pascal smiled with the air of fond reminiscence. "That night was amazing. But now I'm remembering how we put Scott in the pup hood the next day and defiled him."

"Fuck," I said.

"Get the hood, Pascal."

"What?" I whispered.

"I think this is a good opportunity to remind you of your place, Scott," Jericho said, crossing his arms as Pascal went over to the closet.

Pascal was our resident leather pup, and I'd come a long way from thinking the fetish was completely ridiculous, to appreciating how it could enhance Pascal's personality and give him pleasure, but I didn't think of myself as a pup. They had only done it the one time, and it had been hot, yeah. As I was thinking back on it now, I recalled how enjoyable it had been. I wasn't sure why it made me nervous to put on the pup mask and be a mindless animal for an hour.

Pascal brought the well-made hood over and raised his eyebrows at Jericho.

"You can safeword, Scott. Or just tell me you're too tired," Jericho said.

I stared at the hood. It was made from soft black leather, with red trim on the lifelike ears, and a realistic muzzle. I looked at Jericho, then at Pascal—who seemed to be on tenterhooks, hoping I'd agree to this.

"We'll have to be quiet. No way do I want Gerome to hear me barking. He already knows I'm a huge medical slut."

Pascal laughed loudly, then slapped a hand over his mouth. "Sorry."

Jericho smiled. "Mmm. You are a huge medical slut, Scott. And not averse to a different kind of humiliation, it seems." He inclined his chin and stared at the bulge in my jeans.

"Fine," I sighed, pulling my shirt off.

"Yes!" Pascal said, swinging the pup hood on his finger as he gazed at me with a gleeful countenance.

"When you're naked, come and kneel at my feet," Jericho said. He held his hand out for the hood, which Pascal passed to him.

"There you go, Sir."

"Thank you, Pascal."

I got naked, then raised my finger to my lips. We listened. There were only the familiar background noises of our home at night. Once I was certain that Gerome wasn't awake and wandering around, I kneeled on the wood floor in front of Jericho.

"Good boy," he said, ruffling my hair.

This was such a wonderful mind-fuck. I was a professor at the local college, and I'd earned the respect of my students and the faculty. The medical kink was one thing—everyone needed to go to the doctor on occasion, even if they were the Prime Minister or a celebrity, so it was humiliating, but also kind of normal. This was different. And it made me feel very fucking strange.

But I knew from experience that if I trusted Jericho and Pascal and went with it, it would be fun and exciting.

I liked to be under another man's control in the bedroom. I made so many important decisions at my job. I held the success and failure of hundreds of students in my hands. But here, in this safe space, I didn't want to feel like my choices *mattered*. It was a joy and a relief to submit to Jericho, and Pascal brought more fun into it. He was Jericho's faithful assistant in the exam room, and he brought a lighter atmosphere to the bedroom, as he was quick to find amusement in most situations.

Jericho lowered the pup hood over my head and Pascal buckled it behind. Kneeling between the two of them in this humbled way was a singularly arousing experience, and I closed my eyes for a moment, getting used to the leather mask.

"Do you remember what Scott's pup name is?" Jericho asked Pascal.

"Oh damn," Pascal muttered, scratching his chin and scrunching his forehead.

"Rocket," I said, my voice echoing inside the leather hood.

"Well, well, well. Scotty remembers. Isn't that interesting?" Jericho smirked.

I didn't really give a fuck what my pup name was. I didn't connect to this kind of play the way that Pascal did. At least, I didn't think I did.

"All right, now," Jericho said, beckoning to Pascal. "Why don't you come up on the bed and we'll give you a couple of bones to play with?"

So that was how it was gonna be. Well, I could play with bones. I loved to play with them, as a matter of fact.

Pascal and Jericho stripped naked and positioned themselves on the bed, side-by-side, leaning against the headboard.

"Here, puppy, puppy," Pascal whispered, mindful of keeping our cover. "Come and get it." He waved his erection at me while Jericho grinned, stroking himself idly.

I crawled up on the bed, moving forward, and giving a nudge to Pascal's cock with my leather muzzle as I flashed him what I hoped was a lust-filled look.

"Oh my god," he muttered. "Good boy…"

Pascal was beefier and bigger than Jericho, and had a charm that I couldn't deny. He was great at snuggling and an intimidating presence when we were out and about. We didn't have to worry about being rolled when Pascal was around. Even though Jericho was more my physical type, I had learned to love Pascal's laid-back masculinity and easy humor.

I grunted and then opened my mouth, maneuvering into position to get at Pascal's erection. The bottom jaw of the hood was short. In a moment, I had my lips around him.

"Oh, good boy, good boy," Pascal groaned. "Look at him, J. So eager."

"Oh, yes, he's a good boy. A good doggy," Jericho murmured.

I was getting into it, slobbering and slavering over Pascal's cock, when Jericho told me to switch. I slid off and crawled over to where Jericho was lying.

"Suck me, Rocket. Suck my cock."

I obeyed, lost to the soothing routine of doing what I was told. I loved my job, but boy, did I enjoy this more. And if things got too stressful in the work sphere, then an evening of submission and obedience could sort me right out and have me ready to be in charge again. In pup space, I wasn't even required to say anything. I could be a pet—Jericho and Pascal's special pet—and take a simple joy in blind obedience.

I went back and forth between them, crawling over their legs, and bending to their cocks, giving them everything I could, until Jericho told me to stop.

"Turn around."

Slick fingers stroked between my cheeks and rubbed my eager hole, while someone's hand lubed up my erection. I closed my eyes and lowered to my elbows, my submissive ass up in the air for both of them.

Jericho entered me first. I could tell it was him, from the size of his dick and from the ways he moved and dealt with me. And since he was top of the chain in our strange dynamic, he usually got first dibs.

"Oh, yeah. What a good boy," he moaned, sliding in without much trouble.

That familiar feeling of being penetrated by the man I'd grown to love, the man who had seen me hovering on the edges of a pup play Halloween event and approached me, so long ago, gave me a thrill and nostalgia for the time we'd met. He and Pascal had taken me home that night, for what was supposed to be a one-time thing—an introduction to medical kink that had blown my fucking mind. And it had developed over time into this committed, and kinky, polyamorous relationship.

I stifled my bliss-filled noises as Jericho fucked me, slowly and purposefully. I lost myself to the present moment, feeling the tension build. Jericho knew my body, and he knew how to fuck me. After a little bit of time, he climaxed with a quiet moan, then pulled out and slapped my ass.

I felt claimed and safe, and when Pascal pushed in, it brought me up to another level of pleasure. I was closer now and the feeling of impending bliss was within reach. My body sang and hummed with ecstatic energy as he moved, a little rougher and with more urgency than Jericho. He came with a stifled moan as he hunched over me, then kissed my shoulder as he pulled out and played with my jizz-filled hole. Then they flipped me over and took turns sucking my dick until I got off, groaning as quietly as I could while Jericho held his hand over my mouth.

In the morning, I woke first.

My ass was pleasantly sore, and I recalled our tryst from the previous evening. They'd cleaned me up after they were done defiling me, so I wasn't sticky with dried jizz.

I extricated myself from the tangle of familiar bodies without waking them somehow. I pulled on some PJ pants and a t-shirt, then padded down the stairs and peeked into the living room.

Gerome snored lightly, snuggled under a couple of blankets. I was glad to see him getting much-needed sleep and happy that we'd been able to soothe him. I tried not to make much noise as I loaded and started the coffeemaker. The fancy model we had was almost silent as it brewed, making a soft, swishing noise that soothed me. I made a couple of pieces of toast, then spread cherry jam on them and ate them at the kitchen table.

By the time I'd finished, the coffee was ready. I poured myself a cup and sat down in the same spot, checking the news app on my phone.

"Good morning."

I glanced up and saw Gerome in the doorway to the kitchen, wrapped in a blanket, gazing at me out of sleepy eyes.

"Good morning, Gerome. I hope I didn't wake you."

He smiled and shook his head. "Might have been the coffee. It smells so good. Is there enough for me?"

"Of course. Help yourself. Did you sleep well?"

"Yeah. I feel rested for the first time in days."

"I'm so glad," I said, sipping my coffee. "There's milk in the fridge and sugar in the cupboard above the sink, if you need it."

"Thanks."

"And there's bread and cereal and fruit if you'd like something to eat. Although Jericho will probably make pancakes or eggs when he gets up."

Gerome's eyebrows lifted. "You don't say? Maybe I'll wait and enjoy my coffee for now."

"Good idea."

He looked unsure for a moment. "Is that okay? Do you mind if I stick around? I can get going, if that's—"

"Stay. It's lovely having you here," I said. "Mugs are in the cupboard over the sink."

Gerome opened the cupboard and pulled down a cup. He chuckled, then showed it to me.

"Whose is this?"

I stared at it, grinning. It said "I Heart Bingo" on the side.

"It's Pascal's. We gave it to him as a joke, and now it's his favorite."

"Oh. Should I put it back and pick another?"

"Don't you dare. He won't mind."

Gerome poured himself some coffee, added a bit of milk, stirred it, and sat down beside me, taking a sip. "I'm feeling more philosophical today. I think the sleep helped."

"Probably," I said.

"You know, it won't be the end of the world if I test positive."

"Exactly."

"I don't really want to deal with that right now, when I'm so young. But, I could find out next month that I have stage four cancer. I could get killed in a car crash this afternoon. So, if I find out that I..." He took a deep breath and let it out. "Have HIV, then I'll deal with it, and listen to what my doctor recommends."

"I think that's a good way to think about it," I said. "Very mature."

"I'd still rather be negative. I *hope* I'm negative," Gerome said with a sigh. "But if I'm not, I'll deal with it." He smiled over his steaming mug. "Does that mean I'm growing up?"

I laughed. "In a way. A scare like this can have a way of making you reassess things."

"Yeah."

"I think that young people—jeez, I sound like a grandpa—young people tend to think they're immortal, right? That those things they've heard about always happen to other people. I think it's a survival mechanism, but maybe a holdover from when the world was infinitely more dangerous than it is now."

"Huh. Yeah, maybe you're right."

"Then you realize that something *could* happen to you, like *really* understand that it's entirely possible, and your world view changes." I took another sip of my coffee, then nodded. "And when you turn forty, you realize that you've lived half your life already and that you will actually die sometime in the next forty or fifty years."

He stared at me. "Wow."

I raised my eyebrows. "But that also comes with a change of perspective, because you realize that you're not going to be here forever. And you're braver in a different way. Not reckless, but more willing to do those things you were putting off."

He gaped at me. "No way are you forty."

"You're right. I'm forty-one."

"Come on."

"It's true, and I feel it." At the moment the only thing I was feeling was the soreness from my romp with Jericho and Pascal, but it did seem like most days a part of my body was protesting.

"So…what had you put off?"

I blushed. "Well, luckily not a foursome with my loving partners and an adorable twink."

He laughed lightly. "Luckily."

"And I met Jericho and Pascal when I finally braved the leather bar and expressed an interest in medical kink. But I think it was the fact that I could see forty in the headlights, you know? I wanted to seize the day. Before my grip got too weak." I shook my head.

"Well, here's to seizing the day," Gerome said, lifting his mug to clink it with mine. "I'm glad I came to the cottage with you guys that night. Thank you for looking after me so well."

"It's only that we're older, and we know better than to risk your health, and ours, for some quick kicks."

"Hey, did someone mention quick kicks?" Pascal said, yawning as he padded into the kitchen in his boxer briefs and nothing else. He frowned, heading for the coffee pot. "Jeez, say that ten times fast. Bet you can't."

I arched my eyebrow at Pascal and turned back to Gerome. "Forgot to warn you about the bear sightings in the kitchen."

"Oh hey," he said, pointing at the mug Gerome was using. "You love bingo, too?"

"Oh yeah," Gerome said, playing along. "My favorite pastime."

Pascal laughed. "And, Scott, I'm a pup, not a bear."

An alarm pinged in my brain as Pascal continued.

"Well, I'm usually a pup. Except for last night, right, Scotty?"

Gerome sat up. "What? What happened last night?"

"Nothing," I said, giving Pascal a warning look.

"How are you feeling today, Gerome?" Pascal asked, as Jericho ambled into the kitchen.

"I'm good. What happened last night?" Gerome asked Pascal. He cleared his throat. "While I was passed out like a baby down here. Missing everything."

The three of us exchanged looks, then Jericho brought his coffee to the table and sat down, while Pascal continued to sip his where he stood leaning against the counter.

"I just meant that Scott was the pup last night. Not me, for a change."

Gerome's eyes went wide. He looked at me. "*You* were the pup? *You?*"

Pascal broke into more laughter.

"Yes, me. Why is that so hard to believe?" I felt a bit offended, even though the pup identity wasn't something I'd claimed for my own.

"I don't know. I just…can't picture it," Gerome said, gazing at me and obviously trying to.

"Well, I sure can," Pascal said, grinning over his mug at me.

"Knock it off. I don't think Gerome wants to hear about all of that." I waved my hand in the air, as I blushed with embarrassment.

"Oh, yes, I do," Gerome said. "I want to hear about all of it."

"You seem to be feeling better," Jericho said, smiling at Gerome.

"Yeah. Trying not to worry about it until I find out what I'm dealing with. Or not dealing with."

"Good idea," Jericho said, sipping his coffee.

"Which do you prefer, Gerome? Pancakes, French toast or scrambled eggs?" Pascal asked.

Jericho frowned. "Oh, you're making breakfast today? Cool beans."

Pascal laughed. "No. I thought you were going to…"

Jericho shook his head and gazed at Gerome. "I'm telling you. They totally take my astonishing cooking skills for granted in this house."

Gerome shrugged. "I can just make toast…"

"Don't be ridiculous," Jericho scoffed. "Answer Pascal's question and I'll make what you like."

"You really don't have to…"

"I'd like to feed you, Gerome. At least let me have *that* pleasure," Jericho said.

"You'd better do as he says. He's going to make something, so you might as well tell him what you prefer."

"Okay, okay. French toast, please."

I clapped my hands. "Yes!"

We stuffed our faces with Jericho's delicious French toast, then Gerome thanked us and took off. We told him to keep us updated and to feel free to text us or stop by, whenever.

Two days later, I got the text I'd been waiting for.

Gerome: *NEGATIVE!!!*

Me: *CONGRATS!!! I thought so, but it must be a relief to hear it.*

Gerome: *Such a relief. I'm sitting here feeling like I'm going to float up into the air.*

Me: *We should celebrate.*

Gerome: *YES!*

Me: *Come for supper?*

Gerome: *YES!*

Gerome had told me that his HIV positive hook-up had been very relieved when Gerome had told him that he hadn't passed the virus on to him. And that Gerome had offered his shoulder to lean on if the guy ever wanted to talk about things. He'd said he had a lot of support already but thanked Gerome for letting him know about his test results.

I texted the good news to Jericho and Pascal. We invited him for supper that Saturday. When I texted him a time that worked for us, he surprised me with the following:

You know, if you guys don't mind, I would love to meet that HIV positive couple you know…

I called Grant to see if they could come on Saturday, explaining that Gerome had had a recent scare and that we'd told him about them. They were free and said they'd love to come for supper, so I texted Gerome again.

Me: *They're in. Do you have any food restrictions?*

Gerome: *Nope. Although I'm not a huge fan of seafood.*

Me: *Noted. See you Saturday. Don't forget to talk to your doctor about PrEP…*

Gerome: *Yes, Dad. Smiley face.*

Me: *Good boy. Smiley face.*

I wondered if, now that he'd gotten a good test result, perhaps Gerome would be up for some safer sex shenanigans once Grant and Christopher went home on Saturday. I was embarrassed to say how much I'd enjoyed the 'Dad' comment. But I'd put that out of my mind for now.

Jericho and Pascal had originally introduced me to their friends, Grant Firestone and Christopher Ogabwe, shortly after we'd first met. Grant was an event coordinator for a non-profit organization and Christopher owned a flower shop in the Byward Market. They'd been together, at the time, for about five years, and during one of our early meetings, they'd let me know of their HIV status.

They were completely open about it, even to the point of wearing

POZ pins to Pride events and such, which was why I'd felt comfortable telling Gerome about them. They were out and proud about who they were and their positive status, so that other people could see that it was possible to live a full and rewarding life after an HIV diagnosis.

They arrived before Gerome, who had texted that he'd had an emergency—nothing terrible—and was running late.

We hadn't seen Grant and Christopher in ages, so there was a lot of hugging and catching up to do while we waited. Then the conversation turned to our absent dinner guest.

"So…is Gerome the young guy you invited back to Duke's cottage? The one from the restaurant?"

I stared at Grant. "How on earth do you remember that?"

He raised his eyebrows. "How would I forget? I've been fantasizing about it ever since because you never gave me any details."

Jericho smiled. "We don't kiss and tell."

Christopher barked a laugh. "Since when? You told us exactly what happened after the Halloween party."

I felt my cheeks heat, and Jericho looked embarrassed. Pascal glanced at me with sympathy.

"Yes, well, I've learned from my indiscretions," Jericho admitted. "With Scott, we didn't know it was going to be anything more than a one-off. And I was probably showing off."

"You? Showing off?" Grant said, smiling. "Anyway, Scott doesn't care, I'm sure."

I shrugged. "Water under the bridge."

"Or in the enema bag," Christopher muttered.

"Christopher!" Grant admonished.

"What?"

"Oh my God," Grant mumbled.

Christopher glanced at me with regret. "I'm sorry, Scott. I get carried away."

I raised my hands and smiled. "Yeah, so does Dr. Griffin," I said, side-eyeing Jericho, who finger-gunned me as Pascal guffawed.

Grant and Christopher chuckled.

My phone dinged. I glanced at it.

Gerome: *On my way. Ten minutes, I'm not far.*

I tapped a reply while I said, "That was Gerome. He should be here in ten minutes or so."

"Wow. A boy who communicates when he's going to be late. Wonders never cease," Grant said.

"Let's not talk about that," Christopher muttered.

Pascal's eyes widened. "Oh, yes, you should talk about that. Have you been playing?"

"Shhh," Christopher said, glancing at Grant. "Maybe. Once or twice."

"Well, well, well. What's this disrespectful boy's name?" Jericho asked with a grin.

"Dane," Grant said. "He's trans, and he's lovely. However, not always communicative. We're working on it."

"I'll bet you are," Jericho said. "Naughty, naughty."

"Of course, we're playing safe, as he's neg. But he knows about us. We take precautions."

"Be sure to let Gerome know. I think he was terrified of testing positive," Pascal suggested.

Grant shrugged. "People still are. And they should be. It's life changing, for sure, but not like it used to be."

"There is still the stigma. We do encounter it," Christopher admitted.

A timer in the kitchen started dinging.

"Excuse me," Jericho said. "I need to check on the casserole." He went into the kitchen.

The doorbell rang.

"Oh, that's Gerome," I said, getting up.

He came in, apologizing profusely for being late and for holding up dinner.

"Come and meet our friends," I said.

Introductions were made. Pleasantries exchanged. Nobody mentioned at first why we'd arranged this get together.

We sat at the table once the pasta casserole was ready. With eating and praising Jericho's cooking talents the main distraction, Grant finally addressed the elephant in the room.

"I heard you had a bit of a health scare, Gerome."

Gerome blushed. "Yeah. It's…not something I want to go through again."

"I'm sure," Christopher said. "We're glad everything turned out the way you wanted it."

Gerome gazed at the two of them with embarrassed sympathy. "I'm…sorry it didn't turn out that way for you."

Christopher smiled. And it wasn't a fake 'I'm only smiling so you won't feel sorry for me'. It was a genuine, happy smile.

"To be honest, it wasn't the diagnosis I wanted. Of course not. But the change it brought into my life wasn't all bad." He looked at Grant and reached for his hand.

"No, that's true," Grant said. "We wouldn't have found each other. And we're very happy together."

"Most of the time," Christopher said with a wry smile, while Grant put a hand to his chest in mock indignation.

We laughed.

"But…the treatments work pretty well, don't they?" Gerome asked. "That's what Scott told me."

"Yes. Most of the time," Grant said. "They do monitor you, because at any time they may need to make an adjustment. But we've been lucky. As I told the others, we've had zero viral load readings for years. Even if one of us was neg, we wouldn't necessarily need to use condoms. We probably would, but it's nice knowing that there is almost a 0% chance that we would make someone sick."

"That's amazing," Gerome said.

"That being said, I would hope you've been looking into preventative medication, like PrEP," Christopher said. "Pardon me for acting like a grandad, but please protect yourself. You simply don't need the hassle of it all."

"Or the stigma," Grant added. "We were talking to the others about that. There is quite a bit, still, in the straight community, of course, but also in the gay community."

Gerome nodded. "Yeah, I didn't really know much about it until I got that scare. I was lucky to be able to get in touch with Scott."

Christopher and Grant looked at us.

"They are very helpful, these three. Very, very helpful," Christopher said, giving Gerome a wry grin. "In many, many ways."

Gerome blushed. "I guess you heard about how we met…"

I raised my hand. "Now look, we didn't give them all the dirty details, Gerome."

"We wanted to," Pascal said, waggling his eyebrows.

"No, we were very discreet," Jericho confirmed. "Mostly. You really can't blame us for wanting to brag about the beautiful boy we had for dessert that night."

Pascal made a nostalgic sound. "It was an incredible evening."

"Yes, it was," I agreed.

"All right, all right. You don't have to keep bragging," Christopher muttered, eyeing sweet Gerome.

"It's okay," Gerome said. "I bragged to my friends about it, too."

"You did?" I said. "Huh."

"Are you kidding? Of course, I did. Everyone was jealous."

"Well, of course they were," Jericho said. "Now, at this moment, I would like to mention that I have prepared a lovely dessert. Not as lovely as Gerome, but I have a feeling the five of us would be a bit much for him, especially so soon after his recent health scare."

"Jesus Christ," Gerome said. "Yeah, I think I'd like some dessert of the food variety tonight. Not that you aren't all super wonderful and, uh, hot."

"Aren't you sweet," Grant said, nudging Christopher's elbow. "Isn't he adorable?"

"Very. God, remember when we were his age?" Christopher said.

"Barely." Grant raised his glass. "To dessert, of all the varieties."

PART 3

REUNION

After dessert was eaten and we'd relaxed with coffee in the living room, Grant and Christopher took their leave. It was still early, so I brought out Cards Against Humanity, and we played that until we were almost pissing ourselves.

By that time, it was ten-thirty, and Gerome gazed at the three of us as if considering something.

"You know, now that it's only the four of us…"

We looked at Gerome, then at each other.

"Please clarify where you're going with that, Gerome," Jericho murmured, putting an arm around my shoulder and kissing me on the cheek.

"I'm only wondering if…a different kind of dessert is…on the table. Tonight. Maybe. If you want to." He fluttered his eyelashes at us. "I'm game."

We'd only had a bit of wine with dinner. Four sober people thought about what had been suggested while the clock ticked down the hour. Pascal was the first to break the silence.

"I want to," he said, smiling at Gerome. "If we can just convince these two."

I cleared my throat. "No convincing required, on my part." I looked at Jericho and raised my eyebrows.

He grinned. "I'm in. Of course, I'm fucking in."

Gerome lit up like it was suddenly his birthday. "Hell, yes. Really? You guys are still interested in me, in that way?"

"Ah, sweet, sweet, Gerome," Jericho said, pushing up from the sofa and walking over to him. "You underestimate us."

Gerome's eyes widened, and he gazed at Jericho with something like awe. "I really don't think I do."

"I only mean that we held off while you were fragile and stressed. But now that you seem to be feeling *so much better*, we would be more than happy to…entertain you…again," he said. "If that's what you want."

"It is. It is what I want," Gerome said, gazing at the three of us from his spot on the sofa.

My memories flashed back to that night in Wakefield, when we had encountered Gerome in the restaurant and had invited him back to the cottage. We hadn't wanted to pressure him into anything, so we'd started a movie and I'd been scared to make the first move. The others had signaled me to do something, since I was sitting closest. I'd turned to Gerome, and he'd been staring at me the way he was staring at me right now.

"I think we need to talk about safety. Considering that you just had a major scare," I said. I was the oldest, and possibly the most risk-averse.

"Sure," Gerome said, gazing at me like he wanted me for dinner. "Anything you want."

Anything you want…

Pascal gave a nervous chuckle. "I'm okay with a no swallowing rule. I like it when things get messy."

Jerome smiled. "Maybe we should take this to the bedroom, so things don't get messy on our furniture."

Pascal rolled his eyes. "Such a killjoy." He gestured to Gerome. "Come on. We'll discuss the *safety guidelines* and wait for these two to get their acts together."

Gerome got up and followed Pascal upstairs. Before they'd reached the top, Pascal turned.

"Better hurry up, or we'll start without you," he said, with a twinkle in his eyes as Gerome laughed.

When they'd disappeared, I walked over to Jericho. I took his chin and kissed him, hard.

"Do you think this is a good idea?" I asked when I pulled back.

Jericho was gazing at me in a dreamy, horny way, and my body answered the look in his eyes.

"I think it's a fantastic idea. They do say that you should get on the horse right after you fall off." He shrugged. "We know these diseases are out there. But if you take the right precautions, your risks go way down. You only live once, right?"

"He *did* just get a negative test result," I said. "When did we have our tests done last?" I couldn't remember.

"Mmm, November, I think. And the doctor said it was up to us if we still wanted to get tested every six months."

"Oh, right," I said, gazing dreamily at his perfect lips. "The benefits of being in a committed relationship, I suppose."

"I suppose," Jericho agreed. "As long as we trust each other."

"Which we do," I said.

He smiled. "Which we do. And we're smart when sharing…"

I nodded. "Now, let's go deflower the pretty twink."

"Again," Jericho said.

I laughed. "Yes. Again. As many times as he wants."

"You're ambitious."

"I'm so fucking horny."

When we got to the bedroom, it was to be greeted by the vision of Pascal and Gerome, kneeling on the bed, facing each other, while Pascal pulled Gerome's t-shirt over his head.

"Here, catch," he said, throwing it to me.

I did catch it and lifted it to my nose, sniffing Gerome's particular aroma. Vanilla and cinnamon, on top of clean body smell and a tinge of masculine arousal. I closed my eyes.

Gerome watched me while Pascal's fingers went to the fly of Gerome's pants.

"A recent vintage, but complex and full of life," I said, tossing it to Jericho, who sniffed it as well.

"Mmm. The scent of youth and mischief. My favorite."

"Oh fuck me," Gerome murmured, as Pascal slipped a hand into Gerome's pants and found what he wanted.

"He's hard as a baseball bat."

"Is he? We're going to keep him like that all evening," Jericho said, undoing his own trousers. "And maybe, *maybe*, he'll get to come at the end of it."

"Yes, if you're a very good boy and do as you're told," I added, getting my clothes off and joining the others.

"How are you all so fucking hot? *And* so kind. How?" Gerome said, his eyes heavy lidded as we drew his pants off him and laid him out on his back.

We stared down at him, stroking ourselves and simply anticipating the feast.

Pascal grinned. "How adorably sweet. He thinks we're *kind*, Jericho."

"Mmm. Not so kind when we're teaching a boy how to serve his elders," Jericho murmured.

Gerome whimpered, blinking up at us like a baby deer.

"First, though, let's reward him for being so responsible over the past couple of weeks," I suggested. I was so eager to get my mouth and hands on Gerome, it wasn't funny.

Pascal took a shuddering breath. "Dibs on his cock."

"Goddamn," I said, sighing. "Fine. But you can't hog it the whole time. Dibs on his lips, then."

"I'll take those cute little nipples," Jericho muttered.

We descended on the adorable and sexy young man, who sighed and moaned beneath us like a cherished concubine.

I kissed him, softly at first, enjoying the smooth perfection of his lips, and living off the quiet moans he made into my mouth. It was a good thing we had a huge bed—a California King that took up most of the room—because it was crowded with four of us. But we didn't mind being so close and bumping into each other as Gerome suffered our fervent attentions.

"Okay, okay," Jericho muttered after several delicious moments. "Now switch."

Gerome made an eager sound as I pulled from his mouth and saw Jericho go for Gerome's cock as Pascal pulled off. I moved down the mattress and worshipped Gerome's nipples while Pascal went in for a deep, passionate kiss. We kept on like this, moving every few minutes along a clockwise rotation, relishing Gerome's sighs and moans as he squirmed beneath us.

Then the begging started.

"Oh my god. Please, please, please," he moaned, his hands swirling in my hair as he turned from my kiss—I was back on lips.

"Please what, my luscious boy?" Jericho asked, as I bent to lick and kiss Gerome's pale neck.

"*Fuck* me. Nobody fucked me the last time. I want it. So bad," Gerome panted. "Please!"

Jericho smiled. "But how will we choose who gets to fuck you, Gerome? There are three of us, and I'm pretty sure we'd all like to."

Gerome blushed even more. "I want you all. As long as you use condoms and don't take forever to come, I can handle the three of you."

Pascal, Jericho and I exchanged eager looks. When would we ever have this opportunity again?

"Not at the same time, though," Gerome said quickly. "Who's going first?"

It was hilarious how excited and eager he was.

"Who do you want to go first?" I asked, glancing at Jericho. I knew he liked to take control but I didn't think he'd mind my question. He could always tell Gerome that he would decide.

Gerome's gaze went from each to the other of us, then landed on me.

"Scott," he said.

"And then?" Jericho asked. "We'd better get it all straight now."

"Pascal. And then, you finish," he said, looking at Jericho.

"Oh, believe me, I will. Want to go out with a bang, do you?"

"Hell yes. It's been a stressful month."

"You're in good hands with us," I assured him.

"Yes, I know. Thank you."

"Enough gabbing," Jericho said. "Come on, Pascal. Gerome can give us some attention while he's getting fucked."

"Hell yeah," Pascal said, clapping his hands and sitting on the bed, leaning against the cushions, while Gerome went onto all fours.

Jericho sat beside Pascal, holding his dick out to Gerome.

"Whenever you're ready," he said.

"Oh, I'm fucking ready." Gerome scooted forward and got to work.

I grabbed the lube and condoms from the dresser. It didn't take me long to get organized, and once I was sheathed, I dribbled lube down the crack of Gerome's perfect ass.

He gasped at the sensation—the lube was probably cold—but spread his legs to give me more access.

"You have such a pretty hole," I murmured, knowing that I enjoyed compliments in a moment of passion.

He whimpered as he swallowed Jericho's cock to the root.

I met Jericho's pleasure-filled gaze as I dropped the lube bottle onto the bedspread and concentrated on playing with Gerome, loosening him and preparing him for me.

When I finally breached him, he gave a lovely deep groan and came off Jericho's cock.

"Oh god," he moaned, then returned to his worship, while Jericho grabbed his hair and guided him.

"So good. That's it. Let me use your throat the way Scotty's gonna use your ass," Jericho said breathlessly.

Ever since that first escapade at Duke's cottage, I'd thought of Gerome, recalling those wonderful, scandalous memories with fondness and excitement. Now I was actually inside Gerome, buried to the hilt, and watching him suck Jericho's cock and mumble and choke and gasp.

"Oh fuck, that looks so hot," Pascal said, stroking himself and shifting his gaze from me to Jericho and Gerome, then back to me.

But I turned my focus to Gerome as I dug my thumbs into his crack, pulling him wide so I could watch my condom covered cock sliding in and out. It felt so good, and I could tell Gerome was enjoying it.

There was some shuffling, and I heard Jericho telling Gerome to switch to Pascal's cock. When I glanced up, I met Pascal's excited gaze as he slipped into Jericho's spot at the head of the bed.

"Oh my fucking God," Pascal gasped as Gerome bent to his cock. "Oh fuck."

I was so transfixed by what was happening in front of me that I didn't realize Jericho had gone behind until he slapped my ass and told me to hurry up.

"Do that again and I'll come," I panted.

"Promise?" he asked.

"Yeah," I said. I was close.

He slapped me again, hard, and I groaned, emptying into the condom as I crouched over Gerome. I closed my eyes and heard Pascal's muttered words of encouragement to Gerome as I pumped him through my orgasm. Then I let out a shaky breath, grabbed the edge of the condom, and pulled out.

Jericho had gotten onto the bed beside Pascal and pulled him into a passionate and sloppy kiss as he was being attended to by Gerome, who sighed as I pulled out.

I got down from the bed on shaky legs.

"Pascal," I said.

Pascal broke away from Jericho. He gazed down at Gerome, who pulled off his cock with a loud slurp and waited while Pascal came round behind him.

"You all right, Gerome?" Jericho asked, smoothing Gerome's hair behind his ears.

"Perfect. I'm fucking perfect. I'm ready for Pascal. So ready."

Jericho smiled. "All right, get back to work on me while he fucks you. Scott can watch."

I rolled the condom off, tied it, and took it into the bathroom to throw it in the trash. When I came back into the room, Gerome was working on Jericho's cock as Pascal sank inside the eager twink.

Gerome made a gorgeous sound as Pascal went deep with a throaty groan of his own.

I pulled on my boxer briefs and sat in the armchair, where I had a clear view. I'd have to remember this for future wank sessions. Gerome looked profanely beautiful, penetrated at both ends, his muscles tensing and relaxing as he coped with the physical stress of it. His cock hung, heavy and hard, beneath him, the head shiny with pre-ejaculate, as Pascal fucked him in quick, frantic bursts.

"Okay. Okay, fuck. I'm coming. I'm coming," Pascal grunted, pounding the twink's ass as he squeezed his eyes shut and let out a groan.

"Fuck, baby, that's so hot," Jericho mumbled, watching Pascal come apart.

Gerome came off Jericho's cock, causing it to bounce against Jericho's stomach as Gerome whimpered with need.

"Oh please...please...I need to come," he said, reaching for his own cock as he balanced on one arm.

"Not yet, sweetheart," Jericho murmured. "Put your hand back on the mattress. No touchy."

Gerome obeyed, but he whimpered again, and threw Jericho a look of frustration.

"Come on!"

"No. You come while I'm fucking you and not before. Be a good boy, now." He smoothed his fingers through Gerome's hair.

Gerome groaned as Pascal finished and carefully withdrew.

"Jesus Christ. That was so hot," Pascal whispered.

"Yes," I agreed. "Yes, it was."

Jericho cupped Gerome's chin.

"Ready for me?"

"Yes! Please, please, please. Only hurry..."

Jericho laughed and I smiled. Impatient little twink. Then again, he'd had a hell of a month. He deserved an evening of mindless debauchery.

"Maybe Scott will kiss you while I fuck you," Jericho said, glancing over at me.

"Of course," I said, slipping into Jericho's spot. I couldn't offer my cock because it had the remnants of my release on it, so I kept my boxer briefs on and guided Gerome's mouth to mine. I rubbed and pinched his nipple while Jericho got ready and eased inside him.

"Oh fuck me. Such a good boy, Gerome. Such a good, good boy," Jericho murmured, his forehead creased and his eyes dark with desire.

"Fuck, fuck, fuck," Gerome panted. "I'm gonna come if you keep talking like that. Can I come? Can I?"

"Not yet. Let me come first."

"Okay. Okay," Gerome moaned, clenching his hands into fists to keep from touching himself while Jericho quickened his pace.

"Oh fuck yes. Oh fuck yes. Fuck, fuck, fuck," Jericho panted as he reached his climax, pounding Gerome hard and fast as he came with a grunt.

Gerome had abandoned the kiss and laid his head on my thigh as Jericho slowed his pace.

"All right," Jericho sighed, grabbing the lube and squeezing some into his palm. He kept his cock lodged inside Gerome as he met my gaze and wrapped his fingers around Gerome's erection.

"Come now," Jericho ordered, as he used his hand and buried cock to bring Gerome to his own screaming culmination. It was loud and unbelievably erotic, watching Gerome spatter the bedspread like some eccentric impressionist painter with a jizz fetish.

It was too late for Gerome to go home. He fell asleep in Pascal's arms, so Jericho and I slept in the other room.

In the morning, when we went downstairs, Pascal and Gerome were there, arguing politely about which of the latest video games was the most award-worthy.

Jericho slid his hand around Gerome's throat and kissed him on the cheek. "Good morning, my sweet sexy boy."

Gerome beamed at me, then turned and kissed Jericho on the lips.

Jericho kissed him back, then pulled away with a sigh. "Careful. You'll get another pounding if you keep that up."

"Okay by me," Gerome said, shrugging and winking at Pascal who looked very, very excited.

"Now, come on," Jericho said, being the voice of reason for once. "I have stuff planned for today and I believe Scott has plans, too."

"Yeah, yeah," Gerome muttered with a smirk. "Can you blame me for trying?"

Pascal lifted his mug and took a sip of his coffee, calming his expression.

"Gerome is only a text or a phone call away. I'm sure we can arrange another fun evening sometime," Jericho added.

"Absolutely," Gerome said. "You guys are very good for my mental and physical health."

I laughed. "And you're good for our huge egos and, um, adequate other parts."

Jericho clapped his hands together. "Who's making breakfast?"

Pascal, Gerome and I all looked at him.

He sighed and headed for the stove. "Fine. Pancakes?"

There was a chorus of affirmatives as I pulled out a chair and sat between Gerome and Pascal, giving my input on the video game debate.

DAWN

EVIE MCGLYNN

The dawn is not distant, nor is the night starless; love is eternal.
Henry Wadsworth Longfellow

CHAPTER 1

SETH

The mausoleum was cold, even at the height of summer. I walked down the now familiar aisle and stopped in front of the small, engraved marble plaque that marked the final resting place of the man I loved.

David Harding
April 17, 1985 – May 10, 2024
Beloved Husband.

I put my hand on the smooth, cold stone and finally let my tears fall. "It's over, sweetheart. After two years, the lawsuit is finally over. I'm so sorry your family tainted your memory like that. But it's finally done, and you can rest easy." My mind drifted back to a time before all this. A time when we were still discovering each other and learning what love meant for both of us.

But that was nearly two decades ago. And life was good. Until it wasn't. And then we found out how utterly unfair life could be. How cruel and unyielding. Now, there I stood with all that remained of the life David and I had built in the inside pocket of my suit jacket. I patted the outside of my jacket. "Now we can start to pay back the people who helped you over the years."

The twenty-minute drive from the cemetery to my condo in Asbury Park became a forty-minute drive because of summer Shore traffic. The Jersey Shore was a popular summer destination, especially for the residents of North Jersey and New York City—people we locals not-so-lovingly called *Bennys*. I was thankful my building had a parking garage, or I would have had to park in the next town over.

When I walked into the condo I used to share with David, I had just the briefest expectation that I would hear him calling me from the bedroom. I took a breath and shook off the deep sorrow that wrapped around me as I remembered he wasn't there and never would be again.

I paused in the living room to gaze at the painting over the fireplace. It was a picture of Asbury Park's Convention Hall, shown from a beach vantage point and framed by sunset pink clouds and a pale twilight sky. It was the place where we'd first met seventeen years before. We'd had our wedding on the beach right beside it. My finger lovingly traced over the signature on the bottom left corner. I felt that all-too-familiar tightness in my chest. "Oh, David, how I miss you."

I went into my bedroom to change into something more casual and comfortable for the mid-July heat. I was looking forward to my next three appointments. I enjoyed giving people good news, and for them, this would be the best kind of news. I changed into dark-blue cotton shorts and a short-sleeved white linen shirt, slipped the documents I needed into a cross-body bag, grabbed my keys, wallet, and sunglasses, and headed back out into the summer sun.

It was a beautiful, sunny day, and the tourists were out in force. The sidewalks were crowded, and the traffic crawled along Cookman Avenue as people headed toward the beach and boardwalk. I'd decided to walk since my destinations were fairly close to my condo. My first stop was the Visiting Nurses Association's LGBTQ+ clinic. I had an appointment with their clinical director, Tom Kincaid. I'd known the man for ten years and considered him a friend. I was glad I would be able to pay back some of the endless kindness he'd shown David and me. He was the one who'd gotten David into hospice care, which allowed me to keep him at home as he neared the end of his life. Tom had also referred me to a grief counselor after David's death.

There were three patients in the clinic's waiting room when I entered. Gloria, the receptionist, smiled broadly when I walked in. "Seth! How wonderful to see you again."

I kissed her cheek. "Thank you, Gloria. You're looking lovely as always."

Her cheeks got rosy. "You're such a charmer, Seth."

A man dressed in purple scrubs entered the waiting room, and I swore I stopped breathing for a moment. He was gorgeous. Sandy-blond hair touched with sun-streaked highlights fell in soft waves around an angular face. He had cheekbones for days and the most beautiful sea-green eyes I'd ever seen. The laugh lines around his eyes and mouth indicated he was likely in his mid-thirties.

To my embarrassment, he caught me staring. He raised a slender eyebrow. "Can I help you?"

I blinked and cleared my throat. "I'm...uh...here to see Tom, I mean, Mr. Kincaid." *Jesus, what was wrong with me?*

"It's okay, Jon," Gloria said. "He's an old friend of Tom's."

I gave her the side-eye. "Who you calling old?"

She gave me a saucy wink. "There's a lot more salt than there used to be in those lovely locks."

Jon snorted. "Now you're just being mean." He held out his hand to me and smiled brightly. "Jon Taylor. I'm covering for Liam."

"Ah, okay," I replied, taking the proffered hand. "Seth Morgan."

Jon's eyes skimmed up my body, and I didn't miss his look of appreciation. "Nice to meet you, Seth."

Before I had a chance to say anything else, Tom came into the waiting room. "There you are, Seth. Is Gloria giving you a hard time?"

"She called me old." I fake-pouted.

Tom laughed. He ran a hand through his mostly gray hair. "You're younger than me, for what it's worth." He indicated the hallway leading to his office. "Let's go chat. You can tell me all about how today went."

I gave Jon one more lingering glance. "Nice to meet you, Jon."

Once inside Tom's office, my friend chuckled. "I think that's the first time I've seen you check out another man since David died."

I felt my face heat. "I probably embarrassed myself too. I've gone out with a few guys over the past year." I shrugged. "They've mostly ended in a one-and-done. Sometimes, there was a second date, but none of them were all that interesting."

"Well, I have to say, Jon is an interesting man." Tom tapped his temple. "Incredibly smart and amazingly compassionate. He has a private practice as a nurse practitioner, but he'll move appointments around if Liam needs him to cover. He also volunteers at the Center."

"Really? That's good to know."

Tom sat behind his desk. I took the seat in front of it. "How did it go this morning?"

I couldn't help the grin that spread across my face. "The judge ruled in my favor. They didn't get a dime. In fact, they'll have to pay a portion of my attorney fees."

"Ha! Excellent news," he crowed.

"It is indeed," I replied.

"We should go out to dinner tonight to celebrate. Mark is off tomorrow, so we can even stay out late."

"That sounds like a great idea," I said.

"Pascal and Sabine?" he asked.

"You know me so well. It's my favorite restaurant."

"What's next for you?" Tom asked.

I unzipped the cross-body and pulled out one of the three checks I'd written as soon as I'd left the courtroom. "I finally get to do what David asked of me before he died." I slid the check across his desk. "This is the downpayment. I have two more checks. One will go to The Center and the other to Project R.E.A.L."

Tom picked up the check and his brows rose to his hairline. "Seth, this is an incredibly generous donation. What about you? Don't you need some of this now that he's gone?"

I shook my head. "David and I talked about this a long time ago. We planned for the future with this in mind. I've made very good investments, and my condo is paid off."

Tom's eyes got shiny. "Well, bless both of you. This will mean a lot to the people we help."

"It's the least we could do. You and this organization were there for us throughout the whole ordeal. To the last, David never stopped expressing his gratitude for what you all did for him. For both of us."

Tom got up and came around to where I was sitting. "Come on. Get up. This deserves a hug."

I rose, and he wrapped his arms around me in a tight hug. Tears stung my eyes. It felt so good to have some real human contact. It brought home how touch-starved I was. "It's my pleasure, really. I would have been lost without you and Mark."

When Tom finally let me go, we were both a weepy mess. He handed me a tissue and took one for himself. "You said this is just a downpayment. What do you mean by that?" he asked.

"After David got his diagnosis, he went into a frenzy of creativity. I have twenty-three paintings in storage that he painted over the course of three years. I'm going to hold an art auction, and the proceeds will be split between the three organizations here in Asbury Park that help people with HIV and AIDS. It's the least we can do."

"You're a good man, Seth," Tom said. "So was David. He is missed."

"Yes, he is," I replied.

CHAPTER 2

JON

I watched Seth's fine ass walk toward Tom's office. When I turned back to Gloria, she watched me with a knowing smirk. I leaned over her desk and whispered, "Who *was* that?"

She stared at me over the rims of her glasses. "Seth Morgan."

I rolled my eyes. "Yes. Thank you. I got his name. But *who* is he? He's not a patient, but he knows everyone here."

Gloria's expression grew somber. "His husband was a patient here. He died two years ago." She leaned to the side to look around me. "But you have patients waiting, so I'll have to tell you the rest later."

I squeezed my eyes shut. "Great. And they all saw me flirt with the silver fox."

Gloria snickered. "I'm sure it's nothing they haven't seen before." She made a shooing motion. "Go on. Get back to work."

With a last glance in the direction Seth had taken, I called in my next patient.

Seth was long gone by the time I finished with my patients and the accompanying paperwork. As busy as I had been, my thoughts still frequently returned to the handsome man. If I'd been anywhere else, I would have asked for his number. He was clearly interested if his adorable stutter had been any indication.

As I left the small office I shared with the other nurse practitioners who worked here during the week, I almost ran into Tom as he walked down the hallway. I stopped so I didn't knock him over. "Sorry about that."

He smiled. "No worries. I don't blame you for wanting to get out of here. Any plans for the evening?"

I shrugged. "Not sure yet. I'm in the mood for something new. I'm going to try to get my bestie to come out with me."

Tom's brow furrowed. "I thought you had a boyfriend."

My stomach twisted. "I did until he decided to cheat on me with someone half his age. He said I was getting too old and it was bringing him down."

Tom mouthed the words "*Too old*" and pursed his lips. "Wasn't he older than you?"

"Yep. But he started to get obsessed with looking younger." I sighed. "Honestly, he was more form than substance. I should have seen it coming." I gave a wry smile. "I got taken in by dirty talk and a big dick."

Tom snorted and burst out laughing. "Listen, Mark and I are taking Seth out for dinner tonight at Pascal and Sabine. You're welcome to join us if you like. I got the impression you and Seth might hit it off."

"Really? What makes you think that?"

"He couldn't stop staring at you. I've rarely seen him tongue-tied, but he definitely was with you."

My lips twitched up into a smile. "Well, I'm flattered. He seems like a pretty put-together guy."

"Oh, he is," Tom agreed. "He just hasn't dated much since David died two years ago."

"Understandable. Two years isn't a long time after someone you love dies." I checked the time on my phone. Just shy of five-thirty. "What time are you meeting for dinner?"

"I made reservations for seven-thirty," he replied.

Two hours. I considered whether I wanted to take a chance on the unknown quantity that was Seth Morgan. I made a mental shrug. Eh, why not. If nothing else, I'd get dinner, a nice night out, and maybe make a new friend. "Sure, I'll meet you there."

Tom clapped me on the back. "Excellent. I think you two will get along well. You're both intelligent and enjoy the arts."

"I guess we'll find out," I said. "I'll see you later."

I almost changed my mind twice. I was still stinging from Kevin's dishonesty. In addition to my embarrassment, his cruel words about me getting old had made me self-conscious. I had to shake myself. I was going to be forty this year, not four hundred. *Get a grip, Jonathan.*

Seth clearly wasn't self-conscious about getting older. In fact, he wore his silver fox status quite well. He clearly took care of his body. He also didn't dye his hair, instead letting the natural steely gray slowly take over his thick dark locks. I closed my eyes and imagined how his well-trimmed salt-and-pepper beard would feel rubbing against my thighs as he sucked me off.

I grunted as my cock responded to that image, surprised at how quickly it filled and thickened. Damn, I was more attracted to Seth than I'd realized. Good thing I was headed into the shower.

I was barely under the spray when I grabbed my body wash and poured a generous amount into my palm. A groan slipped from my lips as I wrapped my hand around my cock. I shuttled it through my fist, the rapid schlick sound echoing off the bathroom walls. I slid my other hand down to tug on my balls before moving it farther back and slipping a finger into my hole. That was enough to send me off. I gasped as my orgasm barreled through me, whiting out my vision. Thick ropes of cum shot from my dick, hitting the wall before being washed away by the warm spray. I breathed heavily as I held myself up by leaning against the cool tiles. Well damn. That was unexpected.

It had been a long time since someone had caught my attention like Seth had. Kevin was good-looking and could be good in bed, but he'd been self-absorbed and hadn't always concerned himself with my pleasure. I didn't even know Seth, yet just the idea of him had me going off like a rocket.

As I toweled off, I wondered what the night would bring. And if I took more care in getting dressed than usual, it was nobody's business but mine.

CHAPTER 3

SETH

Pascal and Sabine was my favorite restaurant in Asbury Park. It reminded me of the bistros David and I ate in while we were in Paris. I arrived a little before seven-thirty. I'd walked because parking was too difficult with the tourists taking up all the spaces. Even though it was a Thursday night, the place was crowded. That was summer on the Shore for you.

I greeted the woman standing at the host station. "I'm meeting someone here." She nodded and gestured toward the back of the restaurant. "Of course, Mr. Morgan. They're already here."

Tom and Mark were seated in one of the several semi-circular booths the restaurant boasted. I liked the booths because they gave a sense of intimacy to the dining experience, and it was much easier to talk to everyone at the table. When I got to the table, I noticed a fourth place setting. Tom stood to give me a hug. "Good to see you again. It's been ages since we've gone out together."

His husband, Mark, also got up to greet me. "Good to see you again, Seth."

"It is good to be out and about," I said. "I guess I let myself become a hermit for a while." I frowned at the extra place setting. "Are we expecting someone else?"

Mark shot a look at Tom, who looked sheepish. "I invited Jon to join us for dinner."

I narrowed my eyes at Tom. "Are you trying to play matchmaker?"

Mark elbowed Tom. "I told you he wouldn't like it."

"Hear me out," Tom began. "I'm not saying you have to date or anything like that. But what could it hurt to get to know the man? I saw how you looked at him."

I huffed a sigh of resignation. "Fine. Just don't push. If it happens, it happens."

Tom put up his hands in surrender. "I wouldn't dream of it."

"Yes, you would," I scoffed.

"He's got you there, love," Mark said with a chuckle.

I took my seat, buzzing with anticipation. I would never tell Tom this, but I was excited to see Jon again. He was a good-looking man and had seemed interested in me. At least, I hoped he was.

I had just picked up the menu when Mark's eyes widened, and he murmured, "Oh wow."

I turned my head to find Jon coming toward our table. *Oh wow*, indeed. He was wearing a cobalt-blue linen shirt over white linen pants. The blue of his shirt accented the sea green of his eyes and highlighted the golden streaks in his sandy-blond hair.

Tom elbowed his husband. "Hey," he complained.

Mark kissed Tom's cheek. "I'm married, darling, not dead."

Tom rose to greet Jon when he got to the table. "Jon, I'm so glad you're joining us."

Jon gave him a bright smile. "Thanks for inviting me."

Tom gestured toward me. "You've already met Seth, and this is my husband, Mark."

After all the greetings, I scooted over so Jon could fit in the booth next to me. I leaned toward him and said quietly, "Tom thinks he's a matchmaker. It's fine if you aren't interested in anything like that."

Jon turned to face me and gave me another of his brilliant smiles. "But I *am* interested. Very much."

My body flushed hot and cold. Jon was a beautiful man. I hadn't been this truly interested in someone in a long time. All of my previous "dates" and hookups had been me just taking care of my physical needs. I hadn't been interested in getting to know them any better. Jon was different, although I couldn't exactly pinpoint why. I cleared my throat. "All right, then. I guess we'll see where this goes."

"That works for me," he replied.

The server came by to take our drink orders. I noticed Jon ordered a soda while the rest of us got our favorite cocktails. I didn't say anything. First, because it was none of my business, and second, because David had been an alcoholic who'd been sober for thirteen years when he died. Thankfully, neither Tom nor Mark remarked about it either.

The conversation was lively around the table. Mark was teasing Tom about their upcoming vacation. "I swear I'm going to have to pry him out of his office on the day we're supposed to leave because he'll have 'just one more thing' to get done before he hands the reins over to someone else for two weeks."

Tom smiled sheepishly but didn't deny it. "Liam will keep me in line. He'll kick me out when it's time for me to leave. He and Mark have conspired against me before."

We all laughed. "Where *is* Liam?" I asked. "Is he on vacation?"

Tom shook his head. "His husband, Marco, works for a security firm that sometimes does search and rescue missions overseas to rescue kidnapped executives being held for ransom. Liam goes along as a medic for the team."

"Well damn," I said. "And here I was, proud of myself for getting up early and showering."

Jon snorted. "Don't compare yourself to Liam. He's very driven, albeit mostly to keep his husband in one piece. He told me he started going on these missions because the previous medics were doing shoddy work stitching up Marco's wounds."

I shook my head. "He never even mentioned it to me."

Jon shrugged. "He doesn't talk about it much. He told me because he would have to call me in to cover for him at the last minute. He doesn't get a lot of warning before they have to leave."

The server brought our drinks and took our dinner orders. "That reminds me," I said to Jon, "Tom said you have a private practice. Where is it located?"

"It's not far," Jon replied. "In Neptune, close to the hospital."

"I'm guessing you're pretty busy," I mused.

He nodded. "Yeah. I have specialties in psychiatric nursing and family practice nursing. It keeps me busy."

"Now I feel like I need to get a second job to keep up," I joked.

Jon turned his head and leaned in close enough to murmur in my ear. "I'm sure you can keep up just fine."

An honest-to-god shiver ran down my spine and my cock began to fill. This man was not shy and didn't play games. I liked it. I let my lips brush lightly over his cheek. "I'm certainly willing to try."

Tom cleared his throat. "Are we interrupting?"

I narrowed my eyes at his triumphant grin. "Not yet. I'll let you know when you are."

Jon let out a choked laugh. "I would prefer to move any activities that could be interrupted to a more private location."

We paused the conversation when the server arrived with our meals. We were quiet as we dug into the delicious food. When I paused to sip my wine, I leaned close to Jon and said, "Let's go for a walk on the boardwalk after dinner. Then we can decide where we'd like to go from there."

Another of his beautiful smiles graced his lips. "Sounds good to me."

CHAPTER 4

JON

I could listen to Seth talk all night. Tom had been right. Seth was intelligent and incredibly interesting. He'd traveled all over the world, both before and after he got married. I kept getting the niggling feeling that I knew him from somewhere. I knew I'd never met him in person —I would have remembered that. But something about him was familiar.

One of the best things about Seth was his genuine interest in what I had to say. I wasn't used to the men I dated being interested in my career. They heard I was a nurse and pigeon-holed me into a role that wasn't my reality. Not that Seth and I were dating—yet. But I could see it happening if he was ready.

The server brought over the dessert menu, and I groaned. Even though I was full from dinner, I couldn't resist getting their chocolate pot de crème. To my delight, Seth was also a big fan of the delicious dessert. His moan of pleasure when he put the first spoonful in his mouth went straight to my dick. I gave him the side-eye, and he grinned. He knew exactly what he was doing.

By the time dinner was over, I was ready to skip the boardwalk and go straight to his or my place. Screw getting to know each other first. I wanted to fuck or be fucked. I really didn't care which. I couldn't even fault Tom for looking smug as we left the restaurant.

"I'll see you both soon," he said with a smile.

Mark rolled his eyes and tugged on his husband's arm. "Come on, Cupid. Leave them be."

Seth chuckled. "Goodnight, you two. I'll be around more often. I promise."

"I'll hold you to that," Tom said.

As we watched them walk away, Seth shifted nervously. "Are you still up for a walk?"

"Absolutely," I replied, telling my dick to calm the fuck down.

He seemed to relax. "Okay. Good."

We spent the ten-minute walk talking about our favorite places to travel. "Even though it sounds cliché," Seth said, "I really do love Paris in the spring. But I also love Ireland. The people there are so friendly."

"I've never been there," I said. "I haven't been able to travel as much as I would like because I was working on my nurse practitioner specialties. I started in family practice but saw the great need for psychiatric nursing, so I went back to school for that specialty."

"That's impressive," Seth said. "It's a lot of work."

I shrugged. "It took another year of classes to finish. But it was worth it. I'm able to help a lot of people who can't get access to a psychiatrist."

Seth smiled sadly. "I'm glad you did that. David had a hard time finding a prescriber because a lot of psychiatrists didn't take his insurance."

I nodded but didn't ask because it was none of my business. "Access to good mental health care is important to me." We stopped at a crosswalk, waiting for the signal to change. The traffic was still heavy even at nine-thirty on a Thursday night. "What about you?" I asked as we were finally able to cross the street. "You said you're a biomedical engineer. What does a biomedical engineer do?"

Seth pursed his lips. "There are a lot of sub-specialties, and kind of like you, I started in one and switched to another, beginning with biomechanics. I wanted to engineer better prosthetics. I did that for about ten years before moving over to biomaterials."

"Why the switch?" I asked.

He shrugged. "I wanted to try something new. In biomaterials, we work to create better medical devices, like the ones that deliver insulin to diabetics. I lead a team of engineers at a company in Princeton."

"That's a long commute," I commented.

"I know," he replied. "But I love living in Asbury Park. Besides, I work from home three days a week, so it's not too bad."

"You live in Asbury?" I asked. "Me too. Where do you live?"

He pointed behind us. "I have a condo on Lake Avenue. Where do you live?"

"No way. I have an apartment on Cookman," I said.

He grinned. "We live one street away from each other."

"I'm in the apartments over Toast," I said.

Seth's brows rose. "Are you serious? I have breakfast there at least once a week. I can't believe we've never seen each other."

I shrugged. "I don't eat there much. Maybe it's because I live over top of it."

"Could be," he mused. "I'm in the Wesley Grove condos, so we're, at most, a five-minute walk from each other."

"Oh wow," I said. "I went to a party in a condo over there. Those are really nice. Do you have the rooftop patio?"

"Yep," he said with a smile. "It's great on nights like this, and I can watch the Fourth of July Fireworks from the comfort of my home."

"Nice."

We made it to the boardwalk, which still had plenty of people wandering in and out of the various shops, restaurants, and bars. A cool breeze blew off the ocean, whisking away the heat of the mid-July day. The old-fashioned streetlamps dotting the boardwalk's edge gave it the feel of bygone days when the boardwalk was first built.

Of course, that illusion was shattered by the neon lights and loud music from the open-air bars. I didn't mind though. I loved walking the boards at night. I also loved coming down in the early morning and absorbing the peace of that in-between time just before the sun peeked over the horizon. It was like the world held its breath while waiting for the new day.

"Do you want to head toward Convention Hall?" Seth asked.

I gazed at the other end of the boardwalk where Convention Hall stood in all its faded glory. "Sure. It's a nice night for a walk."

We talked more as we walked, and I had to try really hard not to take his hand in mine. Not gonna lie. It was unusual for me to want that from anyone. I wasn't much of a hand-holder. At least I hadn't been. I had no idea what it was about Seth that turned me around like that.

We got to the doors leading into the Grand Arcade, the pass-thru between Convention Hall and the Paramount Theater and stopped. Seth just stared up at the decorative designs set in the brickwork on the outside of the structure for a few moments before saying, "This is where I met David."

"Right here?" I asked, wondering where this was going.

He shook his head. "Inside. He was selling some of his paintings at the Fall Bazaar."

And it hit me like a ton of bricks. "Your David was David Harding, the artist?"

He looked at me in surprise. "Yes. Didn't you know?"

"No," I replied with a shake of my head. "No one mentioned it. That's why you look familiar. I've seen pictures of you with David. You didn't have the beard back then."

He stroked his well-trimmed salt-and-pepper beard. "Yes. This is a new addition. After David died, I didn't take care of myself as well as I should have. I didn't shave for weeks. When I finally started to get myself together, I decided I liked it, so I kept it."

"It certainly suits you," I said. My imaginings from my shower came back and my cock perked up with interest. "I like it." I paused, then decided to just lay it all out there. "I like you. A lot."

Seth stepped closer to me. "I like you too, Jon. I haven't been this genuinely interested in someone for a long time."

I closed the distance between us. "So, what do you want to do about it?"

A large group exited the building right next to us, shattering the moment. Seth growled and took my hand, leading me away from the doors toward the railing separating the boardwalk from the beach below. The moon was barely a crescent, so the water was dark except for the sprinkling of lights from the distant ships.

He crowded me against the cool metal and said, "I want to kiss you. Is that all right with you?"

"Absolutely," I replied.

He cupped my face with his warm hands, brushing his thumbs over my cheeks. "You are a beautiful man," he said softly. He lowered his mouth to mine, his plush lips opening slightly when I teased them with my tongue. His beard felt as good as I'd imagined. I slipped my arms around his waist to pull him closer. Our tongues tangled and a low moan escaped his lips. He tasted like chocolate, wine, and something uniquely Seth. I wanted to do this all night.

My hands slid lower to cup his ass and the hard length of his cock pressed against my abdomen. I ground my hips against his, craving the friction. Someone loudly cleared their throat nearby, and Seth looked over his shoulder at the person. With a sigh, he reluctantly pulled away. He rested his forehead against mine. "Well, that escalated quickly."

I chuckled. "Yes, it did." I kissed him again softly. "Do you want to continue this at your place? Or at my place? I'm okay either way."

He blew out a short breath. "I do. I really do…"

"But…?" I continued his thought.

"But whenever I start with sex first, I end up not taking the time to get to know the man, and it hasn't lasted." He brushed his fingers through my hair. "I really like you. I'd like to get to know you better. I think we could make something good out of this if I can break that pattern." He pursed his lips in frustration. "Does that make sense to you?"

"I think so," I replied. "I'll admit, I'm disappointed. But I'm happy you want to try for something more than a one-and-done."

"Oh, definitely," he said with a rueful smile. "I can honestly say my cock is not very happy with me right now."

"Same," I replied.

"It was a lovely first kiss," Seth said.

I took his hand and raised it to my lips. "It really was."

CHAPTER 5

SETH

I took my morning cup of coffee onto my rooftop patio. There was still more than a half-hour until sunrise and the dawn light filtered over the rooftops. I loved this time of day. The world was still and quiet as it waited for the sun to make its appearance. But that stillness was missing for me this morning.

The closer I got to Jon, the more guilt weighed on me. Intellectually, I knew it was ridiculous for me to feel guilty for being attracted to another man. David and I had talked about it ad nauseam before he died. He'd insisted I not wither away alone. He'd wanted me to find someone to love again. I honestly hadn't thought I'd find anyone who could give me what I'd had with David.

Then Jon came along with his brilliant smile and sunny disposition and blindsided me. I thought about him all the time, even at work. The more I got to know him, the more time I wanted to spend with him. I'd alternated between congratulating myself and kicking myself for not taking Jon up on his offer to come to my place or take me to his. At least I'd gotten his number. It had only been a little more than two weeks since that first dinner and we'd gone out six times already.

This morning, we were meeting for breakfast at Toast, the restaurant right below his apartment. I thought it was funny that he rarely ate there. I hoped it wasn't because he didn't like their food. But then again, Jon wasn't the type to keep quiet if he didn't like something.

I was glad it was Saturday because that meant I might be able to entice Jon to spend the day with me. I honestly wished we'd spent last night together so the breakfast we'd be having would be in my kitchen after spending the night in my bed. Maybe it was time. I knew he wanted sex as much as I did. All I had to do was get past my guilt.

Jon had already gotten a table by the time I made it to the restaurant. The place was packed even though it was only a little after eight-thirty on a Saturday morning. The low murmur of conversation and the clatter of silverware against ceramic filled the space. I wove my way through many long tables and dodged busy servers in my effort to get to where Jon was sitting. A smile lit up his face when he saw me approach. He rose and gave me a hug. I returned the hug and kissed him lightly on the lips. "Good morning, gorgeous."

A light blush bloomed on his cheeks. "Good morning to you too."

I took the seat across from his. "How was dinner with your parents last night?"

"It was good," he said with a shrug. "They're trying to plan a fortieth birthday dinner for me. I told them not to make a big deal out of it, but they like throwing parties."

I blinked in surprise. "You're turning forty?"

He frowned. "Yes. Is that a problem?"

I shook my head quickly. "Not at all. I thought you were younger, that's all."

"Well, thank you," he said with a wry grin. "My ex cheated on me because he thought I was getting too old. It's a bit of a sensitive topic."

I reached across the table and put my hand over his. "The man was obviously blind and an idiot. I'm sorry he did that to you."

"Thank you." He turned his hand over so he could clasp mine. "It turns out he did me a favor. I was a free man when I met you."

I squeezed his hand. "Lucky me."

We released our hold on each other when the server came to take our order and pour us each a cup of coffee. I picked up my cup and breathed deeply. "Mmm, nectar of the gods."

Jon nodded. "There's nothing like your first cup of coffee."

"It's my third," I said before raising my mug to my lips.

Jon's eyes widened. "How are you not vibrating?"

I laughed. "I may have a little addiction." I took another sip. "To be fair. I don't usually have this many in the morning, but I was up early watching the sunrise."

"From your rooftop patio, no doubt," he said.

"Of course," I replied with a grin. "But I want to circle back to your birthday. When is it?"

"Oh. It's August ninth."

I felt a little hurt. "That's just a little over a week away," I said. "You never said anything."

Jon bit his bottom lip. "I wasn't sure if I should ask you to come. You wanted to take things slow. I didn't want to push."

Well, shit. Hello, guilt. Only now it was for making Jon feel uncertain about my feelings for him. I blew out a sigh. "I'm sorry. I never meant to make you feel like you couldn't ask me to participate in important events in your life. I would love to come to your birthday dinner."

"I'd love for you to be there," he said.

The server brought our food, and I asked for orange juice. "All done with coffee?" Jon asked playfully.

"Yeah. I'm really not supposed to drink that much. I just wanted to be awake for our date." I dug into my omelet. "Where is your birthday dinner being held?"

"At the restaurant in the Moonlight Inn," he replied after swallowing his bite of French toast. "Have you been there?"

I nodded. "David and I went there a lot. The last time was a fundraiser held by the pianist, Jeremy Fitzgerald."

"I heard about that," Jon said. "It was a bit too rich for my blood."

"Maybe you can get him to play for your birthday dinner. He is Liam's brother-in-law, after all."

Jon snorted a laugh. "No way am I asking a world-renowned concert pianist to play for my birthday party."

I just smiled. He might not want to ask, but I certainly did. I'd met Jeremy Fitzgerald a few times since the fundraiser. He and his husband, Sean O'Neil, had even gone to David's funeral. David had bequeathed a painting to Moonlight Inn as a thank-you for their support of the LGBTQIA+ community. I hadn't been able to honor his intention because the whole estate had been tied up in litigation by David's greedy relatives. Now, I could give it to them and sneak in a request for Jeremy to play for Jon's birthday. Even if it was just one song, it would be amazing.

We chatted about lighter topics for the rest of the meal, but I had plans. I just hoped Jon would be on board with them. I was pretty sure he would be, but there was always a chance I was wrong.

After we paid the check, we walked outside into the humid summer air. I pulled him into my arms for our first real kiss of the morning. Our tongues tangled and our bodies melded together. When I finally lifted my head, he looked at me with a slightly dazed expression and said, "Well, hello to you too."

I chuckled. "I've been dying to do that since I walked into the restaurant."

"Happy to be of service," he snarked.

I drew him close to me again. "I had an idea for something to do now that we're finished with breakfast."

"What's that?" he asked breathlessly.

"Why don't you show me your apartment?" I ran my nose up his jawline and pressed a kiss behind his ear. "Specifically, your bedroom," I murmured.

Jon tilted his head back to look me in the eye. "Really?" he asked, his voice hoarse with need.

"Yes. Really," I replied with certainty. I was done letting guilt hold me back. I wanted this man so badly that it hurt.

He stepped back and took my hand. "Okay then. My door is right here." As we climbed the stairs to the second floor, he said, "Seth, I want you to be sure. I don't want you to regret anything."

I moved up to the step he was on and stopped. I cupped his face with my hands. "I could never regret anything with you."

CHAPTER 6

JON

This wasn't what I'd expected to happen after having breakfast with Seth. I thought maybe we'd wander around town or go to the beach. Instead, he was following me up to my apartment so we could finally give in to the sexual tension we'd been fighting for the past two weeks. My cock was already hard, anticipating getting my hands on him.

I silently thanked whatever deities existed that I had cleaned my apartment the day before. I opened my door, glad the large front windows let in the morning sunlight. I loved my apartment with its hardwood floors and high ceilings. I also loved living right in the center of downtown Asbury Park.

Seth looked around, a soft smile on his face. "This is really nice. Light and airy."

"Thank you." I turned and slid my arms around his waist. "You said something about wanting a tour?"

"Yes, definitely," he said with a smile. Then he stopped walking and fixed his gaze on the picture over the gas fireplace in my living room. It was a painting of the old carousel house in Asbury Park. Painted by Seth's deceased husband.

"Shit," I murmured.

Seth put his hand on my arm. "It's fine, Jon. I won't fall apart every time I see one of David's paintings. You told me you have a few. I wouldn't expect you to hide them."

Even still, my stomach was twisted in knots. I felt guilty. Seth must have seen it in my expression because he took my face in his hands and kissed me. "Jon, listen to me. I loved David. We had a wonderful life together. Seeing his paintings reminds me his legacy lives on. It makes me happy to see other people enjoying his creativity."

I let out a quiet breath of relief. The last thing I wanted to do was make him feel bad about being in my space. I held out my hand. "So, how about the rest of the tour?"

He took my outstretched hand. "Lead the way."

Since my apartment was open-plan, it was easy to see most of the spaces with just a few steps in either direction. Seth paused when he saw my guitar sitting on a stand in a corner on the other side of the living room.

"You play guitar?"

I nodded. "Since I was in high school. It's just a hobby, but it soothes me and lets me be creative."

"You'll have to play for me sometime," he said.

"I'd love to." I moved closer to him and slid my hand up his body. "Right now, though, I'd like to play with you."

His gaze heated and a slow smile curved his lips. "I'm all yours."

I took his hand again and led him to my bedroom at the far end of the living room. Before I opened the door, I said, "Just so you know, there are two more paintings in my bedroom."

Seth pulled me close. "All I'll be thinking about is you."

The morning light poured in through the large windows in my bedroom. The two paintings hung side by side on the wall above my bed. They were smaller than the one in the living room and both were of two men. One was them sitting on the sand, watching the sunrise. The other was the same two men standing by the boardwalk railing holding hands.

Seth smiled when he saw the paintings. "I remember those. That's

Frank and Ed. They were so excited when David asked them to pose for him."

"Did they just stand there?" I asked.

Seth shook his head. "David took dozens of pictures of them in the poses he wanted and then created the paintings from the photos."

"Wow."

"Speaking of wow," Seth began, sliding his arms around my waist and drawing me close. "That kiss downstairs was pretty amazing. I want to kiss you again—naked."

My cock twitched at the thought of seeing Seth naked. "That sounds great to me," I rasped.

It didn't take us long to get undressed. Seth's body was long and lean. It was clear he took care of himself. He had nice muscle definition, especially in his legs. His dark chest hair had a liberal smattering of gray. He had a little softness around his belly, which I looked forward to nuzzling. "Lie down," Seth said quietly. "I want to explore your body."

I swallowed. My cock was already hard. I had a feeling that Seth exploring me would be the best kind of torture. I situated myself on the pillows. Seth knelt on the bed and ran his hands up my legs, starting at the ankles. Then he leaned down and kissed my ankles, my calves, and my inner thighs. His touch was gentle, almost reverent. His kisses were soft and sensuous.

He moved up my body, ignoring my aching cock, much to my dismay. I groaned in protest. "Seth. Please."

He hummed and let out a low laugh. "I'll get there. Trust me." He continued up my torso, alternating between caressing and kissing my bare skin. I'd been right about his beard feeling good against my flesh. He paused to suck on my already hard nipples, scraping them with his teeth and then soothing them with his tongue. He continued up my neck, behind my ear, and finally to my lips. Even that was an exploration. He pressed his lips to one corner of my mouth and then the other before taking my mouth in a deep, claiming kiss.

I wrapped my arms around him so I could feel his full weight on my body. I slid my hands down to the globes of his ass and rolled my hips. We both groaned as our hard cocks ground together, the friction a relief. "I want to be inside you," Seth growled. "Do you do that?"

"Yes," I gasped. "I'm vers."

"Good to know," he replied. "We can switch up next time." He kissed me again. "I get tested regularly. I'm negative, and I'm on PrEP."

"Same," I replied. "But I'd still prefer to use condoms."

He nodded. "Supplies in the usual place?"

"Of course," I said, pointing to the nightstand beside my bed.

He lifted off me so he could get the condoms and lube out of the nightstand. He paused after he pulled open the drawer, and a wicked grin lit up his face. "You have all sorts of goodies in here. We'll have to try them out sometime."

I was sure my smile matched his. "That sounds great to me."

Seth dropped the condoms and lube on the bed beside me, then took his position over me again. He kissed me slow and deep before asking, "Are you okay with this position?"

"Absolutely," I replied. "I prefer it."

"Excellent," he murmured. He traced a trail of kisses down my body, stopping at the juncture of my hip and thigh. He took a deep breath. "You smell so good."

My whole body tingled in anticipation. I couldn't remember the last time a man had paid this much attention to my pleasure. His mouth moved closer to my aching cock and an actual whimper fell from my lips. I didn't have time to be embarrassed because my dick was suddenly enveloped by the wet heat of Seth's mouth.

My back arched and I let out a groan of pleasure. "So good."

I heard the click of the lube bottle and then felt Seth's cool, slick finger circle my hole. He slid it in up to the first knuckle. "Yes. Like that." He went deeper, and it felt so good, but it wasn't enough. I raised my head. "I need you inside me. I don't need a lot of prep. I like the stretch and burn."

He met my gaze and held it for a long moment. "Are you sure?"

I smirked and tilted my head toward my nightstand. "Those toys aren't there for show."

Seth chuckled. "Duly noted." He rolled on the condom and

slathered on a generous amount of lube. He pushed my legs back and leaned down to kiss me. The head of his cock pressed against my hole. I let out a breath and bore down, allowing him entrance. The stretch and burn were glorious. "Yes," I hissed.

"You feel so good," he ground out. He entered me inch by marvelous inch, filling and stretching me just the way I liked.

When he finally bottomed out, he stilled, allowing me time to adjust. It took a few moments for the burn to turn into pleasure. When it finally did, I said, "I'm good. Don't hold back."

He grunted his acknowledgment and pulled almost all the way out before driving back in. I wrapped my legs around his back as he set a punishing pace. The room filled with our grunts and moans of pleasure and the slap of skin on skin. Sweat dampened his face, and our bodies grew slick with it. More than the heat and the friction, the look in his hazel eyes as he drove into me set my whole body on fire.

My orgasm began to rise, sending sparks of electricity down my spine. "I'm close," I gasped. I went to slip my hand between our writhing bodies, but Seth beat me to it. He wrapped his slick hand around my hard cock and jerked me to the rhythm of his thrusts. My climax exploded through me, whiting out my vision. I threw my head back and cried out, my back arching up off the bed. Hot ropes of cum shot out over my stomach and some even made it to my chest. Seth's rhythm faltered. He thrust once more and let out a loud moan of pleasure as his cock pulsed and filled the condom with his warm cum.

We lay there breathless for a few moments. Seth smiled down at me. "That was...wow."

"Definitely wow," I agreed.

Seth kissed me tenderly, then grasped the base of the condom and slowly pulled out. I gestured toward the small trash can next to the bed. "Just throw it in there."

"I'll get you a washcloth," he said, getting up and heading into my en suite. He was back a few minutes later with a warm, wet washcloth. He gently cleaned off my chest and abdomen and then tossed the washcloth onto the floor. He stood next to the bed, seemingly uncertain what to do next.

I held up one arm so he could snuggle in. He hesitated for a brief moment, then lay beside me and rested his head on my chest. I wrapped my arm around him and held him close. "How are you doing?"

"Not sure," he replied. He lifted his head to meet my gaze. "I didn't expect it to feel like this."

"Like what?"

His eyes got shiny. "Like I haven't felt since David died. Like I've finally connected with someone again."

CHAPTER 7

SETH

Jon's gaze softened. The compassion in his eyes made me want to cry even more. My emotions were a jumble of guilt and hope. He pulled me closer and kissed my forehead. "And now you're feeling guilty?"

I nodded mutely. "It feels like I'm betraying David's memory even though he wanted me to find someone after he died."

"He sounds like a good man," Jon said.

"He was. He really was," I replied, my voice rough with suppressed tears.

Jon turned onto his side and faced me. "Will you tell me about him? I mean, I know some things from reading about him, but it's not the same as hearing it from someone who loved him."

"You want that?" I asked in surprise. "You want to hear about my dead husband?"

He brushed my cheek with his fingertips. "I do. He's part of your life. He'll always be part of your life. I would never want to pretend he didn't exist."

It was no wonder I felt a connection with this man. His empathy and compassion were just what I needed in my life. "I told you we met in Convention Hall, where he was selling his paintings. That was seventeen years ago. I was initially drawn in by his brilliance as an artist. But once I got talking to him, I was more attracted to his intelligence and quick wit."

"Seventeen years?" Jon repeated. "I thought you'd only been together for three or four years."

I shook my head. "Only married for three and half years. We were together for a long time before we got married." I paused, wondering how much of David's story I should share. But then I remembered Jon worked with patients like David all the time. "When I met David, he'd already gotten his HIV diagnosis three years before." I blew out a frustrated breath. "He hadn't gone to the VNA clinic or the A-Team at the hospital to start on the antiretroviral medication. He was on a self-destruct path."

"What changed?" Jon asked.

I let out a self-deprecating laugh. "David would have told you it was me who got him to start taking care of himself." I shifted my position on the bed. Being forty-six didn't lend itself to staying in one position long. "I like to think he finally realized he had something to live for and that his family didn't get to define his worth."

He grimaced. "Don't tell me, let me guess. Uber religious family."

"Got it in one," I acknowledged.

Jon sat up. "That really sucks."

I joined him, moving the pillows so I was leaning comfortably against the headboard. "It does. They threw him out after they caught him kissing another boy. He was fifteen. The things he had to do to survive only reinforced his belief he was worthless."

"And that was likely how he contracted HIV," Jon concluded.

I nodded. "It's hard to say how long he had it before he was diagnosed. When we went to the clinic to start him on the antiretrovirals, his CD4 count was only just above two hundred."

"Oh shit," he whispered.

Oh shit was right. A person with a healthy immune system had a CD4 count of between five hundred to sixteen hundred. David had been close to getting an AIDS diagnosis right then. I shook myself out of the memory. "Thankfully, he responded well to the medications. His viral load went down and his CD4 went up."

Sadness touched Jon's expression. "But his expected lifespan was shortened because he didn't get on the medication right away."

My stomach twisted. "It was. A lot shorter than we expected."

He took my hand. "I'm so sorry, Seth."

I kissed his cheek. "Thank you. We had a good life together. I helped him get his art in galleries and he helped me live in the moment more."

"If you don't mind me asking," Jon began, "why didn't you get married when it became legal in New Jersey?"

"David didn't want to burden me with his diagnosis and potential medical problems. We argued about it quite a bit."

"What changed his mind?" he asked.

I sighed. "It became clear that the medications were no longer slowing down the virus. By that time, David had made quite a name for himself in the art world and had also made a lot of money. I reminded him that if we weren't legally married, his family could be considered the default next of kin if he died. They could get their hands on everything he'd made."

Jon's eyes widened. "I never thought of that."

"As it is, I just spent the last two years fighting a lawsuit they brought against me. They wanted control of David's estate because they said I had exerted undue influence over him and coerced him into marrying me."

"That's awful."

"It was," I agreed. "But it's over now. David's estate will be divided between the three organizations in Asbury Park that help people with HIV and AIDS."

"That's why you were at the clinic the day we met," Jon observed.

"Yes," I replied. "I also gave checks to Project R.E.A.L. and The Center."

"Wow, that's great. They're all good organizations."

"They are," I said. "And they all helped David at one time or another. He wanted to give back."

"And his religious family wanted to keep it all for themselves." Jon scoffed. "And they call us deviant."

I moved over so I could straddle him. "I like being deviant."

A wicked smile turned up his lips. "I might be able to help with that."

After spending a wonderful weekend with Jon, I didn't want to return to work on Monday. I compromised by working from home so I could visit Moonlight Inn and speak with the owner, Sean O'Neil. He'd agreed to meet with me over lunch at the restaurant in the hotel. His husband, Jeremy Fitzgerald, joined us.

Sean greeted me with a hug when I walked into the restaurant. "Seth. It's good to see you. It's been a minute."

Jeremy also gave me a hug. "Nice to see you again."

We sat at a table in a corner close to the Steinway grand piano that was the showpiece of the dining room. It was tucked into a large half-hex alcove with tall leaded-glass windows that let in the summer sunlight that shone on the beautiful instrument.

"Congratulations on getting the lawsuit dismissed," Sean began after we ordered our drinks.

"Thank you," I replied. "It was a brutal two years." I smiled. "I owe Liam and Marco a night out. Marco's brother, Santino, was a nightmare for them."

"Good," Sean said. "They deserved it after what they put you through."

The server brought our drinks and took our food order. After she left, I leaned forward and put my arms on the table. "I had an ulterior motive for meeting you here for lunch." Sean just looked at me with a raised eyebrow. Jeremy gazed at me with avid interest. "There is a painting David wanted you to have here at Moonlight Inn as a thank you for being a good friend and advocating for the LGBTQIA+ community."

Sean blinked in surprise. "Really? That's…wow, I don't know what to say. Thank you."

I pulled out my phone and opened my picture gallery. I found the folder with David's paintings and clicked on the one he'd specified for Sean, expanding it so he could see it better. I passed him my phone. "He painted it specifically for you."

Sean sucked in a breath and his eyes went wide. He leaned toward his husband. "Jeremy, look at this. It's Moonlight Inn done up for Pride."

Jeremy stared at the picture and then looked over at me. "It's beautiful. I don't know how he did it, but he managed to capture the warmth of this place."

I knew the painting well. David had agonized over it for weeks because he'd wanted to get it exactly right. Sean and Jeremy were good friends of ours during the last two years of David's life and continued to be so with me, even when I'd decided to become a hermit. The painting showed the hotel bathed in the bright light of a full moon, the windows glowing with a warm light from within. Pride flags were arrayed all along the wrap-around porch and a banner proclaiming *All Are Welcome Here* hung proudly over the front entrance.

Sean raised shining eyes to me. "Seth, this is gorgeous. I can't thank you and David enough for this gift."

"You're welcome. David was proud of this painting. Your friendship meant a lot to him." Sean handed me my phone and I set it on the table beside me. "I'll be going to the storage unit later this week to pick it up."

"I know exactly where to hang it," Sean said. "Right in the lobby where everyone who walks in will see it."

I shifted in my seat. I was wondering if my brilliant plan wasn't so brilliant after all. But I decided to soldier on. "So," I began, sure my nerves were showing in my voice, "I've started dating someone."

Delight showed on both their faces. "That's great," Sean said. "I know David was worried about you."

"I know. He was a bit of a mother hen," I remarked fondly. "Anyway, Jon's family is having a fortieth birthday dinner for him here."

Sean interrupted me. "Jon? Do you mean Jon Taylor, Liam's friend?"

"That's right. I forgot he was friends with Liam. You probably know him."

Sean shrugged. "Not well. I've only met him a couple times."

"Anyway," I continued. I turned my gaze to Jeremy. "I was wondering if you wouldn't mind playing something for Jon for his birthday. But only if you want," I hastened to add. "I know you're busy and probably have more important things to do than play at a birthday party."

Jeremy held up his hand. He glanced over at Sean. "He's cute when he's flustered." He turned his attention back to me. "Seth, I'm never too busy to do a small favor for a friend."

Relief flooded me. I hadn't realized how important that was to me. "Thank you. Thank you very much."

"Well, we have to help you impress your man," Sean said.

CHAPTER 8

JON

On the morning of my fortieth birthday, I woke to the delicious aroma of bacon and fresh coffee. I took a deep breath and stretched before burrowing deeper into the blankets. The sheets smelled of sex and Seth and felt good on my bare skin. The morning sunlight poured in through the tall windows, and I could hear Seth singing along to an Elton John song downstairs in his kitchen.

Seth had taken me to Pascal and Sabine for a pre-birthday dinner the night before. Then we'd walked hand in hand to the boardwalk and onto the beach. The sky had been clear, with just a sliver of the waning moon giving its faint light. The ocean was cool but not as cold as at the beginning of summer. We'd let it wash over our bare feet as we stood with our arms around each other and our toes wriggling in the wet sand.

Then we'd come to Seth's place and made love. It was the only way I could describe it. The emotions I'd felt while he moved inside me were more than I'd ever felt with any other man. It occurred to me that even though I'd only known him for a little more than a month, I was falling for this wonderful, complicated man. I just wasn't sure if he was ready for something like that again. I didn't know if he ever would be.

I must have drifted back to sleep because I was drawn awake by the feeling of soft lips pressed to my forehead. I opened my eyes to find Seth smiling down at me. "Happy birthday, beautiful."

I slid my hand behind his neck and drew him down for a kiss. "Thank you." I lost myself in the kiss for a moment before I remembered I hadn't brushed my teeth. I pulled back. "Sorry. Morning breath."

Seth smiled tenderly. "No problem at all."

I took a deep breath. "I smell bacon."

He chuckled. "Yes, you do. I made bacon and waffles."

I groaned. "So good. And so bad for me. I can't wait."

He gave me a mischievous grin. "It's your birthday. Calories don't count."

"Don't I wish," I said.

He kissed my cheek. "It's almost ready. I left a pair of pajama pants and a T-shirt out for you to wear."

"Okay. I'll be right down." I got out of bed and headed into his en suite to use the toilet and brush my teeth. I thought about taking a shower but decided I'd wait until after breakfast so I could persuade Seth to join me. I put on the clothes Seth set out and followed my nose down to the kitchen.

When I got downstairs, Seth was setting a plate of waffles and a bottle of maple syrup in the middle of the dining room table. "Those waffles look delicious," I said as I walked around the table to give him a kiss.

He threaded his fingers through my hair and wrapped his other arm around my waist to deepen the kiss. He finally pulled away and rested his forehead against mine. "I like you in my clothes."

"That's good," I replied. "Because I like wearing them."

"Come sit," he said. He got the bacon from the kitchen counter and joined me.

I moaned with pleasure when I took my first bite of waffle. "This is so good. It's light and fluffy on the inside and just crispy enough on the outside. You're a really good cook." When I looked over at him, he was staring at me with a heated gaze. "What?"

"If you keep making sounds like that, we won't be finishing breakfast."

My lips curled up in a smile. "Well, I was going to invite you to join me in the shower."

He leaned over to kiss me. "You have the best ideas."

Despite his protests, I helped Seth clean up after breakfast. "I'm trying to speed up the process," I insisted. "That wonderful shower of yours is calling to me."

"But it's your birthday," he objected.

"You can treat me like a princess after we fuck in the shower," I retorted.

He snorted a laugh. "You're too much."

After we put the dry dishes away, I hung up the dish towel and headed upstairs. Seth stopped me with a hand on my arm. "Before we go back upstairs, I have something for you." He led me into the living room, where I noticed the back of a framed canvas leaning against the wall on the floor next to the fireplace.

Seth kissed me before going to pick up the canvas. "I found this when I was in my storage unit getting the painting for Moonlight Inn. I thought of you." He turned it around to reveal a painting of the same couple who'd posed for the ones in my bedroom. One big difference was that David had painted the two men close-up. In this painting, they looked older. Their hair was now mostly gray. One of them looked thinner and more careworn. The couple held each other in a tight embrace, their eyes alight with love and joy. Tears streamed down both their cheeks, which seemed to belie the happiness on their faces.

I reached out and gently brushed my fingers over the canvas. "Seth, it's gorgeous. They look so happy together. Why are they crying?"

Seth brought one hand around so he could point at the painting. Indicating the thinner man, he said, "Ed had undergone treatment for prostate cancer, and they'd just gotten the news that he was cancer-free."

Tears welled in my own eyes. "That's wonderful. David captured it perfectly."

"He really did," Seth agreed. He looked at me with a tender expression. "I wanted you to have it. So you'd know that there can be happy endings."

I saw a brief flash of pain in his eyes. He and David hadn't gotten their happily ever after. My heart squeezed. Seth didn't have to give me this gift. Everything he'd done for me up to this moment had been plenty. I took the painting from his hands and leaned it against the sofa. I took him in my arms and held him. "I've always believed in happily ever after." I was starting to hope I would get mine with Seth.

My parents loved Seth. They were thrilled when I told them I was bringing someone to the party. They'd hated my last boyfriend—rightly so, as it turned out. My mother had been bugging me for years to settle down. She didn't want me to be alone as I got older. My sister, Bethany, was there with her husband. My best friend, Carrie, had come with her girlfriend. Liam and his husband, Marco, stood by the grand piano talking to Sean O'Neil, owner of the hotel and Liam's brother. To my surprise, Sean's husband, Jeremy, showed up a few minutes later. It was then I realized they were also joining us for dinner.

Seth came up behind me and wrapped his arms around my waist. "We're in illustrious company tonight."

"I know, right? I didn't know my parents knew Sean and Jeremy."

Seth merely hummed in acknowledgment and said, "Let's go sit."

I loved the restaurant in Moonlight Inn, in part because it had been so lovingly renovated to reflect its Victorian roots. The ornately carved mahogany crown molding and wainscoting were reminders of a bygone era brought to life in the twenty-first century. Sean had done an excellent job combining Victorian charm with modern convenience.

A long table set for twelve awaited us. My parents insisted Seth and I sit in the middle seats so everyone could talk to me since it was my birthday. I ended up with Seth on one side and Liam on the other. I noticed my bestie sitting next to Seth. I rolled my eyes. Carrie had told me she would give Seth the "shovel talk" when she finally had him to herself. I leaned over to catch her eye and scowl at her. She just winked and laughed.

Liam leaned in and said, "I'm so glad you and Seth hit it off. He's a great guy. It's nice to see him smiling again."

Warmth filled me at his words. "I really like him," I said. "Probably more than like him, to be honest."

"I can't say I'm surprised," he replied. "He's a good man."

"That he is."

We all fell silent when the food arrived, eager to dig into the delicious meal. To be honest, I was mostly looking forward to dessert. The chef made the best chocolate mousse cake. My parents had promised they would order a whole cake for the table. Seth leaned over to kiss my cheek. "How are you doing?"

I smiled and kissed him back. "Really good. I'm so glad you're here."

"I am too," he replied.

"I hope we get to do this more often," I said. "I like being part of this extended family."

Liam leaned over and said, "There's a lot more of us. Just know, if you're ever in a bind, there'll be someone to help you out."

I believed him too. I'd heard about some of the ways this found family had helped other members of the LGBTQIA+ community. It even included Marco rescuing Liam from Syrian militants four years before. I never had gotten the full story about that. I supposed there was a reason for it.

When everyone was finally done with dinner and the servers had taken our plates, I said, "It's time for cake!"

There was laughter around the table. Sean gestured to someone on the other side of the restaurant. Then he and Jeremy got up and went over to the piano. "No way," I whispered.

Seth grinned at me. "Happy birthday, sweetheart."

Jeremy played the introduction and Sean started the chorus of "Happy Birthday to You." Everyone joined in, even the other patrons. A server brought in a chocolate mousse cake with four lit candles and set it in front of me. Of course there was plenty of sexual innuendo when I blew out the candles, and I mouthed an apology to my parents.

My mother shrugged. "We're used to it."

The server took the cake away to cut it. I glanced at Seth and said, "Would you all excuse us? We'll be right back."

I rose and gestured for him to follow me out of the restaurant and into the hallway that led back to the front lobby. I drew him into a shadowed corner and kissed him deeply. "Thank you," I said when we came up for air. "That was a wonderful surprise."

"I like spoiling you," he said with a smile.

I pulled him closer. "I like being spoiled by you. I'm looking forward to returning the favor."

Seth drew me into a long, languid kiss. When he finally pulled away, he rested his forehead against mine. "If I have anything to say about it, we'll have a long time together to spoil each other."

Tears stung the backs of my eyes. "Oh yeah? I like that idea. A lot." I swallowed hard. "I'm falling for you, Seth. I know it seems fast and I'm not trying to pressure you. I just want you to know."

His eyes shone brightly with tears. "I feel the same way. You've filled the empty spaces inside me. I never thought I'd have something like this again. I feel like David is watching over us, laughing at me and saying, 'I told you so.'"

I let out a wet chuckle. "If he were here, I would thank him for sending you my way. I'd honestly given up on finding my person. And now, here you are."

We stayed there in each other's arms for a long while. We probably would have been there longer, but Liam came out of the restaurant and spotted us. "Sorry to interrupt," he said with an apologetic smile. "They're asking for the birthday boy."

I sighed softly. "Okay. We're coming." I stepped away from Seth and held out my hand. "Ready for a new adventure?"

He grasped my outstretched hand and grinned. "Absolutely."

EPILOGUE

FOUR YEARS LATER

SETH

I blew out the five candles on the birthday cake set in front of me. Cheers and catcalls sounded around the restaurant in Moonlight Inn, reminding me my friends were sometimes twelve-year-olds despite their physical ages.

Jon leaned over to kiss me. "Happy birthday, my love."

I returned his kiss. "Thank you, sweetheart. And thank you for this wonderful dinner."

Jon had arranged to have all the found family we'd accumulated over the past four years join us for my fiftieth birthday celebration. The group had grown in the time since Jon's fortieth birthday party. It now included a whole security firm, several ex-military badasses, the assistant hotel manager and his husband, and four children ranging in age from three to eleven. In the beginning, I kept forgetting who the kids belonged to because the whole group took it upon themselves to watch over them. Woe be to anyone who tried to hurt any of these kids.

The group was so big that Sean had decided to close the restaurant to the public so we could have the whole dining room to ourselves. I sighed and leaned against Jon. "How are you doing?" he asked.

"Good," I replied. "You've given me a lot to celebrate."

He put his arm around my shoulders and pulled me close. "I feel the same way."

I turned my head to kiss the ring on his left hand. For all that I'd been hesitant to start something new after David died, once I had Jon in my life, I'd wanted very much to make him mine. Surprisingly, it was Jon who'd put on the brakes. He'd asked me to wait, to be sure it was what I wanted.

Sure enough, he'd been right. After I auctioned off David's remaining paintings and divided the proceeds between the three charities I'd chosen, I'd fallen apart. I could barely get myself out of bed. Jon had been there with me the whole time. He'd encouraged me to go back to therapy, held me when I cried, and celebrated every small victory with me. We'd taken long walks on the beach or boardwalk, depending on the weather. When it was too cold, we'd snuggled in front of my fireplace and just talked.

It turned out that fighting the lawsuit for two years delayed my grieving process, so the auction hit me harder than I'd expected. It had taken almost a year, but finally, I'd emerged from my depression stronger than before. I'd also been surer than ever that Jon was the one for me. A second chance at love I never thought I'd get. We'd married a year later.

A small commotion by the piano brought me out of my reverie. Jon kissed my cheek and rose from his seat. "That's my cue."

I frowned in confusion. "What?"

"It's part of my gift to you." He walked over to the piano, where eleven-year-old Cody was seated on the bench. Jeremy was leaning over and speaking to him quietly. Jon said something, and both Jeremy and Cody nodded. Cody's Uncle Zach brought up a chair and set it in the curve of the grand piano. Jon went behind the piano and came back carrying his guitar.

"Oh wow," I whispered.

Jon sat on the chair and everyone in the room went quiet. He looked at me and said, "This is for you, Seth. You told me to believe I could have a happily ever after, and then you gave me one. I love you."

He nodded to Cody, who began playing "Your Song" by Elton John. Jon joined on guitar and then started singing. My vision blurred as tears filled my eyes. My heart was so full of love for this sweet, gentle man.

When the song ended, there was a round of enthusiastic applause. Cody's dad, Nico, ran up and pulled his son into a fierce hug. Sean went over and took Jon's guitar from him. I hurried up and threw my arms around my husband, "That was beautiful."

"Thank you," he replied with a smile. "Cody and I worked on it for a month at Jeremy's school in Asbury."

I nuzzled into his neck. "Sneaky."

He gently tugged on my ear with his teeth. "Well, you're nosy. We had to be all Secret Squirrel so you wouldn't find out and spoil the surprise."

I chuckled and kissed him. "I can't help it if I'm observant."

"Like I said," he countered, "nosy."

Later that evening, we went home and made love. We fell asleep wrapped in each other's arms, sated and happy.

As was usual for me, I woke before sunrise. I got out of bed so I didn't wake Jon, made myself a cup of coffee, and went out on the patio. The air was crisp and cold as it was early May, so I brought a blanket with me. The sky was just beginning to lighten when Jon wandered out with his own cup of coffee and joined me under the blanket.

"Good morning," he mumbled.

"You should have stayed in bed," I said.

He shook his head. "I like this time of day, just before sunrise, when the light starts to brighten the sky. It's the promise of a new day. A new beginning."

"It is a new beginning," I agreed. "And I'm so lucky I get to share it with you."

THE KISS

COURTNEY W. DIXON

CHAPTER 1

CHICAGO, ILLINOIS - 2 YEARS AGO

AUSTIN

I sat on top of my large wooden table in my loft apartment, swinging my legs back and forth, my hands fisting in my hair while staring at the large blank canvas, mocking me in all its whiteness.

There was nothing.

No pattern emerged.

No composition jumped out at me.

My mind was blank when it was usually filled with color, chaos, and a vision that would guide my hand to create a world that made me such a successful artist. I never dreamed I'd make it big, but now my mind was filled with doubts and imposter syndrome.

Everything was his fault.

I let go of my hair and ran my hands through the greasy strands, which I hadn't washed since... When was the last time I showered? I sniffed my pits and winced at my ripeness, but I couldn't bring myself to care. My life was in ruins.

Alex was gone.

Five years wasted.

He was my first relationship. My first love.

I was alone. It was only me and my struggling creativity.

All those good times we shared exploded into a rain of ash when he came home last month to pack up his things because he'd found someone else to love. He walked out that door, leaving me to pick up my shattered remains.

"I'm tired of being second best to your art and career. I need to be someone's priority."

Had I neglected him?

I hadn't thought so. He was the love of my life.

Although, when I painted, I tended to get hyper-focused.

But we had sex often enough, right? Then, at least three times a month, we spent our time on dates to make up for me being buried in paint up to my elbows trying to meet deadlines. Hell, I'd done his portrait countless times over the years because Alex had a stunning body and an angelic face.

He never even talked to me about how he felt. I would've listened, dammit!

"Did you find someone else, or did you cheat on me?"

Rage was my first reaction to being gaslighted and told I didn't treat him well enough, and then for him to just up and find someone else instead of talking to me. It left me with suffocating anger.

I had no doubt an opportunity presented itself, so Alex took it and then blamed me for his shitty decision. While he'd been my first relationship, I wasn't a damn idiot. I understood how the world worked.

The look on his face as he stood there with folded arms over his chest and unable to look at me was enough to eviscerate my soul. He just didn't want me anymore and fucked someone else.

"He gives me the attention I need."

Was this the antithesis of love? This manipulating apathy?

"So you kept on fucking me?" I yelled.

Alex winced. "Because I still love you."

That was his excuse for fucking me after he'd fucked someone else. No, not an excuse. It was an outright lie. No one who loves another person would do that. It didn't get any more selfish than that.

"If you love me, you would've talked to me instead of ripping us apart because you couldn't keep your cock in your pants!"

I hadn't begged him to stay. How could I? Once he'd fucked someone else, there was no way could that be fixed. I would never trust him.

I'd been so angry—so betrayed—that I told myself 'good riddance' to him. But as soon as the door slammed behind him and I was left with no presence of him other than his cologne still mingling in the air, I broke apart and crumbled on the floor.

Now, a month later, and I still couldn't get my shit together. I couldn't create. I couldn't think. Alex had ripped out my soul while killing my muse in the process.

It wasn't only his leaving but the cheating while still having sex with me. Not only had Alex stabbed my heart, but he'd stabbed my back.

My phone ringing startled me out of my declining thoughts and growing depression. I lifted it off the table where it sat next to me and looked at the screen. My stomach flipped painfully when I saw the call was from my doctor.

My fingers trembled when I swiped the phone on.

"Hello?"

"Is this Mr. Austin Strauss?"

"Yes."

"This is Dr. Medina. I'm calling about your test results for STIs and HIV."

I swallowed the lump in my throat as my stomach continued to twist in knots.

It's fine. Don't jump to conclusions.

But I knew deep down that it wasn't fine. Had I been free and clear, my doctor wouldn't have called me directly. He would've had a nurse call me or send me a formal letter.

"Okay." It was all I could get out of my dry mouth.

"You're clear of any STIs, but... I'm sorry to say your results came back positive for HIV. I'd like you to come in as soon as you can to talk about your treatment options. Please make an appointment as soon as you can. There are a lot of options today..."

I didn't hear anything else my doctor had said as I slid to the floor, put my head between my legs, and cried. My sobs rang out and bounced off the brick walls of my loft, echoing my pain.

How could Alex have let this happen? Did he know? Was it intentional? Payback? Payback for what? I hadn't done shit to him.

Alex couldn't have punished me anymore had he tried.

I didn't know how long I lay on the floor crying like a baby when I sat up and wiped my face and nose with the back of my hand.

When Alex left, I deleted his contact information, but it didn't matter. I had his number memorized, so I picked my phone off the floor and dialed him.

His phone rang several times, but there was no answer. Asshole. He was probably avoiding me, although I was surprised he didn't block me, too.

I quickly typed out a text.

Me: Fucking pick up your phone! This is an emergency!

A few seconds later, he called.

"What do you want, Austin!" he snapped when I answered.

"Thanks for giving me fucking HIV, you prick. It wasn't enough that you cheated, but you fucked him bare?! Now, you're trying to kill me. Did you do this on purpose?!

"What? Oh, my god! No, of course not."

"What the fuck ever. Get tested, not that I care what the hell happens to you."

"Wait… Austin…"

I hung up on him and then blocked his number.

I really did care. I hated Alex with every fiber of my being, but I didn't want him to die.

"Fuck!" I cried out to no one.

CHAPTER 2

AUSTIN

I needed to get out of this place to breathe and escape Alex's ghost in the loft we shared for three years.

I needed something. Someone. An escape.

Alcohol called to me so I could obliterate my mind for a while and run from this mental hell I was in. But not at home. A bar. Yes, a bar would do. And somewhere close so I wouldn't have to drive. I could just stumble home.

My mind was in chaos. Fear, anger, despair… It was suffocating.

Too much shit dumping on me pushed me over the edge.

I dragged my reeking body to the bathroom and climbed into the shower to wash away two weeks' worth of stink, grease, and filth. Too bad it couldn't wash away my living nightmare.

Even worse, I'd never be able to move on from Alex because this virus would forever remind me of what he'd done to me. How did one recover from that?

After getting dressed, I stepped into the living room area and stopped in my tracks.

Flashes of taking a knife while in a drunken rage and shredding all the art I'd created of Alex suddenly hit me. A pang took hold at the waste —a waste of five years, a waste of my body and soul, and a waste of all that beautiful art. But there was no lingering regret at the loss of all my work. I couldn't look at Alex's form ever again without the rage and fear.

It was time for obliteration.

The October evening was cold and windy, but the gay club was only five blocks away.

When I pushed the doors open to the club, I was hit with warmth, an overabundance of cologne, and stale beer.

I dropped off my coat and scarf with the coat-check person, then shoved my way through the crowd of men straight to the bar.

A cute bartender with blond hair swooped back and a thick blond beard came up to me, wiping down the counter.

"What'll you have, handsome?" he yelled over the heavy dance beat.

"Two shots of your best Anejo tequila and an old-fashioned, with more old and less fashion."

"So, basically bourbon on the rocks?"

"Yep."

By the fourth shot of tequila, I was well on my way toward obliteration, the warmth of alcohol spreading across my skin while my brain tingled and the music buzzed in my ears. It didn't help that I hadn't eaten much in the past month, and I'd lost a lot of weight.

"Yeah, pour me a margarita, will you, with an extra splash of Patrón," said someone with a deliciously deep voice.

I glanced over at the man, standing at least three inches taller than my six feet. With his hair nearly black and dark scruff on his face over pale and creamy skin, he was the opposite of Alex, who'd been tan with blond hair.

The man's tall and lean frame filled his navy blue suit perfectly, keeping his jacket open and the top three buttons of his white dress shirt unbuttoned without a tie. Black hair peeked out of his shirt as if to say hello.

"Tequila? A man after my own heart," I said, buzzed enough not to care how corny that sounded.

He lifted his drink, took a sip, and turned to face me, leaning on the bar with a smirk that exposed dimples on his stunningly rugged and handsome face.

"Next, you're going to ask me if I come here often."

I gulped back the remaining bourbon and ordered another. "Do you? Come here often, that is."

He chuckled, exposing expensively straight white teeth. "First time. Just moved to the area. You?"

"I come here from time to time. How do you like our beloved city of Chicago?"

"I like it just fine. Then again, I'm from boring Little Rock."

A naughty idea formed in my drunken haze. Sex was all I could think about with this man. Not exactly sex. I wasn't drunk enough or cruel enough to hurt someone like that. I definitely wasn't that asshole Alex. But I had this desperate need to discover if this guy tasted as good as he looked. He'd make a perfect distraction.

When I got my fresh drink, I downed half of it, no longer feeling the burn washing over my numbed throat. "You're hot. Want to get blown?"

He choked on his drink as he laughed. "Bolder than I expected. Sure, why not? I'm always game for a good orgasm."

We set our drinks on the counter, and I took his hand in mine. I led him toward the bathrooms, where some couples were already having fun, and shoved him into one of the empty stalls.

"I'm Dallas, by the way," he said.

What were the odds? I would've laughed that we were both named after cities in Texas, but I didn't care. My mind wasn't in a good place. I just needed to fucking forget, and the alcohol wasn't doing enough to help with that.

"I'm Austin."

"Hey, that's cool—"

I smothered him in a kiss to shut him the hell up.

No talking.

No emotions.

No nothing.

I only wanted to feel his cock in my mouth and taste his bitter sweetness exploding on my tongue.

My hands threaded through his thick, cropped hair, pulling him deeper into a kiss. Our tongues clashed and fought for taste and exploration. Dallas tasted divine with tequila and lime while his light and peppery cologne swirled around me, filling my senses as I got lost in his demanding mouth with firm yet buttery-soft lips.

Hands slid under my Henley, smoothing soft palms across my skin. I buzzed with more than alcohol as I got lost in our kiss.

I slid my knee between his legs, feeling his stiff cock pressed against my thigh. Our bodies pressed closer together, seemingly uninterested in anything more than kissing.

We kissed each other as if we were all about to die at any moment, and this would be the last time we ever kissed, putting our entire bodies into it. My drunken dick took notice.

As much as I wanted to push aside my emotions and just have fun, they slid into my periphery unheeded. All the pain and suffering I'd gone through the past month trickled to the surface, threatening to ruin my evening. So, I kissed him harder because our kiss made me forget even for a second.

But Dallas suddenly moaned, pulling me back to reality.

Dammit!

No.

This wasn't why we were here. I needed nothingness.

Our kissing was growing too personal and intimate.

I quickly pulled away, wiped my mouth with the back of my hand, and fell to my knees on the disgusting bathroom floor.

"Holy shit, you can kiss," he breathed. "I've never…"

I said nothing as I lifted his shirt and pried apart his belt. I didn't look up at him when I unzipped his slacks and let them pool around his ankles. His boxer briefs were in black, holding in his ample package.

Unwillingly, I glanced up at him, his blue eyes blown black. He gave me a simple nod and his permission, so I pulled down his underwear, exposing his hard cock. It was pale and smooth except for the head, which was flushed and started to bead pre-cum. He wasn't so thick I wouldn't be able to wrap my lips around him, but he was nice and long with pretty veins. Fuck, his cock was perfect.

When I stroked him a few times, pumping him up, his deft fingers forked through my hair much too gently. It was too goddamn intimate.

This felt all wrong.

I felt all wrong.

My body itched with the sensation of contamination—a month of sweat, grease, eating crap whenever I remembered to eat, and now HIV. Realistically, I knew I couldn't give him HIV from a kiss, but the buzzing fear wouldn't leave me.

I couldn't do this to him. He deserved better, and I didn't give a fuck if I knew him or not.

Alex destroyed me inside and out.

I suddenly stood, struggling to breathe, looking at Dallas wide-eyed as the tears threatened. His worried look grew blurry as the first tears spilled. He quickly pulled up his underwear and pants. This had to end now.

"Oh, god… I shouldn't have come here. I'm so sorry."

The alcohol didn't settle well as it started to burn in my stomach, threatening to come up.

"Austin?"

"I'm so sorry," I said again, pushing my way out of there and wiping my face, which refused to stop leaking.

"Austin!"

This wasn't me.

I wasn't a player.

"Wait!"

This was all wrong.

"Are you okay?"

I was all wrong.

"Let me help you."

Why did he care? I didn't deserve it.

When I stepped out of the bathroom, the music drowned out his calls to me. My pace was wobbly, and bodies jolted me back and forth while the bar spun in my vision, threatening to knock me down. I nearly fell before someone gripped my arm to keep me steady, but I yanked it away.

I needed to get out there.

I couldn't believe Alex had done this to me. He'd changed my life forever.

When I stepped out into the cold night without my coat, I ran.

What day is it?

What time is it?

I lifted my head to grab my phone off my bedside table only to find it was dead because I couldn't remember the last time I'd charged it.

I sat up, tossed the covers off me, and rubbed my scruffy face. My entire body ached from my emotional turmoil, but panic flickered that I was symptomatic already. I felt my throat, checking for swollen lymph nodes, but they seemed normal.

Something had to give.

Something had to change.

I couldn't live like this.

I picked up the phone and called my doctor.

CHAPTER 3
TWO YEARS LATER

DALLAS

I walked around the studio apartment with my hands in my denim pockets, appreciating the brick walls and stunning view of Old Town Chicago. The industrial look really gave it an urban vibe, which contrasted with where I grew up in the Midwest.

I glanced out of the expansive windows to take in the parks and the view of Lake Michigan. Since it was winter, with Christmas just around the corner, the landscape was bare and covered in white, but in the spring and summer, it would all be green and gorgeous.

The condo wasn't massive, but the view from my window each day was well worth the smaller size and higher price tag.

"Amenities include an indoor pool and gym, among other things," said my real estate agent, handing me a brochure. "You'll see more details inside this. Of course, everything is within walking distance with fantastic restaurants and museums." She glanced out of the windows with me. "But between you and me, if this were a closet with this view, I'd take it in a heartbeat."

"I couldn't agree more."

Ally came out of the area where the bed would be with gleaming green eyes. She rushed at me and wrapped her arms around my waist. "God, this place is stunning, Dal. It's perfect."

I tucked a strand of highlighted blond hair behind her ear, then wrapped my arm around her, tucking her close. "Yes, this place really is amazing."

"God, and that view… wow. You're really moving up in the world. It's about time all your hard work and having no life started paying off."

Being a financial advisor wasn't easy, but since I was single, I only had to worry about myself, so I put in the long hours, building my client list and increasing my commissions.

I'd been so busy that I hadn't seen my old college friend for about a year. A few days ago, Ally flew in for the holidays, forcing me to take a break, so I took her house hunting with me.

I'd been doing it for the past two months, and my eyes were set on this condo for a while, finally getting the balls to purchase the place. It wasn't the best idea to buy a home right before Christmas, but I hadn't had any plans to celebrate anyway, not until Ally decided to pop in for a visit.

Mom and Dad begged me to come down to Little Rock to spend the holidays with them, and I needed to, but not this year.

"Are you going to help me move in?"

She lifted her hand, palm down, and inspected her fire engine red manicure. "If you insist, but if I break a nail, you're paying for it."

I chuckled. "Deal."

She was just teasing. We were more than friends. We'd grown to be best friends, and Ally Chambers was someone I could lean on when I needed someone to talk to. And, of course, I was always there for her as well.

I looked at the agent. "When can I move in?"

"As soon as your down payment goes through and the paperwork is approved, which shouldn't take long since it's the slow season."

Ally clapped as I handed the payment to my agent and signed the dotted line… several dotted lines. "This is exciting! Your first and very own place." She walked over to the corner of the living room by the vast windows. "The Christmas tree can go here."

"Christmas tree? I don't even own one ornament."

"Okay, Scrooge. Well, you better get shopping, then. You've got two weeks."

It was a good thing I took some time off—sort of. As a financial advisor, you never really had 'time off.'

That night, Ally and I went to an Italian restaurant a couple of blocks away. She pulled apart some steaming bread, slathering on an excessive amount of butter.

"So, how's your love life?" she asked with her mouth full.

"You know very well I have none. Relationships take time and work—time I don't have."

"You invest in people's money, but you can't invest your heart? Not everyone is so demanding, Dal. You just need to find yourself an introvert or someone who's got a big career, too."

I sipped my Sangiovese and sighed. "Great, then we could guarantee never to see each other. What's the point? Besides, why do I have to have a relationship to complete me? You don't have one."

"You're right, you don't, but do you even get laid?"

I coughed the wine, careful not to spill it all over me. I glared at her as I wiped my mouth with my napkin.

"Rude."

"Please, we tell each other everything."

"I guess I should be grateful you aren't one of those who sets me up with every person who has a dick."

She snorted a laugh, covering her mouth with her hand. "Oh, god. While I love tormenting you, I'm not that cruel."

"The truth is, it's been a while."

Too long, in fact.

There had been flings here and there, but nothing worth noting. Sometimes, I'd use a hookup app just to get a release. But the only one who really stood out to me since I'd been in Chicago was Austin, a name I'd never forget. Nor that kiss.

Jesus.

I'd never been so consumed by a kiss in my life, not like that. There'd been so much emotion behind it, almost like it hadn't really been about a fun blowjob. And I'd been right about the emotional aspect when the look of horror and pain spread across his pale brown eyes. He apologized to me over and over before he ran. Afterward, I spent several days mulling over if I'd done something wrong but then told myself to forget it. He was just a damn stranger in a bar—another hookup. Nothing more. Hell, we hadn't even hooked up. He ran out of there with me wanting to know what was behind that damn kiss.

Regardless, it had been an evening I couldn't forget or shake. I didn't think about it as much anymore, but the memory would hit now and again. That kiss had rocked me to my core as if only I could sustain him somehow, but he ran out of there with me wanting more and to know what was behind that passion.

"I know that look," she said.

"What look?"

Before she could respond, because servers had impeccable timing, he placed Ally's carbonara on the table and then put my bowl of Calabria in front of me.

After he left, she leaned forward as I stabbed the Filega pasta with my fork.

"That lost and far away look you always get when we're talking about dating and relationships. You're thinking about him."

"It was just a missed opportunity for a blow job. Nothing more."

"Awesome, you're lying not only to me but also to yourself. I'm sorry, Dal, but you spent the following couple of weeks going back to that bar so you could run into him again."

Actually, I'd been back to that bar several more times after, but I didn't tell her that. My obsession was embarrassing enough. Eventually, I gave up.

I shrugged to hide how ridiculous it was to crave a kiss from someone I'd never see again. "What can I say? That was a kiss to kill all other kisses." And that, right there, was the truth of the matter, not that I was trying all that hard to find someone in my life.

Ally softened, her green eyes sparkling like gems in the candlelight. "Dallas... There are other men who are great kissers."

It hadn't been about how well he kissed.

"I know," I said to end this conversation.

While I still thought about that kiss, I really had moved on. Besides,

I wasn't interested in dating anyone seriously. There was no time for commitments.

I'd finally hit my Zen and second wind as I ran on the treadmill in my building's gym. My legs burned, and my heart and breathing were heavy, but I was in a place I could push through as the rock music beat into my ears, matching my pace. My sweaty face reflected in the mirror I faced, starting to turn red.

Movement suddenly caught my eyes, and I glanced in the mirror, watching a man walk in with brown hair, his long bangs long falling in his face. He wore a gym shirt exposing lean yet muscular arms and shorts with a towel slung over his shoulder and a water bottle in his hand.

He looked vaguely familiar, and I couldn't take my eyes off his handsome features. It was nice to know I had an attractive neighbor.

The niggling familiarity kept my eyes peeled on him as he walked by me, not even glancing my way. But when he turned to face the mirror, setting up his treadmill, that was when it hit me like a sledgehammer.

That night.

That kiss.

That fear.

No way in hell...

I suddenly lost my rapid pace and started to wobble and sputter before I fell off the damn thing, a searing pain in my knee shot up my spine, but the embarrassment erased most of my suffering.

I righted myself and looked over at the man, who'd been oblivious to my downfall, wearing earbuds so he didn't hear me. I quickly turned off the treadmill and rested my hands on my knees, catching my breath.

Seeing him again made my heart race more than from exertion.

Of all the fucking small worlds.

Austin.

That had to be some fate shit.

Once I was confident I could walk properly, I removed my earbuds, stepped off the machine on numb and weak legs, and moved in his direction. There was no way I was going to walk out of the gym without saying something.

As soon as I stood next to him, Austin looked over at me. You could witness the recognition in those milk chocolate eyes, and then came that fear I'd seen before. He said nothing as he removed his earpieces.

"Hey," I said stupidly.

Nice one, Dallas. You act like you've never talked to a man before.

"It's you," I added because that was so much better. I mentally eye-rolled myself.

When he kept staring at me in the mirror, not saying anything or even moving, I scrambled for words.

"Uhm, what are the chances, right? I mean... Do you remember me? Two years ago? The bar? Ah..."

I rubbed my neck, feeling like an utter moron. He recognized me, right?

"I remember," he said flatly.

His tone didn't bode well, but I swallowed and pushed on. With a deep breath, I exhaled and scraped the bottom of my confidence barrel.

"Look, I'm going to go out on a limb here because this is so coincidental that I'm starting to believe in fate for the first time in my life. I've never forgotten that kiss... our kiss. But you ran out of there so fast, and you didn't give me a chance to fix whatever I did. Let me make it up to you and take you out to dinner. Or better yet, I've just moved in. Why don't you come over and let me make you dinner? I'm a pretty decent cook."

His brows furrowed into worry as he looked away, fisting his towel hard enough to turn his knuckles white.

"I—"

You could see his rejection coming from a mile away, but still, I pushed. I couldn't give up yet.

"Just think about it, Austin. I'm not asking for marriage here. Just a date. We can take it from there, but I would really like to get to know you."

With a sigh, Austin stepped off the treadmill and walked away. My stomach dropped to the ground. Dammit. Maybe there was no such thing as fate. Perhaps I was just an idiot seeing something that wasn't there that night.

But then he stopped without turning around. "You don't want to get to know me."

"I'm in condo number 1016 if you change your mind because I would very much would like to get to know you," I blurted to his retreating back.

CHAPTER 4

AUSTIN

How was that possible? What were the chances of running into Dallas again in such a big city? We'd barely spent fifteen minutes together one night while I was trying to escape my mental hell. Yet that kiss we shared had such an impact on me. It had been too much too fast before the guilt hit, so I ran.

During my better days, I'd often think about that kiss. Eventually, I grew obsessed with it, so much so that I started to sketch it and paint it, creating an entirely new series, which currently sat in a gallery. I'd made a substantial amount of money on that fucking kiss I couldn't forget. It was the only beautiful thing among all that ugliness I'd endured.

After I ran from Dallas for the second time in my life, I stood in front of the massive canvas hanging over my sofa in the open living room, staring at the larger-than-life men, their nude bodies abstractly and sensually entwined in a passionate kiss. It was a mixture of hope and depression. It gave me a small glimpse of all that I could've had, but something I'd denied myself since that fateful night.

Dallas had been my last kiss. No man had ever kissed me again because I hadn't allowed anyone into my life.

Logically, I understood I could have sex again, despite being HIV positive. My helper T-cell and CD4 counts were good, and my blood kept coming back with a negative viral load. It was all under control as long as I consistently got my injections every two months. But there was a lingering fear and stigma.

People understood about it more and more, but if I thought coming out as gay had been hard, coming out as HIV positive was next to impossible. Who would want to date me when they could have someone free of such things? Not to mention, my sexual drive was low... more like non-existent. I couldn't even remember the last time I'd rubbed one out.

But seeing Dallas today did something to me. My body flickered to life like a lightbulb, struggling to stay lit, flickering and flickering until it shone bright. My body was doing that for the first time in two years.

Tormenting thoughts forced their way into my brain.

You're not good enough.

You're ruined.

Why would he want you?

No one will ever love you.

You don't trust anyone, anyway.

I'd been in therapy, but it was still new. It took me a year and a half to even get the balls to do that as I wallowed in self-pity from hell.

My therapist had been working with me to build my confidence and bring my family back into my life, who'd been constantly worried about me, but I'd pushed them out, especially my brother. Sure, I still saw them, but it wasn't often.

I walked over to my fridge, grabbed a bottle of beer, and opened the cap, tossing it into the garbage. Then returned to my living room, and sat in a chair. I leaned back, took a sip, and stared at the painting.

The black abstract lines morphed and twisted along the white space of the canvas, mingling with spatters and scrapes of paint in beige, brown, yellow, and blue. The men shifted in my vision until I started to see more hope than ruin.

Why?

Because Dallas was here, living in my building. Because he felt the same way I had that night.

"You don't have to be alone, Austin. We are learning more about HIV every day. While there is still a stigma associated with it, people are more understanding and less afraid of it. People are even dating more often with partners who have it. I'm certain you'll be able to find love again," my therapist said.

"It's not only the stigma," I whispered, fidgeting my hands on my lap, unable to look at her.

"Yes, then there's Alex's damage. We've been dealing with your trust issues, and we still have a long way to go, but I'd like you to try to remember that even if we've been hurt, we should always start with trust unless they prove otherwise. That's the only way to build a strong foundation. They will never be Alex, Austin. In time, I believe you can open up your heart to someone again and that someone will love you in return."

I wanted to be brave and embrace this weird fate thing with Dallas.

I looked at my half-empty beer bottle with a sudden trembling hand because I was about to leap—a leap I hadn't taken in two years. It was slightly terrifying. Dallas could reject me when he learned the truth, and if he did, there would be others who'd do the same. But how would I know unless I finally got the balls to get out there again?

Life had been fucking lonely.

I stood, raised the beer in cheers to my painting, and chugged the rest of it back.

Who knew how long I stood in front of the door with brass numbers reading 1016, carrying a bottle of Cabernet.

My stomach twisted in painful knots, so much so that I thought I'd be sick a couple of times. And three times, I'd walked away only to turn back around and scowl at the door as if it offended me somehow.

I cursed at my weakness. I cursed at my fear. Most of all, I cursed Dallas for threatening to toss my carefully constructed life into an upheaval mess. But that damn flickering of hope wanted to turn on to full brightness. That was the only thing that kept me rooted in front of his door.

Sweat dripped along my back, and I wiggled at the tickling sensation. I quickly sniffed my pits to make sure my sweat hadn't turned sour. It was all good there. My deodorant was being a trooper. Perhaps I should buy it in bulk, or maybe some stock in the company.

You're digressing, Austin.

Fuck it.

My raised fist hovered over the wooden door until I finally rapped my knuckles on it.

Several seconds later, which felt like hours, the door opened to the scents of something Italian mingled with the spice of his cologne that I couldn't forget had I tried, bringing back a flood of memories from that night.

His pretty blue eyes went wide. "You're… here." His words were breathy, a mere whisper.

Shit, Dallas looked so handsome, wearing a simple button-up in pale blue with the sleeves rolled up and tucked into dark wash jeans while his feet were bare.

"I…ah… Is this a bad time? You're cooking. I'm sorry. I'll…"

I turned on my heels as my face burned so hot it turned to ash, but a gentle hand on my arm pulled me back.

"Don't go."

His earnestness and sincerity kept me from running again.

"Come in," he said, waving me in. "Please."

I paused for a moment before I got the balls to step inside.

His condo was much smaller than mine, but it didn't look dissimilar with its open floor plan and brick walls. But my place was more chaotic, crammed with all things art. His was neat and cozy with simple, modern furniture. Although, he had several cardboard boxes tucked into corners, clearly having just moved in.

"I... did I interrupt your dinner?" I asked.

He smiled brightly, exposing those expensive teeth as his blue eyes, the color of faded denim, twinkled. His nearly black hair made his eyes just pop, especially with those thick lashes. But it was the dimples that really sucked me in.

"Not at all. In fact, the lasagna in the oven is for tomorrow night. I have a friend in town, and we plan to spend the holidays together. I wanted to make something nice for Christmas Eve tomorrow."

"Oh, is this friend..."

"Is just a friend. Ally. We've known each other since college."

He held out his hand. "Is that for me?"

I rubbed my neck as I handed him the bottle. I was entirely out of my element. Two years was all it took for me to forget how to date entirely. "Ah, yeah."

He took it from me and smiled again. "Thank you. I wasn't expecting company tonight, so I don't have anything to eat. I was just going to order some takeout. Would you... like to stay and eat with me?"

God, I wish my stomach would stop flipping around. It was starting to hurt.

"Uh, sure."

"What are you in the mood for?"

I shrugged. "I'm not picky."

"How about Thai?"

"That sounds perfect."

"What do you like?"

"Uhm, some red curry with chicken would be great."

"Sounds good. Let me pour us a glass of this lovely wine, and I'll order it for delivery on my phone app. Why don't you have a seat, and I'll be right there?"

I nodded and smoothed out my sweater, though it wasn't wrinkled. I walked into his living room and sat on his comfortable sofa, which was in the middle, facing out at the stunning view of Lake Michigan. He shared the same view as me.

When he returned, he handed me a glass of wine and sat next to me, curling his leg under him. "So, Austin. Let's talk."

Here goes nothing.

Full transparency. No point in beating around the bush.

This was my make-or-break moment.

CHAPTER 5

DALLAS

When I opened my door, to say I was surprised to see Austin standing there was an understatement. I had a feeling I'd run into him again, but only in passing and nothing more. He had to come to me before I could pursue him further. It had to be on his terms.

My stomach tingled in a good way, and my heart rate kicked up to a thousand notches, seeing him standing there, looking a little sweaty and a lot nervous.

I had no idea what had happened to him, but the same pain I'd seen in those soft brown eyes the last time was still there, lingering like a dark cloud that refused to move on. That he was here now was the most important. He came to me instead of running again. We were connected somehow, and I had every intention of proving that to him.

Once I'd poured us some wine, I sat down next to him on the sofa, my leg curled underneath me. Leaning my side into the back cushions, I watched him take a sip, facing the windows, refusing to look at me. His cheeks were flushed with a cute, rosy color.

He looked beautiful, even in his nervousness. He wore a thick, cable-knit navy blue sweater, and his jeans had strategic holes in them that looked expensive. His brown hair was lighter and straighter than mine. It was long in the front, but instead of swooping it back as most men did, he let it fall naturally. I itched to pluck the strands away to see his face better.

"I'm glad you're here."

He nodded and took another small sip of his wine.

"I'm... scared," he finally said.

My brows rose to my hairline, not expecting him to be so forthcoming. But he needed my patience, and he clearly needed an ear. There was baggage there, and the only reason I was willing to take it on was because I genuinely felt an important connection between us despite being two passing ships in the night.

"What are you afraid of?"

"You... me... everything."

"Can you elaborate more?"

He set his wine glass down on the coffee table and wiped his hands on his jeans.

"I haven't had a kiss or a date or a relationship since that night. I don't know what the hell I'm doing."

My breath caught, but I tried not to show my surprise. Everything hinged on my reaction to him. Austin was a damn flight risk, and I didn't want him going anywhere. Not only did I want to get to know him more, but I was damn curious about his story.

He looked at me with such pleading eyes that I reached out and placed my hand on his shoulder, giving it a gentle squeeze. "It's okay," I said.

He nodded. "So, I feel something there... with you. It's the only reason I'm here right now, and to finally move forward with my life."

"I'm so glad you did, Austin."

"We'll see. Look, I'm just going to come out with it because I don't want to waste your time or mine if you don't want to pursue this."

"But I want to."

"Just... Please let me finish."

"Okay."

"I have HIV."

Well, that explained his resistance to dating. It was definitely a difficult subject to talk about with someone you hardly knew, so I understood his reaction and fears. It was also the best time to bring it up before things got too deep.

"I'm so sorry to hear that. How do you feel?"

His eyes went wide, and his mouth opened and closed, trying to find words. "Why do you act like I'm talking about the weather? You're not freaking out?"

"I hurt for you, Austin. I know that this is a life-long illness, and you have to receive treatment for the rest of your life. You are receiving treatment, right?"

"Definitely. I've, ah, had a negative viral load for a while now."

"That's great news. Congratulations."

"But…"

I raised a hand to stop him so he'd understand why this didn't sway my interest in him. "My cousin has it. He was… careless in his youth. But he's been under treatment for years, and he's doing really well. I know a lot about HIV from him."

I took a bold step and leaned forward, pressing my nose close to his neck, and took a deep breath. He smelled like the forest, so clean and fresh. "Did you think I'd run for the hills?"

His body shuddered, and he quickly nodded. "Yeah."

"Look at me, Austin."

When he did, his pale brown eyes shimmered with wetness. There was still fear in them but also some relief. "I'm interested in you. Now, I understand your fear and resistance to dating. God, my cousin struggled for a long time, too. He hid from family and friends as he came to grips with his life that had completely changed. Now, he has a partner that he's lived with for the past six years. They're doing great, and he's very happy."

Austin squirmed in his seat and coughed. "Good. I'm… glad for them."

"So you see, there's no need to be afraid around me."

"Dallas?"

"Mhm?" My fingers traveled along his neck, brushing the surprisingly soft hair there. I couldn't control myself. I wasn't afraid to date him. While I hadn't had sex in a while, I still needed to get tested and put myself on PrEP. It was no hardship and all in the name of living long lives.

"It's… more than that."

The air grew heavy again as he was about to unleash something else, something I hoped also to get past.

"First, thank you for not judging. I may not be showing it, but it means everything. That was my biggest fear and biggest hurdle, but I've got baggage. You don't want all my baggage."

"We all have baggage. Why don't you let me judge that? But also, I'm a pretty good listener," I chuckled. "Or so Ally says, but she could be biased."

Austin gave me a brief smile, which lit up his face like fucking fireworks. I needed more of that. So did he.

He sighed and rubbed his hands on his thighs again. "I got HIV from my ex. We were together for five years, and he was the love of my life, or so I thought. He came home one day and told me he was leaving me for someone else. He… cheated."

"Jesus. He not only left you and cheated on you, but he couldn't be respectful enough to wrap it up?"

"No. The betrayal and anger I felt… Fuck. It's still holding on to me so tightly, but I am getting professional help. Honestly, that's pretty much the only reason I'm here. I don't think I would've knocked on your door had I not been seeing a therapist."

"I'm glad you're getting help. It's so important."

Austin abruptly stood and tossed his hands in the air, a crackle of anger sizzling. "Don't you get it? I'm a fucking mental wreck! You don't want this. There are so many better men out there. Why are you so… understanding!"

"Should I not be?"

"I…"

"Look at us. We barely know each other, and we're already being honest and open. That's mostly you. But I've also been cheated on. I know what it's like and how it makes you feel like a failure sometimes. But that was a long time ago."

His eyes took on that pleading look again, maybe filled with a bit of hope. I stood and grasped his face. It was bold, but I didn't give a shit.

Everything was on the line, and I wanted another taste of him, dammit. I wasn't going to back away from this, not when he serendipitously stumbled back into my world. Austin was on the right track, but he didn't need to be alone anymore.

"You're so damn brave. Before, I was attracted to you. I felt connected through that insane and much-to-short kiss. But now? I'm in awe of how you've breached your fears and come face-to-face with them with someone you hardly know. I'm honored to be that person."

His hands rested on my wrists, but he didn't pull my hands off, looking at me with red-rimmed eyes. "I've been so lonely."

I inched my face closer to him, almost ghosting his lips. "That ends now."

CHAPTER 6

AUSTIN

As soon as his lips were on mine, instead of the expected stiffness and panic, I melted. I also wanted to fucking cry in relief, but I managed to hold it all back with a will I didn't know I had. His short beard was rough on my skin, and I loved it. His peppery scent was all I could breathe in. It wouldn't take much for me to grow addicted to him.

How was he accepting this?

Don't question, Austin.

His lips were as soft, warm, and as owning as I remembered them.

Hell, I was surprised I even remembered how to kiss.

The noise in my mind was finally silenced when his strong fingers forked through my hair at the back of my head and fisted it, not painfully so, but more like he wouldn't allow me to run this time.

Our heads twisted, and his tongue brushed the seam of my lips. I quickly opened for him, allowing him to explore the inside of my mouth. When he pressed his pelvis against mine, there was no denying how hard he was.

I nearly wept again when my own dick stirred to life, proving, once again, that we were meant to be here at this moment in time. God, it'd been so long.

Soon, our entire bodies went into the kiss, touching everywhere we could as if making up for lost time. This was how it should've been. I never should've used him or anyone to get over my pain that day.

We finally pulled away, resting our foreheads together, trying to catch our breaths.

"That's what I'm talking about," he whispered. "How does a simple kiss feel like coming home? Only our second kiss in as many years? Your energy is so raw and deep. I fucking crave it."

The buzzing of his phone pulled us apart. The food was here.

An idea suddenly hit me. He needed to see it.

I grabbed his hand and pulled him out of his condo. He quickly locked up, and we headed downstairs to the lobby to grab the food. Once back in the elevator, I pushed the sixteenth-floor button.

"We're going to eat at my place," I said.

We held hands again as we rode up, the air quickly filling up with scents of coconut milk and curry. I glanced over at Dallas, who had a slight smile on his face, looking up at the floor numbers blinking by.

When the doors opened, I tugged him toward my condo and unlocked the door.

His pretty blue eyes scanned my place. "So, this is where you live. Damn, your place is so much bigger. And I love what you've done with it. So eclectic."

I took the food from him and brought it to the kitchen, setting it on the counter, but I didn't grab plates for us to eat. We came here for one reason only.

I threaded our fingers together again, tugged him into my living area, and pointed at the painting over my sofa.

"That's a gorgeous piece," he said.

"That's us."

The longer we stood together without him running for the hills, the stronger my confidence grew. If I could handle coming out to Dallas like I had earlier, I could handle anything.

His brows rose, looking at me. "Us?"

"I'm an artist."

"You did this? Holy shit. I had no idea you were an artist. No wonder you're so passionate. It's stunning."

Dallas walked closer to the painting, scrutinizing it. "It's... a bit sad, yet sensual."

My stomach flipped around in excitement that he understood the emotions behind the piece.

"Yes. Exactly. All I could think of was that kiss. It wasn't supposed to happen, not like that. I'd been so angry and upset that day. My life as I knew it was over. I rushed to the bar to get drunk. Not to find someone to kiss... or other things. But there you were. It was spontaneous on my part and not at all like me. It was that kiss and how gentle you were with me when I was on my knees. It wasn't supposed to be like that. I ran because it was wrong of me to do that to you just because I was hurting. But that kiss... It was electric."

He craned his head back, smirking. "So you captured it in art. It's as emotive as that kiss was. Stunning. It truly reflects the pain and passion behind it."

"There are others—so many others that I have an art show going on centered around this theme."

"Oh, hell... now you have to take me."

I smiled, truly smiled, for the first time since I could remember. "I will."

"You need to do that all the time."

"Do what? Art?"

"No, smile."

I smiled shyly and walked over to him.

"For over a month, I couldn't create shit after Alex, but with you... You helped revive my creativity and career."

Dallas slid his arms around my waist. "Hmm, it seems you owe me a substantial amount of money."

My jaw dropped, and he laughed.

"I'm teasing you, Austin. But I would love a piece for my new condo since I don't have anything on my walls."

"I have tons of them you can have."

"Thank you for showing me."

Dallas pulled me into another kiss that was as good, if not better than the last one.

"Are we doing this?" he asked when we pulled away. "Are we going to make a go of something special here?"

"I would like that, but I'm still afraid. I can't promise I won't freak out on you from time to time."

"Then have your freak out, and then we'll talk about it." He cupped my face again in his strong and protective hands. "I've been waiting my whole life for you."

CHAPTER 7

SIX MONTHS LATER

DALLAS

I watched my boyfriend continually glance at me while talking to people about his art at an art show. I leaned against a wall and sipped champagne, waiting for him.

A smile curled on my lips when he managed to escape. He snagged a glass of water from a server and sauntered my way.

"Congratulations, Mr. Strauss. Your art show is a success."

We clinked glass and plastic before he stood next to me, facing the crowd. "Thank you, Mr. Tate. I also appreciate your charitable donation toward Immobile Osculum. I hope it finds a space on your now cluttered walls."

I laughed and sipped on the bubbly drink, going right up my nose.

I'd invested a substantial amount of money toward Austin's art, which was quickly filling up my walls. He'd given me the rest, but I'd insisted on paying for some of it. The last thing I wanted was to make him a starving artist.

"Good boy for drinking water."

He huffed a laugh. "I'd rather have champagne, but I don't want to risk things with alcohol." He leaned his head closer. "Is this 'good boy' thing new?"

I winked. "It is if you want it to be. So, does this mean you're ready to get out of here soon? Are we still on for tonight?"

His body shivered, and he nodded, blushing straight to his ears, which was fucking adorable.

"Yes. I think I'm ready."

"Don't think. Know."

"I'm ready."

"Good."

After dating for six months, we'd yet to have sex, waiting until Austin was comfortable enough. He came to me last week to tell me he was ready, and I was more than eager.

I wrapped my arm around him to pull him close and nipped at his ear. "Let's get out of here."

"Give me thirty minutes to say goodbye."

"I'll give you thirty seconds."

He adorably rolled his eyes as he meandered back to his adoring fans as I stared at his cute ass that I was going to be inside soon.

Not wanting Austin to get cold feet and to show him I was completely on board with having sex with him, as soon as we closed the door to his condo behind us, I jumped him. His back landed against it with a 'thud' as I took his lips in mine and thrust my tongue into his mouth.

God, I was so ready for this. I'd been taking PrEP for months now for when he was finally wanting to try sex. Sure, we gave each other hand jobs, and he'd blown me a few times—and what a mouth he had —but I wanted him viscerally. To join our bodies once and for all. To connect with him more profoundly.

"When we're done, maybe you can create some art of us fucking," I panted on his mouth.

He snorted a laugh. "Maybe."

"You can call it 'The Copulation.'"

Austin threw back his head and laughed as I nibbled his throat, inhaling his forest-green scent. "Sounds cheesy as hell."

"You love this cheeseball."

"I really do."

"I love you, too, baby. Now let's get naked."

"Dal?"

"Yes, sweetheart." I continued to nibble at him as my hands climbed underneath his untucked dress shirt, roaming my palms on his chest dusted with hair.

Our heads rested together as his hands rubbed up and down my arms. "I'm… scared. It's been so long."

"We don't have to, baby. It can wait until you're one hundred percent."

"But I want to. It's just… I kind of forgot what it was like. What if I do a shitty job?"

"That's impossible."

"I know it's irrational. I understand you're protected, and I've got a negative viral load, but I'm still terrified you'll get it."

"We can use condoms for our first time if you want, but there's no way I'll get it, sweetheart. I love how you're looking out for me. I love how protective you are. You decide how you want this to go down."

"Thank you for being so patient with me."

"If you never wanted sex, I would still love you. We can continue as we've been doing it."

His body shuddered with my words. "God, I love you, too. Let's do it."

I looked at him squarely in his pretty milk chocolate eyes. "Are you sure?"

"Yes," he said more firmly.

I snagged his hand and yanked him to his bedroom, where we quickly undressed each other. I shoved him onto the bed before I jumped on him and smothered him in another kiss. Our hands were everywhere, caressing goose-pimply skin.

"I can't wait to be inside you," I growled. "Then next time, if you feel up for it, you can be inside me."

"I'd like that."

My cock was leaking and straining for friction and release. I'd never been so turned on in my life. Austin looked so sexy naked, his neatly combed-back hair already a wreck.

"You're fucking gorgeous, baby. Now, on your stomach. Let's get you prepped."

Austin rolled over and lifted his stunning pert ass in the air. His hole opened and closed, as eager as I was.

"Fuck, has anyone told you how beautiful your ass is?"

He chuckled into his pillow. "You may have mentioned it once or twice… a day."

"Well, because it's perfect."

"You're biased."

I bent over and bit his right ass cheek, making him yelp. "Behave, or I'll bite the other one."

"Yessir…"

I sat up wide-eyed and gasped. Holy hell! Where had that come from, and why did I like it so much?

"Say that again."

"Yes…sir?"

"Fuuuck… I like that."

Austin wiggled his butt playfully, and I gave it a little pat, pleased he was feeling good enough to do so.

I snagged the lube and condom waiting for us on the bedside table, opened the condom wrapper, and rolled it on to be ready. We didn't need it, but I knew he'd feel better with me wearing one.

After flicking open the lube bottle, I poured a generous amount into my hand, spreading it around my fingers and over his begging hole.

"Ready for me?" I'd keep prodding him every step of the way.

"Yes," he breathed.

My cock ached that we were finally doing this. I'd been dying to be inside him, but never complaining. This was his show, and his consenting to sex was everything.

I breached my oiled index finger inside him. Austin froze for a second but let me in. "Are you okay?"

"I forgot how much I liked anal play."

That tugged a smile from me. "Then, we'll have more play. Next time, I'll use my tongue."

Now I worked two fingers, stretching him, pressing on his prostate, pulling out groans and moans, and maybe a few whimpers here and there.

"God, your ass is sexy as hell. Ready for a third finger?"

"I'm ready for your dick."

I snorted a laugh. "Soon, baby. You need more stretching."

After a few more minutes and lots of begging from Austin, I pulled out my fingers and flipped him onto his back because once I was in him, I wanted to see him wrecked when he came. There was no way in hell I was going to miss that. Not for our first time.

CHAPTER 8

AUSTIN

I'd been so torn and guilty for holding back sex from Dallas. It had been a real struggle and required tons of therapy to get past my issues, from my fear of sex to my trust issues.

Over two and a half years. That was how long it'd been since I'd had sex last. It was slightly terrifying, but I worried about Dallas, too. He'd been so fucking patient with me, always so accepting and supportive. He was damn near perfect.

Dallas hovered over me with eyes full of love and understanding. While I appreciated it, his stunning chest and rippling abs were a distraction. I looked down further to see his engorged cock stretching the condom. My dick throbbed and leaked pre-cum in response. Hell, he was sexy.

"Do you still want to do this?" he asked, always making sure I was comfortable and felt safe.

"Don't back out now. I need this, Dal."

I needed to offer Dallas all of me and do this for myself. I loved and trusted him, and that was saying a lot.

"Lift your legs back for me."

I grabbed my thighs and pulled my legs back, exposing myself. The position was vulnerable as hell, but not any more than when I'd had my ass in the air not long ago.

"If you're uncomfortable at any time, you tell me to stop, okay?"

I nodded but huffed at him. "I'm not stopping this. While I appreciate your care, please stop."

Dallas leaned down and smothered me in kisses before he sat up and pushed my thighs back further, lining his cock up to my hole.

"Dallas," I warned when he opened his mouth as his tip started to breach me.

He chuckled and inched his way in while I breathed through the stretch and burning, bearing down on him like how I remembered doing before.

It's like riding a bicycle, right?

He slowly pulled out and pushed back in, and each time, he went deeper and deeper, while all that time, carefully watching for any signs of discomfort or panic.

"Fuck, baby… I'm not going to last with you wrapped so tightly and warmly around me. You're so perfect. We fit like we were made to do this together."

My hands gripped his thighs, planted between my legs as I panted, inhaling his peppery scent with each breath, which was now mingled with the musky smell of arousal.

Once he was fully seated in me, I blew out a sigh of relief. I did it. I didn't freak out. That showed how much my trust had been restored, and that was all thanks to therapy and Dallas.

I reached my hand to his face and eased him down to kiss me. "Thank you for this. I love you so much."

"No, Austin. Thank you for allowing this and trusting me."

"Now move before I combust. I need to feel you hammer into me, and I need to feel it for days afterward."

His grin was crooked, and his eyes turned mischievous. "You got it."

He sat upright, looking down at his cock, and his lips parted before he sucked in his bottom lip to nibble on while he slid in and out of me.

One day, we'd switch positions, but for our first time, I needed to have him inside me.

"Fuck… you should see how hot this looks. I'm definitely not going to last long."

Dallas angled himself, and when he did, lights danced behind my suddenly closed eyes. I wrapped my legs around his hips as my back arched off the bed. "Shit. Yes. Right there… more Dal."

He let my legs go, leaned down, and pressed his lips to mine as his hips punched into me faster and harder. My wrapped legs pulled him tighter, and I wrapped my arms around his slick back.

My heart raced as the burn turned into beautiful pressure and delicious torture, suddenly desperate to come. Every time he hit my prostate, I got closer and closer to falling into the climactic abyss. I so wanted to fall because I knew Dallas would be there to catch me.

"Dal… I need to… come. I'm on fire…"

His chuckle rumbled straight to my chest. He sat up and continued to pump into me. "Grab your cock and make yourself come. I want to see you decorated in it."

"Jesus," I breathed and grabbed my dick.

Once I started rapidly stroking, Dallas pulled out and slammed home. I threw back my head and tugged on my dick faster. He soon hammered into me, grunting with each thrust as my body burned. My flush pulled a sheen of sweat across my skin.

My spine tingled while his cock zapped, electricity coursing through my body every time he hit that pleasure button.

"I need you to come, baby. I'm dying here," Dallas panted, dripping sweat from the tip of his nose onto my hand and abs. His hair was wet and falling over his eyes, and his eyes were hooded. Shit, he looked sexy as hell.

I pumped my dick faster and closed my eyes as the pressure grew too much. Then, without warning, I blew like I'd never orgasmed before.

"Christ!" Dallas yelled. Maybe that was me. I was currently deaf as the rush of blood pumped in my ears.

Hot cum spattered on my abs and over my hand as Dallas whimpered. "Shit… so fucking tight…"

My cock sporadically continued to pump as my body grew limp and numb. I gripped his arms as he slammed into my overly sensitive prostate. He swelled and grew hot inside me as he came. His thrusts lost their rhythm, and his eyes slammed shut while his mouth opened, gasping through his orgasm.

I need to see him like that over and over again.

He fell on me, and his heavy weight blanketed me like a shield as his heart beat heavily against mine.

"Best... sex... ever," he rasped hoarsely.

I chuckled, but I couldn't find the words to agree with him. My fingers trailed gently along his sticky back as our bodies cooled and calmed.

Who knew how long we lay there when he finally pried us apart and climbed out of bed?

"Don't move."

He left toward my bathroom and came out shortly after, carrying a wet washcloth. With caring hands, he cleaned my ass of lube, and the hot water clinging to the rag was soothing. Then he wiped away the cum from my stomach before he cleaned himself.

When he tossed the rag into my hamper, I lifted the blanket, and we both slid underneath. Dallas pulled me tightly against him. I rested my head on his shoulder and my hand on his chest, dragging my fingers through his chest hair.

"If there was ever a moment when I knew with one hundred percent certainty that you're mine, this is it. I'm never letting you go, Austin. I promise never to hurt you and that I'll always love you."

I lifted my head and kissed him. "And you're mine. I promise always to love you, too. Thank you for helping me heal my soul. I'm not sure I could've fully done it without you."

"Yes, you could've. You're so strong and brave. You didn't need me, but I'm so happy you want me."

After so long of being alone and lonely, never believing I'd find love again, I definitely wouldn't give up Dallas... ever.

FEELS DIFFERENT

ESSIE SLOANE

CHAPTER 1

I unlocked the front door to my tiny apartment, grinning over my shoulder at the man laughing behind me: Aaron Rogers, the guy I'd been seeing for about six months. The man who made my stomach flutter every time I laid eyes on him. He was starting to dominate my dreams as well as my every waking thought. I hadn't expected it when I'd swiped on him on that dating app or when I'd met him for our first date, but every time he texted me a quick good morning or good night text, I was thankful.

And tonight, it felt like we were going to cross the final hurdle.

Because Aaron was different than any guy I'd ever met on a dating app. Most of them were looking for one thing, and one thing only. The dinner or drinks or movie or whatever first date cliche they drummed up was a formality before inviting me back to his place for sex. Or me inviting him back to mine. I wasn't going to pretend that I was some innocent who didn't know exactly what he was signing up for when he went on those dates.

Aaron, though, he'd only kissed me good night after our first date. At my car. I'd thought I'd blown it until he'd sent the first good morning text the next day. It had blown me away. (What could I say?

The bar was in hell.) He kept up that pattern for four more dates, an entire month of dating, before I asked him about it. He said he just wanted to take it slow, and so we had.

We'd gone on dates. We'd defined the relationship. We'd gone over to one another's houses and watched movies, making out on couches like teenagers. It made my heart race every time. It also made me desperate for things to push further, to discover more of this magnificent man.

But every time I tried, he caught my wrist and stopped me. The most I'd gotten was a little bit of grinding that only made me want him more. I'd started to get a complex about it. Maybe it was me. Maybe he didn't find me attractive. He might not have been into scrawny guys with floppy carrot orange hair, too many freckles, uneven lips, and a disproportionate nose. A lot of guys hadn't been, not for anything more than a quick one night stand.

Except that he didn't even want that.

I didn't get it.

But that night, things felt different. He'd been more physical during our date. His hand had barely left my thigh during the entire movie, which had me half hard before the end credits rolled. During dinner, he'd been playing footsie with me. When we got out into the parking lot, he pinned me against the car and kissed me so thoroughly that I spent several blocks on the car ride home catching my breath.

And the way he was looking at me now?

Tonight was different.

When the door closed behind us, he crowded against me, pushing me back against the small stretch of wall next to my mounted coat rack. He kissed me the same way he had in the parking lot, tongue probing and searching my mouth. His body caged me in, and I could feel how much he wanted me, his hard dick pressed against my stomach.

Tonight was different.

I lost track of how long we kissed there before he lifted me up and carried me the short distance between my front door and the couch, bravely navigating the clutter on the small apartment floor. He settled with me on his lap, and I could feel him underneath me. I rolled my hips and swallowed down his moan. I didn't know what had changed, but I could feel it heavy in the air between us.

His hands began to explore my back, first over the fabric of the black tee-shirt I'd worn that day, and then, miraculously, underneath it. The sensation of his bare fingers on my skin had me moaning. Actually moaning. It might have had something to do with his hard dick pressing up against my ass though. For the sake of my image, I was going to pretend that was entirely what it was. I tangled my hands into the familiar territory of his ash blonde hair and deepened the kiss.

Yeah, tonight was definitely different.

We lost ourselves in making out. I kept waiting for him to push it to the next level, something beyond hands on my bare back. After all, he'd been the one that wanted to take things slow, and I didn't want to pressure him into something he wasn't ready for. But damn, I needed more. He made me need more every single time he touched me.

Without thinking, I slid my hands down his sides and grabbed the hem of his shirt. He let me take it off of him, and I was drunk on the sight of his bare chest. His lean musculature might not has been as defined as a porn star's, but it wasn't nothing either. His nipples were a pale brown against lightly tanned skin. They were smaller than mine. He had a small black triangle tattoo over his left pec, and I wanted to run my tongue over it. He captured my mouth with his, delaying my plans to get my mouth on that perfect chest.

I settled for running my hands up his bare chest, savoring the new area to explore. I traced my fingers over the delicate lines of his tattoo, grinning into the kiss as goose flesh rose under my fingertips.

Then my shirt was removed, joining his on the floor. We pressed our closer bodies together, and he lowered me down onto the couch. I didn't care about the feeling of the scratchy fabric under my bare skin. I only cared about the weight of the man on top of me. It was everything I'd dreamed it would be. Better even, because it was real.

Because it was him.

Tonight really was different.

I didn't know how long we laid there, making out. I only knew when it became too much, when I needed more again. Given how well my last attempt at bravery had gone, I was empowered to make another move. Maybe he'd been waiting on me to make the next move this whole time. I could kick myself if that were the case. I brought my hands down to his ass. I squeezed his cheeks over his jeans first, pushing him down harder against me. We both groaned at the friction, and he didn't stop me.

I took another small step, reaching underneath his pants and over his boxers. He stilled for a moment, but he let me proceed. He kept his movements controlled, a tease, a taste for what would (hopefully) come later.

I slipped my hands underneath his boxers. My hands sprawled over his bare ass cheeks, and then he pulled away.

I'd barely gotten a chance to touch him. The moment he pulled away from the kiss, I withdrew my hands from his ass, feeling like a chastised child. My heart sank as he pulled himself off of me, planting his feet back firmly on the floor. I stared at him for a moment before following suit. That insecurity was back, the ever echoing question in the back of my mind: was it me?

"Is it me?" I heard my thoughts spoken out loud, in my voice, falling from my tongue. I hated how the words tasted as they left, how they sounded when they hit the air. My voice shook, and the sound made my stomach sink down to the very tips of my toes.

I couldn't look at him. I didn't want to see his face when he heard the pathetic tone of my voice. I didn't want to look at him when he admitted it was me. And when he put his hand on my knee, I didn't want him to be touching me either. Every time he touched me, my brain got all foggy. I convinced myself that he actually liked me, but I didn't want to do that this time. I didn't want to delude myself that this thing that I thought was building with my boyfriend over the past six months was real.

"It's not you." His voice sounded as shaky as mine. I couldn't help looking at him, and the sadness on his face hit me like a sucker punch. He might be gearing up to break my heart, but I still hated seeing him look like that. Feelings were stupid.

Love was stupid. Love. At least I hadn't been dumb enough to tell him that I was in love with him, not if he was about to end it. Because what always followed, it's not you?

"It's me."

Ding, ding, ding. We had a winner. Right on time. It still hurt. The words I knew were coming still made it hard to inhale. "Do you know how cliche that sounds?" I asked him. "If you're breaking up with me—"

"Whoa! Who said I'm breaking up with you?" He sounded confused.

Was he not breaking up with me? Because I'm pretty sure he just used the most cliche break up line known to mankind. If he wasn't breaking up with me, then why would he say that? I groaned. "You're not breaking up with me?"

"No," he said with a shake of his head. He leaned over and planted the most tender kiss of my life on my lips. It had none of the heat from our make out session, but it somehow made me feel warmer than I ever had in my life.

It still didn't answer anything. Was he just not attracted to me? Was he not into sex? It wasn't a deal breaker. I'd figure out a way to cope... through lots of masturbation and sex toys, which had been the past six months for me anyway. If it meant being with him, then I could do that. Because I loved him. The words stayed unspoken on my tongue, but that didn't make them less true.

I still needed to know though. I drew in a deep breath and repositioned myself on the couch, turning to look at him. "Then what it is? Every time we start to get physical, you pull away. This is the first time I've ever seen you shirtless, and it's been six months."

He looked uncomfortable, and I hated myself for prying. I should have been a better person, a more patient person. I should have let him figure out what he wanted to tell me and waited. I wished I could pluck the words from where they hung in the air and stuff them back in my mouth, unheard. Too bad that wasn't possible. Words couldn't be unspoken.

"I didn't mean to push you," I said instead. I gave him the out. "If I was going too fast."

It was his turn to pull in a deep breath. He reached out and took my hands in his, wrapping his fingers around them. "It's not that," he assured me. "Trust me, going slow is kind of new to me."

"Why?" Foot. Meet mouth. "Sorry. I—If it's something you don't want to talk about right now, you can tell me that. I'll stop pushing. We can watch a movie and snuggle or something."

And then, when he went home, because he never stayed the night with me, I'd beat off and then beat myself up for being such an idiot. It was the status quo.

He didn't say anything at first. Maybe he was going to take me up on the offer, but he also didn't let go of my hands so I could grab the remote and move onto the second part of that offer. Turn on the TV, cuddle up, and pretend that I hadn't just made an ass of myself.

He opened and closed his mouth a few times, before he finally spoke. "I need to tell you something, and it might change everything," he started. He sounded scared, terrified actually. I squeezed his hand, glad that he'd grabbed mine. Because it meant I could reassure him without interrupting him. He took the squeeze as an invitation to continue. "A year ago, I was a different person. I was making a lot of bad decisions. Reckless ones."

I hummed, trying to keep from asking more questions. What kinds of wild and reckless decisions had he made? He'd always seemed so steady the entire time I'd known him.

"I was partying with the wrong people. Drugs, hookups, drinking too much. My parents came to visit, and they found me overdosed in my bathroom while they were sleeping in the living room." I drew in a deep breath. That wasn't what I was expecting. It would explain why he wanted to take things slow, if he'd just had that history. "They sent me to rehab, and my doctors did tests, and I came back—" He drew in a deep breath, trying to steady the shake in his voice. "I came back positive."

Positive.

I didn't have to ask for clarification. He wasn't talking about coming back with a positive attitude.

"Are you—are you okay?" That was such a stupid question. He'd just told me he'd gone to rehab and tested positive. And here I was, asking if he was okay. God, I was a damn idiot. "I mean…"

"I'm undetectable. I'm on medicine." I nodded. "But this is the first time I've tried to have something real since I got the diagnosis. I didn't know how to tell you, and honestly, I was afraid of how you'd react."

Another punch to the gut. But then, I didn't know how I was going to react either.

A part of me wanted to tell him that it didn't change anything between us. I wanted to tell him that I loved him and that nothing in his past could change that. I wanted to assure him that he'd made bad choices, but they didn't make him a bad person. I believed the last part of that, and I wanted to believe the rest of it. I wanted to believe the rest of it so bad.

The rest of me though? I was terrified. I knew that undetectable meant that it couldn't be spread. I knew that I wasn't at any increased risk, and I'd been on PrEP since I was eighteen and out of my parents' house. I knew it shouldn't be a big deal, but it was.

I kept my hand in his, though, as I tried to sort through the tangle of thoughts in my head.

I loved him, but I was afraid.

I wanted him, but I didn't know how to have him.

And there were the other fears too. What if something happened? What if I lost him? What if he forgot to take his medicine, and then we forgot to use protection and I forgot my pill that day. It wouldn't be the first time.

The biggest fear screamed at the back of my mind: what if I couldn't handle this?

He studied my face for a moment before leaning in and giving me another gentle kiss. He released my hands and picked his shirt off of the floor. "It's a lot," he told me quietly. "I know it's a lot. I know that you're blindsided. I think... I think I need to go home now."

I wanted to tell him no. That I wanted him to stay. I did want him to stay, but I also knew he was right. It was a lot, and I needed to wrap my head around it. I needed to decide if this was something that I could handle. I caught his hand in mine. "I'll call you tomorrow, okay?"

He nodded and put his shirt back on. He paused with his hand on the doorknob.

"Good night, Adam."

His voice was quiet, reaching me as he opened the door and stepped out. The moment the door closed, I wanted to chase after him.

Instead, I stayed planted on my couch, head swimming with more thoughts than I could manage.

CHAPTER 2

I stared at the wall for an hour before I realized my thoughts were just as tangled up as they'd been when Aaron left. I needed to talk to someone about this, someone who had been there. Unfortunately, none of my friends could help.

I only had one friend in a serious relationship, and they'd been together since high school. They'd lost their virginity to one another, after getting tested together. A few of my other friends hooked up, but as far as I knew, they'd never dealt with this. A few of those friends had dated people in the past, but they'd never mentioned anything like this either. It took me thinking of and turning down another few names before I remembered my boss.

James McMahon took a few weeks off every year, always at the same time. It was in honor of his late husband, a man who had died in the early 2000s from the same disease that was plaguing my mind now. There was a picture of him on his desk in the office at the bar he owned. I'd seen it every time I went in to talk to him about something. He was also the kind of guy that invited confidences, so much that I'd leaned on him every time I had a problem. He was the father I didn't have.

I'd not talked to my own parents since I graduated high school.

They'd been vocal with their opinions regarding my sexuality, and I'd left home a few days after graduation.

The more I thought about James, the more I realized that I needed to talk to him. I pulled out my phone and texted him, asking if he was free for a chat. He replied within minutes, telling me to meet him at the bar.

The drive to the bar took under ten minutes. Getting back to his office took a little longer. Several of my co-workers stopped to chat or give me hell for coming in on my night off. When I finally extricated myself from them, I was somehow more anxious than I'd been in the first place. Probably because every moment between the conversation with Aaron and the potential for answers felt like ten.

James was waiting in his office when I got there, sitting behind his desk, fingers wrapped around a small tumbler of whiskey. A second one sat untouched across from him. "Have a seat," he instructed, pointing toward the uncomfortable folding chair on the other side of his desk.

I walked over and slouched onto the seat. My eyes landed on the back of the picture frame I knew housed a younger picture of James with his late husband, Henry. James' dark hair had yet to get any silver. He'd been clean shaven, and there were fewer lines around his clear blue eyes. The mischief on his face hadn't changed in the twenty-plus years since that picture had been taken. That look wasn't on his face now. It had been replaced by concern, and it was directed at me.

I could feel the weight of his eyes on me, the questions he wanted to ask. I liked that he waited for me to decide what to ask. He was patient, every time. When I didn't say anything for a few minutes, he spoke. "Okay, Adam, what's up?"

I swallowed hard and reached for the whiskey, downing it in one gulp. The liquor loosened my tongue. I put the glass down. "It's about Aaron."

He took a small drink from his own glass and nodded. "Is every-thing okay between you two? You had a date tonight, right?"

I'd forgotten that I'd told him about that before I'd left the night before. I'd been so excited. I'd convinced myself that tonight would be different, even without the evidence of Aaron's lips on mine. I'd been right, just not in the right way. Tonight was different. It had changed our entire relationship.

"We had a date," I confirmed. I wished I had another glass of whiskey, but I knew James wouldn't pour me one yet. Maybe I could get another one out of him before the conversation ended. He kept his steady gaze on me, egging me on. He needed me to say what I needed to say. More than that, I needed to say it. I drew in a deep breath, steeling my nerves. "He left early. After he told me…" I stopped. Was this a violation of his privacy? What if he didn't want some guy he'd never met knowing?

But I needed to talk to someone about it, and James was the only person I had.

"He told me he has HIV."

Silence punctuated my sentence, and it grew more deafening by the second. For the first time, James took his eyes off of me. They rested on the framed picture of him and Henry. I could see the sadness there, the ghosts that had haunted him since Henry died. I regretted saying anything. I should have figured this out on my own, instead of putting this on him and bringing back bad memories.

When he finally spoke, his voice was gravelly. "You two—You've used condoms? Right? You've been safe?" There was no mistaking the concern there, and I wasn't surprised. He kept a large supply of condoms in the break room, so no one had an excuse not to practice safe sex. He also offered to drive people to the clinic if he found out that his staff weren't getting tested regularly. More than a few staff members had taken him up on the offer.

"We haven't gotten that far," I assured him. "He wanted to take it slow. I guess I know why now."

James let out a long breath and nodded. "Okay, good." He stopped. "Not good that you two haven't… Good that he told you. Before."

"Except now I don't know what to do."

"I understand that," James told me. I knew that he understood, because he'd been there. He'd dated someone with HIV when the medicines were still new. He'd married him, unofficially, and he'd loved him until the day Henry died. If anyone understood, it was was James.

That was why I'd come to him with this.

"How did you do it? It was different then, right?"

"It was very different then," he agreed. "But the moment I met Henry, I knew that he was my person. After we met, he convinced me to go to college instead of just slumming around town with my brothers. He understood me in a way that no one else had, and it came so fast. I was in love with him before I even realized that I was falling. It was like something out of a movie. Except that he had HIV. He was on medicine, and we were safe. We were always safe, but there was still that worry. All the damn time."

I couldn't imagine that worry. I knew some of the things he'd gone through, coming of age in the 90s when the AIDS epidemic was running rampant through our community. He'd mentioned old friends, people he'd grown up with who had passed away. He told me about funerals he'd attended, and then he told me about stories he knew from people older than him. Who had gone through the worst of it.

It had to be scarier then.

"How did you handle it when you found out?"

He drew in a deep breath and finished his glass of whiskey. I watched as he poured us both another glass. "I didn't handle it well at first," he started. "I ended things with him. I broke my own heart, because I was terrified. I was afraid of being another dead body, another funeral. I didn't want to leave my family. You've seen them in here." I grinned. I had seen his family. He had four brothers, all loud and raucous, and the moment he joined them at the bar, he was just as wild as his brothers.

"But you two got back together?"

Obviously, they'd gotten back together. Otherwise, they never would have gotten married. The picture on his desk wouldn't exist. He wouldn't be telling me this story, because it would have ended there.

"It took a few weeks. I was miserable without him. My brothers worried about me constantly. I was drunk all the time, fighting everyone that even looked at me wrong. Then, one night, I went to the bar. I was planning on getting trashed, and he was there. He was nursing a beer with this hangdog look on his face. I'd never seen anyone look sadder in my life, except maybe myself in the mirror." A ghost of a smile haunted his face. "I went over to him, and we started talking. I was happier than I'd been since the day I walked away from him. We made plans to talk the next night. Sober. Never looked back after that night."

"So you were okay with it?" He raised an eyebrow. "With his HIV? Even though you were scared?"

"I chose to deal with it, because the alternative meant walking away from someone that I loved. Going back meant I got four years with him."

"Only four years?" The way he spoke about Henry, on the rare instances he spoke about him, he made it out like some epic love story.

Maybe it was.

"Only four years," he repeated wistfully, "and we were only married for a week."

"A week? What... Shit, sorry. That's probably personal, isn't it?" I already knew the answer. Of course, it was personal. How could it not be?

He had a faraway look in his eyes. I assumed he was thinking of different times, of the years he spent with Henry. Of the end of his time with Henry.

"It wasn't legal. It wasn't even something we were thinking about, you know? It was an impossibility. We just figured we'd be those old gay men in town that died holding hands or some shit." He shook his head. "Then he got sick. Some complication with his medicine. I got the call from his mom, saying he was in the hospital. Wasn't the first time he'd been hospitalized, so I wasn't that worried. Not until he was in there two weeks and the doctors came in. Said that things weren't looking too good." His voice cracked. "They didn't think he was going to make it. That night, he asked me to marry him. He didn't have a ring when he asked. Not like he could get one in the hospital."

I wanted to tell him to stop, but that seemed more cruel than having asked him in the first place. I wasn't sure I wanted to hear the end of this story. Not when I already knew what happened.

He kept talking. I wasn't even sure if he realized I was still there, still listening to what he was saying. "The next day, I went to a pawn shop and bought two simple gold bands. We exchanged vows with him in his hospital bed. He was wearing his hospital gown. His parents," he swallowed hard and took another deep breath. "His parents were there. My brothers. We were all crammed into this small hospital room. We kissed, just like any wedding. And we were married. Just like that. Maybe it wasn't legal, but it was still real. A few days later, he went in his sleep. I was sitting beside him, holding his hand." A tear fell from his eyes. I watched as it traced a path down his cheek. I watched as he wiped it away with the back of his hand.

I waited for him to continue his story, but he didn't. It just ended. Like Henry's life. Like his first marriage.

I knew that times were different now. Medication had changed, and there was more information available now. There were fewer deaths.

But that could still be my fate, saying goodbye to the person I loved most in the hospital, watching him fade away while he held my hand.

"Do you ever regret it?"

James looked up at me, shaking his head. "Not for a single minute. Losing him almost destroyed me, but I found my way through it. I moved on. I fell in love again, more than once. I married someone else, even if he turned out to be a piece of shit. But I never stopped thinking about him. Never stopped believing we'd still be together too, if things had been different." He took a small drink from his whiskey. "He was the love of my life. How in the hell could I regret a single minute with him?"

I wanted that. One day, I wanted to look back at my life and remember all the love I had with someone. There had been exactly one person in my life who made me feel even a fraction of that.

Aaron.

"What do you think I should do?"

James reached across the table and clasped his hand on my wrist. "I can't answer that for you, kiddo. You're the only one who knows if you can handle being with him."

"But do you have any advice?"

He looked thoughtful as he leaned back in his chair. "My advice? Follow your heart, but don't stay with him if you're not sure. If you don't think you can handle everything that comes with loving someone with HIV, then don't stay with him. But if you think that he's worth it, then you know what you need to do."

I nodded as his words settled over me. This was a man who had been through hell in the name of love. He'd walked through the valley of the shadow of death, and he'd come out the other side.

Could I do that? Was Aaron worth the risk?

CHAPTER 3

James and I talked a little longer before I left. I had a lot to think about. My thoughts might have been less tangled up, but it felt like they'd multiplied and gotten louder. There were parts of James' story that I hadn't even considered. There were parts of being in a relationship with Aaron that I hadn't even thought about. Not that I had much time to think about any of it yet.

I already knew that night would be a heavy one.

I thought about stopping at the liquor store on the way home, buying some mental lubrication to help the thoughts slide around easier. I decided against it. I needed to be clear headed while I contemplated the future of my relationship, because that's what this was. The future of my relationship. It felt big, and I needed to treat it that way.

I drove past the liquor store and straight to my apartment.

As I sat down on the couch, I remembered every time Aaron had sat there with me. I remembered the first time we'd made out on this couch, a month and a half into our relationship. I'd thought that night would be the one that was different, and instead he told me that he wanted to take things slow. I'd been insecure about it, at first, but I agreed. I liked him a lot, even that early into our relationship. I liked going on dates with him, the calls and texts, the fact that he made me feel seen.

Was I really willing to throw that away because of what he'd told me?

I thought back to the way his hand always rested on my thigh, just above my knee, while we curled up together and watched TV. It felt like it belonged there, and when I was in his arms, I felt like I belonged there. I'd never felt that way before.

But was it enough?

The tale of James and Henry replayed in my mind, but I changed the roles. I was James, a little less handsome and a little older than he'd been in his story, but I filled the role well enough. Aaron was Henry, eyes sparkling the same way Henry's did in the picture on James' desk. I pictured us falling in love. That part was easy. I was already there, in love with someone I didn't know if I could have. I didn't know where Aaron was on that journey, if it was another thing he wanted to take slow. I pictured holidays and birthdays, laughing and crying together as we fell deeper in love. I thought about nights in bed, whispering shared dreams to one another.

And then I imagined how it would feel when the rug was yanked out from underneath us.

"Life isn't guaranteed. Even if you dated someone healthy, shit could still have the same ending," James had advised me.

Just because Aaron was HIV-positive didn't mean that he would die. Just because I wasn't didn't mean that I would live a long life, either. There were too many variables.

That didn't change the question.

I pulled out my laptop and began researching. Maybe if I had more information, I could make my decision easier. Maybe if I knew what I was facing, I could weigh the outcomes. Because I knew what I wanted. I knew it the moment Aaron walked out of my apartment.

I wanted him. I wanted the man I'd gotten to know over the past six months.

I spent the rest of the night researching. I read statistics. I read about the different medications that were available on the market, and then I read the side effects for every one of them. After reading those, I had to talk myself down, because the side effects of medication always sounded terrifying. Even for things as simple as cough syrup. I didn't need to work myself up over side effects, even if that had been what ended James' short marriage to Henry.

The pessimistic voice in my head really needed to shut the fuck up.

I read through things I already knew about prevention. I read articles and blog posts about people in relationships with men with HIV. The articles and blog posts calmed me down the most. There were a lot of people having these relationships, and according to most of the articles, they were the same as any other relationship. Their partner had to take a daily pill or scheduled shots. It would be the same if he had severe allergies or mental health issues. There were even articles stating that condom use and PrEP weren't necessary when the viral load was undetectable.

The sheer number of sources assuring me that this was safe soothed my worries.

And they also kind of made me feel like an idiot. Had I overreacted? Maybe he wouldn't even want to be with me, because I hadn't been able to just look at him and tell him that it changed nothing. That I accepted him and that just being with him made the risk worth it. I wish I'd been able to do that right away.

Because these facts and figures, these personal accounts, talking to James, it all boiled down to one simple fact: being with him made the nominal risk worth it.

I reached for my phone, ignoring my laptop as it clattered to the floor in my rush. I navigated to our text thread and smiled.

Aaron: Good night

He'd still sent me the good night message, even after the way I'd reacted to his announcement. I didn't deserve someone like Aaron, but damn I was glad that I'd found him anyway.

Adam: i'm sorry for how i reacted earlier. can you come over tomorrow?

I didn't expect an answer. Since his good night message had been sent an hour before, I assumed he would be asleep. So when my phone chimed less than fifteen seconds later, I nearly jumped out of my skin. I smiled when I saw the notification of a new text message from Aaron.

Aaron: It's not a big deal.

Adam: i reacted like shit

Aaron: I told you something big. It's okay to take time to come to terms with it and decide what's best for you.

Adam: i'm still sorry. so can you come over tomorrow? lunchtime maybe?

Aaron: Three good for you?

I sent him back a thumbs up and went to take a shower. Right before I fell asleep, I sent him a quick good night.

I didn't sleep very well. I tossed and turned all night, bits and pieces of my conversation with James intermingling with memories of Aaron and dreams of our future. It wasn't a bad dream, though there were some parts that were just weird. Like having dinner with James and Henry, the four of us settled around the table. There was probably some psychological reason for it, something about missing my family or James being a stand in dad.

I didn't really care.

I woke up earlier than I had in a long time, finally deciding to call real sleep a wash. I spent the day anxiously cleaning my entire apartment. By the time three rolled around, I had cleaned the place from top to bottom. It was probably cleaner than the day I moved in. I'd taken a shower and changed into a nicer outfit: jeans and the band tee Aaron had bought me at the concert he'd taken to for my birthday.

He'd bought us tickets to one of my favorite bands, even though he'd told me he didn't really like them. By the end of the night, he'd been converted. We listened to the band when we drove to the orchard to pick apples a month later. He'd made a playlist of some of their more romantic songs when he took me to a moonlit picnic, the band serenading us as we laid on a blanket lookup up at the stars, cuddled together against the cool bite of the autumn air.

I thought about playing their music now, but we needed to talk. It was the kind of conversation that required real attention, and how could I do that if I were singing along or tapping my feet or whatever?

At five past three, I heard the knock on the door.

When I opened the door, he was standing there, looking nervous. I motioned for him to come inside, and he nodded before taking a few steps past the threshold. I wanted to pull him into my arms and kiss him. I wanted to let him know that everything was okay, because it was. I wanted to tell him that I loved him, that nothing else mattered except the way I felt about him.

It would be so easy to just let everything be okay, to never talk about it. But that wouldn't make it go away, and he might have doubts. He might wonder if I was going to walk away one day, and I didn't want that. I wanted forever with him. Maybe six months was too soon to be thinking like that, but I didn't care. I wanted forever with this man.

"Let's sit down," I suggested, motioning him toward the couch.

He followed after me without a word. We sat in the same positions we'd sat in the night before, when he'd told me that he was HIV-positive. I wished it were still the night before, that I hadn't sent him away. I wished that I'd been able to say the right words and prevent this rift between us, but I hadn't been able to do it. Now we had to build a bridge over it.

I didn't know how to start.

We sat in heavy silence. I couldn't find the words that I wanted to say, and he was endlessly patient. For the first time, I wished that he weren't. I wished that he'd push and force me to figure out a way to start the conversation. Every second that he didn't, the silence grew louder until it was deafening. I drew in a deep breath, and he turned his head to look at me better.

"I already said I'm sorry for how I handled your… news," I started. He held up a hand like he was going to silence me, but dropped it after I shook my head. I needed to apologize to him. Out loud, not just over text. "I wish I'd been able to handle it better and tell you that everything was going to be okay and that it didn't change anything between us, but I didn't know."

He nodded. "And if it's not going to be okay and it does change things, then that's okay." Even with his perfect words, he wasn't able to hide the sadness in his tone. My heart broke knowing I was the reason for that. "Just tell me. If things aren't going to be okay or if you can't handle any of this."

I reached out tentatively, placing my hand on his. "I didn't know if I could handle it," I repeated. "I do now. I talked to my boss—"

"James?" he questioned.

Because of course he remembered my boss's name. He remembered every little thing I told him. He was just that kind of guy. How could I have questioned if his diagnosis was worth throwing away what we were building? Of course it was.

"He lost his first husband due to complications with his HIV medicine," I explained. "He was the only person that I could talk to about this. The only person that would understand what I was going through and how I was feeling."

"And how were you feeling?" he prompted.

"I was messed up over it," I admitted. "I didn't know what it meant for us. For me. I didn't know if I could handle everything that came with it."

"With dating a partner who has HIV?"

I nodded. "I didn't know what it would mean. Would we always have to use condoms? Would it mean that I couldn't have the future I want with you?"

"What kind of future do you want? Maybe I can answer that."

Why had I mentioned anything about futures? Because now I had to tell him all of it. I felt my cheeks burn. Oh god. His hand squeezed mine, and I looked into his deep eyes. "I want to grow old with you. I want to come home to you at night and tell you about my day, because I know that you'll listen better than anyone else I've ever known. I want to call you my husband. I might want to have kids with you one day."

"You can have all that with an HIV-positive partner," he interjected.

"Yeah, I know that. I knew that part yesterday too. What I didn't know was how long I'd have you by my side if I decided to be with you. I didn't know if your diagnosis meant that I'd lose you before I was ready." I paused. "I didn't know if I was okay with that either."

"And now?"

I drew in a deep breath and turned to face him, one leg curling up underneath me on the couch. I met his beautiful eyes and smiled. "I know that even if it turns out that I only get four years with you, I won't regret those four years."

He raised an eyebrow as he shifted, his position mirroring mine. "That's oddly specific. Something I should know?"

I laughed. It was the first time I'd laughed since he left the night before. "Not that I know of. Promise it's not some weird psychic vision." It was his turn to laugh. His eyes sparkled, and I felt myself fall even more in love with him. There was no way I could walk away from Aaron. "James and Henry had four years together. I asked him if he regretted it, if he'd have made a different choice knowing how it ended. He told me that he wouldn't. So... four years."

"What if we had more than four years?"

"Then I'd be even happier," I told him simply. "I love you." It was the first time I'd ever said those three little words to anyone. They weren't as scary as I'd once thought. Not when they were being said to the right person. "I did some research. Just because you're positive doesn't mean that we can't still have a long and happy relationship. It doesn't mean that I can't still have that future I want. With you. Because I don't want that future with just anyone. I want it with the guy who took me to my favorite band on my birthday, even though he wasn't a fan. I want it with the guy that made us a picnic under the stars and who always remembers the little details. I want that future with you, Aaron."

"I love you too."

It was the simplest answer to my verbal diarrhea, the only one I needed. I leaned forward, and he met me in the middle in a kiss that felt different. It was a kiss filled with promise of a future that I only wanted with him.

CHAPTER 4

The kiss started slow, just lips brushing one another. It was tender and gentle. It was a sigh, a release of the breath we'd both been holding all day. Twenty-four hours ago, I'd been obsessed with the idea of taking the next steps with him, but I'd been wanting to move the wrong thing forward. I'd wanted to push us physically. Instead, we'd progressed in a different way.

We'd admitted that we were in love with one another. I'd swallowed my fears surrounding those words and him, and I had made the leap. He'd been there to catch me, and then he jumped with me.

I felt safe with him. Even though there were so many things that should've made me feel unsafe, I didn't. Not with him. I sighed into the kiss, and he took the opening to slip his tongue past my lips.

His tongue's exploration of my mouth added the first spark of heat to the kiss. Our bodies moved until we were pressed against each other. I could easily lose myself in his kiss, in the way his hands came to rest on my waist. I could feel his warmth through the cotton of my tee shirt. It was as soothing as the kiss itself. I put my hands on his shoulders, pulling him in closer. Our knees touched, and I struggled not to push things further.

I knew why he wanted to take things slower now, and I had to respect that. When he was ready for those next steps, he'd let me know. But when he pressed me backward and draped his body over mine, I forgot that for a moment. I straightened the leg pressed against the back of the couch and allowed him to slot himself between my legs. He fit comfortably, like he was designed to be there.

The familiar weight of his body on mine teased me, sending blood rushing south. I wanted to touch him and had to remind myself that he was in control now. He was the one who was setting the pace of our physical relationship. I had to remind myself of that fact again as he pressed his half-hard cock against me. I let out a soft exhale into the kiss, trying hard not to moan at the feeling.

I lost the fight when he rolled his hips again. I was more than half-hard, and I knew that he could feel it. How could he not? I rolled my hips up to meet him. Every roll of our hips made me harder, and I could feel his body reacting the same way. When he let out the first breathy groan against my lips, I felt my control waver again. I pulled away from the kiss, and he chased after my lips like they were something he craved.

When he couldn't reach them, he began kissing down my neck. "Aaron," I groaned. How could I keep control over myself if he was constantly tempting me?

He pulled away and hovered over me. He looked concerned, and I could understand why. Every other time we got like this, I was fine. I was the one pushing things, trying to add fire to our relationship. I was never the one to pull back or pump the breaks. "Everything okay?" he asked after a few moments.

"Everything is great," I assured him.

He didn't look convinced. "You sure?"

"I'm sure." The skeptical look in his eyes pushed for more, and I obliged. "I just don't want to push you too far, too fast. I understand now."

"You understand now?" he questioned. He sat up a little, and I followed suit. "Are you sure you understand?"

I thought I did. Maybe I didn't. Was there some other reason he didn't want to sleep with me? I tried to squash down the rising tide of insecurity. "Maybe I don't?"

He laughed and shook his head. "I wanted to tell you before we slept together," he told me softly. "Maybe not the way I did yesterday, but I did want to tell you."

"Then why did you?" He looked confused again. "Tell me yesterday, I mean. Why did you tell me if you weren't ready?"

"I was ready; I was just terrified." Terrified? I was the least scary person that I knew. "I was afraid that you'd be overwhelmed by it." Great. So I'd done exactly what he'd been afraid that I'd do. I hoped it counted for something that I'd come back. That even if I'd been afraid of what a relationship with him would look like, I'd come back after I'd gotten my head together. "But then yesterday, you asked if it was about you. You looked so down about it... I couldn't be the reason for that. Not when I knew that it had nothing to do with you."

"I'm sorry."

"Can you stop apologizing for everything?" He laughed and grabbed my hand. He stood and pulled me off the couch with him. I was confused, but I followed his lead. His arms wrapped around my waist and pulled me closer. He planted a quick kiss on my lips. "The thing is... you know now." He gave me another kiss, walking me backward a step. "You know everything now." Another kiss, and another step. "You know how I see you. You know how I feel about you." Two more kisses and two more steps. I realized what direction he was leading me. "I'm ready now."

I nodded and took the final few steps toward my bedroom door. He'd never been in there before. We'd never taken the first steps over that threshold. It had been an invisible line, like we knew what would happen if we ended up in a bed together. I didn't blame him for that concern. When I was around him, I wanted to push every single boundary.

I reached behind me and found the doorknob, pushing the door open. I walked us backward into the room, stopping when my knees hit the mattress. The kiss broke, and he rested his forehead against mine. "I love you," he whispered again, the words warm on my lips and in my chest.

"I love you too," I repeated. I dropped my hand to his and laced our fingers together. "Are you sure you're ready to do this?"

He pulled his head back. His soulful brown eyes met mine, and there was the smallest smile on his lips. "I am."

"If you change your mind…"

His smile grew larger. "If I change my mind, I'll tell you. Do you have condoms?"

I knew it didn't matter that I was on PrEP. Maybe one day, we'd cross that boundary, but not yet. Neither of us were ready for that. I motioned toward the small table by the side of my bed. "They're in there. With the lube." I sat down on my bed and pulled him down to sit beside me. "James is very vocal about safe sex. He puts condoms out in the break room and encourages us all to take as many as we want or need."

"Really?"

"Yeah. Meaning I always have a supply."

I watched as Aaron reached into the bedside table and pulled out a condom and the small bottle of lube I kept in there. He rested both on the top of the table, and looked back at me. "Saw some other interesting things in there," he teased.

I felt my cheeks burn red. My sex toys. He'd seen my sex toys. "Well, I've been with this amazing guy for six months," I teased, "and I've been taking it slow with him. Meaning I've needed to take care of my own business." I saw the hunger in his eyes. It warmed me from the inside. "Maybe one day, I'll let you watch."

"What about letting me join in?" he questioned.

His voice was a low and sensual purr. Fuck, if he decided to talk dirty to me in that tone, I might just lose my mind. The idea of letting him join in, especially if he was talking to me like that… Fuck me sideways. I nodded. "Yeah. I would let you. You can use them tonight…" I looked down at my hands before finding enough bravery to meet his eyes. "You can use them to get me ready."

He paused, and I could see the hamster wheel turning in his head. He slowly shook his head. "Tonight, I want it to be just us. Nothing else. Not for our first time."

"Okay." I leaned in and gave him another soft kiss.

The kiss heated quickly and after a few moments, we were laying down on my bed, our bodies pressed close together. We found ourselves in the exact position we'd been in on the couch, rolling hips and chasing friction. Our hands began to explore one another's bodies, and every single moment felt heavier than the last. I knew what was coming next.

I swallowed hard as he reached between our bodies and found the button of my jeans.

This was finally happening.

My hands shook as I undid the button to his pants and pushed them down. He rose to his knees and pulled them down further, tugging his boxers down with them. I saw his cock for the first time. I had only felt it through his pants, and it more than lived up to expectation. It wasn't the longest dick I'd ever seen, but it had a nice girth and curved slightly to the left. My mouth watered at the sight of it. I wanted to taste him so badly that I had to clinch my blanket in my fists to hold myself back.

His hands at the waist of my jeans brought me back to the moment, of what was actually happening instead of fantasies. "Lift," he instructed softly. I lifted my hips and he slid my jeans and underwear down, freeing my hard cock from their confines. He crawled down the bed, peeling my pants down until I was left naked with him. Our pants fell to the side of the bed.

Our eyes met before he leaned back over me. The first feeling of his bare cock rubbing against mine sent sparks coursing through my body, and a moan escaped my lips. "Fuuuck."

He rolled his hips again, and another obscenity fell from my lips. It was more intense, skin to skin without fabric separating us. I reached down between our bodies and wrapped my hand around our shafts, making us a tunnel to fuck into. The combined friction of my hand and his dick rubbing against mine was driving me insane. I wanted more, but I was in no hurry to spreed run through this.

His moans vibrated against my lips as we rutted against each other, precum lubricating the slide and making it smoother.

I could feel the precipice coming closer, and I knew that if we didn't slow down, we would go careening over the edge before we were ready. Or maybe that was just me. I loosened my hands. I didn't want everything to be finished yet. I wanted to know what he felt like when he slipped inside of me, how he felt moving in my body.

"You okay?" he whispered, pulling away from the kiss.

I nodded. He raised a skeptical eyebrow, and once again I felt like my innermost feelings were being dragged out. "I didn't want to…" I raised my eyebrows and trailed off. He looked smug.

"Got it." He lifted his body from mine and reached over to grab the lube. "I don't want to finish like that either. I want to finish inside of you."

I wanted it too. I wanted it so badly.

"Please," I whispered.

I watched hungrily as he coated a finger with lube. He rubbed the finger around my rim, and I couldn't fight my moan. It had been so long since someone touched me like this. My noises grew louder the longer he teased me. One finger went in, and as soon as I adjusted to it, he slid in a second, then a third. His fingers grazed my prostate and sent tidal waves of pleasure crashing over me. Obscenities poured from my lips, and it only seemed to egg him on further. He was turning me into an incoherent mess. My cock was leaking onto my stomach, and I thrust into the air, desperate for friction and finding none.

"Please," I whimpered. "Please Aaron. I need… Fuck, please I need you."

His hungry eyes watched me as I continued to beg, and he fucked me harder on his fingers. Shit, why hadn't we been doing this before? Sure, he hadn't been ready for anal, but there was the whole buffet we could have been sampling. His fingers grazed my prostate again, and all thoughts stopped.

There was only pleasure.

I whimpered again when he withdrew his fingers, desperate to be filled with something. He grabbed the condom from the table and tore it open with his teeth. His other hand wrapped around his dick, stroking it slowly. I wanted him more than I'd ever wanted anything in my life. I couldn't disguise my hunger as he slid the condom down over his length. He slicked his cock and positioned the head at my entrance.

"You okay?" he asked softly. When I nodded, he began to push inside, slow and steady. There was the familiar bite of pain followed by a surge of pleasure. He pushed in little by little until he was fully seated. He gave an experimental thrust, pushing a moan from my lips. "You like that?" he questioned. That low and lusty quality was back in his voice, and it drove me insane.

"Yeah," I answered. "Love it."

He began to move, slow strokes, alternating between deep and shallow thrusts. I wrapped my legs around him, and he bent over me, kissing me deeply. Our bodies collided together as our tongues danced. It wasn't fucking. I had been fucked before, and this felt entirely different.

This was a connection of body and soul, of mind and spirit. If we weren't kissing, we were looking deep into one another's eyes. This was the most intense experience I'd ever had.

Making love.

That's what this was. I'd never had anything like this before.

The sounds of our lovemaking filled my small bedroom. Our low moans were music to my ears. "Getting close." His words were soft, spoken directly into our kiss.

I felt his hand wrap around my dick, and in a few strokes, my release spilled over his hand and onto my stomach. His thrusts grew erratic and his moans louder as he came into the condom. When he finished, he collapsed onto my chest.

We kissed lazily for a few more minutes before he pulled out and tied off the condom. I grabbed an old shirt from the floor and haphazardly cleaned myself off.

"That was worth the wait," I exhaled. "Give me a few minutes to find my legs and we can see if we can Tetris ourselves into my shower."

"Sounds perfect." He laid on his back, and I curled up against him.

When his arms wrapped around me, it felt like home.

CHAPTER 5

That night, Aaron stayed at my place until I started to yawn. We talked more about what we wanted, about what his condition meant for those things, and about our different comfort levels with different physical aspects of our relationship. We talked about lighter topics too—movies we wanted to see, a band that was playing in town, our jobs.

I wanted him to stay the night, but he explained that he didn't have his medicine with him.

He returned the next morning with breakfast, and that night, we actually slept together for the first time. I'd never slept better in my life than I did with his arms wrapped around me and his body pressed against mine. We spent another day together, separating only when it was time for me to head into the bar for my shift. I hated leaving him, but unfortunately, we couldn't stay in our loved up bubble forever. The world outside still existed, and it required our attention.

I had a skip in my step when I entered the bar. I greeted all of my coworkers with a smile and chatted with everyone as we got set up for the night. I noticed James watching me, and ten minutes before we were set to open, he pulled me into his office.

"You look like you're feeling better," he noted as I sat down in the same seat where he'd told me the story of him and Henry just a few days before. "I take it that means you and Aaron talked?"

My cheeks hurt from smiling so much, yet my smile somehow grew larger as I nodded. "We did. We're still together," I told him. "Thank you. For helping me through that, I mean."

"Any time kid." James studied me for a few moments. There was an unadulterated look of admiration in his eyes, and I couldn't help shifting under the weight of it. I wasn't used to people my dad's age looking at me like that. I was more used to disapproving looks for not living up to their standards of masculinity. "I'm really glad you're happy."

"I am." I sighed. "I don't think I would've gotten there without you. The fact that you didn't regret anything with Henry, even after how it all turned out? It made me think, and it kept me from running scared."

He grabbed the bottle of whiskey out from his desk drawer. I watched as he pulled out two glasses and wondered if they were the same ones we'd drunk from last time. He poured two small portions of the alcohol and handed one over to me. "To bravery and choosing love, then," he toasted. I clinked my glass with his and downed the small measure of whiskey. It burned it's way down my throat in the very best way. "Okay, now get to work."

I laughed and rose from the chair. I was almost to the door when James cleared his throat. I turned to see that same expression in his dark blue eyes. "Everything okay?"

"I just see a lot of myself in you," he admitted. "Makes it hard to know when ideas I have are crossing the appropriate boundary between boss and employee."

My curiosity piqued. I turned to face him better. "Only one way to find out."

His chuckle filled the space between us. "Well, I was thinking about asking you if you wanted to come over for dinner one night. Bring Aaron. I'd love to meet him."

"I would love that. I'll check with Aaron, and we can figure out a day?"

The smile on James' face when I agreed would probably stay with me for the rest of my life. I'd never seen him look as happy as he did in that moment, and I knew that even if Aaron didn't want to come to dinner, I would. He'd been good to me since he'd hired me. He'd taken care of me. He'd listened to me. He cared about me, and I cared about him too. I just never realized that he might be lonely until that moment.

Every time I saw James for the rest of my shift, that smile was still in place.

It didn't take much convincing to get Aaron to agree to dinner with James. He'd heard a lot of stories about my boss. He knew that I viewed him as a father figure, even if that wasn't information that I'd shared with James himself. Maybe one day I'd find the words to tell him what he meant to me. Or maybe I'd just buy him a Father's Day card and leave it on his desk and let him figure it out for himself. That seemed a bit more likely.

We planned dinner for a week later, and Aaron took great care in how he dressed. He said it was because he wanted to impress James, and I fell even more in love with him. He wanted to impress the person I viewed as a father figure. How had I gotten so lucky to find someone like him?

He even managed to make sure I left the apartment on time. We showed up at James' house ten minutes ahead of schedule.

"I'm a bit nervous," he admitted as he put the car into park.

"Why?" It was a stupid question. He'd already told me why he was nervous when he told me why he took awhile to pick out an outfit for the night. "I mean, don't be nervous."

His laughter filled the car. "That's easier said than done. I've never met a boyfriend's parents before."

"I mean technically, you still aren't."

"Except that I am. James is like your dad, right? At least that's how you think of him. So it's the same thing as meeting your parents." He went quiet for a moment before speaking again. "Besides, it's not like you talk to your parents, right? So this is as close as I'm going to get."

He had a point there. My parents weren't in my life. James was.

Aaron's parents were in his life. "Well, if this is basically you meeting my parents, you realize that means that I have to meet yours soon, right?"

A radiant smile exploded on his face. His eyes practically glowed with happiness. "Really? You want to meet my parents? Already?"

"It's been six months. Besides turnabout's fair play, right?" I noticed movement in a window and nudged Aaron. "I think James knows we're here. Ready?"

"As I'll ever be."

I drew in a deep breath. The next words hurt me to say, but I had to say them. Just in case. It wouldn't be fair not to give him an out if he wanted one. "You can say you don't want to do this. If you're too nervous, I can go have dinner with James and meet you at your place."

I'd just have to catch an Uber or something.

"No." He shook his head and leaned over to give me a quick kiss. "I said I'd do this with you, so we're doing this. I want to do this. Meet James and see more of your world."

He quickly climbed out of the car, as if to prove it to me. Or maybe to prove it to himself. I wasn't entirely sure. I followed him out of the car and led him up the path to James' front door. It opened quickly after we knocked, which only confirmed that I'd seen movement at the window and James had been waiting.

I'd never been inside James' house before. I wasn't sure what I was expecting, but it wasn't what I saw when I walked in. It was neat but sparsely decorated. The furniture was nice, but it would hardly be considered top of the line. The living room was simple, and when he led us into the kitchen, I saw the same aesthetic choices in there. Most of the decorations were framed pictures. There were a few of him and Henry. There were more of him and his brothers from various stages of life. There was even a framed photo from the bar's Christmas party, his arm thrown casually around my shoulders as we chatted with another coworker.

Maybe the familial feelings I had for my boss were mutual.

Dinner smelled amazing, and it looked better when we settled around the round, wooden table. We loaded our plates with food.

Conversation was stilted at first. Small talk combined with shoveling food into our mouth wasn't the best combination for getting to know someone, I guessed.

We slowed down after a few bites, and Aaron asked a more questions about the bar. They were simple questions, easy for James to answer, but questions I'd never thought to ask him. Like why he'd chosen to buy the bar in the first place and some of his favorite parts of owning a bar. I could see Aaron and James both relax as the conversation began to flow. They seemed to get along, and I couldn't be happier about it.

Conversation about the bar somehow led to Henry. James wasn't as forthcoming as he'd been with me. I didn't blame him. I'd seen the emotions in his eyes as he talked about the love of his life. I hoped I never saw that haunted expression staring back at me in the mirror over Aaron.

After Henry, the conversation felt stilted. I didn't like it. I wanted the conversation to flow the way it had before. I felt obligated to make it happen. After all, these two men were only sitting around this table chatting because of me, because they both cared about me in their own ways.

Unfortunately, I wasn't great at small talk.

I sighed, and Aaron's attention turned toward me immediately. "You okay?"

I felt James' eyes on me, but I couldn't acknowledge him. Not with the worry in my boyfriend's voice. I reached out and squeezed his thigh in what I hoped was a reassuring way. "I'm fine," I told him. I could tell he didn't believe me. I probably wouldn't have either if the tables were turned. Everyone knew that I'm fine was always code for the opposite. Why had I chosen those words? Anxiety spiked in my gut another time. I was going to ruin this, somehow. "I'm just trying to think of something to say that isn't small talk."

"I could tell him bar stories about you," James suggested. "All the embarrassing ones."

"Oh, please. I want to hear those," Aaron piped up, freeing my attention from him.

I turned to glare at James, and he looked completely unabashed.

"Okay, so he started out as a barback," James began. My glare was entirely ineffective. I was terrified of whatever tale was going to come from my boss's lips. There were too many from my barback days to choose from. I'd been an absolute mess back then, eighteen and broke and trying to make my way in the world for the first time. "He'd never done any kind of bar work before, but he was determined. Unfortunately..." He grinned a wicked grin, "Well, he's your boyfriend. You know he's a bit clumsy, right?"

"I think that's an understatement," Aaron teased. "I've watched Adam trip over dryer lint."

"Oh my god, that was one time Aaron!" The one and only time I'd allowed him to be around while I was doing laundry. I turned toward my laughing boss. "What he's not telling you is that I didn't trip. I slipped. On linoleum floor." The lint on the linoleum had caused me to slip and fall straight on my ass.

"That's not much defense," James pointed out. "As I was saying... He was carrying a tray of dishes back to the dishwasher, and I hear this loud crashing sound. I go to investigate and I find him on his ass, surrounded by broken glasses and bleeding. Almost had to take him to the hospital."

"Tell the whole story!" I demanded. He was leaving out a very important detail. Aaron and James laughed at my indignation, and I rose to defend myself. "There was a wet floor and no wet floor sign."

Aaron raised an eyebrow at me. "You were in the kitchen by the dishwasher right? Or the sink?" I could see where he was going, and I wished he'd stop talking. Instead, he kept going on toward the obvious conclusion. "Shouldn't you have assumed that the floor would be wet?"

"That's not even the worst one." James looked over at me. There was trouble behind his blue eyes as he stood up. "You two want a drink?"

"I'll take one. Beer for both of us?"

"Please." If James was going to humiliate me, then I was going to have a drink while he did it. It might make the whole thing less terrible.

James kept talking while he went to the fridge. "So, it was his first or second shift bartending. He'd been at the bar for two years? Three?" He looked at me over his shoulder, searching for confirmation that I refused to give him. I wasn't going to provide more details to add to his story. "So two or three years, and this guy comes in. He's hot as fuck. I was about to go do some paperwork in my office, but I stuck around. Talked to a few clients. Couldn't take my eyes off of him."

"Should have gone to your office," I grumbled.

"But then I wouldn't have seen what happened, Adam," James singsonged. He popped the cap off of three bottles of beer and carried them over to the table in a manner befitting a bar owner. He placed one down in front of Aaron and passed the second to me. "The guy came over to order from Adam, and everything was going well. Until he got the drink ready, went to hand it to him, and the guy said something. What did he say, Adam?" I mimed zipping my lips, glaring even harder. I didn't remember the exact words the guy had said, only the gist of it all, but I remembered the rest of the story as clearly as if it had just happened. Years hadn't been enough to dull the humiliation. "It was something flirtatious, I could tell that. Adam ended up dropping the glass, spilling some brightly colored cocktail all over his white shirt."

Aaron was shaking with laughter.

James continued telling stories, each worse than the last. My cheeks were on fire, and Aaron couldn't stop laughing. He started tossing in stories of his own, about me and about himself. It made me feel a little better, him willingly jumping onto the pyre with me. It emboldened me to start telling tales about James and his brothers, things I'd witnessed at the bar.

Unlike me, he didn't seem to feel a flicker of embarrassment about any of it.

The night pressed on. We had a few more beers, and I had that beautiful feeling of being loved.

Warmth settled over me, and I knew that this, right here, was what I wanted for the rest of my life.

WORSE
THINGS

BREANNA RAE

CHAPTER 1

BRANDON

"There are worse things," Casey Morrow says.

On the other end of the call, I have to pause for a moment to process what he's said before I can find the words to respond. "You understand what that means, right?"

"Brandon, I understand. There are worse things than a blood test, okay?" he replies, soft and gentle in a way I don't deserve.

"It's not the blood test," I offer, heart in my throat. "It's what it means."

"I know, but it'll be okay. I trust that it will be okay."

I slump down where I sit on my couch, leaning back against the fabric as I sink into the soft cushions beneath me. My shame spirals through me as I stare down at the prescription papers on my coffee table and my hand shakes where it clutches my phone. "Casey, I am so sorry. I didn't mean to… I didn't know. I…" My throat squeezes shut, and tears threaten from the corners of my eyes as I stumble and flail over these apologies I owe.

Funny.

I never wanted to cry before now. I didn't shed a single tear when I was in the sterile little room with my doctor earlier listening to the news of my new diagnosis, but with Casey on the other end of a phone call I never thought I'd have to make, my entire body is screaming sadness out of every possible inch. I inhale slowly, the breath stuttery and shaky as it enters my lungs only to get caught there.

I hold onto it for a moment, afraid that if I let it go, I will start sobbing and screaming like a child with a broken toy, though that doesn't quite capture the depth of what is inside me.

I am the toy.

I am the broken thing here in this room, and if I have, in turn, broken someone else, I don't know if I will ever get the pieces of me to go back together again.

"Brandon?" Casey says, softly, gently. "I'll be okay, I'm sure. We used a condom. I'm on PrEP. We talked about it before we even got naked, remember?"

"No," I whisper, before the tears choke the rest of what was going to be another apology from my lips. I can't remember anything right now. Not the conversation we may have had before the night we spent together curled around each other in my bed. Not him letting me know he was being safe or agreeing that I was also trying to be safe.

I tried to be safe.

My breath hitches and everything gives way, leaving me a shattered mess on the plush couch I have only owned for two weeks. A special purchase, to replace the old and battered one that used to sit in its place. I'm finally crawling out of the hole I fell into paying for school out of my own pocket, and with my last year of my automotive apprenticeship behind me, I am now able to afford nicer things than I had before.

Except what if I can't anymore?

What if I have to give it back to the store because this takes away my ability to work? What if I shouldn't even be at work anymore because I could infect people? I've smashed my knuckles open on car parts more times than I want to admit while fixing them, what if it happens again and I leave contaminated blood on one of them, and then someone else touches it?

What if?

Tears slip down my cheeks and I do my best to wipe them away, clearing my throat against the thickness my messy thoughts have brought me. Taking a deep breath, I run my hand over the soft fabric of this grey couch, feeling the ridges in it against my fingertips. There is nothing but silence on the other end of this call, but that is okay. I don't deserve any more words from Casey Morrow, especially not the kind and comforting ones he is choosing to offer me when he does speak.

"I should let you go," I say, finding words to offer him instead. "Will you let me know? Your results, I mean?"

"Shark attack," Casey blurts out the moment I finish my question.

"What?"

"A shark attack would be worse than a blood test."

I bite back the strangest laugh that tries to bubble up my thickened throat, letting loose some sort of stifled snorting noise instead.

"It's true," Casey insists. "Sharks are terrifying, dude. I'd rather face a blood test than sharks any day of the week. Or a bear attack, since we're pretty landlocked here, I guess. Bears are more likely in Alberta, but I'd rather have a blood test than a bear attack my face."

"We live in the prairies," I respond, slow and sluggish as tears continue to fall down my cheeks.

"Okay, so maybe, it's more likely that I'd be attacked by feral prairie dogs, but still. Worse than a blood test."

I let loose a slight laugh followed by a slow breath, rubbing my hand on the couch still. I like the feel of it against my skin, soothing and soft when everything else just seems too harsh and cold. My tears have stopped, leaving my face heated and eyes sore. I take a deep breath as Casey snickers into the other end of the call, then sighs audibly. Still running my hand over the couch, I murmur, "You'll tell me, right?"

"I will," Casey responds. "I'll be okay, Brandon."

"Okay."

He pauses for a moment then comes back with a question I don't have an answer for. "Will you?"

Yes.

No.

Maybe so.

The truth is, I should be. If the medications work, and I pay close attention to every aspect of my life moving forward, I should be okay. The doctor rumbled on about a bunch of things, but I can't really remember all of it. One of the nurses came in to give me a packet of information that probably has a bunch of answers to the many questions I have, but I haven't opened it yet. He took down the name and number of my ex to notify him that someone he had been in contact with was diagnosed and he should go get tested himself. The nurse also offered to take a list of everyone else I had sex with to call them on my behalf, promising confidentiality, and while that would have probably been easier, my guilt wouldn't let me take advantage of it. I've only had sex with one person since I parted ways with my former long-term boyfriend who was less faithful to our relationship than I was, and I needed him to know how sorry I was for bringing this disease into his life.

Casey Morrow, the only one-night stand I've ever had.

It's been a handful of weeks since we eyed each other across the crowded dancefloor of The Verve and came together to dance in the middle of the flashing lights and thumping bass. We spent a few songs there, pressed against each other, hips rolling in time with the music, lips pressed together, and arms wrapped around each other's necks. Casey had suggested finding a quiet place away from prying eyes, his hard cock rubbing against mine from behind the confines of our clothing, and I had eagerly agreed at the promise his eyes held.

Now, I wish I hadn't.

I desperately wish I could take it all back.

"Brandon?" Casey asks, sounding concerned at my long pause. "You okay?"

"Yeah," I answer, cheeks sticky with dried tears and eyes burning. "I'll be all right."

"Not sure I believe you," he responds, "but okay. I'll grab a self-test from the pharmacy and let you know what my results are."

"Okay."

"There's worse things, though, than a blood test, remember?"

Sharks. Bears. Feral prairie dogs.

And a positive result for HIV, though he doesn't mention that. I don't mention it either, but it hangs in the conversation unspoken as we say our goodbyes.

CHAPTER 2

CASEY

"This is going to be okay," I mumble to myself as I walk down the aisle at the pharmacy around the corner from my apartment.

It will be okay. While a piece of me is slightly concerned at the news Brandon called to share regarding his positive HIV status, I know I was safe when we were together. Condom and PrEP. Self-testing every three months and lab testing at least twice a year through my family doctor. I don't have a lot of random sex with strangers, but when I do indulge in a hook up, I make damn sure I'm prepared for it. My mother, the sexual health nurse, wouldn't have it any other way. I think I was the only kid growing up who knew more about the birds and the bees than anyone else in my grade. I can still remember sharing information with my grade four classmates on the playground that the teacher hadn't covered in our rudimentary sex education class. I can also remember the conversation my mom had with me after school where she gently informed me that some kids weren't ready for the knowledge I had, and that when it came to anything about the human body, I needed to stay silent and let the teacher teach her curriculum. How was I to know that sex education was more about labeling penises and vaginas at that age than it was understanding what all those parts were meant for? I thought Mrs. Burke had simply forgotten to mention semen and eggs, labia and vas deferens while she was teaching us, and took it upon myself to fill in the blanks with what I knew.

I've been well versed in sexual health since long before I came stumbling out of the closet, wide eyed and terrified about a boner I'd sprung while thinking about kissing Justin Bieber. That's how I know I'm going to be okay here. The chance that I've contracted HIV from Brandon is minimal at best, but I'll still test just to be sure. If only to ease his poor mind in this moment. I will have to test again a few months out because sometimes certain things take time to build up in blood, but for the moment, I can assure him that I am HIV negative since that is what he needs. He was a wreck when he called me, and the sound of him crying into the other end of the phone still rumbles inside my brain, though it's been at least an hour since we hung up.

I grab a couple of self-testing kits off the shelf at the back of the pharmacy, then turn and make my way to the front to pay for them, passing by displays of knickknacks and snacks as I go, but when I reach a small display of discounted items, I stop to take a look. There's a bunch of sale makeup thrown into the bin, but beside them sits a grey fleece blanket printed with blue snowflakes. I reach for it, thinking of Brandon's apartment and the colors he's chosen. He told me that his soft grey couch was the first thing he'd bought for himself when he finished his schooling, and this blanket matches the color I vaguely remember from that night. He'd fucked me in his darkened bedroom, but when we were done and cleaned up, we'd sat in his living room for a few moments with glasses of water in our hands, chatting in that awkward way one does after letting a complete stranger wring pleasure out of their bones.

I can't remember what he does for a living, but I remember the small pride in his voice when I'd commented how comfy his couch was. I remember his smile, the way it curls up one side of his mouth a tiny bit higher than the other, like a friendly smirk, and the dark chocolate of his eyes. His short near black hair, and the tattoos of birds and vines that run up his one arm to crest over his chest like armor, half outlined, half colored in with another booking needed to complete the lot. I remember the back of his right hand, inked with a hawkmoth, and the way his touch was gentle, like butterfly wings against my skin as he'd explored me with his fingers. When I caught his eye from across the club, I had noted he was attractive. I hadn't imagined that he'd be so fucking hot up close and personal, but thinking about Brandon Tremblay's talented fingers and smirky smile has my entire body heating up as much as his phone call has made me feel for the journey he is now on.

I grab the blanket as I think about Brandon and his couch, the truth of what he's learned about himself heavy inside me, and his tears rattling in my ears. He'd said he'd been sick for a few weeks with what had appeared to be flu symptoms, but the tests his doctor had done ruled everything out, except for HIV. I'd been his first phone call when he'd gotten home from his appointment, and that also sits inside me.

Brandon could have called anyone to come be with him in the moments after he learned of his diagnosis. A family member, or a friend, perhaps, who loves him and would sit beside him as he processes this news. Instead, he called me to apologize and let me know that I need to take a test. I didn't think to ask if he had anyone to call to come and be with him so he's not alone right now. Should I have asked? Does he even want anyone there? I've never been in a situation like this before with any of the people I've slept with, but the thought that Brandon is alone after hearing such devastating news doesn't sit right inside me.

With a sigh, I turn and head back into the depths of the pharmacy to grab more items. A box of orange pekoe tea bags. A bag of gummy candy and a box of chocolate chip cookies. A box of chicken noodle soup packets, the good kind that you cook on a stove in a pot, and a sleeve of the best crackers to go along with it. I pile all of this into my hands and carefully make my way to the till to check out, hoping that I can remember the way to Brandon's apartment. If he wants to be alone, I'll drop off this care package for him, but the summer classes

I'm taking for extra credits towards my education degree are done for the day, and with nothing else to do, I have time to sit with him if he needs someone.

There are worse things than spending an afternoon with an incredibly handsome man.

Brandon opens the door to his apartment, his eyes widening as he sees me standing there. It didn't take me long to get my bearings and figure out how to get here. I did stop by the identical building next door first, but a quick look at the names by the front door told me I was off in my assumption. I finally found his name on one of the nameplates by the door of this building, though, and knew I'd made it. I didn't ring the buzzer for his apartment, choosing instead to sneak in when someone else was leaving. I don't know Brandon well at all, and he may have completely ignored the ringing.

"Casey?" he asks, bewildered. His cheeks are red and blotchy, and though he's still stunningly gorgeous with his high cheekbones and scruffy jaw, he looks absolutely shattered. His eyes are sad, and as I offer a smile, they grow even sadder somehow.

"I came to bring you some things," I say, holding up the reusable bag printed with the pharmacy logo on it. "Can I leave it with you, or can I come in, maybe?"

He hesitates, but only for a moment, before opening the door wide and taking a step back to let me in. With a grin, I step into his space, holding out the bag to him. He takes it from me carefully as I kick off my shoes in the entryway, placing them beside his heavy work boots on the tray by the door.

"What are you doing here?" he asks, holding the bag like he's unsure of what it contains.

"I got the feeling you might be alone and that didn't feel right to me. You can kick me out, but I thought maybe you'd want company."

"Oh." Brandon glances down at the bag, then back up at me. "And this is?"

"Supplies for health," I offer, turning to head into the living room beyond the door. Though my heart is a bit fluttery inside me with nerves and the hope that I'm doing the right thing, I make myself at home on his couch. Brandon slowly walks into the room and sits down carefully on the complete opposite end of the couch. He places the bag on the table beside a brown envelope with the logo for a local HIV education non-profit on it and a small stack of white prescription papers.

"You didn't get them filled?" I ask, gesturing to the papers.

"Not yet. I'm not quite there yet in my head, but I will go get them tonight. The doctor said starting them sooner rather than later is best, obviously. I just needed…" He trails off, shrugging his shoulders.

"Time to process?"

"Yeah," he breathes, closing his eyes. "Time to process."

"Have you called anyone else?"

"Nobody to call."

I leave that alone, but I'm a bit saddened that he has nobody else who he'd go to for comfort or reassurance. No parents or friends that he could call for support. Just me, the stranger he fucked three weeks ago. We sit in silence for a few moments until he opens his eyes and looks at me, still seeming a bit confused as to why I'm here. I offer a smile back and gesture to the bag I brought. "Care package. It's all yours."

Brandon nods, opening the bag and pulling items out. He places them one by one on the table beside his unfilled prescription papers, a small smile growing as he sees what I've brought.

"Lipton chicken soup?" he asks, holding up the box.

"It's the best one." I nod. "My mom always made it for me when I wasn't feeling good. It's comfort in a bowl, even though it's from a package."

"Never had it. Soup came in a can when I was growing up." He pulls out the sleeve of crackers and places them beside the soup, then reaches in and lifts the snowflake blanket out of the bag. Brandon holds it for a moment, then suddenly, a tear slips down his cheek. He wipes it away, offering a small, uncomfortable laugh. "Fuck."

"You can totally cry if you need to. It reminded me of your couch, so I grabbed it. Thought it might be nice for you to have. It's super soft, and when I'm not feeling good, I just want soft things."

"Same," he replies, his voice a little hoarse. He sighs and wipes the tears from his cheeks with a hand, then places the folded blanket on his lap, running his hand over the soft fabric again and again, like it's soothing whatever is happening inside of him. Finally, he turns and looks at me, eyes still a bit confused, though now he just looks exhausted. "Did you take a test yet?"

"Not yet. I bought a couple, and I'll take one tonight. I'm sure it'll be okay, though, Brandon, we were so safe that night." He nods, but I don't quite think he believes me. He doesn't have much of a reason to, if I'm being honest. Brandon knows my body, but he doesn't know me aside from the scant pieces of conversation we had after he fucked me that night. "Condom and PrEP."

"I know," he replies with a sigh. "I just keep worrying that I had a cut on my hand from work or something, and that when I put my fingers inside you, I transferred it somehow into you. Casey, I don't know how I'm going to go ahead if I've gotten you sick. I can't even imagine what knowing I did that to you would feel like."

"Who..." I trail off, not sure if I should even ask where he got it from.

"My ex," he responds. "He cheated on me and brought it home to me somewhere along the way. I don't know if he knows yet, and I know he shouldn't get my sympathy, but he does. Even if he cheated on me and gave me HIV, I can't help but feel for him. Stupid, right?"

"I don't think it is at all. I think it's just your heart reminding you that even though it's broken, it exists."

"Maybe." He shrugs, sighing. "I'm more worried about your heart, though, right now."

That my health is his focus strikes me as being wrong, when he is the one with the life changing diagnosis. "What about you, Brandon? Are you worried for you?"

"I don't know. I should be, I suppose. I was thinking earlier about having to take my couch back to the store, and how I was going to let them know that I can't afford the payments anymore. I also sent an email to cancel my booking with my tattoo artist, which sucks, but I won't be able to afford the cost anymore. If I have to leave work permanently instead of the handful of sick days I've been granted, I mean."

"Why would you have to leave work for good?"

"I get banged up a lot," he offers with a small half smile that seems more sad than happy. "Cars have tight spots, and I have big knuckles. I get lots of cuts and scrapes trying to reach in to get the parts I'm working on. What if I cut myself and get someone else infected that way?"

Ah. Mechanic. That tracks with the work boots in the entryway and the faint scent of gasoline and oil coming from his clothing. "Did you work today?"

"Before my appointment, yeah. I called them to say I have the flu and need to be off until I'm not contagious. They understood, but I'm always contagious now, I suppose." He looks down at his hands like he anticipates seeing a plethora of cuts and gouges, blood seeping from beneath his skin.

"Let me see." Without thinking twice, I scoot over on the couch so I'm right beside him and grab his hands, holding them in mine. His palms are callused where they rest on mine, and I smile as I look down at his fingers and the moth tattoo on the back of his right hand. Brandon is shaking a bit in my grasp, but he lets me turn his hands over as I search for hidden cuts and wounds. There's nothing but his skin against me, no blood seeping from whatever cuts he has imagined he may have. "No cuts, Brandon. It's okay."

"But there could be," he responds. "I'm not the most careful."

I glance down again at his hands, seeing the faint lines of a scar that almost encircles his thumb. I run my fingertip over it gently. "What was that?"

He surprises me by laughing. A real, true laugh. "Got my thumb stuck in a can of grease. It had a hole popped in the top of it, and like a dumbass, I thought I'd just stick my thumb in and peel the rest of the tin top off. That fucker was sharp as shit around the rim."

I laugh softly, shaking my head. "Okay, so you may have to be more careful then. That's possible."

Brandon sighs, taking his hands out of mine and putting them on the blanket on his lap. He yawns so wide I can almost count the fillings in his back teeth, then slumps back into his seat. "I don't know what I'm going to do if you're positive, Casey."

"Well, how about we just find out together?" I offer, thinking of the self-tests I have downstairs in my vehicle.

CHAPTER 3

BRANDON

Casey stands in my kitchen, getting the HIV self-test ready. He ran down to his car to grab it, and I thought for a moment he wouldn't come back. I wouldn't have blamed him, I've been a bit of a mess since he arrived, and if he'd have taken the chance to escape, I would have understood entirely.

But he didn't.

He came back to prove to me that he is right about his health and that I can stop worrying about infecting him, which I can appreciate. Standing in my kitchen, he gives me a smile, then pricks his finger like he's done this a hundred times before, a bubble of red blood forming on the pad. I watch in awe as he conducts what looks like a complete science experiment, putting blood in one of the three bottles in the kit, then squeezing the contents onto the small test disc. He picks up bottle number two, shaking it before adding it to the disc as my heart sits in my throat.

"How fast will you know?"

"It's super quick," he offers, adding bottle three to the disc after giving it a good shake. "Should know the moment I finish adding this bottle."

"It doesn't need to sit?"

"Nope, not this one anyway. Some may need a moment or two before they report results, but look," he says, picking up the test disc and giving it a good, long look. He holds the test disc out to me, and I take it from him, staring at the single dot on the circle.

"Positive?" I ask, my heart slamming in my chest and my hands shaking.

"Negative, Brandon. That's a negative result."

"Oh, thank fuck." Negative. HIV negative. I clutch the disc, reaching for the paper that came in the box to double check. Just to be sure that our one night of fun didn't leave him sick. Not that I don't trust his words, but because I need to read it myself to know with absolute certainty that he is safe from the monsters that now live inside my blood and body.

"See? We were safe, Brandon. We were so safe together that night." I don't respond, focusing instead on reading those words on the paper in front of me, comparing the printed list of outcomes with the actual results on the disc. Casey gently takes both away from me and places them on the kitchen counter, and as my eyes meet his, he smiles. He raises his hands to my cheeks, his cool palms meeting my burning skin and soothing some of the anxiety away with his touch. I heave a relieved sigh, sinking a bit where I stand as he smooths his thumbs over my cheekbones. I don't know why he is holding me like this, but I don't want to move away from his hands. "We were safe, Bran. Trust me."

"Okay," I whisper, as his hands smooth the edges of the worry lingering in the back of my mind. I like that he's called me Bran as nobody has done before. It's familiar and intimate in a way that soothes me, though I hardly know this person in front of me. He tilts my head down gently and places his lips to my forehead in a move that has me both rattled inside and full of a sudden sense of loneliness.

I am alone in this now.

Me and my diagnosis. As it should be, if I'm being honest, yet knowing he is negative and I am not, feels like a lead weight inside me.

I had wrapped myself in the idea that if he was okay, then I was okay as well, but that isn't what's coming out of me right now. I'm fucking tired, that much I know, but there's something else hidden inside there that feels lonely and scared.

Maybe I'm not as okay as I thought I'd be.

"Are you hungry?" Casey asks, pulling back and looking into my eyes like he can somehow see that I am not okay.

"I don't know. Not really." I haven't eaten since breakfast, but I don't feel like I want to. "I don't know what I am right now."

"Sharks," Casey whispers back. "Sharks, bears and feral prairie dogs. There are worse things."

"Worse than HIV?"

He pauses for a moment before smiling gently, softly running his fingers over my cheekbones. "That's up to you, Brandon. Medication is the first step if you don't want it to become worse than the rest of the things that could come eat your face off."

I snort a small laugh in spite of myself. "A prairie dog won't eat my face off."

"You don't know that for sure. A feral one might." He grins at me for a moment, and I am caught in his gaze. His blue eyes, eyes I have seen filled with lust and want and need, scan my face, and I catch the way his top teeth bite down on his lower lip for a few seconds. He is every bit as beautiful to me tonight as he was the first night I spotted him, his body moving on the dancefloor like he had no cares, and the world was there for him to simply enjoy.

He can have that again, now that he isn't tainted by my broken blood, and I am overwhelmed by every bit of joy and fear that has lived inside me since the moment he showed up at my door. I'm shaking and nervous, a baby bird in his calm hands, but Casey simply smiles at me like he understands even though he can't possibly.

He leans in and places his lips to my forehead again, followed by temples, cheeks and jaw. His lips leave warmth behind them, and I quiver nervously as Casey takes a chance, pressing his lips gently to mine. I startle at the touch of them, but I don't pull away. Instead, I kiss him back as his arms loop around my neck, gently, like my nature instead of the storm brewing inside of me. I kiss him because he feels good against me, his body meeting mine, and warmth created in the small space between us. Finally, Casey pulls back and smiles again, lips plump and inviting as he looks at me. I grow hard inside my jeans, my cock staring at the zipper that confines me as I stare into his eyes for a moment too long.

Because that is when I panic.

Eyes wide, I glance down at his perfect lips and move away from him. His hands fall from my face and his own eyes go as wide as saucers. "I shouldn't have kissed you. I'm sorry."

I nod, because I know he shouldn't have. I shouldn't have let him either when I am so filthy on the inside and can offer nothing more to him than a few chaste kisses. I take a step away, shame and guilt burning inside me as I look down at the floor. The wall. My feet. Anywhere but Casey's perfect, handsome face.

"Not because of HIV!" he clarifies, reaching for my cheeks and turning my head upwards so my eyes meet his. "Not because of that. No. It's just been a shit day, and I don't want to take advantage. I got carried away because you're hot as hell, and I'm sorry for kissing you out of the blue like that."

I nod, slightly blushing at the admission that he still thinks I'm attractive in spite of it all. I'm also fairly relieved that he's apologizing not out of fear that I infected him somehow, but out of worry he'd overstepped. "I didn't mind it. I just don't know where my head is at right now. Too many thoughts all at once, maybe. I don't exactly know the things I can and can't do anymore, but I know that kissing doesn't pass it."

"Exactly." Casey smiles again, looking relieved that I haven't taken any offense to his words, and lets go of my skin, gesturing towards the small hallway. "Your brain needs rest. Go nap. Or shower, maybe, if that would feel better? I'll make you some soup."

"You don't have to stay, Casey." He didn't have to come in the first place, though I am secretly glad he did. I don't have parents I can call who would support me through this. They still don't understand that being gay isn't a choice I'm making, and the news of my HIV positive test result wouldn't go over well at all. I don't feel much like being shouted at and called a bunch of slurs over the phone today. While I do have some friends, they aren't exactly close enough friends to trust with this information.

"Do you want me to go?" he asks, which is an entirely different question.

"It's kind of strange, don't you think? I mean, we don't know each other that well. If you have better things to do, you don't have to hang out with me here."

"I know you have freckles on your butt cheeks, you're a good kisser, and I know your cock is longer than mine." Casey shrugs, offering me a cheeky grin. "Good enough for me. We can learn the rest as we go, I think. Soup?"

I laugh, nodding. "Soup. Sure."

"Next time, I'll get stuff for grilled cheese sandwiches too."

"Next time?"

Casey doesn't respond with any other than a smile and a kiss pressed to my cheek that warms me somewhere deep inside.

Casey snores softly on my couch, his head in my lap. On the living room table, our empty bowls of soup sit along with the empty packet that once held the crackers we ate with the chicken broth. I had a shower while he cooked and then we sat down together to eat and watch a movie, though he fell asleep almost instantly after he put his spoon down. I can't stop looking at him where he rests on my lap, glancing between his face and the true crime documentary he insisted on watching while we ate, like blood, guts and murder most foul didn't bother him in the least.

In any other world, this could be something. I'm sure of it. If he had come by my apartment for any other reason than to be with me as I try and figure out how the hell I'm supposed to live my life now, I know whatever small threads of attraction and interest that could lie between us would be worth building onto.

We could have the world ahead, instead of the nothing I am able to offer, and it's cruel of the universe to bring him to me now when I am at my worst. I wish I didn't feel so unclean, uncertain of even letting him rest his head on my fabric covered thigh knowing that beneath it lies my skin, and beneath that, the taint of an illness that at one point in history took so many lives of young, beautiful gay men away forever.

I swallow hard as I glance at the unfilled prescriptions on the coffee table. I'll get that sorted out tomorrow morning and get started on healing up what is breaking to pieces inside of me as quickly as possible. The men that came before me diagnosed with HIV didn't have the ability to access anything like the medicine that exists now, and I know without it, I will die.

Casey rolls over in his sleep, his face turned upwards to me now. His hair cascades over my lap, mussed and golden in the glow of the TV across the way. He wrinkles his nose for a moment, before his plump lower lip opens the tiniest bit to release his nearly silent snores. From a distance, his jawbone looks as smooth as the rest of his skin, but I can see traces of faint blonde stubble illuminated in the darkness by the scant light emanating across the way from where we sit. He'd have a soft beard, I know, if he can grow one at all. I reach down and brush the back of my knuckles against the angle of Casey's cheek for some reason I can't put into words other than knowing that I can't resist touching his skin. I stroke his cheeks for a moment, listening to him sigh happily in his sleep. This could have been something, I'm sure, but that potential is gone now, and that stings like salt in a wound. As I pull my hand away from his skin, his eyes pop open and he offers a sleepy smile.

"Sorry," he murmurs, yawning. "Didn't mean to fall asleep on you."

"It's okay."

He sits up, stretching his arms over his head, and I am hit again with that sudden, strange loneliness that came across me before. As he turns on the couch to face me, I have to look away so he doesn't see anything hidden inside my eyes because I don't know how to put it to words and will fail if I try.

"You okay?" he asks, resting his hand on my thigh.

"Yeah. Sorry. Just tired, I think. It's been a long day."

"Sure has." Casey squeezes my thigh but doesn't take his hand away. "You have nice legs."

"Thanks?"

I meet his eyes, and he laughs, giving my thigh another squeeze. "They make good pillows. I noticed it the first night I was here. Thick thighs save lives, Brandon."

"I played rugby in high school," I offer. "Almost went to provincials."

"Why didn't you go? Didn't make it?"

I shake my head. "I made it but had nobody willing to sign the permission slips. It's all right. It doesn't matter much anymore. There are worse things, I suppose."

"No parents?" Casey asks with another yawn.

"Oh, I have parents. They just caught me in my bedroom with a friend the night before the paperwork was due to be turned in. Getting a view of your only son on his knees with a dick in his mouth doesn't exactly equal letting said son travel out of town to play a sport."

Casey frowns. "But if you made the provincial team, you had to have been good at it. Taking away a possible future career for the crime of sucking a dick doesn't seem fair."

I shrug, because I had the same thoughts when my father tore up the permission slips that would have allowed me to travel to Edmonton to play as part of the team. It's so far in my past though, it hardly matters anymore. Not when the present moment and uncertain future feels far worse than something as simple as not playing rugby on the provincial high school team. "It is what it is."

Casey's face scrunches, but he doesn't say anything else. Instead, he stands and stretches, his arms up in the air as he grumbles softly under his breath. When he's done, I stand as well, anticipating that he is about to make his leave.

"I have class first thing tomorrow morning, or I would stay," he says, like it's an apology for needing to go and a goodbye all at once.

"It's all right," I respond, with a half-baked smile. "I should get to bed anyway. Gotta get my prescriptions tomorrow and read whatever is in that info packet they gave me."

Casey nods, then heads for the front door of the apartment. I trail in his wake slowly, yawning into the stillness of the space around me. I wasn't tired before I stood up, but now I feel as if I weigh a thousand pounds and my legs are made of concrete. Casey slips into his running shoes, then stands for a moment, looking at me as I look right back at him. He turns, and I think he's going to open the door, but then he moves to face me again, stepping closer to me than he was before.

"Trust me?" he says, curling his hand around my cheek and brushing my cheekbones with his thumb.

"With what?" I ask, heart tripping over itself behind my ribcage and nerves crackling down my spine.

Casey leans in slowly, my face still cupped in his hand, stubble brushing his soft fingertips. He gives me time to move away, and while I probably should, I don't.

I let him kiss me, savoring the taste of his lips against mine and wishing this was a start instead of an end.

CHAPTER 4

BRANDON

I thought he would leave.

Despite him assuring me that he was interested in getting to know me, I had thought that Casey would disappear after the first night he invited himself over. I was ready for him to go, to know that he had done his good deed and that I was thankful for the time we'd spent because it meant I wasn't alone with my own thoughts and worries.

But he came back and has done so frequently over the last few weeks. Now, he sits on my couch in a pair of green plaid pajama pants and a plain grey T-shirt like he has always been here, long legs curled beneath him and a textbook on his lap. He wears a pair of thick framed tortoiseshell glasses he plucked from somewhere in the backpack on the floor, and every so often, his nose scrunches and he lifts a finger to push them back up onto his face. When he isn't turning pages, he glances up at the TV where some show he's put on to listen to plays episodes he's missed large parts of while studying. It doesn't seem to matter to him though, he laughs softly at whatever he sees on the screen, then turns his head back down to his books.

My apartment is filled with the noise of Casey, and as I stand in the kitchen, waiting for the coffee maker to finish up, I am thankful for it.

As if he knows I'm watching him, he lifts his head from his textbook and smiles, pushing a lock of golden hair behind one of his ears. It's growing long, but he's told me that's the point and that there will be no haircut in his near future.

"Coffee done?" he asks, stretching like a cat in the corner of the couch I've started thinking of as his.

"Almost. Studying done?"

He sighs, then shrugs. "I think so. I'm getting tired of words anyway. I wish textbooks weren't so wordy. Just say what you mean and get on with it."

I laugh softly as he closes the book and drops it on the floor beside him. He's studying to become a teacher. Something tells me there's a whole big future of textbooks ahead for him. I turn back to the coffee maker as it sputters and whooshes, the last few drops falling into the waiting pot. Grabbing it, I pour two mugs, adding sugar to mine and cream to his.

"Extra cream?" he requests, but I'm already turning the contents of his cup to the lightest shade of brown possible. I add just enough cream for it to be the color he likes best, and then pick up both mugs, heading for the living room. I place his mug in front of him and he grins, picking it up and taking a huge sip. He sighs happily as he cradles the mug in his hands, smiling at me over the brim of it. "Perfect."

I sit down on the couch beside him, placing my own mug on the table as he sips at his again. He yawns, pulling off his reading glasses and wiping his eyes with the back of his free hand. Casey's face is paler than usual, his eyes drawn and sunken a bit into his skin. He says he hasn't been sleeping well since the new semester started, and that adjusting to the more packed schedule than he had when he was doing the simple course he took over the summer to gain some extra credits is tough.

"I'm fine," he says before I can even ask if he's all right.

"Just tired?" I clarify anyway, a tiny thread of worry uncurling itself inside me. I quickly check my hands for cuts or open wounds, knowing that while there has been no sex between us, we have kissed, and I have touched his face with my fingers. It's irrational, I know, but I feel like I live with a monster inside my blood that's just waiting to infect him simply because he keeps coming around me.

Touching me and letting me touch him in the little ways I do now.

Casey reaches out and places one of his hands on mine. "Stop. I'm just tired. I promise, Brandon."

I offer a sheepish smile because I know better. I have read the entire packet of information that I was given and learned all the ways I have to be careful now. Holding hands and kissing aren't on the list of super dangerous things, and Casey is quick to remind me every time I get lost in my own anxiety over infecting him.

As if to prove his point, he put his mug down on the table, grabs my hand and presses it to his lips, kissing my knuckles. Instead of releasing me, he places my hand to his cheek and leans his head against it, still holding onto my fingers. "I'm just tired. It happens every year with the ridiculous schedule. There are worse things."

"Sharks," I offer with a smile as I uncurl my hand on his cheek to hold him. I run my thumb over his cheekbone, and he leans into the touch.

"Exactly," he murmurs, shuffling closer to me on the couch. Casey leans over and presses his lips to mine, and I revel in the feel of him against me, dropping my hand from his face to rest on his warm thigh. Usually, he stops the kiss by now, but today he doesn't move away.

Instead, he moves closer to me, hands gently coming to rest on my chest. I'm wearing a thin T-shirt, and I can feel the heat of his fingers against my skin, sending thrills through me. Casey doesn't move away from the kiss, but he does move himself onto my lap, straddling my thighs. I pull back as he comes to rest on my lap, need and want coursing through me at the pressure of his thighs against mine, splayed open over my body. He wraps his arms around my neck, looking into my eyes as he pushes his hips forward, applying delicious pressure to the front of my sweatpants. I am growing hard beneath them as he pushes himself forward again, but my heart starts racing inside my chest, and my worry is bubbling up from inside me like a freight train.

"Casey," I choke out as he pushes his hips forward again, sending shivers down my spine.

"It's okay," he murmurs, pressing his forehead against mine. "We're safe. This is safe. You could fuck me, and it would be safe, Brandon."

"I don't know," I murmur as my breath hitches in my throat. He feels so good against me, hips gyrating against my pelvis and his cock behind his pants rubbing against mine, but my entire brain is at war with my body. I know the things I know about safe sex with HIV, but that doesn't help me at all, and I am tensing beneath him as much as I never want him to stop writhing against me. I remember what it felt like to take him, to have him bent over in front of me, my cock slipping in and out of his body as he moaned and gripped my pillows tight in his fists. I want him, but I don't want to hurt him at the same time, and now that he's offering himself to me again knowing full well what I am now made of, I am screaming inside my own head that I will take this beautiful thing and make it worse. I will ruin him and wreck him with what I carry inside me. It's too much, and I can't get the rational side of my brain to kick in to remind me that I know we could be safe in enjoying each other's bodies. I let loose a small noise of what can only be called distress, and Casey stops moving and pulls back, looking down into my eyes with concern written into his own.

"Hey," he whispers, gently caressing my face with his hands again. "You can say no, and I will stop. We don't have to do anything until you are ready for it, okay?"

"I don't want you to get sick."

"Oh, Brandon. Do you want me, though?"

"Yes." I do. I want to explore his body without hesitation, take what he is offering me and wring his own pleasure out of every inch of him. I want to hear my name on his lips as he releases, knowing that I am the one that gave that to him. I just don't know if I can let myself do it when everything else feels off-kilter and ugly inside me.

"Then let me show you how you can have me. I trust you," he says, pressing his hips forward again, his cock rubbing against mine to send shivers down my spine.

My heart beats a rapid pace behind my ribs and my lungs squeeze as I force breath in and out of them, my cock straining beneath my pants and my head on fire with thoughts of infecting him. "I don't know, Casey."

What I mean is, I don't know what to do here.

What I mean is, I don't know if I can trust my own body.

What I mean is, I'm scared.

I'm so scared.

"Do you trust that I would not let myself get HIV from you?" he asks, looking down into my eyes.

That strikes me in a strange place inside, jolting my brain out of the fear and worry threatening to consume me. "Trust you?"

"Yes. If you are uncertain of yourself, then that is a better question. Do you trust me, Brandon? Do you trust that I know we can have sex safely and that I would not put myself into a position where I would get HIV from you?"

I go silent, thoughts rumbling through my brain like a train on a track. "I've never thought of it like that."

Casey smiles, leaning forward and pressing his lips to mine briefly before pulling away. He crawls off my lap and sits beside me, leaning into my side as I put my arm around him. "Then think of it like that, and when you're ready for it, Brandon, I'm here."

CHAPTER 5

CASEY

"Why do you always say there are worse things?" Brandon asks, placing a steaming cup of coffee on the table in front of me.

"Because there are always worse things," I reply, picking up the mug and blowing some of the heat off the top. It doesn't really work, and I burn my mouth on the first sip anyway, but the effort was there. I wince as I swallow, the burn tracking down my throat.

"It's hot," Brandon offers with a small grin.

"No shit." I take another sip anyway before putting the mug down on the table. I'm curled up on the couch in his living room beneath the blanket I brought him last month because he keeps this place impossibly cold all the time. "Burning your mouth with coffee is a worse thing."

"Worse than sharks?" he asks, sitting down beside me.

"Not worse than sharks. Or bears. There's always something worse." It may seem like a flippant thing to say in light of what he's been going through, but it's something I've lived by since I was little. I used to get so upset when I failed tests or didn't achieve to the level I thought I should. I was so hard on myself as a kid, forgoing playing at recess in favor of reading books by myself or scratching math problems into the dirt of the playground with a stick. I even got to the point in junior high where I wasn't sleeping some nights, choosing to stay up and study with a flashlight, doing flashcards by myself in the darkness of my bedroom. My mom, at her wit's end with trying to help me understand that one thing wrong on a math test wasn't the end of the world, had given me those words, and for some reason, they'd stuck in my head. It took a lot of practice to realize what they really meant, but they help me keep things in perspective, I suppose.

I know there are worse things in the world than failing a math test, and I know that what Brandon has going on inside of him could potentially be one of them. He's been taking his medication daily, though, for nearly a whole month, and we've been getting to know each other more and more each day. In this case, worse things could be that the medicines don't work well, or that the doctor discovers he has a strain of HIV that doesn't respond to them. Worse things means he dies young, like countless others have in the past from this disease. Worse means I don't get to keep getting to know the quiet man filled with worry for everyone but himself that I am becoming quite fond of.

There are worse things, yes, but they don't belong here in this space with us.

Brandon settles into the couch and grabs the remote for the TV, turning it on and gesturing meaningfully down at my abandoned textbook. "Still working?"

"Nope," I reply. "We're going to go out tonight."

"Out?"

"Yes, somewhere outside of these four walls, Brandon. We're going out."

"Where are we going?"

"Somewhere. Anywhere. I don't really care where, but we've spent so much time together in this apartment that I'm starting to feel like I'm about to grow into the couch and become a permanent part of it."

"That wouldn't be so bad," he replies with a small smile.

"It would be terrible," I correct. "Becoming part of your life as a couch-Casey hybrid isn't the vibe I'm trying for." Brandon laughs and I grin at the sound of it. "So, where are we going?"

He hesitates, then offers a smile that seems hopeful. "You can say no, but a band I really like is playing a show tonight at The Warehouse."

"Okay," I agree, plastering a smile on my face. The Warehouse is the worst music venue in this city in my opinion, but I know he loves that screechy metal music so much that I won't say no to going to a show with him. Brandon snorts out a laugh that nearly rattles the walls around us. "What's so funny?"

"Your face looks like my suggestion was kicking puppies and burning buildings to the ground. We don't have to go, it's okay. We can do something else."

"Oh no. We're going. I have no other plans and if this is a band you really like, I won't make you miss it for me."

He smiles, leaning over to press a kiss on my cheek, and I revel for a moment in the feel of his lips against my skin. Brandon rarely kisses me or touches me without hesitation and whenever he lets himself move without thinking it through a thousand times first, it feels like the best gift I could possibly be given.

I'm about to let him know he's going to have to lend me some clothes so I don't stick out like a sore thumb when the alarm on his phone goes off and his expression sobers. It's his reminder to take his medication, I know. Brandon rises from his spot on the couch and heads to the bathroom, giving me an apologetic smile over his shoulder as he goes.

I rise to follow him, my feet soft on the carpet beneath them as I go join him in the bathroom. He stands in front of the small counter, filling the plastic cup he keeps by the sink with water and pulling his three pill bottles from the shelf above the sink, the air around him suddenly heavier than it was just moments ago. It won't always be these three, some people only have to take one a day, but this is where he's starting, and so far, there's been no side effects with them. Brandon uncaps the first bottle, and I reach around him to pluck it from his hand, shaking the first tablet into my own palm as he turns to watch.

"What are you doing?" he asks as I scoot between him and the counter. I hop up onto it, settling myself on the small ledge in front of the sink.

"Open up," I say, holding the pill out to him.

His cheeks burn a little bit pink beneath his scruff on his cheeks, but he does as I've said, parting his lips and letting me place his first pill on his pink tongue. He swallows it down with a sip of water from his cup. I pop open the second bottle and then the third, adding the last two pills to my palm before leaning forward and kissing him gently on the lips.

He laughs softly, shaking his head at me, but opens his mouth again as I hold up the second pill. I place it on his tongue, waiting for him to swallow it with some water before rewarding him with another gentle kiss. We do the third one the same, but this time instead of ending the kiss, I hold onto him with my lips, placing my hands on his ribcage to feel the rise and fall of his breath. When I do let him go, he takes a small step back, offering me a small smile.

"There is nothing sexier than seeing you take care of yourself," I whisper, hands still on his sides, his ribcage rising and falling with measured, even breaths beneath my touch. He leans forward and kisses me, breathing life into the space between us as I get lost in the touch of his skin against mine.

A reminder that there are worse things than taking pills.

"It's so loud!" I shout as we walk into The Warehouse.

Brandon nods, grinning at me over his shoulder. We're running a bit late, owing to me needing to change from my comfy blue hoodie with the logo for the college I attend on it into something more appropriate for the venue. I'm dressed in Brandon tonight, his tight black shirt with a white spraypainted rabbit on the front stretched across my chest and his studded leather belt wrapped around my waist, holding his loose dark wash jeans in place around my narrower hips. They almost fit me exactly right, and I was thrilled to find that we match a little bit in size. Despite everything that's different between us, we match in some way, and that makes me smile.

Brandon holds tightly to my hand, and I let him take the lead, weaving through the people by the door and trusting that I'm safe with him here even if there are some scary looking people in the crowd ahead. He won't take me into the pit, that much I know. He used to get in there, he'd said as we'd driven over here, but he can't do that anymore. While eventually he may be able to hop into the pit again with the rest of the thrashing bodies, when he hopefully reaches undetectable and untransmittable through the daily use of his pills, it's risky right now in a way he can't afford. He can't be in a position to be pushed, punched and pummeled into the ground.

That doesn't mean he can't afford to be here on the edge of the crowd though, and that is where we come to a stop, behind everyone else. In front of the stage, the floor is packed with jostling bodies and the lead singer screeches into the microphone, sending them higher into their flurry of movement. I wince, but when I glance over at Brandon, the smile on his face is so wide I wouldn't give this up for all the money in the world.

He is at peace here in the chaos, his lips moving to mouth the lyrics to whatever song the singer is singing. I can't make out what the words are, but I can watch Brandon and know that he does. He knows them all off by heart, he'd told me, and I don't doubt that for a second. In the flash of the overhead lights and the strobes emanating from the stage, I can see him as he was the night we met at the club, but this is somehow more than even that.

I know the taste of him now. His touches that he hesitates to give and the ones that he doesn't hold back from. I know his voice and as he mouths the words, I can imagine what they sound like falling from his lips. I know him more than I thought I ever would now that he's no longer that hot as sin one-night stand in my past.

I could love him someday, but I don't know if he'd want me to, so I keep that to myself.

The song changes and the bodies leave the crowd, sweat slicking their faces as they move towards the doors at the back of the hall. There's a concourse out there with cold drinks and snacks, and as the door opens and closes letting bodies in and out, I catch little breezes on my skin from the space beyond them. We listen to a few more songs,

Brandon mouthing the words to every single one of them as the heat in the space builds. Sweat drips down my face and I wipe it away, glancing at the door that leads to the concourse where I know there are cool drinks awaiting me.

"Thirsty?" Brandon asks, as I glance at the door again.

"Yeah," I shout back, nodding.

"Let's go grab something before the next song starts. This song is a bad one anyway. It's from their newest album and it's kind of shit."

I don't comment that it all sounds kind of shitty to me but nod my agreement to going to get a drink. I'm sure Brandon feels the same way about the soft, dreamy folk music I play sometimes when I'm studying, but he hasn't complained once, and I will keep my thoughts to myself tonight for him.

We head through the doors to the concourse and make our way over to grab a couple bottles of water from one of the vendors. I'm tempted to grab a beer, but I know that alcohol is one of the things Brandon is trying to cut down on so I join him in a cool, crisp water. I uncap the bottle as we move to stand at a table by the doors to the venue and take a long sip. Brandon does the same, smiling as he swallows his mouthful.

"Thanks for coming," he says as I sip my water again.

"Anytime."

"We can pick your music next time as long as you promise that if my ears start bleeding, you'll let me leave."

"If your ears bleed?" I laugh, gesturing at the door. "What about your music, huh? I was being nice before, Tremblay, but if you're gonna come at me about my music, all bets are off. I'll be lucky if I can hear by the end of the night."

"You'll be fine," Brandon responds, leaning in and kissing my sweaty cheek.

"Brandon?" a voice asks from my left as he pulls away from my skin. Brandon startles beside me and he whirls around to see who has said his name.

A man stands there, his black hair pulled off his face in a ponytail that cascades down his back like a waterfall and a friendly smile on his face. He is handsome and broad chested, his wide shoulders tapering down to a trim waist where a simple pair of jeans cling. His shirt carries a logo for a local tattoo shop, and he reaches out a heavily inked hand towards Brandon, who hesitates a moment before clasping it in his own.

"Nolan," he says with a relieved smile. "I wondered if you'd be here."

"Of course," the man, Nolan, responds with a smile of his own. "Someone has to keep Chase safe."

"And of course it has to be you."

Nolan grins, shrugging his shoulders. "Best friend duties. You know how it is."

"Best friends. Right."

"Shut up, Tremblay," Nolan says, shoving Brandon's shoulder with a hand as he shakes his head. His cheeks are burning red though, so I gather that this Chase person isn't exactly stuck in the friendzone. At least not as far as Nolan is concerned anyway.

Brandon catches my eye as I look between him and Nolan, then finally makes an introduction. "Casey, this is Nolan. He's the one responsible for the ink on my body. Nolan, this is Casey. He's my… boyfriend?"

"Yeah," I reply, turning to face Nolan. "Boyfriend. You did all that work?"

"All of it." Nolan nods, offering his hand out to me. "Nice to meet you, Casey."

I shake his hand, then smile at the tall man. "It's beautiful art."

"It is. Still have some to finish up though. I'm surprised you cancelled off my booking sheet. When I got your email, I nearly called you to demand that you come in so I can finish the piece. If it's a money thing, I can hold the cost or we can work out payments, Brandon. You know that."

Brandon falls silent, glancing between the floor, me and Nolan. I can feel him quivering slightly beside me and the silence is deafening where it sits in our small circle, even with the music crashing from behind the doors of the ballroom.

"Unless I did bad work?" Nolan asks, clearly confused as to why Brandon is behaving odd.

Finally, Brandon takes a deep breath and gestures for Nolan to step closer. The taller man does, looking very confused. Brandon leans his head up to his ear, and though I can't hear the words, I can make them out by the way his lips move.

"I'm HIV positive," he says, and Nolan's eyes widen as he steps away slightly, my heart aching as the space between them grows.

"For real?" Nolan asks, eyebrows raised in surprise. Brandon nods slowly, shame creeping onto his features, but Nolan surprises me then, reaching out a meaty hand to rest it on Brandon's shoulder. "Sorry to hear, dude. But still, we take precautions, man. We treat everyone like they have something because they might. We're all trained in that shit from the moment we pick up our first fake skin to practice. Certified and everything. You book in if you want to, I don't give a fuck. I just want to finish the work I've started because it's going to be fucking great when it's done." He cranes his neck upwards as the song ends behind the doors of the ball room. "You two heading back in?"

I nod, glancing at Brandon who nods as well. We follow Nolan into the ballroom as a new song starts, but he sighs as we walk in. A heavily tattooed blond-haired man emerges from the crowd by the stage, holding onto his bare ribcage and scowling back at the pit of people mashing their bodies together. Nolan smiles tenderly at the man, then turns to us again. "I'm gonna go see who slammed Chicken Little's ribs. See you soon?"

Brandon nods, clearly relieved and a bit confused as Nolan takes off across the open area at the back of the arena. He meets up with the blond man, who I assume is both Chicken Little and possibly also this Chase person he mentioned before, and I watch them for a few seconds before turning to Brandon.

"Nolan has a crush," I comment.

"Yeah," Brandon responds, but I can tell his head is elsewhere.

"What's going on?"

"Safe." He shakes his head like he can't quite understand that word. "Everyone seems to be so certain that things are just fine. That they're totally safe around me. It's strange, when all I can feel is this illness creeping around inside my blood."

"So let it creep around. You're killing it off and pushing it back day by day with those pills. Hopefully, it won't be detectable in time. You're fighting it off, but you're also fighting yourself and what you think about you. We can be safe, Brandon, if you let us." I take a chance and lift myself up to his ear so he can hear every single word I'm about to say. "You could fuck me, like you did before, and it will be safe."

I lower myself down and look into his eyes, seeing the worry and doubt hidden inside them, but I also see desire. He scans my body slowly, like he is taking stock of every inch of me, then he slowly, carefully nods. I run my hand down my chest, then rest my fingers on the belt he loaned me for the night, tilting my head in question, my body an offering to him tonight.

Any night.

And this time, instead of shaking my offer away, he nods an agreement, his eyes filled with the same lust I know from the first night we met.

CHAPTER 6

BRANDON

I'm shaking.

Trembling like a leaf as Casey carefully peels off the shirt I lent him. He drops it to the floor of my bedroom at my feet, and I swallow hard, staring at his perfect, pink nipples. We left the concert behind, and I thought I was ready, but now that we are back in my apartment, I'm not so sure.

I'm breaking into pieces as he strips in front of me, not sure what to do to quell the fear creeping up my throat.

Maybe this is too much to want. Too much to think I could have from him, even if he says it isn't. I was bold before, but now I'm crumbling inside again.

"Safe," Casey whispers, unzipping the pants I lent him to expose his teal boxers.

I nod, reaching for the hem of my shirt. I pull it off as he steps out of the last of his clothing, coming to stand in front of me, naked and beautiful. My breath hitches in my throat as he reaches for me, pulling me closer to him using the belt loop on my jeans. Casey presses a kiss to my lips that feels like a promise, then lets me go. He runs a hand down my chest, swirling a finger across the vines that tangle across my pecs.

"You're so fucking hot, Brandon," he murmurs as his hand moves from my skin to trail down his own bare chest. His eyes fill with desire as he takes his cock in hand, giving himself a few slow, needy strokes while I watch, getting lost in the movement of his hand on himself. "You wanna fuck me?"

"Yeah," I reply, my mouth dry as Casey moans softly, then lets go of himself to lick his palm before taking his cock back into his slick fist.

I shuffle out of my own clothing, watching him touch himself as my need for him grows. My own cock juts out from my pelvis, the tip glistening with precum, but I don't dare touch myself. I don't want to risk anything without a condom on, and I'm too enthralled watching him pleasure himself to move at the moment. He grins at me as he touches his bare skin, his free hand coming to pluck at his pert, pink nipples, like he knows I am enjoying whatever show he is putting on for me.

"Lube?" Casey asks, crawling onto the bed, his cock swinging between his legs.

"Bedside table," I say, but he already has the drawer open and is fishing around inside for the bottle. When he finds it, he pulls it out and sits back on the bed, making a show for me of slicking his fingers and spreading his legs. That is when I snap into movement, crossing the bedroom to grab a condom from the same bedside table the lube was kept in.

"Brandon," Casey whispers, and I glance down at him, condom in hand and cock twitching with need and want. He closes his eyes and slides a slicked-up finger into his hole, whimpering slightly at the pressure of it.

"Fucking hell," I murmur back, as he moves his finger in and out of himself, letting loose soft little moans with every tiny thrust. "Casey, that's so hot."

I tear open the condom, heart racing and hands shaking still as Casey touches himself, playing with the rim of his slick hole before delving back inside with a finger. He pulls out, then adds another finger inside, wincing and panting at the pressure that two, thick digits give him. I take care with slipping the condom onto my cock, taking my eyes off him for a second to make sure that I am covered and safe. When I look back, Casey is watching me, his eyes filled with lust as I reach for the lube and slick my length with it. His fingers move in and out of his body and his cock rests on his belly, the tip deeper pink than the rest of his shaft.

He stops moving his hands on himself and gestures for me to come closer to him, but the moment I crawl onto the bed, he seems to change his mind about where he wants me. Finally, he gets on his knees and gestures towards the headboard. "Sit."

I give him a mock salute, hands shaking, and stomach filled with nerves and fear as I do as he says, crawling onto the bed and propping myself up on the headboard. I inhale a shaky breath, watching with anticipation as he moves to straddle me, his bare cock bumping along my sheathed one. I almost make him stop, rattled by seeing his bare cock so close to touching mine even with the condom on, but he looks at me then, like I am a thing of beauty instead of dread, and I hold off the words that want to come loose from my lips.

Casey lifts his body and steadies himself, reaching down to grip my cock in his hands. His forehead crinkles as he places my tip at his entrance, then slides me back and forth over his hole a few times. Finally, he presses down against me, lowering his body onto mine as his head tips backwards. I can feel myself slide into him deep and reach forward to grip his hips in my hands as he takes me into him.

"Bran," he moans as his warmth squeezes my cock, his body rippling around mine. He tilts his head forward as he raises himself off me, the slide just as slow now as it was when he first opened himself for my cock. Slowly, he pulls off then pushes back on, riding me carefully, his forehead scrunching at either the effort of it, or because he is in pain.

"Okay?" I ask as his body grips me impossibly tight.

"You feel so good," he responds.

Casey moves his hips and moans, his hands resting on my shoulders. He leans forward and catches my lips with his, kissing me as he starts moving on my body at a faster pace. I skate my hands up his sides as he rides me, moving my thumbs over to rub his nipples as I know he likes.

We've been here before. In another world, far before worse things like HIV came into the picture. I remember his body and the way he lets loose those soft little noises with every thrust like he is embarrassed of them yet can't stop them at the same time.

They are beautiful, and he is beautiful, hair no longer tucked behind his ear but falling forwards as he kisses me, tickling my cheeks. Casey ends the kiss and tips his head backwards, a smile on his face as his cock rubs against my warm stomach. He reaches a hand down and grabs himself, stroking as he rides me. I move my own hand down, covering his to take over as he moans and writhes on my cock.

He comes with a shout, spilling clean, white cum over my stomach in spurts. Sweat bears on his forehead and he reaches up to wipe his hair off his face, then leans down to kiss me again, wrapping his arms around my neck. I'm so deep into him that I don't know where I end and he begins. Casey moans softly and lifts himself off my cock, then pushes his body back downwards, drawing pleasure out of me along with the tendrils of fear that live inside me now.

I'm close. So close, and that is where fear lives.

That is where I start losing my composure. The closer I get to release, the more the dread creeps up inside me, but Casey feels so good wrapped around my cock, and I am starting to unravel inside my own head.

"Casey," I choke out, needing him to know. Begging him to understand that I'm becoming untethered inside, fears and doubts rattling through me, shaking loose from the bones that build me up.

"Trust me," Casey whispers, gently placing his hands on my cheeks as he moves his body on mine. His thumbs stroke my cheekbones, and I lean into him, letting him cradle me there in his safety. Every muscle in my body tenses and flickers with his touch, and there is a threat growing inside me. To run. To fall. To break into pieces here in front of him. Any. Or all.

"Just breathe, Brandon. That's all you have to do. Trust and breathe."

I close my eyes because it's easier.

I close my eyes because I can feel tears prickling at the backs of them, and while I trust him, I don't trust myself.

I close my eyes and breathe him, taking him deep into places nobody has ever gone. Places nobody understands, but I know Casey would, if I let him.

I know Casey will.

I lean in more to his touch as he gently tilts my head down and places his lips against my forehead. His hips move at a steady pace, bringing him away from me and then closer than anyone's been before. My heart, my lungs, my everything becomes his as he rides my cock and presses his lips to my sweaty skin. I am falling apart beneath him as my orgasm creeps closer to the surface, tension rippling up my spine. I hold my breath, like that will help. Like that will stave off the pleasure I suddenly don't want.

Don't need.

Yet am getting anyway.

I hold my breath as everything inside me gives way, my body loosening as I fill the condom deep inside of Casey's warm body. I moan softly at the feel of it because his body is beautiful and his hands are kind, releasing the air into the space between us, then find I'm holding my breath again as I wait for things to get worse.

For him to realize what we've done and what this could mean.

For the panic to set in.

"Breathe, Bran. Just breathe. Everything is perfect," he whispers, stroking my cheeks, kissing my forehead, giving me what I deserve least and need most.

Giving me himself, despite knowing that I contain monsters being locked away by medications I will be on for the rest of my life. This will not be easy, though they will become undetectable in time. They will always be there inside of me, yet he doesn't care. Casey gives me himself without hesitation, and I am not worthy of any of him, but I know that I will spend a lifetime earning his hands, lips, words.

"I could love you," I whisper, and that thought scares me. Draws breath from lung and makes heart hammer behind my fragile ribcage. "Do you know how scary that is, Casey?"

"There are worse things," Casey Morrow says.

AND THEN CAME BLISS

L.C. CHASE

CHAPTER 1

"Here you are, love," Blair said to Greta, one of his favorite repeat customers, as he slid a chai latte across the counter for her.

Greta tittered, as she did every day. She was in her early nineties but gave most fifty-year-olds a run for their money. Full of life and laughter and always with a kind word for Blair.

"I met a lovely young man today," she said. Another thing she did on the regular: try to couple Blair up. "I think you two would get along famously."

"Now, Greta," Blair teased, as he did whenever she mentioned some new potential beau. "You know I'm quite happy being single. I have my coffee shop, my cat, and you to flirt with."

"Oh, you." She fanned a hand over her face, and a light blush colored her cheeks. She picked up her to-go cup. "See you tomorrow, darling."

"You should take her up on that," Traci, his full-time barista, said as she returned from the stockroom, arms laden with two bags of fresh coffee beans.

"On what?" He played it off.

Traci rolled her eyes. "Let her matchmake you. You need a boyfriend."

Blair snorted. He didn't *need* a boyfriend. So what if he sometimes saw happy couples in public and felt a twinge of longing for the same. Didn't mean he had to do anything about it.

"Like I told Greta, I'm happy as I am." And he was. Most of the time.

"Uh-huh." Traci didn't sound convinced, but let it go.

Blair knew she cared. She'd been his first hire when he'd opened his coffee shop in Vancouver's West End, and over the years had become one of his dearest friends. But he truly wasn't interested in the dating scene. Dating was exhausting. Not to mention, lingering stigmas regarding his status narrowed the pool of eligible men.

Greta's visits signaled the end of the morning rush, so Blair took advantage of a quiet shop to do a little extra cleaning before the lunch crowd arrived. The bell over the front door jingled with the arrival of a new customer. Blair looked up and his breath caught.

He'd never seen the man before, but hoped he'd become a new regular, because *wow*. The newcomer appeared a little older than Blair's thirty-six, a few inches over six feet—thanks to the height chart on the inside of the door frame—with a lean frame. Stylishly dressed in a tan-colored three-quarter length coat over a white mock-neck sweater, black jeans, and suede loafers. Square jaw sporting dark stubble, full lips, and straight nose, but Blair couldn't tell his eye color from across the shop. His hair was a messy, dirty blond, either styled so or because of the ever-present winds that rolled off the waters of English Bay across the street.

Blair imagined what those shiny locks would feel like sliding through his fingers. He sighed inside. That was a man Blair could be convinced to dip back into the dating waters for. He was completely Blair's type, and, unfortunately, out of his league.

"Welcome to Bliss Beans," Blair greeted, fighting the urge to bounce on his toes. His excitement growing with each step the man took toward him.

The handsome stranger nodded in Blair's direction, but didn't make eye contact. He stopped a few feet away from the counter and looked at the menu board. Except Blair wasn't sure the man was *seeing* the writing on it. Up closer, his eyes were a beautiful chestnut brown but held a haunted look similar to those Blair had seen too many times in the weekly support group he helped with. Not that *that* was the reason, but he recognized the signs of shock and despair when he saw them.

The bell jingled again, ushering in a trio of ladies who stopped in for coffees and lattes after their yoga class around the corner twice a week. Blair glanced at the troubled man, who seemed no closer to ordering, and shifted his attention to the ladies. After taking care of their drinks, and shrugging off Traci's waggling eyebrows, he turned his focus to the haunted man who still stood in the same spot. Expressionless, shoulders slumped, and gaze distant.

"I'm thinking you might like an iced cinnamon honey latte," Blair said, pushing a full smile into his words. A little boost of sugar usually helped with the aftereffects of shock.

The man jerked. His features tight as he shifted on his feet and cleared his throat.

"Sorry. I guess I zoned out there." His words were apologetic, and his chuckle was self-deprecating, but that dazed look remained in his pretty eyes.

That didn't stop Blair from biting back a whimper at the man's smooth, deep-timbred voice.

"No worries. I know there's a lot to choose from," Blair said, keeping his voice soft and tone light.

The man nodded. "What you said sounded good."

"The iced cinnamon honey latte?" Blair confirmed, and at the man's nod, he smiled. "Coming right up. May I get your name?"

He seemed confused for a second, and then said, "Jake."

Jake of my dreams.

Jake paid and then stepped to the end of the counter while Blair started making his drink.

"Nice out there today. Now the rain has stopped, eh." Blair cringed inside. He wasn't one for small talk, especially about the weather, but he found his thoughts and tongue oddly tangled up around Jake. Something he hadn't encountered since he was a teen, where his mind went completely blank when his high school crush was nearby.

Jake nodded but remained silent, while Blair's brain got stuck on an alphabet hamster wheel, trying to come up with something witty and flirty to say. Maybe get a phone number.

Traci flashed a knowing smile at Blair and winked. *Ugh.* Was he blushing? His cheeks felt hot. Great. Crushing on a customer who looked like he was having the worst day of his life. *Go, Blair.*

"I hope you enjoy the latte," Blair said as he placed it on the counter.

A hint of a smile teased the edges of Jake's mouth, and he mumbled a quiet *thank you* before turning and leaving.

Blair stared after him with a strange sensation of loss tugging at him. He watched as Jake stood on the sidewalk for a minute before crossing the street. Watched as he sat down on a bench overlooking the bay. And continued watching as Jake sat there, still as a statue. The only movement was the breeze ruffling though his hair.

"Wow." Blair started at Traci's voice right beside him. "If I didn't know any better, I'd say you just met the love of your life."

"*Puh-lease.*" Blair rolled his eyes and nudged her shoulder, but her words were already burrowing under his skin. "Get back to work, slacker."

She laughed, singing about a crazy little thing called love, as she wiped the counter.

"That song is before your time," he called after her, an annoying pout in his voice.

Traci sang louder.

Blair shook his head and went back to work, too, but he couldn't stop thinking about Jake. Wondering what had put that troubled look on his face, wishing he could do something about it, whatever *it* was. He bet Jake had an amazing smile. Too bad he'd probably never see Jake again.

CHAPTER 2

"I'm so sorry, Mr. Sheraton."

Words no one ever wanted to hear their doctor start a sentence with replayed over and over in Jake's mind.

He'd left his doctor's office and started walking with no idea where he was going. His head buzzing and his feet shuffling were the only things that registered. He just needed to keep moving, as though movement would prevent him from thinking. Walking had worked on the thinking part, but had done nothing about remembering.

Jake looked down at his hand, which held a to-go cup full of something hot he didn't remember ordering, or from where. Frowning, he stared out at the tanker ships anchored farther out as he mentally retraced his steps. The doctor's office. His doctor's mouth moving but the words coming out of it not making any sense. Standing on the street until someone bumped into him. Walking, walking, walking. Past the Queen Elizabeth Theatre, past the Vancouver Public Library, and through Robson Square. Past St. Paul's Hospital, and along Davie Street. Wandering until he reached the sandy shore of English Bay Beach.

Not a long distance, but he felt as though hours had passed. Just now registering how far he'd walked, his legs grew shaky, and his knees weakened. He spied an empty bench and sat before he fell. Jake placed the to-go cup on the bench beside him and shoved his hands into his pockets. His knuckles scraped the envelope containing a week's supply of pills the doctor had given him to start taking immediately. The physical reminder of his new reality sent a jolt of panic spiking through him. He yanked his hands out of his pockets and clasped them in his lap.

"I'm so sorry, Mr. Sheraton."

That low buzzing sound filled his ears again. He closed his eyes and focused on breathing slow and even, until the steady breaking of waves over the shoreline drowned it out.

"I'm so sorry, Mr. Sheraton," his doctor had said. "Your results came back positive for HIV."

Jake had tuned out the rest of what his doctor had said. At first because the words didn't compute, and then because there had to be a mistake. He couldn't understand how he, mister monogamous and faithfully married, could test positive. Not unless he'd stepped into some sort of alternate universe.

He'd been a child at the tail end of the AIDS crisis. He hadn't seen or experienced what those before him had, but he had watched his favorite uncle lose his battle with AIDS. After that, Jake had always been careful with his sexual partners. Not that he'd had many. One boyfriend in college and then Andy, who he'd been married to for the last sixteen years.

Until the day Andy had come home looking distraught, and, in one fell swoop, pulled the rug out from under Jake's world. Jake hadn't been able to parse which revelation was the worst. That Andy had been bored with their sex life and been hooking up with random strangers for years; that his careless and selfish lifestyle had led to him contracting HIV; or that he'd met someone new—aka someone younger—and wanted a divorce.

Jake had never signed a legal document faster. The divorce made easy by him not wanting any reminders of his life with Andy. They'd sold their condo downtown and their cabin in Whistler, and Jake had taken his share of the proceeds to purchase a new condo overlooking Stanley Park and the North Shore.

And now here he was, somewhere he'd never imagined he'd be at forty-three years old: divorced, alone, and HIV positive.

How had he not seen the signs that Andy was unhappy? That Andy was stepping out on him? That his life wasn't the perfect successful vision he'd strived for and, so he'd thought, had achieved? And what did he do now? He'd be alone for the rest of his life. Sure, his doctor had told him that HIV wasn't the death sentence that it was in the early days of the crisis. That with medication and proper care, he could not only live a full and healthy life, but he could find love again.

Jake snorted. *Find love again.* Had he even had love with Andy? Jake had thought so, but clearly Andy had a different notion of what love and committed relationships looked like. And how could he ever be with anyone ever again, knowing he could pass this disease on to them, too? How did he shift into this new reality? How did he let go of the before and move forward into the after?

Seagulls squawked and cried above, but none had any answers for him. Boats sailed back and forth in the bay. Traffic along Denman Street increased and decreased. Afternoon gave way to twilight as the sun began its descent into the Pacific Ocean. Still Jake sat. Feeling an odd sense of detachment from the world. Detachment from himself. And time that no longer had meaning marched on.

What did he do now?

CHAPTER 3

Blair forgot all about the handsome stranger with the wounded eyes when the lunch rush hit. A rush that hadn't let up until near closing time. He paused wiping tabletops to watch the sun set and noticed a figure sitting on a bench across the street. The same jacket, the same wind-blown hair, the same defeated roll to his shoulders. And the same tug in Blair's chest to ease whatever pain Jake was suffering.

"Nice one tonight, eh, boss?" Traci said as she came up beside him, a tray of dirty coffee cups hugged to her side. They always paused for the sunset.

"Sure is," he said, but he wasn't looking at the sun anymore. He turned to Traci. "Do you mind closing up?"

She grinned. "Got a date?"

With Jake, if I'm lucky. "It's Thursday," he said instead.

"Right. I forgot," Traci said. The doorbell jingled and a last-minute customer rushed in. She turned. "I got this. You go have a good night."

Blair left Traci to finish up and start closing, while he prepared another iced cinnamon honey latte for Jake, a regular coffee in case he hadn't liked the latte, and a cup of peach tea for himself. He put four rainbow cheese crisps in a bag. He pulled on his jacket from the back and, gathering the drinks and snacks, headed across the street.

"Hi," Blair said as he sat down and put the drink tray on the bench between them.

Jake remained motionless, like a living statue. His gaze was distant and unfocused. Lost somewhere in his mind. The Bliss Beans to-go cup rested on the bench near Jake's thigh, but when Blair picked it up to throw it into the recycle bin, it was still full. Either Jake hadn't touched it, or he hadn't liked it. Blair tossed it and when he sat back down, he took a moment to study Jake. His expression was drawn, the skin around his eyes and mouth tight. His shoulders were rigid, and his hands fisted in his lap.

The top corner of a pamphlet sticking out of Jakes's coat pocket caught his attention. Blair didn't need to see the whole thing to know what it was. He recognized the familiar artwork, considering he was the one who had designed it. The title on the front of that pamphlet read *Living with HIV*.

His heart ached for Jake, who, Blair knew from experience, must have just received a positive diagnosis. Blair cleared his throat and angled fully toward Jake.

"Hi, Jake," he said louder.

Jake startled out of his fugue, turning wide, confused eyes on Blair.

"I'm Blair." He smiled and pointed to the tray of drinks between them before hooking a thumb over his shoulder. "I own the coffee shop across the way and noticed you've been sitting here for hours."

Frowning, Jake looked at his watch and cursed.

"I thought you might like a drink and a snack. I brought another iced cinnamon honey latte, and a coffee in case you didn't like that. Or you could have the peach tea?" He opened the bag. "I brought some rainbow cheese crisps, too. You must be hungry."

In response, Jake's stomach growled loud enough to be heard down the street. He ran his hands through his hair and Blair's stomach dropped as Jake stood up.

"Sorry I-I can't," Jake said, his broken voice as distant as his gaze.

The man had barely said two words since Blair had first met him, but Blair didn't want him to go just yet. The pull toward Jake he'd felt earlier shifted into a mild panic. He couldn't let Jake go now. Not after Blair knew what had put that haunted look in Jake's eyes.

"Just a drink?" Blair pleaded, offering his softest smile and trying to be outwardly casual while inside begging, *please, please, please.*

"Okay. Yeah." Jake dropped back down to the bench with a heavy sigh. Exhaustion rolling off him in waves. "That fancy latte sounds good. Sorry I didn't try the last one." A strained sounding huff-laugh burst from Jake's mouth. "I don't even remember getting it."

"No worries," Blair said as he handed the latte over. His fingers brushing Jake's cool skin sent an electric charge up his arm.

"Thank you." Jake took a sip and then lifted the cup in salute. "This is good."

Blair grinned. He'd known Jake would like it. That was his super-power. Knowing which drink or snack was just the right one for his customers.

"Rainbow cheese crisps?" Jake's brows furrowed. "What are those?"

"My special savory snack," Blair preened. He loved coming up with new and healthy items to put on the menu. "Three kinds of cheese, grated zucchini and carrot, sprinkled with chia and flax seeds, and baked to perfection."

"Okay, I'll try one," Jake said, but Blair didn't miss the hesitancy in his voice.

Blair snorted. "One taste and you'll be hooked. I promise."

Jake flicked a skeptical glance at him, but he took the treat and carefully bit into it. His eyebrows shot up as he chewed. "This is amazing."

Warmth spread through Blair. Nothing felt better than making someone happy with the food or drinks he'd made.

Jake didn't speak again, as he ate his cheese crisp and sipped his latte, and Blair found he enjoyed the moment of solitude between them. While he'd only just met Jake, the silence felt comfortable in a way that surprised him as much as it didn't.

The fiery sunset had given way to deepening indigo. As though the enveloping darkness created a safe space for talking about hard things, Blair pointed to the pamphlet sticking out of Jake's pocket.

"I have one of those, too."

Jake glanced down and fear slashed across his face like a dagger. He shoved the pamphlet deeper into his pocket and jumped from the bench. Blair knew this time Jake wouldn't sit back down with a simple plea.

Without forethought, Blair reached out and put his hand on Jake's biceps. Jake froze.

"No, please. Don't go." Blair swallowed. He didn't want to invade Jake's privacy, but he also knew from experience that newly diagnosed people needed to know they weren't alone. "I didn't mean to pry, but I recognize the pamphlet because I have one, too. I've been living with HIV for over a decade now."

Jake's eyebrows shot to his hairline. "Over a decade? But you're— You're just a kid."

"I'm actually thirty-six." Blair shrugged and offered a smile. "But thank you for the flattery. I'll take it."

Blair swore he could see every wheel in Jake's head turning as Jake stared down at him. Jake exhaled so deep Blair was sure he had no breath left in his lungs. His shoulders dropped along with his head.

"Okay."

Jake lowered himself to the bench and sighed. Silence stretched between them again. Not so much uncomfortable, but charged with an intangible energy. That gut-deep feeling that something was about to happen—good or bad remained to be seen, but a change was on the horizon.

"Go ahead," Blair spoke softly, as though speaking too loudly might scare Jake off. "You can ask me anything."

Jake turned fully toward him and studied his face in the low light of early evening. He pursed his lips.

"Over a decade?" Jake repeated.

"I was twenty-two when I was diagnosed," Blair said, remembering that day and feeling much like he was sure Jake was right now. "I was a bit of a partier, let's say. Thought I was invincible and nothing bad would ever happen to me. Turned out I wasn't immortal after all." Blair smiled, but he knew it was a weak attempt. "It took a while to get my viral load stabilized, but once I finally accepted this was my life now, I took my health more seriously. I've been undetectable for years now."

"You look so young and healthy," Jake said, and then winced, as though he'd said the wrong thing.

"Youthful comes from good genes and healthy comes from a good lifestyle." Blair took a sip of his tea. "You can live a full and happy life with HIV, just like anyone else. But you do have to take care of yourself. Stick to your medication regime, get tested regularly, eat healthy, exercise. And luckily for you, these days you only need to take one pill a day. When I was first diagnosed, I had to take two. Treatments are always improving."

Jake scraped his hands down his face. "I just never thought this would happen to me. Especially at forty-three."

"It can happen to anyone anytime," Blair said. "And you could have had it for years before showing any symptoms."

Jake raised an eyebrow at that. His tone haughty when he said, "I've been married—*was* married—for sixteen years."

"And yet, here you are."

Jake stared at him and then slumped back on the bench. "And here I am." His next words were a whisper. "I don't know what to do now."

"Now, you come with me." Blair stood and held his hand out.

Jake frowned, gaze bouncing from Blair's open palm to his face and back. "Where?"

"Somewhere that will be good for you," Blair implored.

Jake stood and placed his hand in Blair's. Even though they'd been sitting outside in the cooling evening with a chill breeze coasting off the water, his skin was warm and soft, and his hand fit perfectly in Blair's. Blair gave him a squeeze of reassurance.

"Come on." Blair gave a little tug. "I just have to stop in the coffee shop and grab my salad."

Confusion etched across Jake's face, but he didn't say anything as he let himself be led by Blair.

CHAPTER 4

The Before Jake would have never let a near stranger lead him somewhere unknown with an ambiguous "somewhere good for you". As if said stranger had any idea at all about who Jake was and what would or wouldn't be good for him. But the After Jake, oddly, trusted Blair. He didn't have any concrete reason to trust Blair—or not to—but something in his gut said to follow. So he did.

He waited in the main café area of the Bliss Beans coffee shop that he vaguely remembered being in earlier, while Blair disappeared into the back. When Blair returned, he had one of those large eco-friendly salad bowls in his hand.

"This is a broccoli salad I made for the meeting tonight," Blair said, lifting the bowl. "Once a month, we have a potluck dinner to share healthy recipes you can make on a budget."

"We're going to a potluck?" Jake frowned as his nerves jangled. "I'm not sure I'm up for that. Even if I had something to bring."

"You're with me, so you don't need anything." Blair stopped in front of Jake. There was a quietness to his rich brown eyes, and his voice was soft and somehow soothing to Jake's anxiety. "You don't have to stay for dinner either. It's a low-key thing, and we don't eat until after."

"After?"

Blair's smile felt like sitting by a fire under a warm blanket. Like coming home and leaving the world's worries and stresses outside the door. Jake marveled at how a single smile could do all of that, but there it was again: he trusted Blair.

"What's your last name?"

Blair grinned. "Blissett."

Blair Blissett. Even his name was happy. Hopeful. Jake shifted his gaze to the menu board, and the name of the café handwritten across the top.

Jake chuckled, waving his arm to encompass the coffee shop. "Bliss Beans."

Blair's grin widened into a blinding smile. "You got it."

Bliss fit Blair. At least, fit the first impression Jake had of him. That he was one of those sunshine-y type people who saw the positive in everything. One side of Jake's mouth tipped up in an attempt at a smile. He slipped his hand into Blair's as easy and comfortable as though they'd been holding hands their whole lives.

"How do you do that?" Jake mused, not realizing he'd spoken his thought aloud until Blair turned a questioning look on him. Jake cleared his throat. "Uh . . . Make me feel like there's hope on the worst day of my life?"

"There is always hope," Blair said with all the sage wisdom of someone well beyond his years, and solidifying Jake's image of him.

Blair led Jake down the street and around the corner to Davie Street, where they hopped on an eastbound bus as a light rain began to fall from the dark skies. A dozen minutes later, they disembarked in Yaletown and walked another block to a local community center.

The look Blair sent over his shoulder at Jake was reassuring as he steered Jake into a large meeting room. Chairs set in a circle that took up most of the room sent a sliver of apprehension shooting up Jake's spine. He jerked his gaze away, toward the back corner of the room that sported a small kitchenette with two fridges. In front of a wall of windows that reflected the interior back to him was a large table with plates, cutlery and glasses stacked at one end, and an eclectic collection of food containers spreading across the center as though spilling from a horn of plenty. A crowd of mostly men and a few women, ranging in age from teen to senior, mingled and chatted amiably. But what had the air freezing in Jake's lungs and a chill of panic racing up his spine, was the welcome sign on a floor stand just inside the door.

Blair had brought him to a support group for people living with HIV and AIDS.

Jake's lungs released, and he gulped in air, but it wasn't enough. His breath hitched and heaved, coming faster and shallower. *Holy fuck. I have HIV.* His head swam and his vision wavered. *Christ. I'm going to pass out.*

Hands gripped his biceps, firm and steady. Blair's youthful, elfin face formed in front of him, his words low and soothing and somehow bringing Jake back to earth, even though Jake couldn't make out a single word. All he knew at that moment was that Blair was there. Blair had him and wouldn't let him go spiraling down the endless rabbit hole of despair.

Jake's gaze darted around the room, expecting everyone to be staring at him. Mocking him, even. But they quietly continued their conversations, as though knowing Jake needed space to find his equilibrium again.

"Hey," Blair said, his voice pitched low. "Right here."

Jake met his eyes and fell into their warm depths. A safe harbor in a new and frightening world. Jake inhaled deeply, the tightness easing from his chest and the fog clearing from his mind.

"There you are," Blair said.

He slid his palms down Jake's arms, but Jake gripped his hands before Blair let go, afraid he'd shatter apart without that calm connection.

"Sorry," Jake breathed.

Blair shook his head. "You have nothing to be sorry for. This is a safe space."

Jake nodded, taking another deep breath. He could do this. Blair had been living with HIV for fourteen years and seemed happy and healthy. Surely, he could too. Right?

"Okay." Jake reluctantly released his death grip on Blair. "I'm good. Thank you."

Blair put a hand on his shoulder and gave him a reassuring squeeze. "You've got this."

A bell jingled, drawing the attention of the small crowd. A tall man, casually dressed in jeans, a heather-gray henley, and orange sneakers, stood at the edge of the chair circle with a little silver bell in his hand. He wore a kind smile on his face as he watched everyone settle themselves in the chairs.

"Come on," Blair said, threading his fingers through Jake's and guiding him toward two empty seats.

Jake sat beside Blair but didn't let go of his hand. The only thing keeping him from bolting out the door, running home, and burying himself under the covers until this nightmare—where Andy cheated and dumped him for another man, and left him with an incurable parting gift—ended.

All eyes turned to the bell ringer as he sat in a chair directly across from Jake.

"Welcome to Bright Light. An HIV and AIDS support group," the man said. His voice was soft and carried a note of kindness. "For those of you new to the group, my name is Trent. I've been living with HIV for eighteen years and running this support group in one form or another for seven years."

"Hi, Trent," the group said in unison, apart from Jake and a slender young woman sitting a few seats over.

"This is a stigma and judgment-free space where we can share our experiences, both good and bad," Trent said, making eye contact with everyone while not singling anyone out. "Where we can find connection and friendship through shared experience, learn about new treatments and therapies, find an array of resources and programs, and learn to develop new coping mechanisms." Trent leaned back in his seat. "Who would like to start today?"

One by one, people shared their experiences with HIV and AIDS. No one looked at Jake expectantly, waiting for him to speak, and he relaxed as each person told their stories. Stories about how they'd contracted HIV or how they were there to support a loved one who was HIV positive. About how the diagnosis had affected their lives, and how they managed their disease and coped with the mental ups and downs.

There was the young man who'd been born with HIV, contracted in the womb by his drug-using mother, which Jake hadn't known until now was rare. A man who, much like Jake, had never thought it could happen to him, but who, unlike Jake, had lived recklessly. A trans woman who had contracted HIV from her partner. A man and woman who was there in support of their HIV positive son.

But the person who had moved Jake the most was an elderly man with the brightest blue eyes Jake had ever seen.

"Hi, everyone. I'm David," the man began, his voice strong and clear. "Yesterday was my seventy-third birthday."

Clapping and happy birthday wishes circled around the room. David stood—a blush streaking across his cheeks and his smile wide— and took a bow.

"I was living it up before AIDS hit, without a care in the world," David said. "That age of indestructibility known as my twenties. Except my twenties blended into my thirties without me noticing."

The small crowd chuckled.

"While I'd naively thought AIDS could never touch me, I'd lost too many good friends to the disease." David paused, his gaze going distant. He shook his head, as though clearing the memories, and continued. "When I turned forty, I realized it was time to grow up and do something with my life, so I started with a full physical. I'll never forget that day, when my doctor told me I had contracted HIV and to get my affairs in order because I wouldn't live to see forty-one." He held his arms out, his smile mischievous. "Clearly, he was mistaken."

The crowd clapped and whistled.

David spoke a little more about the changes he'd made in his life, and how he'd beaten the odds. He still walked three miles every day, performed in the local theater, and hosted a weekly brunch for those with HIV.

"Thank you, David," Trent said when David finished. "I know I speak for everyone when I say we're so grateful you're with us."

Jake found he was glad David was there, too. David had beaten the odds at a time when the odds were stacked heavily against him. Hope bloomed in Jake's chest.

He glanced around the room at the mix of faces that looked different now that he'd heard their stories. Even though those stories and journeys were all diverse and difficult to hear, there was an underlying thread they all shared. They all looked at the good side of life—at least the people here tonight did. They were eager to share and learn new ways to live with the disease. And most of all, they didn't let HIV dictate their quality of life.

Jake had HIV. But he wasn't alone. His diagnosis wasn't the end of his world. There would be life after—a happy and full life, even. The melancholy that had shrouded him like a two-ton thing began to ease. He had work to do. Change was on the horizon. But he was going to be okay.

Conversation moved on from personal stories to the latest research and new local resources, and then everyone rose from their chairs, some stretching backs stiff from sitting, and made their way toward the long table loaded with food.

"So . . .?" Blair turned to him, a wrinkle of worry creasing his forehead. "What did you think?"

"I think you were right," Jake said, fighting an unexpected urge to lean closer and kiss Blair. "That *was* good for me."

Blair's smile rivaled the sun. And for the first time since Andy had betrayed Jake in the worst imaginable way, that little bloom of hope he'd felt earlier began to spread.

CHAPTER 5

"Thank you again," Jake said when they exited the community hall and began walking back toward the bus stop while a light rain fell. "That was exactly what I needed."

"I'm glad," Blair said, as they stopped at the corner, waiting for the light to change.

Jake shrugged the collar of his jacket up, but didn't seem to mind the rain, while Blair tugged a beanie from his jacket pocket and pulled it on. Jake shoved his hands in his pockets and tipped his head to the sky. Eyes closed and a tilt to his mouth that threatened a smile. Blair selfishly took the moment to study Jake again. So different from the man he'd met mere hours ago. Now Jake stood taller. His shoulders were back and relaxed. The tension from around his eyes all but vanished, and the air surrounding him lighter.

A fully relaxed and at peace Jake was someone Blair wanted to know more. He wasn't fooling himself that there wouldn't be hard times ahead for Jake, but if Jake would let him, Blair would be there for him.

Jake lowered his head and turned a grin on Blair, who smiled back. The light changed and Blair walked silently beside him. He wanted to say so many things, but didn't know where to start, what exactly to say.

"So," Jake said as they reached the opposite corner. "About sex."

An unexpected laugh burst from Blair's lungs. "What about sex?"

"If two people are HIV positive," Jake began with a grin. "Then they can have all the sex they want without worry. Right?"

Blair stared at him for a second. Was that a hypothetical two people, or did Jake possibly mean them? Or was that just Blair's own wishful thinking?

"Not exactly," Blair said, drawing a frown from Jake. "There are different strains of the virus. Kind of like the flu, and now Covid-19. You can get a vaccine for one strain but still get sick from another. Except with HIV, it's a superinfection. HIV-SI. And it can increase viral load and disease progression."

"Oh." Jake looked down at the ground as he walked, his mouth flattened and the tightness back around his eyes. The odd raindrop dripped from the ends of his hair. "Blood tests would tell you what strain you have, though, right? So, you'd be okay then?"

"Yes, blood tests would tell you the strain you have." Blair dodged a couple coming the other direction down the sidewalk. "Even then, unless you're in a monogamous relationship, stick to your antiretroviral therapy, and your viral load is undetectable, you should always use condoms."

Jake was quiet the rest of the way. He had a lot to process, and everyone had to process in their own time and their own way. Fortunately, Blair had been able to introduce Jake to the support group on a day he needed it most. That Blair and all the members of the group made sure Jake knew they would all be there for him. That he was going to be okay.

When they reached the bus stop, Jake turned to face him.

"Do you live downtown?"

Blair raised his eyebrows. He'd expected Jake to ask more questions about life moving forward. Or sex. He shook his head.

"No. I have a condo in Kits."

"Nice." Jake rocked on his heels and looked down the street.

The bus that would take him back to the West End was approaching, and something squeezed in Blair's chest. He didn't want tonight to be over yet. Didn't want to say goodbye to Jake. Not now. Maybe never.

"I'd really like to see you again," Blair blurted. *Shit.* "As friends. I mean. To help with anything you need. With—" he waved his hand in the air "—you know. Ugh. Stop me now."

The bus drew closer, and a mix of panic and embarrassment roiled in Blair's stomach.

"I would like that," Jake said with a smile in his deep-timbred voice.

The bus stopped in front of them, and Jake took a couple of steps back.

"Your bus . . ." Blair pointed.

"I'll get the next one." Jake retrieved a cell phone from his inner jacket pocket and held it out toward Blair. "Let's exchange numbers."

Relief flooded Blair's veins. He swapped his phone for Jake's and entered his digits, while Jake did the same as the bus pulled away from the curb.

"I'm really happy I met you today," Jake said, his gaze steady and intense as he pocketed his phone but held onto Blair's hand.

"Me too."

The world could have been burning down around them for all Blair cared, so lost in Jake's chestnut stare as he was. Distantly, he was aware of people walking past them and the whoosh of tires on wet roads. A horn honked. A siren wailed from somewhere deeper in the city. The rain eased again, offering a no doubt brief reprieve.

Time ticked on, but in minutes or hours Blair couldn't say.

Jake looked away, running a hand over the back of his neck. But when his gaze returned to Blair's, there was a naked honesty in his eyes. A vulnerability in them that stole Blair's breath.

"I just really want to give you a kiss right now."

Oh my god, yes.

Blair opened his arms, and Jake fell into his embrace as though he'd always been there. Jake's kiss, the first touch of his lips, was tentative.

A gentle press of mouths. A question. The answer was yes. Blair had a feeling the answer would always be yes where Jake was concerned. He pulled Jake tighter to him but didn't push for more. Jake needed to be the one to take the lead. For tonight, at least.

Jake's tongue pressed at the seam of Blair's mouth, and he opened, letting Jake inside while shivers of delight raced from his head to his toes. How was it he'd only met this man today, when their lips and tongues moved together in blissful harmony, as though this had been a dance they'd perfected over shared years?

"Get a room!" someone shouted, and Jake chuckled against Blair's lips.

Jake rested his forehead against Blair's and then stepped back. He shoved his hands into his pockets as another bus approached. This time Jake moved toward the curb, but he was smiling. The light in his eyes sparking with desire and hope.

"See you soon, Blair Bliss . . . *ett*."

Blair returned the smile, not wanting Jake to go as the bus stopped, but confident this was only the start of something special for them. "See you soon, Jake I-Don't-Know-Your-Last-Name."

"Sheraton," Jake said, stepping up into the bus. "Like the hotel."

"See you Jake Sheraton, like the hotel," Blair joked.

Jake's laughter, full-bodied and free sounding, filled Blair's chest with warmth and promise.

He watched as Jake walked toward the back of the bus and sat down, watching Blair the whole way. Blair waved as the bus pulled away and his smile faded. He stood there, staring after the bus until it disappeared around a corner.

His phone pinged with a text message, but he ignored it. When it pinged again, he pulled his phone from his pocket and his mouth curved up at the sender's name.

Jake: *Thank you for everything today. For giving me hope.*

Jake: *I'm looking forward to getting to know you more. Is tomorrow too soon?*

Blair's heart fluttered, doing a little happy dance in the cage of his ribs, as he typed his reply.

Blair: *Anytime. I'm glad I was there for you. And tomorrow is perfect.*

He pocketed his phone and headed up the street with a skip in his step, to catch his own ride home.

"Tomorrow is perfect," he said aloud.

CHAPTER 6
FIVE MONTHS LATER

Jake pushed the front door of Bliss Beans open and entered with a bounce in his step. The jingling of the bell overhead drew Blair's attention. A smile stretched across his face that never failed to send a flush of warmth through Jake's chest.

"Hey, babe," Blair said as he crossed the floor and pulled him in for a kiss.

Blair leaned back, an expectant expression on his face, but Jake only grinned as he took in the coffee shop, which was closed for a private event tonight. Blair and Traci had already moved the back tables against the wall and formed a circle with the chairs.

He and Blair had started their own HIV and AIDS support group a couple of months after they'd started dating—the day after Jake had first met Blair—holding it at Bliss Beans, and so far, it had been well-attended. Jake was certain a good part of that had to do with the snacks and drinks Blair made specially for those nights. Speaking of which, Blair had arranged an array of healthy treats on one of the larger tables. Jake's stomach rumbled. He hadn't eaten since an early lunch. His nerves had been strung too tight to keep anything down.

"Is there anything left for me to do?" Jake slipped out of his jacket, snatching a smoked salmon cucumber bite on his way to the back room to hang his coat up.

"Hey! Those are for the members." Blair huffed at Jake's chuckle, following on Jake's heels. "What did the doctor say?"

"Mmm. This is amazing," Jake said around the fresh and smokey appetizer, hoping Blair made extra.

He hooked his jacket on the back of the office door and spun around. He reached for Blair, pulling him into his arms.

"Well?"

"Priorities, Bliss," Jake said before leaning in and claiming Blair's mouth.

It had been hours since he'd last felt Blair's silken lips against his own, and he wasn't about to let another second pass him by. That and Blair was fun to tease.

Blair snaked a hand behind Jake's neck, sliding his fingers into Jake's hair and sending a rush of desire through his veins. How could it be that every time he touched Blair was like the first time? That giddy feeling when the butterflies in his stomach took flight and promised something magical ahead. And that promise had never failed to deliver. Every single time.

Jake leaned back, reining himself in. "If we don't stop now, we'll be late for our own meeting."

"You started it," Blair said with a playful note in his soft voice. "And I'm waiting for an answer."

Jake grinned at the impatience in those warm brown eyes. Blair's hair was due for a trim, but Jake liked the extra bit of length. Liked how his brunet strands curled at the end and wrapped around Jake's fingers and framed Blair's youthful face. God, he was beautiful. Jake didn't know what forces had been at work to put Blair in his path, but he sent a silent *thank you* out into the universe. For the gazillionth time.

"I love you," Jake whispered, twirling a curl around his index finger.

"I know."

"Cheeky."

Blair snorted. "I love you, too. Now *please*, tell me."

"So . . ."

"Ugh. You're killing me here," Blair groused. "Out with it."

"Undetectable." Jake couldn't have stopped the smile that stretched across his face if he'd tried. He'd stuck to his regime until the new habit had become autopilot. And with Blair's help, he'd changed his lifestyle for the better. Eating healthy, though, that was because of Blair and the magic he worked in the kitchen, and working out regularly. One of his favorite times of day was when he and Blair ran around the seawall in the mornings before work.

"I knew it." Blair cupped his face in both hands and kissed him. "I had no doubt you'd get your viral load there."

"I couldn't have done it without you," Jake said between Blair's kisses.

And he meant it. He didn't know what he would have done if he hadn't stumbled into Bliss Beans all those months ago. He remembered feeling so lost, with no idea how to move forward or what to do next. But Blair had been there and had taken the time to show a total stranger that he had a full life ahead of him. That all his dreams were still attainable.

"You did the work," Blair countered and kissed him again. "This calls for a celebration."

"Yeah?" Jake slid his hands down Blair's back and cupped his butt cheeks. "I know just how, too."

The door swung open, and Traci poked her head inside. She froze, as did Blair, and Jake started laughing.

"Well." Traci quickly recovered. One eyebrow raised and a hand on her hip, the other still on the doorknob. "At least you've both got your pants on this time."

Blair dropped his head back and sighed. "That was *one* time."

"Whatever." Traci turned away with a smile she couldn't hide, mumbling something about not being paid enough. A second later, her voice echoed down the short hall. "Right yourselves and get out here. People are arriving."

"You heard the lady," Jake teased.

He pulled Blair in for another kiss, keeping this one rated-PG, and slid his hands down Blair's chest before putting some distance between them.

"After you," Blair said.

Half a dozen people were already mingling by the snack table when Jake returned to the main dining room.

"Hey, Jake. Blair," David said, his eyes bright and glittering. "Traci catch you two naked in the office again?"

"Oh my god," Blair groaned as Jake and David laughed. "*One time.*"

"Good to see you, David," Jake said, giving the older man a hug.

Since that first support group meeting Jake had attended with Blair, David had become one of his favorite people. He always had a new story to tell about his youth and his experiences living with HIV, and always in a humorous way. Jake and Blair were now regulars at David's weekend brunches. Just as David had become a regular at their support group. He still attended Trent's group, as did Jake and Blair, though not as often.

"I invited a friend tonight," David said as he loaded a plate with appetizers. That man had an appetite that could put an Olympic athlete to shame.

"Oh? What kind of friend?" Jake only now realized he'd never seen David with a partner.

David snickered. "Not that kind of friend. A Jake."

Blair frowned. "A *Jake*?"

The door swung open, the merrily jingling bell at odds with the young man who walked in with a dark cloud over his head so tangible, Jake felt the weight of it all the way across the room. Was that how he'd looked when he'd been first diagnosed? At his first support meeting? Probably. Though he'd had Blair there to help guide him through it.

"Ah. There he is now," David said.

Jake turned to meet Blair's gaze. Understanding in the warm depths of his eyes.

"A Jake," Jake said softly.

At Blair's nod, Jake planted a quick kiss on his lips before crossing the room to meet David's new friend.

"Welcome. I'm Jake." He extended a hand in greeting to the newcomer. "Don't worry, we've got you."

TO BE
BOLD
J.L. GRIBBLE

CHAPTER 1

DIMA

The last person Dima expected in his office on a Monday morning was the twink who'd sucked him off in a club bathroom about thirty-six hours earlier.

They both froze, Dima half-standing from his desk chair and the man hesitating in the doorway. "Please, come in," Dima said, and the potential study participant slipped inside.

A thick bubble of silence enveloped them as he tugged the office door closed and cut off the conversations in the hall. No photo accompanied the paperwork marking Jacob Nichols as next on Dima's interview schedule, and, well, they never exactly exchanged names. Dima also hadn't pegged him as twenty-five, but his black-framed glasses and smart casual attire were a far cry from Saturday night's body glitter and crop top. Of course, Dima assumed his lab coat came as a surprise after his own tight leathers. "Jacob Nichols?" he asked, half in confirmation of the guy's identity and half in hope he had stumbled into the wrong office.

At Jacob's jerky nod, Dima suppressed a sigh and waved to the chairs before his desk. "I'm Dr. Dmitri Moroz. Thank you for taking the time to meet with me about the long-term therapy trial."

Jacob sat across from him with the same grace that attracted Dima across the crowded dance floor. "Thanks. Erm. Pleasure to meet you?"

Dima chuckled. "Nice to meet you too."

Jake's worry lifted by the way he broke into a sweet grin. If his moves had called to Dima, his smile had sealed the deal. Memories of his mouth's delicious heat assaulted Dima. He shoved them away before they reached his cock and made this meeting even more uncomfortable.

Then Jacob's smile vanished as quickly as it appeared. "Oh. I suppose I don't qualify for the study anymore?"

Dima had already read over the contents of Jacob's application more than once. He shut the folder and moved it to the side of his desk. Jacob's face fell further, but Dima lifted a hand to stall any protests. "You're a good candidate. I'll give your file to one of my study assistants and make a note the other project lead should be consulted on anything relating to your care. By the time we review results in a few months, all data will be deidentified and our... previous involvement will not create any conflict of interest."

"Okay. Good." Jacob toyed with the sharp crease of his pants near his knee. "I'm glad you're not mad."

"Why would I be mad?" Dima swallowed the *sweetheart* that nearly followed his question. Jacob was no longer one of the unnamed men he showered with affection to ease the ache in his heart. Even if Jacob would also never be his patient, this ache was why Dima never wanted to learn their names.

Learning names was dangerous, especially when accompanied by the adorable crinkle of Jacob's nose as he gestured to his file. "Because I didn't tell you..."

"You told me you were on PrEP when I asked whether you'd be more comfortable if I wore a condom."

Jacob offered either a half-shrug or simply how he squirmed under Dima's sharp gaze. "I've been undetectable for over a year, and blow jobs are considered low risk. I feel like I should still be sorry for lying."

"Don't be. You gave me all the information I needed to weigh the risks on my end. Ultimately, all parties of a sexual encounter have to be responsible for themselves." Dima used the protective armor of his desk and lab coat to distance himself from the conversation. He'd pretend Jacob was one of hundreds of patients with whom he'd discussed the thorny topics of risk and disclosure. "Though I can only speak for myself," he added.

"Thank you. I appreciate it." Jacob peered at Dima through his eyelashes. "So, I'm not going to be your patient now. You wouldn't be...interested in getting together again sometime?" The pitch of his voice rose at the end, making obvious the question in his indirect words.

Dima had a physical type, which Jacob fit to a tee. The backbone and courage exhibited by the query acted as much as an aphrodisiac to Dima as Jacob's slender frame and wide doe eyes. Did Dima want a repeat, or more, with Jacob? Hell, yeah. But even as his body reacted, his heart shunned the idea, retreating to the safety of its hardened shell.

"I'm sorry." Dima steeled himself against Jacob's disappointment. "I don't think it would be appropriate."

Voice steady, he replied, "I understand. The study, and all."

Not quite, but allowing Jacob to blame the research trial on his rejection wasn't the worst option. Not when the alternative was the half-assed explanation Dima had given too often. He hooked up away from home, one and done, and the men stayed nameless for a reason.

"I do apologize that you'll have to return for another intake appointment with Dr. Paredes. The assistant who directed you to my office—please tell her I asked you to reschedule with her instead of online, so you can bypass repeating the review process." Dima rose from his chair, and Jacob echoed the action a beat later. This time, masochist that he was, Dima extended his hand across his desk.

"Thank you, Dr. Moroz." Jacob's handshake was firm, professional...and way too tempting. As was how his lips twitched with a touch of sass when he added, "Maybe I'll see you around."

"Maybe," Dima said, simultaneously praying for and dreading any future glimpse of Jacob in the halls outside.

Jacob exited Dima's office on the same light steps he'd entered.

Dima collapsed back into his chair, feeling every minute of his thirty-nine years. Even if they never encountered each other again, Jacob's file shined like a beacon atop his desk, containing phone number and email address in juicy temptation. Temptation Dima should not, and would never, take. As soon as enough time passed for Jacob to make his new appointment and leave the building, he'd bring the file to Amy and erase the man from his mind.

As always, when Dima craved peace and steadiness, his gaze sought the pictures framed in the corner of his desk. Jacob was younger than his brother Val, who grinned at Dima from one of the images. An irrelevant age difference for a club hookup but inappropriate for more.

Perfect for Sipho, though, frozen forever at twenty-seven. Sipho had loved boys whose sweet exteriors hid strong cores. He'd have brought Jacob home from the club the same night and not let him out of bed for days.

Dima's strong core remained, but Sipho's loss had stripped him of all sweetness. Except for the tiny bits he borrowed in clubs from gorgeous men he'd never see again.

CHAPTER 2

JAKE

"There you are!" Val popped up in the corner of the kitchen where Jake had retreated for a moment of solitude under the guise of refilling the chip bowls. "Someone else you should meet got here."

Jake did not want to meet anyone else, despite Val's golden retriever energy insisting otherwise. Jake was already peopled out an hour into this party, in fact, but he allowed Val to snag his hand and tug him back onto the patio. After all, Val was being kind enough to allow Jake to crash in his basement while he searched for a place to live for the next year. The least he could do was participate in the 'Welcome to Maryland' barbeque Val organized on his behalf.

He'd already forgotten many of the names of those Val introduced so far, and now he exchanged polite nods with them as Val hauled him past. At least when he ran into their fellow Space Force folks on base, their uniform nametapes would serve as a handy reminder. Currently, he only recognized Val's husband Sage and their roommate Weston on sight, and he'd already given up remembering their Air National Guard buddies. "I will meet everyone at work this week, you know," Jake tried to remind Val.

"Not this one," Val said. "He's not military." They reached the far corner of the patio where they'd set the drink coolers.

Weston spoke with animated arms to another man there, breaking off when he spotted them. "Sage owes me five bucks. I didn't think Dima would show."

Val clapped his hand on the newcomer's broad shoulder. "My brother loves our parties."

"Your brother loves you." The man smacked a kiss to Val's cheek and turned more fully toward them. His eyes widened for a fraction of a second before his face smoothed into bland politeness. "You must be the friend I heard so much about when Val lived in California. A pleasure to finally meet you, Jake."

Jake prayed he maintained half as much control over his own reaction, especially when shaking Dr. Moroz's hand resulted in the same sparks across his skin as when they touched in his office earlier that week.

As when he'd gotten to his knees for the stunning older man who'd allowed Jake to lose himself in giving pleasure the weekend before. The man who also happened to be his ex-boyfriend's older brother. Fuck his life.

Doctor-patient confidentiality probably also explained why Dr. Moroz acted as if this was their first encounter, and Jake blessed him for it. "You too, ah—" Jake cut himself off, not wanting to assume the privilege of the nickname Val used for his brother and definitely not wanting to reveal he'd met Val's brother in a professional capacity…or any other capacity. Val's half-brother, he finally remembered, given the different last names and their opposite coloring. Side-by-side, Jake picked out the minute family resemblances in the shape of their shoulders, the arc of their strong noses.

Sage darted through the crowd and zeroed in on his spouse. "Val, we should get another round of burgers on the grill."

Weston lit up at the request. "I'll help."

"Absolutely not," Val said. He nudged Jake forward. "Help Dima find a drink, will you?"

Panic surged in Jake's chest, but before he had a chance to suggest he help at the grill instead, Val and Weston vanished after Sage.

Leaving him alone with Val's brother, the heat of the man's touch lingering on his palm.

Not ready to face him, Jake dropped into a crouch and popped the cooler open. "Uh, what are you in the mood for? There's beer, soda, some hard seltzer…" As he trailed off, he risked a glance over his shoulder. A drastic error. Under bright afternoon sun, wearing cargo shorts and a casual T-shirt, Dr. Moroz exuded the same pure sexual appeal here as in a dark club with a harness crossing his deliciously furred chest. Though his shorts might be looser, Jake was already intimately familiar with the beast behind the fabric at his groin.

Dr. Moroz cleared his throat, and Jake jerked his attention to the man's face. "A Coke, please."

"Sure, got it." Jake wanted to bury his face in the ice to relieve the flames surely reddening his cheeks. Instead, he retrieved the requested can, along with a seltzer for himself, and handed it to Dr. Moroz before backing away. Not far enough to be impolite, but more than enough to keep him from succumbing to the urge to drop to his knees and rub his face against the tempting bulge. Because that would be ridiculous.

This was Val's *brother*. Forget either of their previous exchanges. That fact should be reason enough alone for Jake to erase the sexy older man from of his mind once and for all.

While he sipped his drink and tried to look anywhere but Val's brother, Dr. Moroz's dark gaze remained firmly locked on him. As if finally coming to some sort of decision, he released Jake from his inscrutable stare, peering across the patio and shaking his head. "I'm going to rescue my brother and Sage from Weston trying to help with the grill. There's a reason I don't practice emergency medicine."

His wink invited Jake to share the joke, and he laughed. Less than two weeks sharing a house with the man was more than long enough to know Weston's whirlwind energy shouldn't mix with fire. "Good call."

Instead of moving away as the other man passed, Jake indulged in a last whiff of Dr. Moroz's spicy cologne, a last brush of his body heat. He got more than he bargained for when the man paused in Jake's personal space, gripping his elbow and ducking to whisper in Jake's ear. "Relax, Jake. Your secrets are safe with me. And please, call me Dima."

Jake shivered in the warm summer air at the brush of the soft words. He resisted the urge to lean closer. "Thank you…Dima."

Dima smiled, maybe the first true one Jake had seen from him by the way the skin crinkled at the corner of his eyes. Then, he released Jake and moved away through the crowd.

They'd now crossed each other's paths three times in barely a week. What were the odds Jake could make it through a year stationed in Maryland without running into his ex's brother again?

Jake stuck to his fellow military personnel after, his new coworkers at Joint Base Andrews. Easy enough to avoid another conversation with Dima, but not to ignore the heat of his stare. Dima had no reason to stare at him. Jake was just the military buddy crashing with Dima's little brother. Their worlds shared nothing in common. They had no reason to chat.

Nothing to see here, move along.

The strategy worked like a charm the rest of the afternoon and evening. Until the last of the guests cleared out, leaving Jake and Dima at the patio table with the remnants of the fudge brownies Val baked for dessert. Jake had avoided sitting beside Dima, who lounged lazily at the opposite side of the table. Now he couldn't look at the others without also catching Val's brother's eye.

Weston pointed the neck of his beer toward Jake, "I learned a previously undisclosed fact this afternoon. That you and Val dated out in California."

Jake might have grown nervous if not for Weston's lips teasing a grin and the outright laughter from Sage. He might have expected this line of inquiry from Val's actual husband, but he'd gleaned from Val's stories over the years that few boundaries existed between the three long-time friends. "We may have gone on a few dates." The easiest way to explain their handful of less than satisfying physical encounters, neither man able to give the other what he wanted or needed, until they decided they'd be much better suited as friends than lovers.

"Is that what the kids are calling it these days?" Weston asked.

Val smacked his shoulder. "I told you about Jake!"

Weston turned to Sage. "Did you know about Jake?" Sage rolled his eyes and snagged the last brownie from the tray between them.

"I knew about Jake." Dima tipped his water bottle to Jake in a silent salute, and Jake flushed. How did the man stay so unruffled? Wasn't this as awkward to Dima as to Jake, knowing he'd been intimate with the same man as his younger brother?

"A few dates, huh? Val wasn't good enough for you?" Weston asked.

Jake could give as well as he got. "I'd call Val the one that got away, except I never actually had him. He was always too busy pining after someone back home."

"Aww, I love you too, boo." Sage leaned into Val's space for a kiss.

Val indulged him a quick peck before turning to Dima. "Speaking of Jake...I wanted to run something by you."

Jake froze. Oh no. Val had mentioned the day before that he had an idea about Jake's living situation, but he'd forgotten in all the stress of the party. He couldn't rely on Val's hospitality forever, especially with the daily commute he'd start on Monday. But this area provided slim pickings for a single sergeant.

"Jake should rent your spare room," Val continued, oblivious to Jake's mental attempts to cut him off.

No way would Dima go for it. The list of reasons not to agree to Val's proposal ran a mile long, beginning with Dima's role in the injectable medication trial and ending with Jake's knees on a club floor. He was sure to have some smooth excuse about why Jake couldn't stay with him. Monday, Jake would look into his last-case plan of moving into a room on base. Turned out to be second-last.

"Sure. Happy to help any friend of Val's."

Blood rushed in Jake's ears like a record scratch. Dima couldn't be serious. The man was so even-keeled that maybe Jake missed a layer of sarcasm. But when he chanced a quick peek at Dima, Val's brother gifted Jake with a tiny smile and slow blink, as if reassuring him all was well.

All was not well.

"Uh, thanks," Jake said, mouth dry and wishing he hadn't finished his last drink. "That would be—yeah. That could work."

Val beamed at the success of his brilliant plan before peppering Dima with questions about the state of his condo and other logistics. Jake should have participated in the conversation, as the renter in question. Instead, he grabbed the empty brownie tray and a few left-over bottles from his side of the table and escaped to the kitchen.

The running sink as he scrubbed the baking dish covered Dima's entrance. Jake jerked, splashing water onto his shirt, when the bigger man leaned his hip on the counter nearby. Why Dima ever accepted a hookup with him was a mystery, because clearly Jake was a mess. No wonder he'd rebuffed Jake's attempted flirting in his office. Jake finished rinsing the dish and shut off the water, plunging the kitchen into silence.

They had mere moments of privacy before one of the others came inside. "Why?" he asked, voice almost a whisper. "You turned me down last time."

Dima stared at the tile floor, then glanced up at Jake with a soft huff of laughter. "I'm still turning you down," he said. "But I'll never turn Val down. You need a place to stay. That's all this is."

The last of the alcohol Jake drank should have worn off by now. But only lingering tipsiness explained the flash of longing he caught on Dima's face. Or maybe Jake was projecting. He needed to suck it up and find a shitty place on base.

Instead, he pulled his phone from of his pocket. "I guess I should get your address."

CHAPTER 3

DIMA

Dima has never lived with a roommate. Not in college, when he stayed with his paternal grandparents, nor during medical school or residency, renting a string of studios barely big enough for the bed he never saw. Val didn't count, even during the times they lived together as adults, because Dima once changed his brother's diapers. Sharing an apartment with Sipho in Cape Town didn't count either, because they'd created a home together as partners. Val and Sipho were family.

Roommates, by definition, were not family. They were supposed to be stressful, a constant exercise in compromise. Yet sharing space with Jake came a million times easier than living with either his brother or lover.

Footsteps hit the stairs to the condo's second level. By the time Jake poked his head into the condo's supposed third bedroom Dima used as an office, Dima had saved his work. He greeted the young man with a smile. "Good morning, Jake." He'd learned the first week that not smiling at Jake was impossible.

"Morning!" Jake clutched a giant travel mug, but he placed a steaming coffee at Dima's elbow. He wore his weekend usual, tight jeans and a colorful graphic T-shirt. Today's featured old-school Rainbow Brite, which fit his personality much better than the drab military uniform he donned the rest of the week. "I wanted to check whether you needed to add anything to the list on the fridge before I leave."

"Not unless you used the last of the milk by spoiling me again." Dima picked up the fresh cup and inhaled the vanilla sweetness mingled with the stronger notes of dark espresso. As he predicted, Jake brought him a latte brewed to perfection and doctored with one of the fancy syrups that had joined his plain sugar bowl in the pantry.

Jake wrinkled his nose. "What's the point of having a machine that can make all the fun drinks otherwise?"

"Only weekends, Jake." Otherwise, Dima needed to find room in his schedule to spend way more time at the gym to burn the extra calories. "I'll keep it black on work mornings, please."

"Fine." Jake huffed in mock irritation. "Black like your soul," he added with an adorable giggle that was a better hit than a triple shot of espresso.

"Exactly." Dima maintained his stern expression, but his eyes shut in bliss at the first sip. Anyone would melt at the taste of such perfection.

"We still on for the next season of *Unsolved Mysteries* tonight?" Jake asked. "I was thinking of homemade pizza while we watch since I know we'll want to mainline a bunch of episodes."

"Good idea." Dima had quietly become addicted to spending time with him. He loved sitting on the couch with someone else who appreciated his surround sound setup as much as he adored listening to Jake speculate about the subject matter. "It's a—"

He cut himself off. A casual night in wasn't a date. It was two roommates splitting dinner while watching TV. Nothing more.

Though his mouth twitched, Jake didn't call Dima on the slip. "Cool, I'll add toppings to the list." He plucked Dima's empty coffee cup from earlier off his desk and left the office, calling over his shoulder, "Don't work too hard, it's Saturday!"

Jake didn't have to tidy Dima's mess, but he'd never once balked at doing a few extra dishes or asking whether Dima needed to add to a load of washing. He'd also accepted a few regular household tasks like shopping for basics, taking advantage of his access to the tax-free grocery on his military base. Jake made his life easier in a thousand tiny ways. Dima didn't deserve to have such a sweet boy caring for him, even preparing his morning coffee since Jake left for work about ten minutes earlier.

Fuck, he had stop thinking of Jake as a boy. Jake may be younger, but he was Dima's tenant. Jake used to date Dima's baby brother. No matter the circumstances of their first meeting, Jake was off limits to Dima. Jake was not, and would never be, Dima's boy.

The front door closed downstairs. Dima rose from his desk and crossed the hall into his bedroom, still nursing the latte as he sank to the edge of his bed. He'd returned to the U.S. with few mementoes of his time in South Africa, but the large framed print across the room of sunset painting the mountains over Cape Town never failed to soothe him with the reminder of better times. Earlier times, as in the picture of him and Sipho at his bedside, when he was much closer to Jake's age and carried none of the black marks now staining his soul. He and Sipho might have happily lusted after Jake together, but too much time and too many issues separated Dima and Jake now.

Such as the difference in their ages and how Dima knew Jake's name. He'd already carved one name into his heart. He'd have to be content with Jake existing on the outside. At least there, Dima was privileged enough to enjoy his smile.

And his untapped barista talents, as Dima drained the last of the latte.

CHAPTER 4

JAKE

Jake lived for the moments when Dima forgot himself. When he put his hand to the small of Jake's back as he moved past him in the condo's kitchen. When he stretched his arm along the couch and teased a finger through the light hair at the nape of Jake's neck. When he cracked up at one of Jake's dumb puns, losing his studied reserve and the chronic lines of tension along his eyes and plush lips.

He should feel guiltier about all the ways he'd imagined those lips on his body. But now, nine weeks after moving in with Dr. Dmitri Moroz, eleven weeks after the last time Jake had his mouth on him—so he was counting, sue him—he'd wondered whether the chemistry between them was entirely one-sided.

No matter how many amazing espressos Jake brewed, or how many cute outfits he wore on the weekends, or how many times he wandered between his first-floor bathroom and bedroom wearing a towel when he knew Dima had a clear line of sight from the living area, he barely needed both hands to count the times Dima forgot himself and teased glimpses of the potential between them.

Dima rented him a room simply because Val asked. It wasn't as if

Jake could afford no place else and was trying to take advantage of Dima.

Okay, at least not take advantage of him that way.

Jake glared at his reflection as he splashed water on his face, rinsing away the last of the shaving cream. He shaved once a week, using an electric razor in his car the rest of the time, and the Sunday-evening ritual was his time to reset. Gear himself up for the work week and resume the professional persona that, despite his age, meant the U.S. government entrusted him with millions of dollars of electronics.

He opened the medicine cabinet to stow away his razor and shaving cream, the pill bottle on the lowest shelf catching his eye. His daily reminder that he'd be reliant on medication for the rest of his life to keep himself, and everyone around him, healthy. At least until he heard whether he'd made it into the injection trial. One shot every three or four months to keep his viral load undetectable? Sign him the fuck up.

With the pills also serving as a recurring reminder of his second encounter with Dr. Dmitri Moroz, a tiny part of Jake wondered whether something more kept Dima from getting too close. He shut the cabinet door and wrinkled his nose at himself in the bathroom mirror. Ridiculous. Dima's entire job revolved around working with people with HIV. He'd barely twitched when Jake disclosed his status after their hookup.

For all Dima's mouth-wateringly assertive toppy vibes their night at the club, he'd been nothing but respectful the times they met after and since Jake moved into the condo. He wasn't sure how else to convey to Dima that he was open to so much more without crossing actual lines.

As expected, he found Dima clicking through Netflix summaries while he lounged like the king of his domain in the corner of his comfortable sectional sofa. His threadbare USAF tank top probably once belonged to Val and showed tantalizing hints of chest hair. To say nothing of the sweats that showed equally tempting evidence he wore nothing underneath. The sight made Jake want to drop to his knees and mouth at Dima through the soft cotton. Maybe he needed to abandon subtlety and serve himself up on a silver platter.

Instead of a spot at a far end of the sectional, Jake dropped onto the cushion next to Dima. He tugged his feet up until he sat cross-legged, one of his knees pressing into Dima's thigh. Jake spared a moment to wish he'd donned one of his tiny pairs of sleep shorts instead of pajama pants, but the bigger man radiated heat even through two layers of fabric.

"Have you watched this one?" Dima asked, attention not leaving the screen as he gestured with the remote. "I can't tell whether it's trying to take itself seriously or not."

Jake promptly forgot what the screen displayed. He was too busy trying not to freak out that, in his distraction, Dima dropped his free arm from the back of the couch and around Jake's shoulders. With a single tug, Dima could tuck Jake into his side, against all the firm, solid warmth he'd craved for weeks. Had the move worked? Or would Jake break the spell the moment he answered, shattering the moment?

He was certain he tried for some sort of suave response, not the high-pitched squeak which emerged. The relaxed arm curled around Jake's narrow shoulders froze, then vanished, as Dima retreated inward. When Jake peeked sideways, a ruddy flush stained Dima's cheeks under his evening scruff.

Not meeting Jake's eyes, he muttered, "Sorry."

At least he hadn't lunged to the far side of the couch, like the first guy Jake disclosed his status to after his diagnosis—months after the guy before failed to disclose his.

Though he'd better learned to bite his tongue under the not-so-gentle ministrations of drill instructors, sometimes Jake's mouth still ran away from him. "I get it, okay?" he snapped. "Don't get too close to the infected guy."

Dima opened his mouth. Closed it before speaking. He leapt to his feet, pacing away from the couch before whirling on Jake. He strangled another response with a vicious shake of his head.

With a groan, Jake dropped his face into his cupped hands, and he sensed more than heard Dima move farther away. Did he chase after him and apologize for overstepping or run to his room and start packing? Jake's confidence in a dark club had led him into the arms of the sexiest man he'd ever been with. Now, his attitude meant that man kicking him to the curb.

"Here."

Jake lifted his head in time to catch the orange bottle Dima tossed to him. His stomach sank to the floor and beyond. Despite his outburst, he'd never expected his worst-case fear to be *true*. He squeezed the bottle and laughed, the sound harsh as it escaped his throat. "What, you think I needed proof of why you don't want to touch me?"

Dima dragged his hands down his face. "That'd make me pretty fucking hypocritical. Read the name on the prescription, Jacob."

He released tingling fingers, and the print on the label slowly resolved itself into words. Dmitri Moroz. Triumeq.

Which meant…

When Jake looked up at Dima, the other man nodded once. "Fuck," Jake whispered. He placed the bottle on the coffee table with a trembling hand and resisted the urge to hide his face again.

Dima edged around the coffee table and returned to the couch. To Jake's shock, he resumed his original position and, telegraphing the motion, lifted his arm until it once again rested around Jake's shoulders.

Though Jake fucked up their evening, Dima's hesitancy wouldn't do. Dima should never wonder whether he could touch Jake, because the answer was always yes, yes, yes. He leaned sideways and burrowed himself into Dima's chest until both the man's arms wrapped around his smaller frame. "Sorry I'm an asshole," he whispered, wanting to shut his eyes but fearing that if he did so, he'd open them again to find the embrace nothing but a dream.

Dima's body slowly loosened, his shoulders lowering and arms relaxing. Maybe he'd needed this wall broken down just as much. "It's okay," Dima said. He followed the assurance by pressing a kiss to the crown of Jake's head. "I'm an asshole sometimes too, sweetheart."

Jake lifted his head slowly, braced for Dima to put space between them once more. Instead, Dima rearranged them on the sofa until Jake sat half in his lap, where Jake remained nestled in Dima's grasp.

"I haven't seen this one," Jake said. Confusion clouded Dima's face for a beat, until Jake jerked his chin at the television, still showing the Netflix info for a true crime special. "But I heard it's supposed to be pretty good despite the silly title."

"Guess we should check it out." Dima settled them again, until they could both view the screen without straining their necks. As he snagged the remote and hit play, another ghost of a kiss dropped against Jake's hair.

CHAPTER 5

DIMA

Dima was a right bastard for not keeping strict boundaries from day one, allowing Jake to so seamlessly insert himself into Dima's daily routines. Jake had made his desire for more clear through every look, every gesture, from the moment he moved in. No wonder his mixed signals led to Jake's snap the other night. Sharing his status with Jake, then consoling him, had been an easy decision in the moment.

Despite erasing one barrier, Jake never pressed for more. After the TV episode, he'd kissed Dima's shoulder through his shirt and retreated to his bedroom. Too bad Dima's vow the next morning to better distance himself had crumbled over a mug of freshly brewed coffee and Jake's bright-eyed cheer. The next night found them together on the couch again. And the next night, and the next.

Dima loved his work, but he found himself counting the hours until he returned to the condo that had gone from a place he lived to one that suddenly felt like home. But aside from the evening snuggle sessions, nothing else changed. Jake still prepared his morning coffee, they still coordinated which of them cooked dinner each night, and neither man gave words to the shift occurring between them, as if addressing the topic might shatter the fragile balance. For a man so young, Jake had the patience of a saint. Maybe it was a military thing. Val was the same way. Even-keeled and accepting of all life threw at him.

Dima should not be thinking about his little brother while he curled around Jake, holding him firmly against his body.

He shouldn't be cuddling Jake at all, spooning him on the couch, one of his hands sweeping up and down the smaller man's bare torso. Each time his fingers brushed a sensitive spot, every wriggle of Jake's adorable ass sent shocks of pleasure straight to Dima's cock. The documentary narrator droned on the television screen, but the boy in his arms captured Dima's sole focus the moment he dropped onto the couch and nestled into Dima's chest.

His cock rested heavy against his thigh, but he resisted rocking his hips against Jake no matter how much the man in his arms squirmed. A few short months ago, Saturday night might have found Dima in Baltimore or DC, but he hadn't made the trek since Jake moved in. He enjoyed this quiet dance so much more than the messy, writhing heat of a deafening club.

Dima nuzzled his face into Jake's soft hair until he caught the sweet vanilla echoes of his shampoo. He swept his hand low again, teasing his fingers through the fuzz below Jake's navel but stopping short of dipping under the waistband of the sinfully tiny shorts Jake called pajamas. He craved the wiggle that came next even as he braced for it. Jake's whimper, though, rocked through him like lightning.

Even though they played with fire, Jake was the last person he wanted to burn. Dima shifted, intending to withdraw.

In a flash, Jake snagged his wrist and kept Dima's hand in place. "Don't you dare."

Jake's ragged whisper should have been lost under the volume of the television, but all of Dima's senses had tuned to a single channel. "I'm crossing lines I shouldn't."

When Jake released Dima's arm, he didn't move away. Instead, he twisted on the narrow strip of couch until they lay face to face, straining Dima's self-control further. Jake made no attempt to hide the evidence of his matching arousal, and the heat of his erection seared through the flimsy protection of Dima's shirt. A matching heat flared in Jake's expression. "We can keep pretending the lines exist," he said, "or we can—"

The front door swung open, cutting off Jake's words. A familiar voice called, "Brother, I come bearing gifts!"

The couch blocked them from immediate view. Dima tightened his hold on Jake when the other man tried to slither to the floor. Val's ill-timed arrival promised an awkward conversation, but the condo's open-plan living area allowed no escape. Their intimate proximity would be obvious the moment they sat up. Dima maneuvered them both, making sure his larger frame didn't dump Jake to the floor as he stood. He turned to Val, facing the inevitable head-on. "Ever hear of knocking?"

That wasn't quite fair. Dima had always maintained an open-door policy for Val. This was the first time in his brother's entire adult life Dima ever had anything to keep private. Not to hide, though. Dima would never allow Jake to think Dima was ashamed of him. Even if he had no idea where they currently stood.

Any smart remark from Val fizzled out. Dima saw his brother's brain short-circuit in real time as Jake rose from the couch next to him. Jake's tiny shorts would have hidden no secrets, but at least Val's inter-ruption had shriveled their erections. Jake jabbed a thumb toward his bedroom, already moving that direction. "I'm gonna..."

His door shut moments later. Dima didn't blame Jake for aban-doning him. Val was Dima's idiot baby brother. He'd take the first hit.

Val's strike didn't disappoint. "No. Not him."

Trust, Dima had been telling himself that for weeks. Funny how Val skipped over the bigger elephant in the room first. "This wasn't how I expected to come out to you."

Scoffing, Val rolled his eyes. "Please, I've known you were some flavor of queer since I was a kid. We'd have a much bigger problem if I thought you were using Jake as an experiment."

"I'm glad you have that much faith in me, at least." Dima edged around the couch but left distance between himself and Val, who had yet to move further inside than the tiled foyer. His brother clutched a paper bag with a white-knuckled grip. "You said something about gifts?"

"Nope." Val tucked the package closer to his body. "You don't deserve the good baklava."

This explained the unexpected drop-in. Sage adored a Greek restaurant nearby, and Val never hesitated to stop by when in the neighborhood. His love language was food, though, so withholding one of Dima's favorite desserts meant real trouble. "I get why you might be upset," Dima said, measuring his tone the same way he would with an irate patient.

"Do you?" Val shoved the bag onto the kitchen counter, the better to wave his hands as he ranted. "Jake's one of my best friends. He's way too young for you. And if neither of those things weren't enough on their own, you've never dated anyone for as long as I can remember. I figured you might be ace, or maybe aromantic like Weston. But no, you were just hiding from me." Hurt seeped into his voice around the terse words.

"Not ace or aro." Dima dragged his hands over his face. "I know I owe you an apology." Definitely for hiding for so long, especially when Val had called him so often from California agonizing about his own sexuality. Not for Jake, though, even if Val's arguments echoed those Dima had with himself many times over through the past weeks.

"I literally gave you a fucking list," Val said. "But that's okay, because I'm not ready to hear one."

"Val—"

"Not tonight, Dmitri." Val broke out the big guns with his use of Dima's full name. He pointed to Jake's bedroom. "That man is one of the sweetest people on earth. I don't know whether you've got no dating experience, or if you've been quietly leaving a string of broken hearts behind you. Either way, Jake doesn't deserve anyone who won't go all in. And I'm not sure you're capable of that."

Therein lay the problem. Dima wasn't sure either. He'd already given away his heart and lost it forever. In the nearly two decades since, keeping any emotional ties at arm's length had been so much easier. He'd siloed away such a huge part of himself that he'd never even confided in his own brother.

And now he'd remained quiet too long. Val uttered another snort of disgust. "Yeah, that's what I figured. Leave him alone, Dima." He flung the front door open and exited without another word.

He did, however, forget the baklava.

After Dima turned the lock behind Val, Jake's bedroom door pulled him like a magnet. Val thought him incapable of going all-in with a relationship. Maybe that had been true before, when pretending a huge part of his life never happened had been so much easier.

But whatever brewed between them was no longer a private push and pull between Dima and Jake alone. And somewhere between a club bathroom and early morning coffee, Jake made Dima not want to pretend anymore.

CHAPTER 6

JAKE

"No. Not him."

Jake didn't need to hear more after he finished tugging on joggers and a long-sleeve shirt. He buried his head under his pillow to block the rest of the brothers' conversation. He didn't want to hear Val list all the reasons Jake hadn't been good enough, and for Dima to agree Jake also wasn't good enough for him. Their relationship may have been fleeting, and the split mutual, but no one ever kept Jake around for long. Though their physical chemistry wasn't in question, and they coexisted well as roommates, that didn't mean Jake and Dima had a shot at anything more.

Maybe he should accept the timing of Val's interruption as a blessing in disguise.

A gentle rap at the bedroom door roused Jake from his mental spiral. He shifted the pillow and called, "Yeah?"

Would Val enter to warn Jake off his brother? Or worse, had Dima arrived to inform Jake things weren't working out, and he needed to find someplace else to live as soon as possible?

The door swung open, the hall light framing Dima in the threshold.

The second option, then. Except after the briefest pause, Dima entered the room and perched on the side of the mattress. He lifted his hand, froze for no more than a second, and ran gentle fingers through Jake's mussed hair. "Val left. I'm sorry about all that."

Jake wanted to rub his scalp against Dima's fingers like a cat. He settled for a half-shrug. "Not your fault. Everything okay?"

Dima chuckled humorlessly. "No. But Val is angry with me, not you. He's not fond of the idea of you and I in a relationship."

"I'm sure you told him we weren't in one." Jake hated to move away from Dima's touch, but this wasn't a conversation to have lying down. He shifted until he sat cross-legged on the bed, one knee brushing Dima's thigh.

"I may not have been transparent with him about certain aspects of my life, but I do my best not to lie to my brother." When Jake gaped at him, he added, "I'm pretty sure you and I qualify as having been in a relationship for at least the past week, if not the last month."

"Because I crossed so many lines," Jake said, echoing Dima's concern from earlier and evading his gaze.

Dima caught Jake's chin with his fingers. "None of that. We both crossed them. Which should speak for itself, yes?"

He'd leaned closer, leaving Jake simultaneously trapped by Dima's piercing gaze and freer than ever before. He closed his eyes, but not to hide. Their mouths crashed together in a kiss. Messy and uncoordinated for a beat, until Jake yielded under the hand Dima curled around his nape.

As much as Jake enjoyed the thrill of a partner who was a blank slate, he adored the connection that came from knowing the person in his arms. Or in this case, the person who held Jake in his arms, tugging him closer until he sat half in Dima's lap. Dressing had seemed a good plan in the moment, but he wanted to rewind time before Val's arrival, when Dima ran his hands over Jake's bare skin. This was already a million times better than their long-ago club encounter, and they were still fully dressed. Jake broke away, catching his breath and reaching for the hem of his shirt.

"Wait," Dima whispered, squeezing Jake's neck.

Jake froze, panic threatening as Dima stood. Had he read this all wrong?

But Dima never let Jake go, collecting both his hands and kissing each set of Jake's knuckles in turn as he drew him off the bed. The smile lines at Dima's eyes crinkled. "If I get to have my hands all over you this time, and I plan to, we're not going about this half-assed when I have a much bigger bed upstairs."

Dima's gaze rake down his front like a physical touch, which only made him crave more. Jake stole his hands back to tug off his shirt. "I support this plan." The double in Dima's spare room accommodated Jake's slight frame fine, but he'd happily follow wherever Dima led. He'd return to his knees for Dima, or whatever other position the man desired. Especially if he followed through on the promise of hands all over him.

True to his word, Dima's touch never left Jake's skin. They stumbled more than once as they moved upstairs, laughing together between more kisses that left them both breathless. When Dima pushed his bedroom door open, though, Jake broke away. He'd never stepped foot in this space before, and he hungered for more than the other man's body.

A stunning sunset print claimed point of pride as the room's statement piece, but the simple framed photograph atop a nightstand drew Jake's greater curiosity. A younger Dima, maybe even less than Jake's current age, stood behind a gorgeous Black man. Together, their smiles outshone the sun on the opposite wall. "Who's this?" he asked, drawing a finger along the edge of the frame.

Dumb question. The man was obviously someone important to Dima. And likely someone long gone, judging from the age of the picture and his absence in Dima's current life. Dima stepped behind Jake and wrapped his arms around him once again, resting his chin on Jake's shoulder. "Sipho." Dima's simple response carried only happiness, not sorrow or longing. He ran his nose along the edge of Jake's ear, adding, "We were together when I lived in South Africa, but he passed away before I returned to the U.S."

"I'm sorry."

Where awkwardness might have ensued, Dima's confident touch

never faltered. "Thank you," he said. "He's why I closed myself off for so many years. I guess, over time, it simply became habit. To never let anyone close enough to risk the pain of such loss again."

Jake spun in Dima's arms, rising on his tiptoes to brush the gentlest kiss yet across his lips. "Until I moved in. Because you don't lie to Val, but you can't tell him no, either."

"An ability you two have in common, apparently." Dima tugged at the elastic waistband of Jake's joggers, dragging them down Jake's thighs until he stepped out of them. "I've been wanting to see all of you since the night at the club."

He might not win any lifting competitions, but military fitness standards meant Jake had nothing to be ashamed of. He loosely circled his stiff cock and smirked, happy to fish for compliments. "And?"

Almost dazed, Dima replied, "You are absolute perfection." He shot a glance at the picture behind Jake, and his grin widened. "Sipho would have adored you. Would have dragged you home that first night and never let you leave."

"What about you?" Jake asked as he helped Dima shuck his own shirt and sweats. "Always wanted a houseboy of your own?"

The joke didn't fall flat so much as it melted under Dima's heat. He drew Jake onto the bed until they pressed together skin-to-skin. The pressure of Dima's hard cock against his eased one of the needs crawling under Jake's skin and awakened a dozen more.

"You're worth so much more than a simple houseboy," Dima said. "And it's my turn to show you how much you've driven me out of my mind the best ways possible since the night we met."

The last of the barriers, physical or otherwise, crumbled between them as Dima caught Jake in another fierce kiss, holding him close. So close that the heat of their bodies mingled with the heat that had already simmered so long, now erupting into a boil. Jake had assumed he'd take the lead, coaxing Dima toward the bliss he deserved. He urged Dima to roll atop him, to cover Jake with his larger body until he filled all Jake's senses. To Jake's surprise and pleasure, zero hesitancy slowed Dima's movements as they writhed together in a dirty grind that ruined both the neatly made bed and Jake for all other men.

He was no pillow princess, giving as much as he took, but the intensity threatened to send him to his peak way too soon. Jake tried to flip them again, plotting to get his mouth further south than Dima's mouth and neck. Dima lifted to his elbows instead, pressing a hand to Jake's chest when Jake surged after him.

Jake froze, not from Dima's touch but at the emotion that swirled in his dark eyes. No man had ever stared at him like this. He was used to partners who looked on him with hunger, but not this deeper need. "This isn't like at the club, is it," Jake blurted. This wasn't anything like the hookup that had first brought them together.

Alone, the statement didn't make much sense. A crooked grin teased at Dima's kiss-swollen lips, though, showing those dark eyes saw everything Jake couldn't put into words. Dima kissed and nipped his way down Jake's front until he hovered over his aching cock. "No, it's not." His rough whisper made Jake's cock jump, and he chuckled. "I thought shallow and meaningless was all I needed, but all that did was keep me trapped by my past."

"And now? Here?" Jake's questions ended in a moan as Dima dipped to mouth at him, enveloping his length in a heat even better than when they'd rutted together.

"Now," Dima said, releasing Jake with a dirty pop, "you've reminded me I don't have to fear beginnings." He chuckled as Jake tilted his hips, urging him back to where Jake now needed him more than he needed his next breath. "Along with how much I've missed doing this in a bed."

Dima once again sucked Jake into his mouth, and he abandoned any further attempts at introspection. As hot as their encounter at the club had been, it had merely scratched an itch. For both of them, it seemed. Now, he abandoned himself to the delight of sharing his body with a man who already knew and understood everything that usually forced himself to keep a portion of his mind wary and distant. He sank into the plush mattress and gripped the duvet so he didn't float away from the joy that thrummed through his body alongside sheer pleasure.

Too soon, Dima's talented lips and tongue brought Jake to the precipice—then hurled him straight over. His previous overwhelm had nothing on the orgasm Dima dragged from him, leaving Jake with ringing ears and lungs heaving for breath. The weight on his legs vanished and he wrenched his eyes open in time to see Dima kneeling above him, hand almost a blur as he worked the thick cock Jake already craved deep inside him.

Dima roared out his own orgasm as he spilled across Jake's chest, coming so hard the thick drops reached Jake's neck and chin. He swayed after, eyes cracking open with a languid smile. The smile brightened as Jake dragged Dima down into his arms, heedless of the mess.

They cuddled close, trading pleasure-drunk kisses. Jake had almost resigned himself to never making his way into Dima's bed. Now that he was here, he swore to show Dima how good beginnings could be... so that his time in Dima's arms never had to end.

CHAPTER 7

DIMA

Not once had Dima brought home one of his infrequent hookups since he bought the condo a few years ago. Jake was the first man he'd shared this bed with. Having him here should have felt weird, invasive. But much like how Jake had fit himself into the empty cracks of Dima's everyday life, he fit here, as well.

They'd cuddled close after coming down from the high of orgasm. Cleaning up would be necessary sooner rather than later, though Dima chuckled to himself at the thought of Jake unable to leave his side because they'd become stuck together with dry come.

"Hmm?" Jake's blissed out state rendered him nonverbal, apparently.

If Dima allowed this sweet man to leave his arms, he wanted to ensure Jake had a reason to return. Val left a convenient excuse in the kitchen. "Want some baklava?"

Jake jerked. "There's baklava? How the hell did you hide baklava from me?"

"I didn't. Val brought it."

"Hell yeah, I want baklava." Jake dipped his head for a kiss, which turned into two, then three.

Dima wished he was young enough for a second round so soon. He stretched his hand lower, content to lavish pleasure on the other man instead. He'd relish getting his mouth back on Jake's perfect cock as a more than equivalent dessert.

Jake batted him away, wrenching from Dima's grasp. "Nope, you promised me baklava."

And Dima didn't dare renege. They cleaned up together, shifting around each other in Dima's en suite as naturally as they'd shared everything else. Jake did leave Dima's reach when they finally returned downstairs, ducking into his bedroom for a moment and emerging with his cell phone. He slid into what had become his seat at the small dining table as he tapped at the screen. Dima unpacked the dessert and split it between two plates before joining him.

Sweetness exploded across his tongue as he savored the first bite. Dima couldn't wait to lick the taste from Jake's mouth after they finished their treat. He hoped to tempt Jake back to his bed, not bearing the idea of them sleeping apart when his pillows now carried Jake's scent.

Jake's fork clattered against his plate. "Fuck." He stared at his phone, his cheeks losing their rosy hue as the blood drained from his face.

Pastry stuck in Dima's throat. "What's wrong?"

"My orders got changed." Mingled fear and dismay replaced all Jake's earlier pleasure. "I have to report back to Vandenberg next week."

CHAPTER 8

JAKE

Vandenberg Space Force Base offered Jake two reasonable lodging options while he underwent this bullshit medical board review. His parents' house, which happened to be less than an hour away. Or breaking his mother's heart by staying at the base hotel.

He pulled into the driveway and shut off the engine of his mom's old Toyota. Today had been...a lot. Endless meetings, which he'd expected from the few emails he'd traded with Lieutenant Colonel Olsen over the weekend before leaving Maryland. And emotionally difficult, which he had not prepared for in the slightest. He dug his phone out of his pocket and found Dima's contact. He'd gotten into town too late to call last night, thanks to the time difference. Better to call now before entering the house, since he learned during his teenage years that his mom was the queen of unintentional eavesdropping.

The connection went through right away, audio and video. Seeing Dima through the small screen soothed a few of his frayed edges. "Hey, sweetheart," Dima said, easing them more.

"Hey." Jake bit his lip. "So, I got the scoop today."

"Yeah?" Dima's image shifted, the view behind him angling. He sat in his study, and Jake wanted nothing more than to be with him right now for this conversation. They'd never done so, but he so easily imagined curling up in Dima's lap behind the big desk.

"So, you know how I'm supposed to be in Maryland for a year?" Dima's brow curled for a brief flicker before he nodded once. "Well, it's technically a deployment with the communications squadron at Andrews, not a PCS—permanent change of station. And the military has regs about what medical conditions you're allowed to have during a deployment."

Dima's eyes widened in realization, then his frown deepened. "Maryland isn't exactly the middle of the desert, where regular access to your meds might become an issue."

"I know." Jake huffed. "Trust me, logic and the military have never gone hand-in-hand. Anyway, someone in medical doing a chart review flagged my deployment status, so now it's a whole thing. Except no one wants to admit they signed off on something in error, so now I think they're overcompensating. I'm getting med boarded."

"Which means…?"

"I've been referred to the Medical Evaluation Board for a review of my physical fitness for military service."

"Do they need a subject matter expert to come tell them they're being idiots?"

Jake chuckled at Dima's professional outrage, grasping at any point of levity. "I'm pretty sure we're far, far past the point of no return where conflict of interest is concerned. But I appreciate the offer."

"Anything for you, sweetheart."

Dima's dark gaze bored into him from three thousand miles away, and for a moment, Jake didn't feel so alone. His immediate leadership here at Vandenberg had always been cool about the gay thing, one of the perks of working in the military's version of nerd central. But HIV created a host of wrinkles no matter a person's sexual orientation. Bracing himself through every meeting for negative reactions to the disclosure left him exhausted. "Thank you." Dima deserved so much more than trite gratitude after battling his own demons to allow Jake into his affections.

"What happens next?"

"More meetings. And I'm going to visit the legal office tomorrow."

"What?" Dima asked. "You're not in trouble, are you?"

"No, not exactly." Jake didn't want to say the next bit out loud, scared of manifesting his fears into being. "I might get medically discharged. Worst-case scenario," he added, more to reassure himself than Dima.

"You can get kicked out of the military for having HIV?" Now, Dima's outrage grew personal.

"Not technically? All the rules are complicated." Jake shrugged helplessly. "The military doesn't love when a medical condition affects your deployment status. But the military also doesn't love accepting the blame for their own mistakes. Like yanking me home in the middle of a massive project with the National Military Command Center for something dumb." His sudden departure had blindsided his team at Andrews, creating issues for their already complicated schedule.

They shared silence for a few beats. Dima asked, "Are you going to be okay?"

"Yeah." What other option did Jake have? "I'm sitting in my parents' driveway. I should go in before Mom comes to check on me."

"Thank you for calling me." Dima seemed like he might say more, but he settled for a warm smile.

Jake wanted to say more, too, but he hesitated to bind them closer with certain words of affection when regular life had been so rudely interrupted. Dima hadn't even wanted Jake at first, and he deserved someone who wasn't such a mess right now, his future uncertain.

"Been wanting to hear your voice all day," he said instead. "Can I call you tomorrow?"

"I'll be here." Dima blew him a kiss through the screen before signing off.

His phone showed text messages, likely from teammates in Maryland, or from Val demanding more information than the scant email Jake found time to shoot him earlier in the day. But he'd lingered out here too long, especially when a second car pulled into the driveway next to him.

Time to head inside.

"How was work today, sweetie?" His mom glanced from the pot

she stirred atop the stove when Jake entered the kitchen. Her face brightened. "Oh, don't you look handsome."

"Thanks, Mom." He pressed the expected kiss to her cheek and dropped into one of the chairs at the table to work off his boots. He wore his everyday fatigue-patterned ACUs, not his service dress uniform, but Jennifer Nichols never failed to support Jake in the ways she knew how. They weren't a military family by any stretch, aside from one uncle's short stint in the Army around the first Gulf War, but few avenues existed for Jake to pursue a tech career without the funds for college. She'd been thrilled about Jake's assignment to Vandenberg when he transferred to the newly formed Space Force.

His father's subsequent arrival in the kitchen saved Jake from answering about his day. The family fell into old patterns of Jake's childhood, and he set the table quietly while his mom dished the pasta. Dad popping open a second beer and placing it next to Jake's plate was new, but after his day of meetings with leadership and medical, he needed it.

Even after Mom returned to work full-time once Jake entered high school, her cooking skills remained top-notch. "I have to get this recipe from you," Jake said, spinning more noodles onto his fork. "I can never get the sauce right."

"Oh, are you cooking again?" she asked. "I know you hated the stove in your apartment here."

"Dima's kitchen is perfect. No complaints there." Except Dima hated cooking for one, and he'd probably resumed all his poor habits without Jake there for them to trade meal prep. The shitty light beer didn't help when Jake tried to wash away the bad taste left by the thought.

"Dima?" his father asked.

"Yeah, Dmitri Moroz. I told you I was renting a room in the condo owned by Val's brother."

"I thought Val's brother was a doctor." Dad frowned. "What sort of doctor needs the extra income of a roommate?"

"One who works in academia, not his own practice. He's a researcher at the University of Maryland."

"How interesting," Mom said. "What type of research?"

"Infectious diseases. He's currently working on a trial for long-acting HIV meds, actually."

"Does he know—?" His father cut himself off with a grunt as he selected a piece of garlic bread.

"Yeah, Dad. It's come up." Jake's parents trained him too well for him to roll his eyes, but he was old enough now that he didn't bother to keep exasperation from his response. They had never once blinked at him being gay, which had been glaringly obvious from a young age. They'd had a much harder time hiding their disappointment at his HIV after how much they emphasized safety as he grew up. His parents didn't blame him, exactly, but the topic never failed to turn any conversation stilted.

He'd told them he'd returned to California as part of the project he'd been sent to Andrews for. No way was he revealing that his HIV threw his entire military future into question before he had definite news either way. The wait with them for his final diagnosis confirmation had been brutal enough.

"That's good, I guess," Dad finally said. "Since you're sharing space and all."

"And how is Val these days?" Bless his mom for trying to change the subject, even if she had no clue what raised Jake's hackles.

"He's doing well. I told you he got married?"

His mood improved while he and his mom traded gossip about mutual friends through the rest of dinner, but tanked again the moment he finished loading the dishwasher and escaped to the relative privacy of his childhood bedroom. Eighteen years spent in this space, but the condo in Maryland felt so much more like home after mere months. And though he'd only shared Dima's massive bed for four nights, half-pinned under the larger man's warm limbs, he'd never felt more untethered and adrift curled up on this twin mattress alone.

CHAPTER 9

DIMA

Val's invitation to meet for dinner was an unexpected surprise, one Dima dared not decline. Val's hug when they met outside the front door loosened the knot of nerves tangled in Dima's gut, as did the easy small talk they exchanged through waiting to be seated, then ordering their food.

His brother waited until they'd finished most of the queso before asking, "Heard from Jake lately?"

"We chatted on the phone last night." His nerves returned with a vengeance, and Dima wished he'd popped an antacid before leaving work. Or ordered a larger margarita. "We talk most nights, actually," he added. He broke apart a large tortilla chip and chanced a glance across the table. He welcomed Val's contemplative expression over the anger of the last time they'd met in person. Almost a full month ago, which meant nearly as long since he'd watched Jake disappear through airport security with a last wave goodbye.

"Good. He's texted me here and there. He finally told me why they recalled him, even though it's total bullshit, so I'm...glad he has you to lean on." Val tugged the queso bowl closer and dug through the basket for the perfect chip. "Not a fling, then?"

"A fling implies both casual and more than once." Dima shrugged at Val's questioning noise. "I've spent a long time sticking to casual hookups. Jake is the first person in ages who's been…more than once."

"Spare me the TMI, please, brother. This is why I wanted you to leave him alone," Val said, glaring. "Jake deserves way more than a fling."

"And I never said Jake was casual," Dima shot back.

The server arrived with their meals, interrupting their rising tempers. Dima didn't want another fight with his brother, which meant putting all his cards on the table. Sharing truths about himself long hidden. This conversation was long overdue, but Jake only formed a small part of it. "I was with someone, a long time ago. During my fellowship in South Africa."

He'd meant the reveal as an olive branch, but Val's face darkened further. "You returned to the U.S. to accept guardianship of me when Mom died. You left them behind?"

No. Sipho left Dima first, losing his life in a senseless car accident and shattering Dima's heart. "No, he…passed away. Shortly before I returned home."

All traces of anger vanished as Val grabbed Dima's hand from across the table. "Shit. I'm so sorry."

"Thank you." He'd abandoned his original plan to assume custody of his brother and bring him to Cape Town, unable to spend a moment more in the city where the echoes of happiness taunted him around every corner. "For a long time, I was mourning him, and mourning Mom, and raising you. Not interesting in finding anything else, and then it was easy to use you as a distraction. Guess it became habit, even when you grew older."

Habit. Excuse. Same difference. Dima squeezed Val's hand, then stole his back to resume eating.

Val frowned at his enchilada. "I feel bad you were alone for so long."

"I wasn't alone," Dima said. "I had you, Valera."

As he intended, Val rolled his eyes at the traditional diminutive of his full name, which he claimed was inefficient and defeated the purpose of a nickname. "And now you have Jake, I guess? Because he, uh, made it clear in his texts that he wants you."

"He made it pretty clear to me too. Took him a while to wear me down, but now... It should have been easy to lose my attachment when he's been gone for weeks, but I can't imagine letting him go."

Too late, he realized how that might come across, but Val nodded. "Yeah, that's why I worked so hard to keep him as a friend when we didn't work out."

"Not that I'm complaining, but why didn't—?"

"Nope." Val swiped his fork through the air, interrupting Dima's question as a blush bloomed on his cheeks. "That way lies more TMI."

Dima chuckled. "I can't believe I raised such a prude."

"And I can't believe you were slutting around this whole time and I never knew." Cocking his head, Val asked, "Wait, so Sage did run into you at a club? I figured he was fucking with me."

"We're not continuing this line of conversation," Dima said, "because Sage is now your husband, and what I know about that club means TMI for me." He drained the last of his margarita.

"Yes, fair," Val agreed in a rush. Then, he paused, eyebrows knitting together. "But here's what I don't get. You were so open with me about your HIV diagnosis from day one when you came home. And even when I was a dumb teenager still thinking I was straight, you were always so awesome and supportive about Sage and Weston being queer that I never once hesitated about coming to you when I thought I might be too. Why keep that part of yourself from me? Why trust me with your health, but not with your heart?"

Dima fiddled with his fork, searching for an answer. "The first part was because I was protecting you. The second part...putting up all these walls meant putting them up around you, too. I guess that was me protecting myself. But maybe I don't need to anymore."

"From Jake? No," Val said. "I think I got mad because I wanted to protect both of you. And then I stayed mad because I realized you'd been keeping things from me. But I get it, now. And, honestly? There's no one I trust more with Jake's heart—or yours."

"Thank you." His brother's support lifted Dima's spirits almost as high as if he had Jake tucked next to him in this booth. "It won't be as good as yours, but split a piece of flan with me for dessert?"

"Yes, and damn straight it's not as good as mine."

The snarky banter they exchanged through the rest of the meal truly meant a return to their status quo, and Dima snatched away the bill before Val tried to hand over his credit card to split the cost. After, as they exited the restaurant into the brisk autumn air, only the knots of missing Jake lingered in Dima's stomach. He hoped that, someday soon, evenings like this included both Jake and Sage—and even Weston.

As if he sensed the direction Dima's thoughts travelled, Val said, "Say hi to Jake when you talk tonight."

"I will." His phone vibrated in his pocket, and Dima dug it out. Jake's photo flashed on the screen. Maybe he'd sensed them. Dima waved Val closer and answered, putting them on speaker. "Hey, I just got out of dinner with Val. I promise we're both in one piece."

"Hi, Jake!" Val called. "Only minor scrapes and bruises."

"Good. That's—I'm glad. Good."

Dima had hoped for laughter, not the obvious stress edging Jake's words. He dragged his brother out of the flow of sidewalk traffic until they huddled over the device against the restaurant's brick exterior. "What's wrong, sweetheart?"

"Nothing. Maybe. Or everything?" Now a laugh came, but one devoid of humor. "Depends on Monday."

"What happens Monday, buddy?" Val's concerned expression as he asked likely mirrored Dima's

Jake's shaky exhale whooshed over the connection. "Just a meeting with leadership where I learn whether I get to stay in the military or not."

"They're not gonna discharge you over this," Val said. "Did you hear from Finn? I asked him to call you last week."

Dima had met their friend Finn a few times, a nurse with the Air National Guard at the base where Sage worked. Dima also spoke to him the other day, and the guy knew his stuff, especially since he used to work in whatever department approved people for deployment. Dima wished he shared Val's optimism, but working in academia meant a more cynical view of bureaucratic structures and the military-industrial complex than his little brother.

"Yeah, he called," Jake said. "But you know how this shit works. It's not about HIV anymore. Now it's whether I'm worth all the trouble that's been caused over me."

Dima barely had a handle on the medical side of this drama. Joining the military never crossed his mind, even before his own HIV diagnosis, and so much about his brother's world remained truly alien to him. He didn't have the knowledge or experience to do more than listen and support over the past few weeks, hating he was too far away to wrap Jake in his arms.

Val scoffed. "They'd be crazy to let you go. And if they did, you'd go and get a cushy civilian contracting gig making twice as much."

Silence from the other end of the phone. "Jake?" Dima asked.

"No, I won't. I don't even have an associate's degree yet. I barely have all my certifications for the job I already do. That means no career prospects. No job means no health insurance, and I'm not counting on the VA for shit. So, the only way I can afford my meds is if I stay here with my parents."

Dima had heard enough about Mr. and Mrs. Nichols over the past few weeks not to look forward to meeting them anytime soon. No way in hell would he allow Jake to remain in a tiny town with barely any job opportunities, and none in the fields Jake had trained in. Found his passion in.

"Fuck that," Val said, beating Dima to the punch. "You'll come back to Maryland."

"What, and live in your basement?"

"No," Dima said. "You'll stay with me." The offer spilled from his lips with no conscious thought. But once the words were out in the world, he knew without a trace of doubt he meant them with his whole heart. Jake being anywhere else than with Dima was... unthinkable.

"I just said I can't afford rent and my meds!"

Jake's pitch rose along with his anxiety, and Dima gripped his phone tighter. "Jake!" he said. Gentling his tone, he continued, "Sweetheart, I never needed to charge you rent. I miss you like hell. I want you with me. The rest we can figure out."

Silence dragged again, this time long enough to be painful. In a quiet voice, Jake asked, "Really?"

"Really." Staring Val straight in the eye, wishing he could also assure Jake with more than words alone, Dima repeated, "You will always have a home with me."

"Okay." Jake's breath hitched. Dima had never seen Jake cry. If hearing his tears over the phone wrecked him this much, he vowed to do everything in his power to ensure Jake never had reason to cry again. "Okay," he said again, voice stronger. "Shit, I have to go. I'm calling from the driveway again, and Mom is watching me from the front window."

"Call me later, please," Dima said.

"It'll be late when we finish dinner—"

As if Dima cared about the time difference. "It's Friday. Call me before you go to bed. Please."

"I will," Jake said. "I gotta go. Bye."

"Bye, sweetheart." Val echoed the farewell without the endearment, and Dima ended the call. He blew a heavy sigh and tucked his phone away. "Fuck. You really think they won't discharge him?"

"I stand by what I said. They'd be idiots to let him go. But…it's the military. Things don't always make sense." Val's eyes narrowed under the streetlights as he studied Dima for a beat. "You love him."

Dima might be a medical doctor, with multiple degrees, but he'd known since Val was young that his baby brother was the smarter of them. "I'm not having this conversation with you before I've had it with Jake." He wouldn't deny it, either.

"That's not a no, Dmitri."

He shook his head and shoved his brother down the sidewalk. He refused to engage in Val's knowing smirk until they arrived at the parking lot, where Dima had found a spot next to Val's Tesla. Before they split to go their separate ways, he tugged Val into a long, tight hug.

Val clutched him close, then patted the side of Dima's face before stepping away. He opened his car door and paused. "Hey, Dima."

Dima fumbled with his keys at the driver's side door of his Mazda. "Yeah?"

"What was his name?"

He didn't need to ask who Val meant. "Sipho Theron."

"I wish I'd gotten to meet him."

"Me too, Valera." The smiles he and his brother exchanged carried none of the tension of the past month. "Me too."

CHAPTER 10

JAKE

"Is that all you're going to eat, sweetie?"

Half his stir fry remained in his bowl, but Jake had been pushing the food around with his fork more than eating for the past five minutes. He set the utensil aside and summoned a smile for his mother. "Not hungry, I guess."

That she patted Jake's arm instead of ordering him to clear his plate must be some marker of adulthood. "Well, there's plenty left, so help yourself to leftovers later if you want them."

"You will always have a home with me."

Dima's voice had run on repeat through Jake's mind from the moment the call ended, through the meal he had no appetite for, and as he helped tidy the kitchen. He desperately wanted to believe the words. He wanted more time with Dima, to explore the shape of a real relationship. He'd never much cared about the age difference between them, nor the disparity in their life experiences and income levels. Not while he pursued his own career and contributed in what ways he could.

But to rely on the other man completely? At best, keep house for him while Jake worked some dead-end retail or food service job that barely covered the out-of-pocket costs of his meds and labs and office visits? Those scenarios formed a tougher pill to swallow than the one he already took every day.

"Hey, Dad?"

His dad relaxed at the cleared kitchen table, nursing a beer while he scrolled on the tablet Jake gave him last Christmas. "Yeah, son?"

Mom had gone upstairs, but Jake already knew her answer to this question. "What would you think about me not re-enlisting? If I stayed here while I used the GI Bill to pay for online courses to finish my degree instead?"

Scratching his chin, Dad looked up from his tablet. "That'd be fine, I guess. You'd have to cover your own bills, but we'd never charge you room and board. This is your home."

"Yeah, I know. Thanks, Dad."

"You'd still be able to see your doc at Vandenberg?" Dad asked. "Or would you have to go down to Thousand Oaks for the VA?"

Jake leaned against the kitchen counter and fiddled with the damp dish cloth. "I'd probably have to transfer to the civilian practice here in town."

Even from the corner of his eye, he caught the face his dad made. "Doc Diaz has probably never seen a patient with HIV in his entire career. This is a small town, son, and you know how—" Dad cleared his throat. "You know you're too old to be on our insurance now."

He appreciated the attempt at a course correction, but he translated his dad's original thought easily. This was a small town, and he knew how people talked. Neither Doc Diaz nor the local pharmacist would violate his privacy, but before long, everyone would know *something* was up with Jake's health.

They'd ask his parents.

His parents would be embarrassed. Ashamed.

And this validated why Jake still hadn't told them why he was back in California. He hated lying to them, because they really would open their doors to him again if he moved home to finish college. It's not as though he'd have to go back into the closet. But he'd have to stay in the medicine cabinet, which made Jake snort in private amusement. "I know, Dad. Anyway, I haven't decided anything yet. Just wanted to run the idea by you."

He patted his dad's shoulder as he exited the kitchen and headed to his bedroom. He shucked off his uniform top and snagged his laptop, dropping onto his bed as he flipped open the screen. He didn't want to stay in the house all weekend and drive himself crazy worrying about the results of Monday's meeting.

A quick Google search revealed…not much. In Maryland, he'd have dozens of options between Washington DC and Baltimore and beyond. Joining the military had expanded his world. Like his dad said, this would always be Jake's home. But this wasn't his place anymore.

He could stay, if he had no other options. And yet, if he could accept a home from people who loved him but also caused him constant guilt over something outside his control…

Then he had no reason not to accept a home from a man who'd quietly proven he loved every part of Jake over the past weeks, even without speaking those exact words. They'd been lovers for mere days, but Dima stayed in contact with Jake as if they'd been together for months or years. Jake had spent enough time in the military to know this sort of devotion, over such a long distance with no return date in sight, was rare and precious. Meant to be treasured.

Jake's current reality remained the same until Monday. Time to change the facts to suit the reality Jake wanted. He had no control over Monday's outcome. The distance between him and Dima and when they'd see each other again, on the other hand, were malleable details under his control.

Five minutes and slightly more credit card debt later, he closed his laptop and selected Dima's contact in his phone. The other man answered immediately.

"Hey, sweetheart." Dima smiled out of the screen at the strange angle he held his phone in bed. "I'm glad you called."

"You asked." Jake wanted to run his hands over Dima's broad shoulders. To pepper kisses to each tiny gray hair sprinkled through his sexy scruff. "I need a favor."

"Anything." The video blurred as Dima sat up.

"Pick me up at the airport next week?"

"Of course." His brow furrowed. "But won't you find out Monday whether you'll be sent back here to finish the project at Andrews?"

"Whatever happens on Monday happens. My orders to Andrews could be reinstated. Or, I'll have to start the process of military separation. But either way, I want to come home to you."

EPILOGUE

DIMA

Jake stood at one end of the long kitchen counter, clutching an empty plate as he studied the pot luck spread. With a gentle hip check, Dima nudged him to the side and reached for the cranberry sauce. "What's wrong?"

"Why is there sauerkraut?" Jake asked. "Who the hell eats sauerkraut for Thanksgiving?"

"Baltimore does," Val explained, joining them with the dish Jake handed over when they arrived. He released the plastic lid to reveal mashed sweet potatoes. "I don't get it either, but Weston's grandmother made it, so…"

"Got it." Jake mimed zipping his lips, so adorably that Dima couldn't resist pressing a kiss to his boyfriend's cheek.

Boyfriend. At his age, and after so long. Dima adored it. Adored Jake, and loved him even more. Behind them, Val made some sort of gagging noise. Dima ignored him, since Val and his husband were much, much worse.

Once they finished loading their plates, Val led them through the crowded house. They thread their way through the loud teens who'd gathered in the den and emerged into the relative calm of the sun room claimed by the crop of cousins around Weston's age. Jake had been surprised to learn Dima spent Thanksgiving with Weston's family, considering how much they enjoyed needling each other, but the tradition dated to Val and Weston's close friendship in high school, when Weston's parents learned the brothers had no relatives in the United States. On their arrival, Mrs. Kelley had greeted Jake with the same enthusiasm she did all other significant others of her adopted horde. Dima hoped being surrounded by such a welcoming family eased the sting of Jake being so far from his own parents for the holiday.

Val claimed on the arm of the love seat where Sage and Weston ate. Dima gestured for Jake to use the chair next to them, but Jake rolled his eyes and sank gracefully to the floor. After Dima sat instead, Jake squirmed his way between Dima's legs.

"Jake," Weston said, pointing his turkey-laden fork, "when I'm at Andrews next week—"

"You guys promised one meal free from work talk," Dima interrupted. Dating one of his brother's friends meant more meals with his brother, but the downside to being the odd civilian out often meant little to contribute. Jake had thrown himself into work the past month, catching up on the project at Joint Base Andrews. He'd made such a good impression, despite leaving them in the lurch for a few weeks, that the leadership there was apparently making noises about poaching him permanently.

"We don't keep you from talking about work." Weston shoved his food in his mouth.

"You want to hear about my work?" Challenge accepted. "Well, there's this patient I saw while on service last month…"

Jake groaned between his knees, and not in the fun way. "We're eating, baby. I'm still scarred from when you told me. New topic. Sauerkraut. Explain it to me like I'm five."

The topic soon absorbed others in the room, and Dima enjoyed his meal as Jake slowly relaxed against him. Soon, the discussion over appropriate Thanksgiving foods turned to the never-ending canned versus homemade cranberry sauce argument. When the debate ended on a draw, favorite foods for other holidays entered the fray, and Dima found himself offering one of his own.

"Sosaties, fresh from the barbecue." At the blank looks from those around him, he explained, "Christmas is a summer holiday in South Africa. My partner Sipho once grilled us these amazing kebabs marinated in apricot and curry."

The memory absorbed him all at once. Bright sun atop the roof of their apartment building. Sipho, adorned by the paper crown from his Christmas cracker, as he shared stories of past holidays with his family while he grilled lunch. The stars had aligned to give both of them the day free from the hospital. Sipho hadn't seen his parents for years, but he and Dima still toasted them with glasses of the sweet and creamy amarula they'd enjoyed for dessert.

A hand tightened around his ankle, and Dima yanked himself to the present to find Jake staring up at him with a sweet smile. When Val patted his shoulder, he realized this was the first time he'd ever mentioned Sipho in casual conversation. Dima had sequestered all these memories for so long, but acknowledging his first love by sharing the good moments with his family and friends felt—good. Felt right.

Even better, none of them made a big deal of it. To be fair, Weston's extended family was oblivious to the magnitude of what he'd revealed. Still, a load lifted from his shoulders that Dima didn't realize he'd carried for so long.

Jake snuck a kiss to his knee before turning back to the conversation. Dima trailed his hand through his boy's soft hair and settled into his seat, ready to enjoy new holidays with a new love. Sipho would always keep his space in Dima's heart, right beside where Jake enjoyed plenty room of his own.

PHOENIX

MARIE SINCLAIR

CHAPTER 1

MAX

Max found the box in the very back of his closet buried beneath an accumulation of no-longer-worn clothing, bags of costumes and holiday decorations, suitcases, and a few boxes of old cassettes and VHS tapes.

At one time, this box contained the only legacy his twenty-five-year-old self thought he'd leave behind when he died: a panel for the AIDS Quilt. Max was sure creating it wasn't what his doctors had meant when they told him to get his affairs in order because his T-cell count was at zero, and he was so sick they thought death was imminent, but it had been the only thing he could think of to mark his time on the planet.

The symbolism wasn't lost on Max that he was digging this box out from under everything he'd accumulated in the thirty years since that doomsday pronouncement, nor was the irony that he'd had to retrieve it from the closet.

At one time, he'd displayed the panel in his living room as an act of defiance. *Look, world, I fucking survived even though you were trying to kill me.* But after losing so many friends—some of whom had helped him create it and for whom he had made panels—he'd wondered what he was actually celebrating and taken it down. Then tried his best to move forward and live a life he didn't always believe he deserved to have.

Max brushed the dust off from the box, but didn't open it. The weight of it in his hands as he picked it up and carried it to the living room was another bit of irony. It was so light in comparison to what it represented and the memories it brought to the surface, but he didn't have to see it to remember all that. And today's excavation had nothing to do with taking a walk down memory lane.

At one o'clock, Max was exactly where he'd agreed to be, sitting alongside four other men in front of a group of teens at the Sam Mitchell Queer Youth Center prepared to talk about his journey as a long-time survivor of AIDS. The panel—his panel—was displayed behind him: a white ribbon chalk outline on a black background, red hearts with the names of those he had already lost or was getting ready to leave behind filling the outline, his own name and years of birth and death sewn into the upper corners of the panel.

Max hadn't looked at it. When he arrived at the center, he had handed the box off to Ess, one of the center's residence supervisors, then gratefully accepted a cup of coffee from Diego, the center's counselor and the organizer of this event, then gone to sit in one of the comfortable chairs in the front space while people bustled around to finish setting up.

The other presenters had arrived shortly after him, welcomed by Diego and Ess, given coffee, then all of them had been brought into the classroom and shown to the seats at the front of the room. The teens trickled in slowly, talking while their fingers flew over their phone screens, laughing with each other. They were vibrant in their youth and so free with expressing themselves.

Max couldn't help but feel a pang in his heart, a combination of jealousy and grief, and wondered if this hadn't been a great idea. He wasn't usually this morose or morbid, and he'd welcomed the prospect of talking to the kids about his experiences when first asked if he was willing to do so. It was important that they know their history and also that it wasn't the end of the world if they tested positive. AIDS was still out there, as were other STIs, and talking about it was crucial. Now that he was here, now that he was confronted with his own past, his own ghosts, and the young faces before him, he was having second thoughts.

"Having second thoughts?"

Max looked up at the question, and smiled at his friend. "Somewhat."

Sydney Carlton—Cart, for short—smiled back at him. "I can imagine."

Cart was the executive director of the youth center, a role he'd taken on the death of his first husband and the center's founder, Sam Mitchell. Brain cancer had taken Sam whom Max had known as a passionate and tireless AIDS and queer rights activist. Now Cart and his second husband, Ry, were keeping Sam's legacy alive. The baby cooing on Cart's hip was a testament to the way life kept moving forward.

Standing, Max touched his hand to the baby's foot. "I didn't realize you and Ry had had another."

"Yup. Mei was a baby trap and Ry's sister agreed to be our surrogate again, so we decided to go for it, and ended up with this little hellion." Cart shifted from foot to foot in the universal baby-parent rock. He turned slightly so the baby faced Max. "Meet Xian."

"Nice to meet you, Xian, I'm Max."

"Max is a good friend to your daddies," Cart continued. "He knew your bàbá's Sam, and he's helped us out many times."

Xian cooed contentedly and tried to stuff his fist into his mouth while Max fought against the boulder that had lodged itself in his throat. He thought he had himself under control when Cart reached out and put a hand on his shoulder.

"If it's too much for you, you don't have to say anything. The kids will understand if you tell them it's harder than you expected."

Max was on the verge of taking the out Cart offered him when he caught sight of a young man entering the room as if he was trying to be invisible.

"Ah," Cart had followed Max's gaze and turned toward the entrance just as Ess caught sight of the newcomer and rushed to greet him with a happy shout. The young man looked like he was about to bolt, but Ess caught him first and wrapped him in a tight hug.

"Good for you, Ess," Cart said, and Max could tell the comment and nod was for what he was observing, especially when Cart turned toward Max again. "I do hope you'll stay and talk, there are definitely some people here who need to hear what you have to say."

At that moment, Diego stepped to the front of the room and asked for everyone to take their seat. Cart patted Max on the arm, then stepped away to stand on the side, bouncing a little more as the baby started to fuss.

It was too late to make a run for it, so Max sat in his chair, and listened to Diego welcome everyone and thank them for coming.

"It's been forty-three years since the first death due to AIDS was recorded in this country," Diego said. "And though we've come a long way since then, according to CDC statistics, more than 30,000 people will become infected this year. Which is why we asked these wonderful people to come and talk to you about what their lives are like, and how their status has affected them."

The counselor gestured at Max and the other people at the front of the room, and Max took a moment to take them in. He knew a couple of them from volunteering, but the other three were strangers, and he wondered if they were all as conflicted as he was, wanting to help the teens understand and revisiting ghosts of their own. From their expressions, and the glances a few of them made at Max's quilt panel, he thought he was correct. It was difficult but necessary.

As each person introduced themself, Max found his attention drawn back to the young man who'd arrived while he was talking to Cart. Something was familiar about him, but Max could not figure out why. He was too young for Max to have known him anywhere but from the center, but too old to be one of the current teens Max had met during his volunteer shifts.

Nevertheless, the young man kept Max's attention as he slowly realized he might not be able to identify who he was, but he definitely recognized the young man's expression. Shell-shocked, defeated, terrified. Max had seen that look all too often on his friends' faces, and then on his own when he received his diagnosis.

HIV might no longer be the death sentence it was when Max was younger, but it still changed the way you saw your life playing out. Depending on who and how he'd gotten the virus, it could alter the way you interacted with other people, the amount of trust you could give them, the sense that you were going to wind up alone for the rest of your life.

Max had lived through all that, the feeling of being a walking corpse still surfacing even after all this time. His heart went out to this young man, and he knew, if he got the chance, he had to talk to him.

Then it was his turn to speak and tell his story.

CHAPTER 2

MARCELLO

Ess had been so persistent in asking Marcello to come to the World AIDS Day program at the youth center that Marcello had finally agreed just to shut him up. Though he dearly loved his friend, sometimes Ess acted like the center could solve everyone's problems. While Marcello might have agreed with them a year ago—some of his best memories came from the time he'd spent hanging out with the other teens there—he didn't think listening to a bunch of old guys talking about being positive was going to solve anything for him.

Hell, he still carried around the paper with his test results as if he needed to remind himself of his own stupidity, as if seeing the word "positive" in the column for HIV results would make it more real. So how would listening to people talk about their diagnosis and experiences help him?

Marcello didn't know, but he also knew he couldn't let Ess down. Ess was his best friend, and had been really down since their partner, Xave, moved to Los Angeles for his career in fashion design the previous year. As far as Marcello was concerned, relationships sucked no matter how you did them, but at least Ess knew they could trust Xave.

And Xave, man, they were destined for great things. In the days when Marcello was known as Marisol to everyone at the center, Xave had designed all his outfits and helped him shop for things they couldn't make. Marcello longed to slip into his glitter gold heels or grab the near-perfect faux Birkin Xave had found for him in LA. Those days were over, though, and Marcello left home without looking in Marisol's closet.

The classroom was packed by the time Marcello arrived at the center and snuck in. Ess still spotted him immediately and hurried over to give him a hug.

"I'm glad you're here," they said, breathless and bouncy, and leaving Marcello with no doubt his friend meant what he said.

Marcello still double-checked Ess's expression, looking for hints that Ess was just saying what they thought Marcello wanted to hear, and hating himself for the thread of suspicion that ran through all his interactions. Fool me once, he thought before turning his attention to the front of the room where, sure enough, the panel of speakers contained a couple of gray-haired guys. There was also a woman who was closer to Marcello's age, and a guy who looked to be in his thirties.

The center's executive director, Cart, was talking to someone, obscuring them from Marcello's view, but Marcello was more interested in the baby strapped to Cart's chest. He'd known Cart and his husband had had a daughter, but that was a couple of years ago now, so this had to be baby number two, which was cool. Cart had been kind of a mentor for Marcello, helping him finish high school and get into San Francisco State, and letting him volunteer at the center until he graduated—with honors—even though he hadn't been twenty-one yet.

And, fuck, what have you done in the four years since then? Not fucking much. Just stayed in the same shit job scooping overpriced ice cream for tech bros, and, oh yeah, gotten infected with HIV because of my boyfriend's cheating ass. Yeah, me. The bitter voice inside Marcello's head was a familiar companion these days.

Cart moved to the side, and Marcello got a glimpse of the guy he'd been talking to before Diego, the center's counselor, stepped to the front of the room to welcome everyone. Marcello tuned him out, his attention riveted on the guy who seemed vaguely familiar. He'd probably been a volunteer at the center at some point and their paths had crossed. Still, the guy was a stone-cold silver fox, and Marcello had a weakness for older men.

Nope. Not going there, man. Those days are O-V-E-R over. Older does not mean safer.

Fuck off, Marcello told that inner voice because the guy was introducing himself and nothing could have prepared him for what the guy said or how it would feel to know the guy was looking right at him when he said, "I'm Max Allbright, and I was twenty-five when I was diagnosed with full-blown AIDS."

Marcello was rooted to the spot as the guy—Max—gestured to the rectangle of fabric behind him. "This is the quilt panel my friends and I made for me because I was that close to death by the time I went to the doctor. I didn't want to face it. I didn't want to deal with it. I don't know why I'm still here and so many of my friends aren't, and for a long time that was a difficult thing to deal with."

Max's gaze swept the room, and then zeroed back in on Marcello. "I don't have a lot of answers, and far too many questions still, but I will always remember how it felt to get that diagnosis and feel like my life was over. I saw it happen to too many people while I worked at the health clinic, and that's why I said yes when Diego asked me to speak today. Because this diagnosis isn't the end of the world. It changes things, puts some things in perspective, but I want you all to know, if this happens to you, it doesn't mean your life is over."

Those final words unstuck Marcello. His mind buzzing with static, he turned and fled toward the main room of the youth center, thankful he'd remained standing by the exit. He'd almost made it to the front door when Ess caught up with him and placed a gentle hand on Marcello's arm to interrupt his panicked dash for freedom.

"I can't do this, man," Marcello said without looking at Ess, eyes still turned toward the street where a couple walked hand-in-hand. "It was a good idea, and I know you wanted to help, but I can't…"

Marcello didn't get any further in his protests before Ess pulled him into their arms.

"It's okay," Ess whispered as they rubbed circles on Marcello's back.

From the time Marcello met Ess, he'd admired his friend's gentleness and the way it masked a fierce determination to make the world a better place. They'd been outspoken, always willing to throw down in someone's defense, and take the adult volunteers and staff to task for outdated language. Nothing seemed daunting to Ess until they'd fallen for Xave, and the couple's first kiss had become a crisis when the center's landlord used it as a way to try and evict the youth center. Ess had been mortified as their personal life became public and threatened the existence of a place all the teens loved and on which some relied for a place to live.

Thinking about those dark days and the way Marcello and others in their group had rallied around Ess and Xave, he remembered the days collecting signatures in a last-ditch effort to convince the San Francisco Board of Supervisors to help.

"That's who he is," Marcello murmured.

"Who?" Ess asked without letting go. If anything they wrapped their arms tighter around Marcello.

"That Max guy. I think he signed my petition. I remember him talking to Cart about Sam and wanting to volunteer."

Ess shook his head against Marcello's shoulder. "Maybe. I was kind of out of things back then."

Now it was Marcello's turn to hold Ess tighter remembering how distraught his friend had been. Those had been dark days, the darkest Marcello had ever experienced until he got his test results back six months ago and found out he was HIV-positive.

"Didn't mean to bring up bad memories," Marcello whispered.

"And I didn't mean for you to be overwhelmed. I thought it would help."

"Yeah. I know. Love you for trying, boo, but it's going to take time to figure out, and hearing a bunch of people talk about moving on and feeling empowered and all that shit…I can't do it."

"I understand."

Their embrace continued for a few more minutes, but then someone came up and told Ess they needed to take care of something upstairs on the residence floors.

"Don't go away," Ess said before they left. "I still want to take you to lunch."

Marcello touched his fingers to his forehead. "Yes, boss."

Ess laughed as they headed toward the doors that led to the kitchen and the stairs for the upper levels of the building where the center maintained a shelter for teens who needed a safe place to live. As a residence director, Ess lived in an apartment upstairs and was responsible for taking care of the teens who lived here. The shelter had come about after the center had received a gift of their current building from a friend of Cart's husband, and Marcello wished that such a place had been possible for him when he was younger and facing issues with his family after coming out as gay and revealing that he wanted to be a drag queen.

"Are you doing all right?"

Marcello turned to find Cart approaching, the baby he'd been carrying nowhere in sight.

"I'm fine." Marcello smiled and held out his hand. "Long time no see."

Cart took his hand and shook it, then pulled Marcello in for a hug. "We're always here," he said as he let Marcello go, then regarded him with a contemplative expression. "Did you stop by to say hello, or…?"

Fuck. Marcello hadn't had a lot of experience telling people about his status, and had followed his doctor's advice so far that letting someone know was entirely up to him and on a need-to-know basis. But this was Cart, and Cart wouldn't judge him or recoil from him.

"Ess thought the panel would help me come deal with being positive," Marcello said.

True to form, Cart nodded. "How long?"

"Six months."

"And your family?"

Marcello shook his head. "I haven't told them." He shrugged. "I don't live at home anymore and rarely see them. I'm sure that doesn't surprise you."

"To be honest? No. I'm sorry. You know, you can always come talk to Diego if you need to."

"That would be good."

"And I'm sure Max would be willing to listen as well, if you want." Cart inclined his head toward the classroom just as a burst of laughter came from the teens inside. "You know, we're not doing the typical safer sex talk or history of the epidemic, but having a conversation about the day-to-day stuff like dating and talking to partners about their status, that kind of thing. Diego wanted to do something to make the diagnosis less scary if it happens, less of something to be ashamed of or feel as if you did something wrong."

In spite of himself, Marcello flinched. Cart nodded again. "I think Ess's instincts were on the money about asking you to be here today."

"I don't know…" Marcello turned to look at the open door to the classroom.

"How about if we step back inside for a bit, and if it's still too much, you can hang out in my office, and I'll ask one of the speakers to come talk to you. How's that sound?"

Marcello took a deep breath, while still staring through the door. He was lined up perfectly so that guy—Max—was right in his line of sight. As he contemplated going back inside, Max looked up, met his eye, and smiled while inclining his head as if in invitation. Maybe he was really looking at someone else or responding to something one of the other speakers had said, but Marcello felt as if that smile had been meant for him and agreed to return to the classroom with Cart.

"So, tell me something you've done that you never thought you'd be able to do when you got your diagnosis," Diego asked as Marcello and Cart found a space to lean against the back wall.

"I did the AIDS Lifecycle last year," one of the women said. "I was never really active or considered myself an athlete at all, but I did it. All five hundred and forty-five miles of it, and raised nearly two thousand dollars."

The audience and other panelists applauded.

"I bought a house," Max said. "That was about ten years ago now. It took me several years to accept that my docs were telling me my life expectancy was pretty much normal for a man of my age and start thinking about what kind of life I wanted to live. Signing the papers for the house was such an affirmation about the future. I couldn't have imagined that when I was younger." He gestured to the panel again with the birth and death dates only twenty-five years apart. "I mean, that was all the future I thought I was going to have."

There was more applause, and a couple of the other panelists spoke about milestone moments before Diego said, "Okay, let's turn to talking about dating and how your status has affected you and your partners."

Marcello leaned forward because this was the thing he most wanted to know. He'd always wanted the fairy tale, the white wedding, the happily ever after with the man of his dreams. Those things had felt unrealistic when he'd first come to the center as a teen, but then he'd come to understand that wasn't the case. Now, he was back to worrying he'd need to give up that dream after all. He wanted to believe that wasn't the case, and, for some reason, he looked to Max to be the one who gave him that hope.

CHAPTER 3

MAX

The young man was back, and Max couldn't keep his eyes off him. He'd worried what he said had sent the young man fleeing and considered going after him until he watched Ess catch up and give him a hug. And then Cart had talked to him and brought him back into the classroom. Now, he was staring at Max as the discussion turned to dating and how their status had affected their love life, and Max wished he had something as uplifting to say as the thing about his house.

The truth was, Max hadn't done a lot of dating in the previous thirty years. All thoughts of hooking up or having casual sex, all desire for it, had evaporated when he got his diagnosis and thought he was about to die. After that failed to happen, he was too busy recovering and building his body back, learning to live healthier even while friends continued to die around him. Then, once anti-retrovirals meant a diagnosis was no longer a death sentence, Max found there weren't a lot of men his age left to choose from, and he decided to focus on earning the money he'd now need to live by going back to school, getting his degree, and becoming an accountant. It was the most stable thing he could think of, and he'd always been good with numbers. It eventually led him to becoming a financial advisor, at which he'd been very successful, so he didn't have to worry about the future which, until he was in his late thirties, he hadn't planned on having.

The conversation around him was pretty lively despite touching on some heavy topics like when to tell a potential partner you were positive—"I put it right on my dating profile," the guy to Max's right said. "If it's going to be an issue, I don't want to have to deal with it."—and how creepy it was to find some people were interested *because* you were positive. "Virus chasers," the young man on the end called them. "I've had a couple of guys beg me to infect them. That's an instant block. I don't want that on my conscience." The panelists discussed condom usage and safer sex practices—"Even if you're with someone who's also positive, there are a whole host of other STIs you need to protect yourself from," the woman who'd done the AIDS Lifecycle said.

Max watched the young man standing next to Cart begin to deflate and could tell he wasn't getting the answers he wanted. He was looking for hope, and Max wanted to give him some.

"I'll be honest," Max found himself saying. "I haven't done a lot of dating or been with a lot of guys since my diagnosis, but I have had a couple of long-term relationships with people who could see me for me and not my status. We broke up for reasons besides me being positive or my partners worrying about catching the virus from me." As he spoke, he stayed focused on the young man, hoping that something he said would help bring back that smile Max had seen when Ess hugged the guy. "For me, at least, my status is no longer the thing that puts a limit on my love life, it's the fact that I'm closing in on old geezer status in this community."

That got a smile and a head shake from the young man, and a couple of wolf whistles from the teens in the audience which made Max blush.

"Look," Max continued. "Rejection is always going to be part of dating, and I wish I could say that rejection because of your status isn't going to happen, or that when it does, it isn't going to hurt. Someday, it'll be one hundred percent safe to date someone who is HIV-positive, but that's not the case yet. The truth is, you need to take care of yourself. Use condoms, take PrEP, and trust your gut about the people you're with. Relationships of any kind require trust. If you don't feel comfortable with someone or you're not getting the answers you need to feel safe, get out of there. You don't have to be a jerk about it, and this diagnosis is not the end of the world, but your first responsibility is to yourself."

The young man in the back of the room took a deep breath, then turned and walked out again. Max's heart stuttered and ached for someone who was so clearly hurting, but there wasn't anything he could do about it right now except continue to answer questions from the teens who had taken time out on a Saturday to learn about life with HIV.

Half an hour later, Max stood with his fellow panelists as the teens filed out of the room. Some of them hung back and approached with additional questions, or went to Diego and whispered their inquiries to him. Max fielded a couple of questions before Cart touched him on the arm and motioned him to the side.

"I've got someone in my office who wants to speak to you," Cart said, then smiled when Max raised an eyebrow. "It would mean a lot if you would speak to Marcello. You can probably guess why, but it's not my place to tell you. If you're not comfortable, I can ask someone else, but he said he wanted you."

"Why?" Max asked.

Cart shrugged. "Only one way to find out."

Which was how Max found himself climbing the stairs to the offices on the third floor and opening the door to find the young man who had captivated him during the talk. He was presently turned toward the window, which gave Max a moment to study him—Cart had called him Marcello—and admire his slender body and dark wavy hair which reached to his shoulders. The lower half of it was streaked with highlights, but the top half was completely dark. Max wondered if that was an indication of how long it had been since Marcello found out he was positive because he now had no doubt that was what this young man wanted to talk about.

"Hi, Marcello," Max said. "It's nice to meet you. I'm Max. Cart said you wanted to speak with me."

The young man turned, and his beauty took Max's breath away. His face was flawless with smooth, golden skin, sharply defined cheekbones, and dark brown eyes framed by thick black lashes. Max tried not to stare at his lips which were full and a luscious shade of dark pink.

"Hi," Marcello said, his voice a husky breath and much quieter than Max had anticipated. "We've met before."

"We have?"

"Yeah. You signed my petition a couple of years ago when we were trying to save the center from eviction at the old place."

Max squinted while Marcello shifted his weight. He shook his head. "I'm sorry, I don't remember."

"It's okay. I looked a lot different then. Before."

Max chose to ignore the obvious question in favor of getting Marcello to relax. "How so?"

Marcello pulled his phone from the back pocket of his jeans and scrolled through a lot of photos until he found the one he wanted and turned the screen so Max could see. The image made him smile. It was definitely Marcello, but he was dressed in a flamenco-style dress, hair tied up with colorful ribbons, and wearing glittery heels that were so tall, Max got dizzy just looking at the photo.

"Ah, yes," Max said as he gazed at an image of the young man in front of him dressed in his baby drag finery holding out a clipboard. "I do remember you."

Blushing, Marcello dipped his head as he turned his phone off and tucked it into the back pocket of his jeans.

"Are you still doing drag?" Max asked, his heart breaking when Marcello shook his head. "Do you mind if I ask why not?"

They sat in the chairs in front of Cart's desk, facing each other as Marcello haltingly told Max about the guy he'd started seeing two years before, how they'd gotten serious and moved in together, and always got their tests done at the same time.

"We decided we'd be exclusive about a year ago," Marcello said, and Max knew what was coming. "We got tested again, and went bare for the first time after we were clear across the board."

Max longed to finish the story for Marcello to save him the pain of saying it out loud, but he held his tongue, knowing the power that came in speaking the details one's self. When Marcello remained silent, worrying at his fingers and staring at the floor, Max reached out and took the young man's hands in his own. They were warm and soft, and Max found himself absently stroking his thumb over the pulse point on Marcello's wrist.

"I didn't know he'd been cheating on me the whole time we were together." Marcello's fingers gripped Max's. "I wouldn't have gone bare with him if I'd known. And I feel so stupid for not getting on PrEP, for believing him when he told me he was safe."

Marcello's voice had risen, anger present in his tone, in the tension in his body, the fierceness with which he held on to Max's hands.

"He kicked me out when I got sick because he knew what it was. The whole time he kept accusing *me* of cheating on *him*."

"Where did you go?" Max asked, and his heart dropped when Marcello shook his head.

"My family hasn't wanted anything to do with me since I came out, so there's no way they would want me back knowing I had HIV. They'd freak out and tell me it was all my fault. I ended up staying with some friends of Cart's. They had an apartment on the top floor of their house, and they let me stay there until I was able to find someplace permanent."

"Thank God for that," Max said.

He wanted to ask more, but at that moment, Cart returned with baby Xian. "I hate to interrupt," he said. "But someone needs to be changed, and the diaper bag's in here."

Max looked at Marcello, knowing there was more the young man needed to say. "Do you want to get coffee?" he asked, smiling at the nod he received in response. He looked up at Cart as he stood. "We'll get out of your hair."

As Marcello stood, Cart smiled at him. "Would you mind holding Xian while I get what I need?"

At Marcello's terrified expression, Max reached out his hands for the baby. "I'll take him."

There was a quick shuffling of positions, and then Max's arms were full of a wriggly baby who cooed at him while trying to grab for his hair. "Hey, dude," Max said with a laugh. "None of that. I need to keep what I've got left."

"What you've got is plenty," Marcello said quietly, but Max caught it along with the blush that had risen to the young man's cheeks. He was about to say something when Xian made another grab for him.

"Hey, hey," Max said, but he wasn't pissed off. Xian was a firecracker, and Max loved the little boy's giggles.

By the time Cart reclaimed his son, Marcello was laughing along with Max, who gratefully surrendered the baby to his father. "You weren't kidding about hellion, were you?"

Cart shook his head. "Not a bit." He snuggled his face close to Xian's and rubbed noses with him, laughing when Xian opened his mouth and put his lips on the tip of Cart's nose. "But we love our little monster, yes, we do."

"Better you than me," Max said as he motioned for Marcello to precede him through the door. "And tell Diego thanks for including me today. I enjoyed it." He patted the messenger bag at his side, feeling the weight of the panel it contained against his leg. "It dug up a lot of memories, but that's not a bad thing."

"I agree," Cart said. He nodded toward a photo on his desk, and Max glanced at it, immediately recognizing it as a photo of Cart and Sam in front of the old youth center. Right next to it was a photo of Cart and Ry taken at the Forbidden City in Beijing. Max knew they'd gone to China to visit Ry's extended family a few years before. "Not always a bad thing at all. And, Marcello, it was good to see you around again. If you want to come back to volunteer, we'd be happy to have you."

Marcello ducked his head, his cheeks turning an endearing shade of pink that only made him more attractive in Max's opinion. "Thank you. I'll think about it."

With that, Max headed down the stairs to the ground floor with Marcello on his heels.

"Let's head over to Thorough Bread," Max said. "They've got good coffee, and it's quieter in the back than at Spike's, so we can talk."

"Okay."

They headed down 18th to Church and walked the two and a half blocks to the bakery. Marcello was quiet the entire way, and Max didn't try to fill the silence with idle talk. The young man had some serious questions to ask, Max was sure of it, and it was probably better to give him some space to organize his thoughts.

For his part, Max spent the walk turning over things that had been said at the panel, and marveling at the way the Castro kept changing. Sometimes, it depressed him as he found parts of his past that had been erased by a new business or overwritten with a new building, but today, it felt energizing. The streets were full of people, coffee shops and restaurants teeming with patrons. He and Marcello passed a walking tour, catching a snippet of the history the tour guide was talking about and dodging the tourists who had their phones out. Max often wondered how many photos of himself were scattered about on social media because of all the Castro tours he'd encountered. Today, it amused him to think of himself as some tourist's encounter with an actual gay man in the Castro.

They reached the bakery, and Max told Marcello to get whatever he wanted, it was Max's treat. They each ordered coffee—a decaf Americano for Max and a vanilla latte for Marcello— and slices of quiche, then found a table in the back corner of the rear garden. The space was expansive and filled with plants and trees that provided privacy for each of the tables. Max loved this place because it felt like a jungle oasis in the middle of the city. But today, he loved it even more because it gave him a chance to get to know Marcello a bit better.

CHAPTER 4

MARCELLO

Getting a crush on a sexy silver fox had not been on Marcello's to do list when he woke up that day, yet here he was as tongue-tied as he'd been the first time he asked a boy out. He had no idea what he wanted to say to Max, only that he hadn't been about to let the man disappear into the anonymous masses of San Francisco without at least seeing him up close. That he'd told Cart he wanted to speak to Max in private had shocked the hell out of him. Pre-diagnosis Marcello would have done that without batting an eyelash. Hell, pre-diagnosis Marcello would have walked right up to the man and asked him out, never mind asking Cart to intercede.

Post-diagnosis Marcello was an entirely different person, though, and quietly sipped his coffee and toyed with his quiche hoping Max would lead the conversation. After a few minutes, Marcello realized that wasn't going to happen, but strangely, the silence between them was comfortable. He chanced a glance at Max, and found the man watching him with a curious expression. When Max smiled at him, Marcello felt his insides flutter and heat rising into his cheeks. How often had he blushed in the past hour? He had no clue, but it seemed to be a regular occurrence when he was near Max.

"What did you want to talk about?" Max asked.

"Are you seeing anyone?" Marcello blurted, then felt his face flame with embarrassment. "I...sorry...I have no—"

"It's fine. And to answer your question, no, I'm not. I haven't been in a relationship for several years."

"Why not?" Marcello asked. "I mean, you're really sexy, I can't imagine guys aren't interested." Marcello stopped himself before he said anything more embarrassing. This was pre-diagnosis Marcello choosing to reappear at the most inopportune time.

Max laughed. "Thank you for the ego boost."

"I mean it," Marcello said, then buried his face in his hands. "Why can't I stop myself from saying things like that?" Still laughing, Max took Marcello's hands in his and pulled them away from his face so Marcello had to look at him. "This is so awkward."

"Why?" Max asked.

"Can we...can we just start over and pretend I didn't say any of that?"

"We could, but if it's all the same to you, I'm going to hold on to the fact that a very attractive young man thinks I'm sexy."

"You think I'm attractive?"

The smile Marcello was quickly becoming addicted to got even broader.

"I do," Max said.

There was a pause as they both stared at each other, and Marcello wasn't aware of anyone else existing at that moment except for the two of them. It felt as if so much was being communicated in their gaze, as if Max was whispering in Marcello's ear but it wasn't in words he could hear, it was more in an understanding, a feeling, a shared reality that went deeper than two people in the same place at the same time.

When Max let go of Marcello's hands, he instantly regretted the loss of their warmth, but the connection he'd felt continued even without the contact.

"So, what did you want to talk to me about?" Max asked.

It was Marcello's turn to laugh. "Well..." He cocked an eyebrow at Max, which made Max laugh again. It was the best sound in the world.

"I am definitely *not* going to pretend this conversation never happened," Max said.

They continued talking for hours, and Marcello found himself opening up about how he hadn't been able to get into his drag persona since his diagnosis.

"Marisol is about fun and play, and I haven't been able to get there," Marcello said. "I miss her." He raised the mug to his mouth to cover the vulnerability he felt at the admission, but he'd already finished the coffee, so he stood and asked if Max wanted another cup because he couldn't think of anything else to do and he wanted this conversation to continue. Max was fascinating, funny, not to mention sexy as sin, and Marcello hadn't been this attracted to anyone in his life.

Max looked at his watch, and Marcello's heart sank anticipating that Max was going to say he needed to get going. But then Max handed him his empty mug and said he'd love another decaf Americano.

Heart beating double time, Marcello headed back inside to order their coffee drinks. He also asked for a couple of pastries—a square of coffee cake and a fruit tart—and returned to the table. Max had his phone out and was tapping out a message to someone, so Marcello took his seat and slid the plates onto the table noting how Max's eyes lit up when he saw them. As if the man weren't gorgeous enough, Marcello just about melted from the way he looked when he smiled. Thank God for the table because he was half-hard for the first time in months.

He scooted his chair closer, which not only gave him more cover from Max seeing, but also meant his thigh brushed against Max's. Marcello froze, holding his leg rigid a hair's breadth from Max's, but then he felt Max close that distance with a tentative touch. Marcello ducked his head, but he also followed when Max moved his leg away until they were touching once again.

Their coffee's arrived, both with steamed milk hearts on top, and Marcello felt his cheeks heat again. "I didn't ask them to do that," he said.

Max only smiled as he lifted the mug to his mouth and blew on the hot liquid before taking a sip. A thin line of foam clung to his top lip, and Marcello fought hard to keep himself from reaching over and wiping it clean with his thumb or, worse, his own lips. Max seemed to know what he was thinking because his tongue flicked out and licked away the foam.

"Shit," Marcello sighed, and Max laughed.

"I can't tell you how long it's been since someone looked at me the way you are," Max said. "It's doing wonders for my ego."

"You keep saying that, but I don't understand why."

Canting his head to one side, Max looked at Marcello. In point of fact, "looked" was too passive a term. Marcello was scrutinized, examined, and seen in a way that had him squirming in his seat and biting his lip. Max's thigh was back, pressing against Marcello's, and the feeling was electric, zipping through his body like a bolt of lightning.

At that inopportune moment, Max's phone chimed with a text, breaking the mood. Max glanced down at the screen and smiled at what he saw. Marcello expected that Max was going to make some excuse to leave and braced himself for the brush-off he knew was coming. Instead, Max put his phone back on the table and turned to face him.

"What else do you want to talk about?" Max asked.

Marcello shrugged. He didn't really have any idea, and he had never mastered the art of small talk. Getting to know someone to whom he was attracted was difficult for him. Even before his diagnosis, he had a hard time figuring out what to say without blurting out something embarrassing. The other teens used to tease him for having no game whatsoever, and he'd hardly ever been in a position to dispute the truth of that statement. He wanted things to be different with Max.

"I wish I was better at this," Marcello said.

Again, Max tilted his head to the side. "Better at what?" he asked.

With someone else, Marcello might think he was being made fun of, but Max had a way of looking at him with kind eyes and a gentle smile that said nothing was further from the truth. Max was interested, so Marcello decided to take a risk.

"Talking to someone I like," he said.

"Someone you like." Max's tone was neutral, steady, as he repeated Marcello's words, but his eyes sparkled and that gentle smile turned sly.

To buy time, Marcello sipped his coffee, carefully putting the cup back on its saucer before he turned to face Max more fully. "Someone I'd like to know better," he said.

And there was that beautiful smile that made Marcello's insides turn all bubbly.

"Well," Max said. "I'm a bit rusty at this myself, but I think the best thing to do is to continue talking and see what happens."

Marcello took a deep breath, and then licked his lips, thrilled when Max's gaze dropped to his mouth, so he did it again.

"Stop it," Max said, but he was laughing. And more than that, he reached out and put his hand over Marcello's.

"Oh," was the only sound that came from Marcello's mouth.

"Is this okay?" Max asked.

"Yeah." Marcello turned his hand so they were palm-to-palm, and Max interlaced their fingers. "Very okay." And if his voice had turned somewhat breathless, Marcello found he was okay with that. "So, what should we talk about?"

Max considered the question. "How about if we start with the mundane stuff like where we grew up, and see where things go."

Which is what they did, and the longer they'd talked, the more it began to feel like a date. Marcello was too worried about jinxing how well it was going to say anything or ask what Max thought, but he secretly hoped that he'd get to see Max again.

☒

That night, Marcello lay in his bed replaying his conversation with Max and texting with Ess who was teasing him mercilessly about the sexy, silver fox.

Are you going to ask him out? Ess asked.

I don't know.

Liar.

Probably.

Ess sent back a laughing emoji.

Marcello stared at his screen. He and Max had exchanged contact info, and he'd been hoping to get at least a "I had a good time talking to you" if not a "I'd like to see you again" message, but it was already evening, and so far, Ess was the only one reaching out to him.

You should ask him out, Ess typed.

I want to, but...what if he thinks I'm too young for him?

Did he say anything to you that made you think that?

No.

In fact, it had been quite the opposite. Once they'd gotten through the initial awkward small talk—awkward, Marcello hoped, because Max was as anxious to make a good impression as Marcello had been —they hadn't stopped talking for more than two hours. Marcello had loved when Max asked about Marisol and said he'd like to see her in all her glory all while holding his hand, his thumb gently stroking Marcello's wrist. That small bit of contact had sent shivers up and down Marcello's spine and even made his dick perk up.

Then what's the problem? Ess broke through Marcello's reverie.

The problem had come as they were leaving and one of the servers made a comment about how nice it was to see fathers taking their sons out for coffee. They'd been walking toward the door, Max's hand brushing against Marcello's, and Marcello had been hoping they'd link up the way they had earlier. He wanted to walk out of the bakery hand-in-hand with Max, but that comment had been like an ice-cold bath that had made Max jerk his hand away and put distance between them. Then they'd been on the sidewalk, an awkward moment of shifting feet and averted gazes as they figured out how to say goodbye. No kiss, not even a peck on the cheek, or a question about seeing each other again. Just Max shrugging, thanking Marcello for a pleasant afternoon, and walking away into the twilight.

Do you think he's too old for me? Marcello typed out.

What I think isn't important.

Marcello silently cursed that Ess was studying to become a counselor.

But do you? I need friend Ess not therapist Ess.

A laughing emoji followed by the shrug one appeared on Marcello's screen. **Are you looking for reasons you shouldn't ask him out?**

Marcello considered that idea. **Maybe.**

It would make sense that you'd be nervous about seeing someone.

I guess so. Marcello waffled, unwilling to let himself hope for more.

But you shouldn't. You're amazing, and Max would be lucky to go out with you.

Staring at the screen, Marcello couldn't get his fingers to move to dispute what Ess had said. He didn't feel as if anyone would be lucky to go out with him let alone someone who had their life as together as Max.

You still there? Ess asked.

Yeaj, Marcello typed, then corrected it to, **Yeah. Just thinking.**

The three dots appeared, then disappeared and came back. **Gotta go take care of something. BRB**

K

Marcello watched his screen for a bit, then scrolled through his social media accounts and ended up watching YouTube videos while waiting to see if Ess would come back. As a resident director on the shelter floors dealing with abused and abandoned teens, Ess sometimes had their hands full. Tempers flared easily, anger sometimes sparking into something more dangerous. Marcello didn't take it personally when Ess didn't come back to their conversation after more than half an hour though his mind was full of thoughts about Max and fantasies about what it would be like to be with the sexy silver fox.

For the first time since he'd gotten that life-changing test result, Marcello was aroused. Thoughts of Max were making his dick hard, and he found himself gently rocking and thrusting his hips up as he lay on his bed watching videos of drag queens.

At first, he tried to ignore the insistent throb as his cock thickened, but eventually, he gave in to the desire to touch himself. His hand slid under the waistband of his sweats and glided across his still flat belly. Marcello suppressed a pang of regret that his abs weren't as defined as they'd been the year before. His motivation for working out had taken a hike at the same time as his libido, but at least one of them seemed to be rallying.

Taking hold of himself, Marcello gave his dick a long downward stroke, shivering at how good it felt. He moaned as he drew his hand back up, fingers tightening just under the glans before he slid his hand back down.

It felt amazing, but he needed lube. It had been too long since he'd jerked off, and what he had was dried out and gummy. Marcello headed to the kitchen, grateful his housemate wasn't home to see him grab the bottle of olive oil and head back to his bedroom.

Once again behind a closed door, Marcello lay back on his bed and poured a small amount of oil into his hand. He pictured Max—the sexy smile, the beautiful blue eyes that twinkled when he laughed, the way their hands had looked entwined—and then thought about what the man would look like without clothes. Marcello had no problem imagining that he'd be built with a trim waist, flat stomach, but it was thinking about what Max's cock would look like that got Marcello's hand moving faster on his own.

The slick slide along his shaft sped up, and Marcello moaned at the way his balls drew up, tension building in them and climbing into his belly. He rolled onto his side, thrusting his cock into his tight fist, and thought about Max lying naked beside him, imagined it was Max's hand on his dick, his hand on Max's, mouths devouring each other. He gasped at the thought of Max coming, his imagination showing him Max falling apart, lips parted in a scream as searing hot cum bathed his hand.

Marcello rolled onto his back, breathing hard as he stared at his ceiling, then grinned to himself at how quickly he'd come. *Too long, man, way too long,* he thought, and then, *I wish that had been real. I wish Max was here right now.*

Almost in answer to his thought, Marcello's phone buzzed. He turned his head to the side in time to catch the text preview and Max's name before the screen went dark again.

Grabbing for the phone, Marcello didn't care that his hands were still sticky with cum and slick from oil. Max had texted him. That had to be good news, right? And there was only one way to find out.

The text made Marcello's heart stop, and then start to pound in his chest.

Can't stop thinking about you. When can I take you on a real date?

CHAPTER 5

MAX

Walking away from Marcello outside the bakery was more difficult than Max imagined it would be, but he needed to clear his head and think things through. As he walked toward the Muni, he pulled his phone out and looked at the text he'd gotten from Cart while Marcello had been getting them another round of coffee.

How's the date going? Cart had asked.

It's not a date.

Sure. Sure. Be nice to the kid, old man.

Max knew Cart had been teasing, but that text coupled with the guy who'd thought he was Marcello's father had put a damper on the connection he'd been feeling while he talked to Marcello.

He hadn't intended for coffee to feel like a first date. Sure, he'd noticed Marcello during the discussion at the center and been first sad at the young man's departure then overjoyed at his return. And when Cart said there was someone in his office who wanted to talk to Max? Max had hoped it was Marcello and been thrilled to find it was. Even as he'd thought Marcello only wanted to talk about what Max had suspected and then confirmed in Cart's office, he'd wondered if he could ask Marcello out.

Max half suspected that Cart's return with baby Xian had been a way to get the two of them into a more date-like setting, which is why he tapped out a text for Cart as he walked away from Marcello.

Got time to talk to an old man?

Cart texted back almost immediately with an invitation to come over to his house, and Max ordered a Lyft car to take him up the hill.

Ry answered the door with a little girl who could only be Mei standing to his side. Ry and Cart's daughter was the spitting image of the man standing in the doorway with a wide smile on his face, except for her eyes, which were the same green as Cart's.

"Come on in," Ry said as he stood aside to let Max through the doorway. "And welcome to the zoo."

Max was about to ask what that meant, but then he heard Xian wailing from the back of the house.

"Rough day?" he asked.

"Xian doesn't like to go to bed," Mei said and wrinkled her nose. "Bǎbá's walking with him." She said something in Chinese to Ry that made him laugh. Whatever he said to her made Mei smile and head toward the kitchen.

"I told her she could have another custard bun for second dessert," Ry said. "Come on in. I'll take Xian upstairs and see if the rocking chair will do the trick."

"Cart told me he was a bit of a handful," Max said as he followed Ry down the hallway. The house had a beautiful craftsman interior full of dark wood and had been lovingly and sympathetically modernized. The hallway opened into the open-plan kitchen where Mei sat at a poured concrete island munching away on her bun. On the opposite side, three steps descended into the family room where Cart was slowly rocking back and forth with Xian in his arms. Xian wailed as if his tiny world had crashed and burned around him.

"A bit more than Mei, but my parents said my sister was like this, so we're blaming her genes. Jen insists Xian's cutting his first tooth and says her daughter did the same thing, and it'll get better." Ry kissed his daughter's head as he passed the island, said something to her Max couldn't decipher, and continued down the steps to take Xian from Cart.

Max watched the tender way in which Cart kissed Xian on the top of his head, then kissed Ry, and had to swallow hard against the tide of emotion that threatened to overwhelm him. He remembered Cart's first husband, Sam, had been friends with the man he'd met as an AIDS activist in the early 90s. This house in which he stood was familiar to him, had been the location of so many meetings, but, like the couple who now lived here, what Max remembered had changed. Sam was gone, and Cart had been reunited with his first love. It was a testament to the way life moved on, and that happiness could grow out of tragedy.

I want that, Max thought. With Marcello? Max mentally shrugged. The possibility was there, but he was unsure about turning it into reality.

Ry passed Max with Xian nestled against the crook of his neck. The baby still cried and whimpered, but he'd settled a bit.

"Xian always quiets down for bǎbí," Mei said as she slid from her stool at the island.

"That's because bǎbí has more patience, and bǎbá's tired," Cart said. He scooped the little girl up in his arms and blew a raspberry on her cheek, which made her giggle, then set her back on her feet.

The look on Cart's face as his daughter followed his husband out of the kitchen was one of pure love and adoration. As soon as the kids and Ry disappeared up the stairs, Cart sagged against the island and rubbed his forehead, but he grinned at Max.

"Somedays…" he said with a shake of his head.

"But you love it," Max said.

"I do." Cart straightened and walked around the island to pick up a bottle of wine from the counter. "Red or white?" he asked.

"Either," Max said. "Whatever you're having."

Cart got a couple of wine glasses out and filled them with red wine. "Let's head outside," he said as he handed Max a glass.

Cart turned on the lights that were strung across the backyard, and led Max outside. The space was gorgeous with a couple of terraces, a koi pond, and a small gazebo, which is where Cart led him. Max noted the toys scattered on the ground, and felt a pang of sadness that Sam wasn't there to see how full of love his house was. He knew that Cart and Sam had only had a few years before brain cancer took his friend, and that Cart had turned inward, devoting all his time and energy to his job as a human rights lawyer and serving as executive director of the youth center.

Putting his glass down on the table in the gazebo, Cart lit the propane heater and adjusted it so a nice bubble of warmth formed around them.

"Okay," Cart said as he sat. "What's going on?"

Max laughed at Cart's directness and took a sip of wine. It was delicious, and Max made appreciative noises.

Cart swirled the wine in his glass before raising it to his lips. "It's from a winery Ry and I visited in Paso Robles before Xian was born."

"It's delicious." Max took another sip, then placed his glass on the table and looked at Cart. "I'd ask if you thought there was a time limit on finding love, but it's obvious you don't."

"Nope." Cart grinned. "If you'd asked me that a few years ago, I'd have said differently, though." He cocked his head to the side, studying Max. "Are you asking if I think you're too old for Marcello?"

"Way to be direct," Max said and reached for his glass to take a larger gulp of wine.

"Not much to be gained from doing otherwise," Cart said. He nodded toward the house. "Both Sam and Ry have taught me that. But you haven't answered my question."

Max nodded. "I think it's more, wondering if…" Max shrugged and swirled the wine in his glass while he thought. "If it's worth trying."

"With Marcello?"

"He's the first person who piqued my interest in a long time, Cart. I'd begun thinking my time has passed."

"That's something I completely understand," Cart said. He stared into the dark liquid in his glass. "When Ry showed up, I hadn't seen him in twelve years. Not since our senior year in college. Losing Ry then was a wound that took a long time to heal. And then I found Sam, and lost him as well. I wasn't sure I could survive if I opened up my heart to Ry again only for him to go away again. Losing people is something we've both had to experience, and it's difficult to open up after living through loss after loss, after your friends have died or moved away. I saw that in Sam. Almost every day, he encountered a reminder of someone who was no longer with us, and each time it brought that grief back to the surface. I see that with Ry as well. Even though his experiences are different from yours and Sam's, he's still dealing with his parents not being a part of his life anymore. Their choice, but it still hurt him deeply, and having Mei and Xian brought all that pain back to life for him. As much as they add to our life, and as much as we love them, I know Ry misses being able to share all this with the people who brought him into this world." Cart smiled. "We do have a wonderful set of lǎo rén, family friends who looked out for Ry and Jen when they were younger and have kind of stepped in as honorary grandparents. They've helped fill that space for Ry."

He took a sip of wine, lost in thought, and Max let him drift in his memories while he contemplated what Cart had said. Losing so many people in such a short period of time had made it difficult for Max to open up when new people came along because he didn't want to risk opening his heart only to have another name to add to his list of losses. He'd left his messenger bag with the quilt panel inside the house, but he could still feel the weight of it on his shoulder. Talking with Marcello earlier that day had been the first time in years Max hadn't felt all those losses so acutely.

"You know," Cart said, and Max was grateful for the interruption of his thoughts. "Sam was your age when I met him, and I wasn't much older than Marcello."

"But you're you," Max said, meaning that when Cart met Sam he'd already finished law school and was working at a prestigious law firm.

"And Marcello is Marcello. Don't sell him short just because he's young or hasn't finished school. We all have challenges that educate us in ways that aren't apparent on the surface. Working with the teens has taught me not to judge by what's on the outside, but to look to what's in a person's heart, what they've done in response to the challenges life has given them."

Max inclined his head in acknowledgement. "How did you get so wise in your forty years?" he asked with a smile.

"It's not the years, my friend, it's the mileage." Cart raised his glass and tapped it against Max's, the sound clear and pure in the quiet backyard. They feel into a comfortable silence again until Cart asked, "Are you asking for my blessing to date Marcello?"

"Maybe," Max acknowledged. "I just don't know why he'd want to date me."

"Who knows why anyone falls in love with anyone. It's one of the amazing mysteries of this life. It's a blessing to love and to be loved in return." Cart pursed his lips and gazed toward the house. "I can't tell you what to do," he said. "But I can tell you, if this is what you want, don't wait. Sam and I danced around each other for two years because he thought I was too young, and I couldn't imagine someone like him would want to be with me. We lost so much time being idiots. Don't do that. If you and Marcello have a connection, trust that. And don't wait."

Cart shrugged. "Who knows. Maybe you go on a date and it's a total failure, and you're no worse off than you are now. But on the other hand, you could go on a date and discover you've got something that will endure forever. You're not going to know unless you try. But you know that."

"Yeah, I do."

Ry exited the house with his own glass of wine and joined them under the gazebo. "Noble Intrigue?" he asked as he sat.

Nodding, Cart reached over and took his husband's hand. "Last bottle of it, actually. Think Jen and Stephen will take the kiddos so we can get away and replenish our supply?"

"Probably." He took a sip of his wine. "Xian finally went down. Thank God. Mei's watching a video."

Max watched Cart raise Ry's hands to his lips and kiss them softly, feeling again that longing to have someone with whom he shared such a powerful connection. *Could I have that with Marcello?* There was only one way to find out. He pulled out his phone and tapped out a message.

Can't stop thinking about you. When can I take you on a real date?

When he looked up from his screen, both Cart and Ry were watching him, a knowing smile teasing at the corners of Cart's mouth. Without saying a word, he raised his glass toward Max and nodded. Max picked up his own glass and touched it to Cart's.

"Here's hoping…" Max was cut off by the buzz of an incoming message. He grinned at the string of smiley faces and kissy lips that flashed across his screen.

"What's going on?" Ry asked.

"I believe Max is going to be going on a date," Cart replied.

A week later, Max was nervously pacing behind his front door waiting for Marcello to arrive. Their first official date had been a low-key dinner at La Mediterranée on Monday. It had gone well enough that Marcello agreed to a second date. Even better, Marcello had agreed to come to Max's house so Max could cook for them.

Max mentally ran through a checklist for this date as he opened the door, checked the street, then closed it again. Dinner was prepped. He had steaks seasoned and ready for grilling, a salad in the fridge, and twice-baked potatoes in the oven. A bottle of red wine was open on the counter, ready to be poured into the waiting glasses. The table on the deck was laid with a tablecloth, candles, and place settings for two. He'd turned the heaters on before coming up the short flight of stairs to wait at the door and fret, pulling out his phone to stare at Marcello's **OMW** text a dozen times.

Each time he looked at it, the string of texts leading up to that message made him grin. He and Marcello had been texting almost nonstop since their date. Silly texts, memes—Marcello was much better at that than Max—and jokes had gradually morphed into sweet questions and gentle explorations. There'd also been some photos exchanged, but Max wasn't going to look at those nor think about how many times he'd jerked off to the sight of Marcello's gorgeous cock in the past two days since the pic had arrived. Points to Marcello for making Max specifically ask to see it before he sent it, and the tease of waiting had resulted in a spectacular orgasm. Max had no expectation that he would see the real thing tonight, but he definitely had hopes.

Two more minutes ticked by, and Max started to feel sick in his stomach. Something had happened. Marcello had changed his mind. The Lyft Max insisted on sending for Marcello had gotten into an accident. Each scenario became more outrageous as Max's thoughts spiraled into a whirlwind of doubts.

He was about to call Marcello, when he heard a car door shut. His internal debate turned to whether he should open the door or wait until Marcello rang the bell.

Fuck it. Max threw open the door just as Marcello arrived on the front stoop and gasped. The Marcello who stood before him wasn't quite as flamboyant as the Marisol Max remembered from the day they first met, but there were some definite signs that Marisol was rising again.

Marcello was dressed in a gauzy red shirt that billowed around him and set off his dark hair, dark eyes, and rich olive skin. He wore high-waisted black palazzo pants cinched at the waist with a gold belt, and balanced on the glitter-gold heels Max remembered very well. As gorgeous as the young man looked in his clothes, it was his face that truly captured Max's attention. Marcello's eyes were outlined in gold with rays of red, yellow, and orange adorning his lids and spreading out from the corners of his eyes. His lips were bright red, and his cheeks dramatically contoured to highlight his already sharp cheekbones.

"You look amazing," Max said. "Stunning."

He wanted nothing so much as to pull Marcello into his arms and kiss him senseless, but he was afraid to mess up the look that had clearly taken Marcello some time to do. Settling for a quick peck on the cheek, Max led Marcello into the house. He loved how easily Marcello's hand rested in his, how their fingers automatically intertwined and fell into a comfortable hold as if they had been doing this for some time instead of a few days.

"Your house is gorgeous," Marcello said as Max guided him up the stairs and they emerged into the living room with its floor-to-ceiling windows that looked out over the city. "I've always wondered what the view looked like from up here."

"Now you know," Max said softly. Ordinarily, he would be sharing his guest's appreciation of the view. It was one of the reasons why he'd bought the run-down bungalow-style house perched high above the Castro at the top of 24th and Grand View Terrace. The other reason was the enormous backyard that he'd had landscaped into an urban paradise with plenty of solitary spots to hide away from the city that surrounded the space. But Max's attention was captured whole-heartedly by Marcello.

Marcello turned to face him. "Now I know, and somehow, it's not what I want to be looking at."

Max grinned. "Why's that?" he asked as Marcello drew him closer.

"Because you didn't kiss me at the door."

"I did." Max leaned in and touched his lips to Marcello's cheek. "Like this."

The tease made Marcello's eyes start to smolder. "Is that really all you want to do?" he asked.

"For now," Max said and turned away to head for the kitchen leaving Marcello to follow, laughing the whole way.

At least he was laughing until he stepped into the chef's kitchen with its gleaming stainless steel appliances and hand-built cabinetry. Max had bought the house with the idea of flipping it. At the time, he still wasn't sure he trusted the doctor's prognosis or that his T-cell count wouldn't plummet again, and the idea of a future was something he couldn't quite accept. He'd renovated the place with the idea that he was doing it for someone else, designing the kitchen of another person's dreams, laying out a garden that would delight a future owner. Only when the construction dust settled and the painters finished the interior and the decorator fluffed their final pillow, Max realized he didn't want to sell the house and had moved in instead still not sure why because he had so few friends left to invite over.

He'd never been more grateful to have gained a future he never expected than in this moment watching Marcello take in the space with awe.

"What do you see in me?" Marcello asked, and Max realized what he'd thought was awe was really fear. He immediately closed the distance between the two of them and took Marcello's hands in his own.

"I see someone who is strong and beautiful both inside and out," Max said as he raised those hands to his lips and kissed them lightly. "Someone I can't resist and want to know better. You're fun and surprising, and..." Max shrugged, then gave a helpless smile. "And completely unexpected. You're someone I like. A lot. And am attracted to more than anyone I've ever met."

As Max spoke, Marcello moved closer until his hands were pressed against Max's chest.

"I could ask you the same thing," Max said, his voice husky and tight, knowing Marcello could feel every beat of his heart, would soon feel how much Max wanted him if he kept moving closer.

Marcello shook his head. "Who wouldn't want you? You're sexy and kind, successful and accomplished. I don't have much to offer you."

"Are you kidding?" Max asked. "You have everything to offer. You're you."

This time, Max didn't stop at a quick kiss to Marcello's cheek. He freed his hands and cupped Marcello's face as he drew them together, lips touching softly at first, then more insistent as the kiss lingered. Marcello sighed and opened his mouth, and Max got his first taste of this man who had captivated him. It was too fast, Max knew, but he was pretty sure he was losing his heart to Marcello and that this was going to be the first kiss of many, many more.

They were both panting lightly when they broke apart, trading quick kisses until Max needed to either take the potatoes out of the oven or turn the oven off. Reluctantly, he stepped away from Marcello, missing the feel of him as soon as there was space between them. He poured them both a glass of wine, and they chatted while Max cooked and then plated their dinner, carrying the plates out to the deck while Marcello brought their glasses and the bottle.

Although it was a chilly night, the heaters had created a nice bubble of warmth in which Max and Marcello continued to talk, pausing every now and then to take a bite of food. Max barely tasted anything, too caught up in watching Marcello's animated expressions as he told Max about something that had happened at work. He was pretty sure he laughed in all the right places, but Max was so distracted by how vibrant and alive Marcello seemed to really pay attention.

Is that because of me? he wondered, and when it was his turn to talk, he saw the same expression of desire and devotion on Marcello's face that he was sure had been on his own.

They had dessert inside, sitting on the couch to eat slices of flourless chocolate torte Max had gotten from Thorough Bread and drinking coffee while staring at the city spread out below them. The huge Pride flag marking Harvey Milk Plaza and the heart of the Castro was illuminated and rippling in the breeze while fog rolled over their heads and sent its tendrils floating between sky and land.

With a sigh, Marcello put his plate on the coffee table and finished off his wine. Max feared the night was coming to an end, but Marcello not only settled back, but leaned against him. Max put his own plate and glass on the side table, unwilling to break contact with Marcello more than necessary. When he found his original position, Marcello had shifted closer, and Max put his arm around the younger man's shoulders. Marcello tipped his chin up. His lips were right there, and Max wanted nothing more than to kiss them again, but he waited.

"Please?" Marcello whispered.

"As you wish," Max answered.

Kissing Marcello this time was unlike anything Max had ever experienced before. Even their earlier kisses had only been a prelude to this moment when Marcello leaned against him, hands free to touch and explore. It wasn't long before Marcello had straddled him and slid his clever hands under Max's shirt to caress and seek out all the places where Max's skin was most sensitive.

He shivered as Marcello stroked his sides, the contact coming just short of ticklish, but causing Max's hips to rock against Marcello's. They were both hard, their cocks touching through their clothes, but neither of them was in any hurry. They had time to get to know each other, time to find out each other's secrets, and time for everything.

With a start, Max pulled away from Marcello, leaning back so he could stare into Marcello's eyes. The wonder of the moment, the sheer audacity of what he had been thinking, and the joy that he had found this person, made Max shake his head. He wished he could find the words to express to Marcello how much this evening meant to him, but he knew he didn't have to. What shone from Marcello's eyes reflected what Max already knew in his heart. Marcello was his forever person.

Later, they moved to Max's bedroom, both naked, both eager, and Max thought how lucky he was to have found Marcello, and how much he was looking forward to the future it had taken him three decades to believe could be his.

EPILOGUE
ONE YEAR LATER

MAX

The crowd was bigger than last year, but that was probably due to the fact that the discussion had been moved to the evening so the teens could bring the adults in their lives to the event.

Max sat on a folding chair at the front of the room, the same as he had the previous year, although nothing else was similar, which was mostly on account of the young man currently talking to Ess and Xave at the back of the room. Xave was visiting from LA, and Marisol had immediately co-opted the up-and-coming designer to fashion something spectacular for this event. The result? Marisol was resplendent in a fiery outfit that was reminiscent of the makeup Marcello had worn the first time he'd come to Max's house.

Phoenix Fire, Marcello had called it when he showed the sketches to Max a few days before, and it suited Marisol to perfection. Max had watched the transformation take place in the bedroom of the house he now shared with Marcello, one of his bedrooms rapidly filling with Marisol's outfits as Marcello reclaimed his passion for drag. He hadn't performed in public yet, but Max knew that would happen soon enough. Especially if Xave kept designing Marisol outfits like this one.

As Marisol made her way to the front of the room, Max admired the way the sheer fabric floated around her in shimmering and shifting hues of red, orange, and yellow, mimicking flames even as they hugged Marisol's slender body.

"Hello, love," Marisol said as she sat next to Max and took his hand.

"Hello, sweetheart," Max said and leaned over to kiss Marisol just as Diego stepped to the front of the room and asked everyone to take a seat so they could get started.

Like the year before, there was general discussion talking about HIV and AIDS, where research and medication stood, prevention and PrEP, and then they got to the personal stuff. Unlike last year, Max was eager to talk about his life, and he squeezed Marisol's hand as Diego pointed out the quilt panel that had been hung behind both of them. The birth and death dates were still there, but now there was an infinity symbol after the latter. Marcello had asked if they could add it, and Max had enthusiastically agreed.

"So let's talk about the positives in your lives," Diego said, and Marisol immediately had her hand up.

"I found the love of my life," Marisol proclaimed when Diego called on her. "I wasn't expecting it. I pretty much thought that it wasn't going to happen, that my status was going to scare everyone away. But that's not what happened at all."

"And how about you, Max?" Diego asked with a twinkle in his eye.

Max took a long look at Marisol, then faced the audience. "Not only have I found the love of my life, I've also found a life worth loving. For the first time in a long time, I want that life to last forever."

CONTRIBUTING AUTHORS
LISTED ALPHABETICALLY

A.M. ARTHUR – SOLVING THE PUZZLE

A.M. Arthur was born and raised in the same kind of small town that she likes to write about, a stone's throw from both beach resorts and generational farmland. She's been creating stories in her head since she was a child and scribbling them down nearly as long, in a losing battle to make the fictional voices stop. When not exorcising the voices in her head, she toils away in a retail job that tests her patience and gives her lots of story fodder. She can also be found in her kitchen, pretending she's an amateur chef and trying to not poison herself or others with her cuisine experiments. A.M. Arthur's work is available from Carina Press, SMP Swerve, and Briggs-King Books.

"Solving the Puzzle" features characters and locations from A.M. Arthur's Belonging, Restoration and All Saints series. However, no previous knowledge of these books is necessary to enjoy this story.

Connect with A. M. Arthur
Email: am_arthur@yahoo.com
Facebook: facebook.com / A.M.Arthur.M.A
Newsletter: bit.ly / 3TWy8Pw

ANA ASHLEY - BITTERSWEET

Ana has been lost in the pages of books for as long as she can remember, taking a few amusing missteps with her childhood writing attempts. But everything changed when she discovered the magical world of LGBTQ+ romance—cue the confetti! Ana's books offer sweet and sexy romance with a charming mix of humor and heart. Getting her guys together wouldn't be the same without the meddling but well-intentioned cast of secondary characters, who always insist on having their own story. When she's not crafting heartfelt tales, you can find her indulging in her favorite pastime of baking delicious treats, enjoying quality time with friends, or staying up late immersed in the pages of a good book.

About "Bittersweet" and Ana's other books: Are you curious about how Fletcher and Harrison met? How about Kay's dad and his significant other? If you love the single dad trope you'll love my Dads of Stillwater series. And you'll find out just how long our dear Julius has been waiting for his perfect Connie to arrive.

Connect with Ana Ashley
Facebook Group: facebook.com/groups/CafeRoMMance
Instagram: instagram.com/anawritesmm
Newsletter: bit.ly/AnaAshley

LEE BLAIR – UNDER MY SKEIN

Lee Blair is a queer author and screenwriter from Oregon who writes low angst queer contemporary romance full of sweet, steam, fun, and laughs. She's constantly amused by the antics of her two ginger cats, spends too much time daydreaming about her next trip to Scotland, and considers starting hobbies its own hobby. Much like buying books and reading books are separate hobbies. Lee also hosts a podcast for readers of low angst queer romance called the Low Angst Library.

"Under My Skein" is a heartwarming story with no relationship angst but some non-relationship emotional challenges are present. This includes an AIDS- related death in the distant past where a main character lost his uncle from AIDS when he was a child. That loss is still felt and is a central part of the story. Also, there is a parent death from cancer in the recent past. A main character lost his dad from cancer two years prior to the story's beginning. The grief and loss are still fresh and prominent, but you will find the uplifting side of grief and how it can bring people together.

Content Warning for discussion of cancer treatment: a main character is an oncology nurse, and there's a scene set at his work, discussing chemo treatment. There's also a brief mention of losing one of his patients.

Connect with Lee Blair
Facebook Group: facebook.com/groups/LeeBlairsBuddies
Instagram: instagram.com/LeeBlairBooks
Website: LeeBlairBooks.com

L.C. CHASE – AND THEN CAME BLISS

Cover artist by day, author by night, L.C. Chase is a two-time Lambda Literary Award finalist, an EPIC eBook Awards winner, and Foreword Reviews IndieFab finalist. In cover design, she is a nine-time Ariana eBook Cover Art Awards winner. A hopeless romantic and free spirit, L.C. is an adventure seeker who loves hitting the open road just to see where it takes her. When not writing sensual tales of men falling in love, she can be found designing romance novel covers, photographing the world around her, drawing, horseback riding, or hiking the trails with her goofy four-legged roommate. You can find L.C.'s full booklist at lcchase.com, and while you're there, subscribe to her totally sporadic newsletter for more about works in progress, new releases, newsletter exclusives, and more. On social media you can follow her on Instagram and Bookbub, and join her Facebook reader group, Chasing Ever After.

L.C. is also the designer of our beautiful cover.

Connect with L.C. Chase
Instagram: instagram.com/authorlcchase
Facebook Group: facebook.com/groups/ChasingEverAfter

COURTNEY W. DIXON - THE KISS

Courtney W. Dixon is solely an MM author as of January 2023, who loves to write steamy romance, but in each story, she gives her characters challenges, struggles, and sometimes trauma. She loves to add variety and multiple tropes in her stories. And she writes her characters as having flaws, imperfections, and who don't always do the right thing. Humans are never perfect and make a lot of mistakes in their lives. You can find Courtney working in Central Texas with her husband, two boys, two crazy dogs, and two cats, none of whom know how to knock on a door while she's working.

Connect with Courtney W. Dixon
Amazon: amazon.com/author/courtneywdixon
Instagram: instagram.com/cwdixonauthor
Facebook Group: facebook.com/groups/courtneyscorruptreaders
Website: courtneywdixon.com

ARIES FRANCE – SUMMER FLING

Aries is a romantic at heart that wears her heart on her sleeve. Writing MM romance is her next great adventure.

"Summer Fling" is a romance. That is to say, this story is mainly about love found between two people. This story is also about AIDS and HIV. In this story, there is reference to a court case. The facts as presented in this fictional case are similar to those found all around the country. In particular, these facts are inspired by the case of the *Estate of Calude Green v. Robert Bowman*, a 2006 case from West Virginia. I wanted to note that for the readers for a few reasons. One, these stories need to be told. All too often deals and NDA's keep people from knowing what truly goes on. Two, Mr. Green's case was brought by the ACLU, who continues to do work in this arena. It is important to acknowledge their work and the work of attorneys everywhere to discuss these issues.

This story is set primarily in the fictional town of Bear Valley, Colorado, and is in the same universe as Aries' Bear Valley series. It is not necessary to have read any of the Bear Valley series prior to reading this story. This story is a stand-alone that simply shares the same address, and some side-characters, as the Bear Valley Series.

Connect with Aries France
Website: ariesfrancewrites.com

J.L. GRIBBLE – TO BE BOLD

J.L. Gribble writes speculative fiction and romance, but she's happiest when combining the two and adding a dose of the unexpected or nontraditional. When not writing, Gribble reads an eclectic range of books, adds to her LEGO collection, and plays video games. She lives in Ellicott City, Maryland, with her husband and vocal Siamese cats.

"To Be Bold" is part of the Core Values collection, because the other 99% of the military deserves love too. Other titles include the full-length novel Service Before Self and Val's story, "Toward Unity," which is free to read at the author's website.

Connect with J.L. Gribble
Website: jlgribble.com
Social media: linktr.ee/jlgribble
Read Service Before Self, an M/M military romance: books2read.com/
servicebeforeself

AE LISTER – A FRIENDLY PRESCRIPTION

AE Lister writes erotic queer romance in multiple genres. She has been writing off and on since the age of fourteen and publishing queer romance since 2011.

"A Friendly Prescription" features the characters from AE Lister's contemporary medical play series, Paging Dr. Griffin! (Skeletal Equation, A Spoonful of Sugar, Alternative Medicine), three stories that were written in response to seasonal callouts from Pride Publishing and featured in multi-author collections.

Connect with AE Lister
Instagram: instagram.com/aelisterauthor
Linktr.ee: linktr.ee/aelisterauthor

EVIE MCGLYNN - DAWN

Evie is a newish author who has always been an avid reader, mostly fantasy, science fiction and, of course, romance. After raising three children into adulthood, acquiring a master's degree, and opening a counseling practice, she figured she didn't have enough to do, so she decided to write books. Evie lives "down the shore" in New Jersey with her husband, her youngest son, his fiancée, and her goofy Rottweiler. Every summer she complains about "the bennies" coming down and snarling up the traffic, but she's a Jersey Girl through and through.

"Dawn" is set in my Down the Shore universe. The MCs in this story interact with characters from the books in the series several years after the end of the last book.

Connect with Evie McGlynn
Facebook Group: facebook.com/groups/eviesexceptionals
Instagram: instagram.com/authorevie1337
Bookbub: bookbub.com/authors/evie-mcglynn

SHANE K. MORTON – MY UNCLE CHARLIE

Shane lives in Studio city with his husband and their fur babies, Bette Davis and Dick Grayson. His novels include: The Trouble With Off-Campus Housing, Private Waterloos, The Year of the Cock, Fault Lines, Drag Queen Detective Series, Bluegrass Boys Series and The Point Pleasant Holiday Series as well as Red Carpet Disaster (Valleywood) and The Diamond Dandy (Tin Star Witches). His Dark Romance books, written under Sean Azinsalt, include: It's in My Blood, Bound, and Dark Eros. When not writing, Shane can usually be found at a film festival or performing cabaret in a dark dive bar.

Shane writes, "Growing up in the 70's and 80's my life was touched by quite a few people I met doing theatre and lost when I was young to the virus. This story is for them. I wish I had taken the time to know them better - but I was too young to understand."

Connect with Shane K. Morton
Amazon: author.to/ShaneKMorton
Facebook Group: facebook.com/groups/shanessweetandsalty
Bookbub: bookbub.com/profile/shane-k-morton

BREANNA RAE – WORSE THINGS

Breanna is a self described weirdo from the wild prairies of Alberta, Canada who lives on a diet of coffee, hockey and horror movies. Along with her collection of increasingly strange art and slightly off-putting oddities, Breanna lives with her husband and collection of pets in a house that looks like Halloween threw up everywhere. Her love language is music, and she collects coffee mugs and garden gnomes, but only really ugly ones. Breanna Rae is the contemporary pen name for B. Ripley.

Connect with Breanna Rae
Instagram: instagram.com/authorbreannarae
Facebook Group: facebook.com/groups/bripleyhive

MARIE SINCLAIR – PHOENIX

Marie Sinclair is a queer author living and writing in San Francisco. As a member of the LGBTQIA+ community, they believe in rooting their stories in the real world of queer culture and showing how love can survive even in challenging times. Their first book, *A Kind of Forever*, was nominated for two Goodreads Member Choice awards, and her third, *Forever After*, was a 2023 Lambda Literary Award finalist in Gay Romance and 2024 IPPY Gold Medalist for best romance ebook.

"Phoenix" brings readers back to the world of Marie's Finding Forever series with a World AIDS Day presentation at the Sam Mitchell Queer Youth Center. Ry and Cart, as well as their kids, make a special appearance, as do Ess and Diego.

Marie is the editor and coordinator for the *Say Their Names* charity anthology.

Connect with Marie Sinclair
Social media, newsletter, website, and a free novella: linktr.ee/marie_sinclair

ESSIE SLOANE – FEELS DIFFERENT

Essie Sloane currently lives in Louisville, Kentucky with her daughter, cat, and ancient black lab. She's a life long reader and has dreamed of being a writer since she was a child. When they're not reading, they enjoy doing small craft projects - crocheting and diamond painting, mainly. She also enjoys listening to music, studying queer history, and playing on her computer. You can reach out to them on Facebook or Instagram.

Connect with Essie Sloane
Facebook: facebook.com/groups/essiesloaneselite
Newsletter, social media, and more: linktr.ee/essiesloane

Printed by Amazon Italia Logistica S.r.l.
Torrazza Piemonte (TO), Italy

66795733R00351